De

This book is dedicated to Tintagon for her companionship while I did the writing and to our mutual friend, ‘P.P.’

Acknowledgements

The author is indebted to the Royal Naval Museum, the National Maritime Museum, The Maritime Trust and the Lancaster Maritime Museum for information used in reconstructing the historical events in this novel. Authors such as C. S. Forester, Dudley Pope, Alexander Kent and Patrick O'Brien stirred my interest in stories of naval adventures. *Nelson's Captains* by Ludovic Kennedy, *Nelson* by David Walder, *The Illustrated Companion to Nelson's Navy* by Nicholas Blake and Richard Lawrence, and *Nelson's Battles* by Nicholas Tracy were all invaluable in providing insights into the life of seamen of the times. I am grateful to Jim Meals of The Pelham Literary Agency for help with editing the manuscript. Thanks to Karen Kennedy for assistance with computer work.

Mediterranean Madness

The Luckless Leftenant Benjamin Rundel

A Historical Novel by

N. Beetham Stark

MEDITERRANEAN MADNESS
THE LUCKLESS LEFTENANT BENJAMIN RUNDEL

First Published in the UK by
Paul Mould Publishing www.GetPublished.co.uk
p.mould@yahoo.com

In association with
Empire Publishing Service www.ppeps.com
P.O. Box 1344, Studio City, CA 91614-0344

A CIP Catalogue record for this book is available from the British Library or from the US Library of Congress.

Simultaneously published in
Australia, Canada, Germany, UK, USA

Printed in Great Britain
First Printing 2009

US 13 ISBN 978-1-58690-094-6
UK 13 ISBN 978-1-904959-90-8

Table of Contents

Introduction

Leftenant Benjamin Rundel has just passed the leftenant's exam in London and has met up with an old friend, Thomas Murphy, midshipman. The two young men are about to engage in a series of battles and adventures together, pieced together from the elements of history sweetened by imagination. But no sooner than they are reunited than an east wind separates them, cutting them adrift to each go his separate way again.

When they are reunited, they forge an even stronger friendship, in spite of their difference in station. During that time, Ben loses his other closest friend and must bear up under an unrealistic burden of guilt that it may be his fault that his friend died. The two young men sail off to Cape St. Vincent, then to Tenerife, but are separated at Camperdown and the escapade on the *Hermione* which Ben must face alone. Ben faces a strange challenge when he is sent to rescue a reluctant Italian woman and her children from French territory. Ben nearly loses his patience with the little brats and their mother, whom he comes to despise for good reason. Ben begins to feel the twinges of pain that is the price of command, and he tries his best to cope with it. There is an escapade with the royal family at Palermo and Naples and the speedy execution of the traitor Admiral Caricciolo by Rear Admiral Nelson.

When the fleet comes up short on beef, Ben is sent to collect 400 head of cattle, but his small ship, with no cargo aboard, is driven ashore in a fierce storm. The ship is driven aground, and they are surprised in the night and captured by a French ship. They are taken to Toulon and marched to a nearby prison. Ben suffers terrible guilt at losing his second ship and dreads the inevitable court martial, desiring death rather than escape. But he is weakened by an attack of malaria which he picked up earlier in the Caribbean. In time, his strong survivor spirit surfaces and takes control. He bribes a guard to teach him French and he quickly learns the language, thus whiling away the dreadfully long days. After six months, his crew is restless and he has to devise a plan of escape. He succeeds in using an underground stream as their escape route, retakes his ship laden with stolen British beef and returns to Gibraltar, over five months late.

Ben returns to his ship and Lord Nelson in time to take part in the battle of Aboukir Bay where he faces some real challenges. After Aboukir, they return to Naples and Ben begins to see his boyhood idle, the British Navy, fall apart. Lord Nelson is enamoured with Lady Hamilton, wife of the ambassador to Naples. When Ben learns that she is carrying Nelson's child, and when news comes of the poor showing of the Mediterranean fleet under Keith, Ben suffers depression and is saved by the advice of the older, wiser Captain Hardy who befriends him.

Many of the events above actually happened somewhat as depicted here. I doubt that Captain Horatio Nelson was at Portsmouth on December 18, 1796, but his presence there is necessary to the maturation of the story. Also, the mutiny on the *Hermione* occurred several months earlier than depicted here, but our hero must develop his skills in handling men. He was in the Caribbean when the Spithead mutiny occurred. Otherwise, the events are portrayed by Ben's faithful shipmate and steward, as he saw them or as told to him by Ben himself. When some of his most trying moments occur, the steward lets us hear how Ben felt in his own words.

This is the third of the adventures of Benjamin Rundel. One needs to read the first two in order to understand why he reacts as he does to the tribulations of life. 'Humble

Launching' sets the story into action with an orphan boy who does not know who his parents are and who escapes from the workhouse to be educated aboard a British ship by a kindly Captain Bailey. 'The Wandering Midshipman' takes up Ben's career after he joins a most unhappy ship *Hawk* under a sickly Captain Sharpe. While on shore in the Caribbean, he is captured and set aboard an American slaver where he must serve as surgeon to the slaves. After his escape from the 'blackbirder,' he is taken at gunpoint with ten of his men to serve on a pirate crew which has lost most of its' men to tropical fevers. Ben and his men escape and return to Barbados with three prize ships under his command. Then he is shipped back to England to take his leftenant's exam and passes on his second try. At that point, he reappears in '*Mediterranean Madness*.'

Chapter One

False Alarm At Bantry Bay, Strange Bedfellows In The Fog

Ben came aboard the *Agamemnon* late that night with Tom Murphy and his gear. He was tired from the long coach ride from London and fell promptly to sleep, Tagon, his cat, by his side. No wonder he was amazed and confused when at 4 a.m. according to his new chronometer, he was awakened and told to, "Report to the Commodore at once." *And why should I need to see the Commodore at 4 a.m.? Should I not need to see the Captain instead? Have I heard correctly? As a leftenant I will take all of my orders from the Captain, not the Commodore. What is brewing?* he thought.

He lifted his cat Tagon gently from his chest and slid quietly to the deck. *Best not to light a candle. I will wake up the rest of the men and I don't want to start off on the wrong foot with them,* he thought. It was going to be great fun dressing in the dark. He had done as any man does when it is late and he is tired. He had slipped out of his trousers and left them in a heap on the deck, a sock under each leg. His coat was, where did he leave it? Must be by the stool next to the bulkhead. He knew he could never tie his neck piece correctly in the dark. He could still not master the tie even in daylight. He would have to do his best. He found his boots and pulled them on and then headed towards where he expected the Commodore's cabin should be. Yes, there was a light there, but the captain's cabin was dark. He approached the sentry standing as stiff as a frozen stick.

"M... Leftenant Rundel reporting to the Commodore." *I'll have to get used to this confounded new title. I am not used to referring to myself as, 'leftenant anybody'.*

A voice from within bade him enter. Ben stepped forward and had his first glimpse of Commodore Nelson.

"Leftenant Rundel reporting for duty, sir." He offered a smart salute.

Ben saw the Commodore eying him closely and returned the favour. The man was small, almost slight of build, with delicate looking hands and a mild voice. He looked unwell to Ben's trained eye. There were dark circles around his large, most expressive eyes. A large nose that protruded rather far and two large eyes seemed all that there was to his face. One could not overlook the large, full lips, protruding, almost pouting. He had a gentle chin, nearly pointed, completing an oval face and light, wavy hair that seemed to disobey all the rules of hair discipline, *much like my own,* he thought.

The Commodore saw before him a tall, slim youth, with a fine figure, broad shoulders, a trim waist and a most handsome face. His face was long with a prominent cleft chin, a small nose and two sparkling green eyes. His hair was dark, wavy and brown and surely had not been disciplined in a long time. He was, of course, unshaven at this ungodly hour. *Yes, the lad has earned the title of the poorest dressed officer in His Majesty's Navy, no doubt about that,* thought Nelson.

The Commodore cleared his throat. "Sorry to roust you out at such an ungodly hour, Mr. Rundel, but the wind appears to be changing, veering to blow from the east. If that trend continues, you should be able to get off to Ireland. Have you heard what is about to happen in Ireland, lad?"

"No, sir. We have been traveling and have no news."

"You are about to become the only man to serve as fourth leftenant for what, six hours, in the British Navy. You see, the French have sailed from Brest with a sizable fleet, some seventeen sail-of-the-line, thirteen frigates and fifteen other transports under General Hoche. He has some 13,000 soldiers and plans to join up with the rebel Wolfe Tone near Bantry Bay against our troops in Ireland.

They have many of our guns from the disaster at Quiberon Bay. The Fencibles will never be able to hold them off. They are too few. You know how hard it is for us to sail the channel in winter, especially with such perverse south-westerly winds. The French are taking advantage of the situation and plan to attack before we can send any ships to intervene. We received word of this planned attack from my friend, Emma Hamilton, in a letter that was passed on to me by the Queen of Naples. But the French did not plan on this shift of wind. We will be able to sail in a matter of minutes. Unfortunately, I and the *Agamemnon* are ordered to stay in port, but the *Indefatigable* will sail within the hour, sooner, I hope. Captain Pellew has lost his third leftenant to a senseless duel yesterday and needs a replacement. I have offered you to serve as third leftenant aboard the *'Indy'* until Captain Pellew can find a replacement. Then I expect you to report back to the *Agamemnon.* I want to hear more about your exploits as a pirate. Now, off with you. Oh, who is this?"

Ben looked behind him thinking that someone had come in, but there was no one there. Then he felt a gentle pressure against his leg. He looked down and there stood Tagon. She looked up at him as if to say that she was not going to be left behind yet another time.

"She is my cat, sir, a fine mouser," Ben offered somewhat lamely. It was embarrassing to stand before this great man and confess that he had a cat, but there was no helping it now.

The Commodore bent down and picked up the sleek grey animal and held it close to his chest, making clucking sounds to her. She snuggled in close to him and seemed quite at home.

"I suppose you are taking her with you," said the Commodore as he stroked her soft coat appreciatively.

"Yes sir, I am afraid that she would have it no other way. She is somewhat upset with me for having been away from her for much of the last year."

"Well, off quickly and tend to the French," said Nelson.

He handed Tagon to Ben, with a look that said that he would not mind keeping her company while Ben was away.

Getting off quickly would be easy. Captain Berry, who was on deck, had already called out the jolly boat and men were preparing to lower it into the water. Ben's things were still packed from the night before, so he put Tagon into her cage and picked up his gear to head on deck. *I have to leave a message for Tom, at least a message.* He fumbled in his duffel for some paper and found a piece of chalk by the binnacle. He scribbled a note.

"Dear Tom:

I have been called away to the *Indefatigable* on a mission to Ireland. Wish you could be there. Tagon is with me. I shall return. Ben."

Then he was over the side and in the boat.

The order came for "up oars," and Ben put Tagon on his shoulder and grabbed for the battens. As he climbed aboard and straightened up, he came face to face with Captain Pellew. Ben managed a quick salute and, "M...Leftenant Rundel reporting for duty, sir."

"Welcome aboard, Leftenant Rundel and I hope that you are not prone to dueling," said Captain Pellew.

"Not I, sir." Ben had seen enough good talent spilled onto the ground as one man shot another over some senseless misunderstanding to realize that he would do all in his power to avoid a duel.

"Does your cat always refuse to salute her superior officer?" said Pellew with a whimsical smile on his face.

"No sir, but she does serve His Majesty most faithfully. She is a fine mouser, sir."

"I hope that she can catch rats. We have had a sudden increase in rat population since we made port. Report to First Leftenant Warfield and he will get you assigned to duties."

Then Pellew turned and called out, "All hands aloft, Mr. Munk and prepare to up anchor. Clue up the headsl's."

Ben felt the cold breeze against his cheek and it was coming from the east. They could sail to Ireland, Tom's home that he had told Ben so much about. Ben hastened below and found the leftenant's quarters. He put Tagon in her cage and left her for the time being with a pat and a kindly word.

It was cold, but Ben soon fell into his duty. The first memory that he had of that cruise was that of seeing a bosun's mate with a starter or rattan in his hand slashing at the back of a reluctant sailor.

Ben yelled, "Hold there, sir! What is the problem?"

This lubber here won't climb the shrouds and handle sails like 'e is supposed to, sir."

Ben looked at the lad. He was lucky if he was sixteen and he was shaking uncontrollably. Ben was only seventeen and could remember when the shrouds seemed too much of a challenge for him.

"What's your name, son?"

"Crafty, sir, Crafty Malone, an' beggin' your pardon, sir, I am afraid of heights."

"Well, Mr. Crafty, it's not so bad when you get the hang of it. It's all in the trying, lad, and all in the mind. Here, follow me."

Now even a third leftenant would rarely leave deck for the tops, but then most of them had come up as midshipmen, young gentlemen with no training as able-bodied seamen. Ben could not contain himself. After all, he was about the same age as the lad and he still loved to be in the tops. One look convinced him that his men were a wild lot. He had to win their confidence and their trust if they were going to beat the French. Ben bolted up to the rail and grabbed the shrouds and began to climb. Someone gave Malone a push and he was soon struggling along behind Ben. Ben could hear his heavy breathing over the whining of the wind in the shrouds as he struggled with fear and the exertion of climbing.

"Come along, lad, you're doing just fine. Don't look down now, always look up. That's where God is. If you look down, you may see the real face of God sooner than you would like. Come on!" coaxed Ben.

When they reached the masthead, Ben pulled the lad over onto the platform and they stood there together for a few minutes, admiring the beauty of the wild sea. The boy had stopped trembling and began to smile at what he saw. His death-like grip on Ben's arm loosened slowly. He was conquering his fear.

"It's not bad up here at all, lad. There's no starters up here. Always remember that," shouted Ben.

"Now to descend, all you do is this," and Ben grabbed a rope, making sure the boy knew the right one to grab and how to hold on. He slid to the deck and the lad followed, with a grin on his face. No sooner had his feet hit the deck and Malone was back scrambling clumsily up the shrouds. He had the message. It *was better* in the tops than it was on deck, most of the time.

Back on deck, Ben stopped the bosun's mate.

"I don't mind your caning a man if he deserves it, but make sure that he knows how to do the work before you lay into him."

Captain Pellew stood on the quarter deck watching the whole affair, with that strange 'almost' smile on his face. Ben wondered what he was thinking. In fact, for the entire cruise, he wondered what went through the mind of this able captain. He was sure he could learn a good bit if he only knew what Pellew knew. He took a decided liking to the man and would watch him carefully to learn all that he might.

His division was a motley lot, mostly jail birds who agreed to serve in the Navy in exchange for release from jail. Most had been aboard only a few hours more than Ben. Whoever his predecessor had been, he was not much of a disciplinarian. Ben found any number of his men wanting in dress and appearance, here an unshaven face, a sloppy shirt, failure to address him as, 'sir,' and many other deficiencies. *This is going to be a challenging tour.* The next day, he requested permission to exercise his men at the guns, in spite of the cold weather. He could not consider going into battle with his division so poorly prepared. Captain Pellew granted his wish and he grilled them mercilessly for the next three days. Much of the time he had them go through the motions with no powder charge in the guns. A good crew could discharge a broadside every one and a half minutes. Often the outcome of the battle depended on how rapidly and accurately the men could service the guns. Half of these men had never served a gun before and the old timers were surly and reluctant to teach the newer men. Ben was not contented until he could get off a round every minute and a half.

"The sooner the enemy is mortally injured, the less time they would have to injure us and the sooner they will surrender," said Ben to his men. "Your ability to hit fast, accurately and hard may save your lives."

On the second day they threw a target overboard and the men practiced with powder and shot. One particular gun was so poorly served that Ben finally ran forward and pulled the men away from the gun.

"This is how it is done, lads," he said a bit impatiently. Ben instructed the men to put in the charge, wad, then a shot and had each rammed home. He pricked the cartridge and poured in some powder in the touch hole and then at the last minute, cocked the trigger.

"Now elevate, more, well," as he swung his hand sharply down to call the point where the gun was properly elevated. Then he motioned the idlers to use hand spikes to move the gun to the starboard so that the bobbing barrel was exactly in line. "Well," he called stepping back. "Clear," and he pulled the lanyard. The gun lurched into the air, barked and spewed smoke, and the floating barrel flew into pieces, settling back into the ocean like a flock of sea birds coming to roost.

"Hurrah, hurrah for Leftenant Rundel!" A great cheer went up and Ben knew that he had made some progress with these ornery men. No crew on the port side had hit the target that day. Ben gambled that he could still aim as well as he used to aboard the *Faithful,* and luckily he won. The rest of the day, he spent time with each gun crew explaining the fine points of aiming and firing rapidly. The next day the men felt ashamed of their performance of the day before and Ben saw a definite improvement in their attitude, rate of fire and their aim. The *'Indy'* was a 44 gun frigate and his 22 guns had struck the target sixteen times on the first firing. That was much better. That was what he wanted.

"Good firing lads. Now you have the hang of it. Keep at it now." He had little trouble with his divisions after that. He had won them over completely. He was learning what they fail to print in the navigation books, that success as an officer demands the ability to lead and understand men.

Then a day later the call for, "All hands! Man your guns and clear for action," was accompanied by the shrilling of the bosun's whistle and the hammering of the marine drums. Feet padded in all directions and the ship was cleared for action in a little over five minutes. Ben was pleased and he knew that Mr. Warfield and Mr. Marks, the other two leftenants were delighted as well. Mr. Warfield walked over to Ben.

"The port divisions were always the laggards, but since you have taken over, the lads have shaped up into a fine crew. Look how they work together now. You would not have seen that a week ago, not that lot."

Apparently the lookout had sighted five frigate sails to port and Captain Pellew wanted to engage them. He looked through the glass at the ships and then because they were scattered over a ten mile area, directed the helmsman to "steer south southwest, if you please."

"Mr. Riggs, would you signal the closest ship, the *Amazon,* to follow suit and we'll take on the ship farthest to port, which I believe is a ship-of-the-line. We may not be able to capture her, but we can leave our calling card at best."

"Aye, aye sir."

"All hands aloft to put on sail. Ensign Shepherd to the signal book if you please."

Ben made sure that his port division was ready, each man at his proper position. They were still green yet, but he was amazed at the progress they had made.

Then came the waiting. The guns were trained, the slow matches lit over the water bucket and every one poised to rush into action. All that was needed was that one deadly word, "fire." Powder boys stood idly by, well out of harms way. Their grimy little faces told of several trips to the powder room to bring up the needed cartridges and shot.

But the ship that they singled out was still a mile away, too far for a fair shot to do any good. They must wait. The wind was whipping up and they were racing along at a good pace, but the enemy ship crowded on more sails and was moving rapidly through the water, leaving a rippled wake of frothy black water. The wind sung as it fled past the rigging, taut ropes straining to hold the sails, but they were gaining on her.

"Point to larboard, Mr. Pitts, if you please," said Captain Pellew.

As they drew closer, Ben could see that she was a fine ship-of-the-line, a 74, but not well handled.

"Look there, Mr. Warfield. Their sails are poorly handled and they must soon tack and reduce sail," said Pellew.

"Aye, sir, and look at her handling. She'll be on the rocks soon if she does not tack."

"Give the signal to fire, Mr. Warfield."

Then the magic word spread down the deck from midshipman to midshipman, "Fire!" Ben told of the action in his own words.

"We were ready and I watched eagerly as my men made the last corrections and fired their guns. The enemy was under a quarter of a mile away and all but two of Ben's port guns scored. They could see yards sinking to the deck, held back by the tangled mass of ropes and rigging, for a second, and then plummeting to the deck, crushing everything in the way. There were shouts of pain too, just audible in the cold, damp fog."

"Visibility could be better, but I think that we have a good start, sir," said Warfield to the Captain.

"Aye and keep up the firing. Pump her full of shot. The *Amazon* is tacking and will engage her from the port side. Between us we can reduce her to rubble."

"The battle went on for several hours. The two British frigates played bird dog with the larger French ship, chasing her ever farther off course and into dense fog, only to emerge from some unexpected quarter and lay yet another round of shot into her. Our fire was concentrated on her rigging. It was the captain's intention to take her as a prize ship. Other ships from our small fleet of twelve ships were hard at work on the scattered French fleet. We passed behind her often enough to see that she was the *Droits de l'Homme,* a 74, but she continued to be poorly handled. With each pass behind her stern, we were able to get off at least one round of grape shot and twelve pounders to rake her decks. We could see guns upended and only a few men struggling to work their way through the mass of wreckage on her decks. She was losing steerage way because so much debris was dragging from her decks in the water on the starb'rd side. The *Amazon* was ably handled and poured shot into her from both stern and for'ard.

"We were not immune from damage. Although the *Droits* was still firing sporadically and with a low degree of accuracy, she had so many guns that we were hit many times, all above the water line and mostly for'ard. We had lost a yard on the main mast and one on the mizzen and two guns had been put out of action, but the hounds had done their work well and the prey was about to go to its watery grave. The *Droits* caught fire after one of our shots hit near her magazine. She exploded in a burst of red and yellow flames, then belched a great column of black smoke and exploded again. We could see her masts fall like great trees felled by a mighty axe. Her decks seemed to heave and then she plunged forward, ever so slowly, dipping her bowsprit into the cold ocean, and began to settle. Huge bubbles rose out of the ship and we could hear a groaning and sighing sound, most eery. Yes, I remembered the day when as a tiny child in my mother's arms I had watched a ship catch fire and sink in the English Channel. The sounds and sights were much the same, the groaning, the almost sighing sounds, the showers of sparks hissing as they hit the icy water, and the billowing smoke, the flames reaching high, giving off a roaring sound. All was the same, except the realization that I had helped to bring about her death. My men performed well and since the port battery was most often in contact with the enemy, we inflicted most of the damage. While I regretted the loss of so fine a ship and so many lives, it was necessary in wartime and I knew it. We had done our duty. I was proud of my men and I told them so.

"When the battle was over, we stood by the rail and watched the last wisps of smoke disappear. We had suffered minor damages, two damaged yards and about six men wounded. One lad would die before the night was over, but it had been an easy battle. Repairs were made and I was able to look for my supper at 4 p.m. as usual.

"It was when I was supervising the repairs that I realized my own loss. There on the gun deck, amidst a pile of splinters from the bulwark, lay my Tagon. She had apparently tried to get below and had been caught by splinters from a lucky shot. I went to her limp body, hoping that she still lived, but a splinter had pierced her abdomen and she lay totally still, cold and dead in my hands. I must admit that I cried a little, maybe more than a little. Fortunately, there was no one close by, so no one ever really knew what had happened to me and my pet. No one saw me at my worst hour. We were together for over nine years. True, she was getting old and needed more assistance than she had as a younger cat, but we had worked that all out. She was going to be fine. *I will not have to leave her ever again*, I thought. I said, "Goodbye," to my best friend, and went on with my busy life."

As near as they could tell, the French did not land a single man at Bantry Bay on the 23rd of December. Then it began to snow, large driving flakes that clung to everything in site. The ships were beautiful indeed with snow on their rigging and yards, but devils to handle. The weather continued foul, with thick winter fogs and poor visibility for the last two days. They came to anchor each night because of the problems caused by snow accumulating on the yeads and sails. Each morning the men moved cautiously aloft and shoveled down the snow, making life on deck most uncomfortable. Ben could not keep the snow from trickling down his neck as it fell from the yards, making him cold and damp the entire day.

Their twelve ships hindered the Frenchman's every attempt to approach land. Several more of the French ships were sunk or taken and by late on the 23rd it was clear that they were in for a fierce winter storm. Great waves began to pile up on the rocky headlands and pound the beaches. Ben saw one French ship after another try to beat back to sea, only to be driven back to land and wrecked on the jagged rocks. Some ships scattered never to be seen again and some simply turned and headed back to France. The British ships stood far off the land with only foretops'ls, keeping well away from the treacherous coast. Two ships that passed them by in the dark of night had lost masts from the storm and were in bad shape.

Captain Pellew said that "In all, only thirty three of the French ships ever returned to Brest. The loss of life must have been considerable."

After the battle we beat back to Portsmouth and a fine Christmas dinner shared with friends aboard ship.

After dinner Captain Pellew summoned Ben and spoke quietly to him.

"You are to report back to Commodore Nelson and

Captain Miller on the *Agamemnon.* They will sail soon to the eastern Mediterranean and you must be aboard. Sorry there has not been more time to get to know you, Mr. Rundel. You are a good officer and I am sorry to see you leave. You performed miracles with your port division. I should like to know you better and perhaps, someday, we will sail together again. Oh, and I am sorry for your loss." *So he did know about Tagon.* Ben had said nothing to anyone aboard about the loss of Tagon. She was his personal loss.

The trip aboard the *Swallow from* Portsmouth to London was swift and uneventful. Ben carried a leather packet with letters and orders to the Commodore. Once aboard the *Agamemnon* he found his old bunk waiting for him. *Am I to serve as third or fourth leftenant?* That mystery would soon be resolved. It seemed that Mr. Hughes had been called home because of a death in the family. That left Ben the position of third leftenant, which pleased him considerably.

Ben told me about his time aboard *Agamemnon.*

"As soon as Tom received word of my return, he came to my berth aboard *Agamemnon* and we chatted for a time. He wanted to know all about Ireland and what had happened."

"Did you get to set a foot on the land?" he asked.

He had to disappoint him there, but added, "But the French didn't get to see the land either, so it was not all that bad. Many ships were lost and the French fleet was scattered. The sharks are eating French steaks from Bantry Bay clear to Bishop Rock. The weather was howling like a banshee on the day that we left. We saw several luckless ships pile up on the rocks."

Tom smiled at that. "And how is my favourite cat?"

Tom could see from Ben's eyes at once that all had not gone well for her.

He looked at him and said, "I'm sorry that I asked."

"It happened during our battle with the *Droits de*

l'Homme which we totally destroyed. I found her dead afterwards below deck, skewered by a splinter. I buried her at sea, but will always miss her. It's my fault. I should have put her in her cage and taken her to a safe place as I always did."

Tom reached over and shook Ben by the shoulder and tried to comfort him. "She had a good life. You gave her that. From what you have said, she would have perished as a kitten if you had not found food for her. You cannot blame yourself for any negligence. She might just as well have been hit in the cage an' unable to run for safety, which would have been all the worse, wouldn't it now. Your first duty is to the King and you did that right well."

For some reason, Tom's words always seemed to comfort Ben. He had that special way about him and Ben would cherish his unique talents for the rest of his life. No more was said about Tagon.

Ben's first impressions of the new division were favourable. His port division was made up of a stalwart group of seasoned seamen and they hit it off quite well. Captain Miller was a fine seaman and kept the ship in good order. Knowledge about the men on board came as bits of conversation here and there. Apparently Commodore Nelson was a man of action, moody, often unwell but decisive and not one to be questioned about his decisions. His skills lay in his ability to weigh the positive and negative aspects of a wild gamble and then to act on his convictions, orders be damned. He was a fine sailor, but paid little heed to the fine points of keeping things ship-shape. His other strength became apparent the first day aboard ship. He was skilled at bringing his officers together and giving them a sense of importance. He frequently asked for their opinions and acted as if they mattered. His rapport with the common seamen was equally commendable. He seemed to be able to inspire everyone with a sense of national pride, pride in King and Country and to give everyone credit when a job was well-done. *This man will bear some study,* thought Ben. *I may be able to learn much from him, but I should keep an eye on Captain Miller too, for his skills as a Captain are most notable.* Now Ben was pleased because he was beginning to learn the things that he had needed for his first leftenant's exam, things that are not written in books and cannot be learned effectively from reading.

About an hour after Ben came aboard, he was summoned by a ship's boy to the Commodore's cabin.

"Leftenant Benjamin Rundel reporting, sir," as he offered a smart salute.

"Welcome aboard, Mr. Rundel. I have awaited your return. You may have heard by now that Mr. Hughes has left the ship. You will fill his position as third leftenant. Remember, I told you when you left for the *Indy* that you would have the shortest career in His Majesty's Navy as a fourth leftenant. I just didn't know how it would all come about. Have a seat, lad." He had an engaging way of smiling that left little lines to port of his mouth.

Ben sat down and the two men began to talk about the future.

"Leftenant Quickstone will acquaint you with your duties. We are headed off to the eastern Mediterranean where we must evacuate people and ships to a safer port. Britain just does not have enough ships to protect all ports in the Mediterranean and still fight a war, and our partial withdrawal in '96 now has to be completed speedily. When we are through, we will rendezvous with Rear Admiral John Jervis and the fleet off Cadiz. We are expecting a visit from the Spanish fleet and should be ready for a sharp engagement. You may want to drill your gun crews while we are on our way to the eastern Mediterranean. Oh, and I would appreciate your attendance at supper in my cabin at say, 4 bells.

"Thank you, sir."

"Oh, and how is your little grey friend?"

Ben could not help but show his feelings. He would always be poor at hiding his emotions. With his head hung low and a long, sombre face, he said, "She did not survive Ireland, sir."

"I am sorry to hear that. I had great plans for her against the French. She will be missed."

Ben could not help but smile at the Commodore's humour. *He is trying to cheer me up,* he thought. The title 'Commodore' had been bestowed on Captain Nelson on 15 December, 1796 when he was sent to evacuate Elba with a small squadron detached from the main fleet.

After meeting the other officers, Mr. Hardy, Mr. Culverhouse and Mr. Runkle and a host of midshipmen, including his friend Tom, Ben went about settling in. He lined up all of the men under his command and inspected them for cleanness, neatness, proper dress. He also tried to learn as many of their names as he could. He found that it helped to know where each man came from. "Miles from Wiltshire, sir," was somehow easier to remember than simply, "Justin Miles." His men came from all over England, Ireland and Scotland and there were a few Germans, Dutch, Americans and one negro fellow who could hardly speak any English. He must try to remedy that when he had time. In general, the men were clean and orderly. When he had finished his inspection, he called out, "Anyone here play a musical instrument, you know, a fiddle or accordion?"

Ben hoped to break the ice since it was a Sunday and there would be free time. He hoped to get some of the men to bring their instruments out and they could play together below decks, since it was late December and a harsh, cold wind whipped the deck. They had been lucky. The east wind had returned briefly after the severe storm and they were able to beat down Channel and head off to the Mediterranean. One older, almost toothless seaman raised his hand.

"I got a fiddle, sir." But he seemed to be the only one who could play. That afternoon, after Ben had made a thorough inspection of the *Agamemnon* he brought out 'laika' his balalaika. It was badly out of tune with all of the moving about and he spent some time getting the strings properly tightened. Then he leaned back against the stanchion and began to play and sing. At once his men looked up from their games and sewing, enchanted by the sweet tinkling strains of the strange little triangular instrument. Several came over to sit by him. Then more came. He wondered why he was tempted to play for the seamen instead of the officers, but there was growing within him something that he could not name, something unnoticed so far, a sense of how to win the loyalty of his men. During the afternoon, the old seaman appeared with his fiddle and they began to play together. Several of the men joined in and they had a fine time singing old sea shanties. Best of all was their rendition of "God Save The King," which was sung with such gusto that most of the officers came below to see what was going on. Even Commodore Nelson popped his head in through the passageway and smiled appreciatively at the good spirit of his men. The ability of his new leftenant to raise the spirit of the men did not go unnoticed. The Commodore was heard to mutter as he turned to leave, "This Rundel bears watching. He shows promise."

That evening Ben appeared at the Commodore's cabin in his best clothes. He commandeered Tom to help get his neck cloth straight and his hose in proper place. His short dress coat buttoned across the front with gold ribbing on the edges, exposing broad white lapels. The cuffs were white with gold buttons bearing a fouled anchor. His black Hessian style boots were shining and new and he wore smart breeches that showed off his fine, slim waist. He wore a new hat too, a bicorn worn fore and aft with a device upon it that noted his rank.

Ben was bade to enter and faced the Commodore, his eight midshipmen and Leftenant Hardy. Leftenant Culverhouse was officer of the watch. Often a Commodore had only three or four ships, mostly frigates under his command and did not need a captain. But Captain Miller was sent aboard because the Admiralty expected a major engagement at Naples and someone might need to take charge of the ship while the Commodore saw to the tactics of battle.

"Welcome, Mr. Rundel. I trust that you have met all of these gentlemen?" said the Commodore.

"All but this gentleman," said Ben as he held his hand out to a smartly dressed man who by his demeanour clearly was well-educated and used to London society.

"Let me introduce our surgeon to you. Leftenant Rundel, this is Mr. Wilfred Bowers. He is new at sea and has left his London practice to patch up us poor Jack tars when we get in the way of a bullet or a cannon ball. He will have some new experiences aboard the *"'Agamemnon',* I am sure."

Ben extended his hand and sent a charming smile with it. "Pleased to meet you, sir and I hope not to need your services."

The meal was exquisite with a citrus drink, steaming hot bread, and chicken in a fine sauce with beans. The Commodore did enjoy good food. Many topics came to the table, not the least was Naples, their destination, women, the war and Napoleon, women and the weather, women, and *Agamemnon* which was making record speed for this time of year.

Then they brought out the port and sherry and hard cheeses. The latter met with Ben's approval and he was about to shove another wedge of cheese into his mouth when someone asked him if he had ever lived down the title of "Little Pee-in-a Bottle."

Ben's face turned a deep pink under his fading tan. "Until now I thought that I had outgrown that title. Where did you ever hear about that story?"

"Oh we know a lot about you. You have made the London Naval Chronicle several times and they do not spare details. But I once knew a shipmate of yours, a Mr. Wilcott, who had come on the tale somehow and passed it on to me," said Mr. Will Benson, one of the midshipmen, a dapper little fellow.

Ben now became the focus of their attentions. "You cannot sit here and eat this fine cheese without telling us about your exploits as a pirate captain, now can you," said the Commodore. "Here, have some wine and tell us all."

Ben waved his hand respectfully, but he must refuse the wine. "I rarely drink wine, sir, thank you."

The Commodore looked most surprised. His eyebrows shot up to meet his unruly hair. "I have never met a seaman of any rank that would turn down good wine."

"I acquired a bad taste for the drink as a small boy, sir. As for my pirate days, you know that I was kidnapped against my will. I would rather forget the whole affair," replied Ben.

"Oh, but we have no other entertainment planned for tonight. Come, lad don't be so modest and bashful. We are all friends here," said the Commodore. Ben realized that Commodore Nelson enjoyed the limelight and eagerly sought it for his own benefit. *I am not cut out of the same cloth,* thought Ben, *so I will make this short and then switch the attention back to him.*

"Well, I suppose that I ought not to disappoint so many of my new ship mates," said Ben. So he launched into a brief account of how he and ten of his crew had been captured by Spanish pirates during a wooding expedition in the Caribbean.

"I heard that you were a well-trained surgeon and had been quite successful in curing some of those devastating tropical fevers while you were in the Caribbean. Lots of our lads suffered and died of fever when we were in the West Indies and especially in the swamps of Nicaragua," said the Commodore.

"I should like to speak with you sometime on the subject of tropical fevers, Mr. Rundel. I may be unlucky enough to be assigned to a ship that is sailing to the Caribbean someday myself," said Mr. Bowers. Ben nodded his willingness and they would surely talk again on the matter.

Ben knew that the Commodore had spent time in the ship *Boreas* and had met and married Frances Nisbet at Nevis before returning home to Burnham Thorpe sometime in 1787.

"I believe that you contracted yellow fever while at Antigua, or was it Jamaica? It is now possible to cure it using certain native herbs which I was able to procure from a local shaman." said Ben.

"I can't be certain where I contracted the blasted fever, but I can say that I wish you had been around to cure me of it then. I have some bad effects of it even today," answered the Commodore.

Ben backed off by asking the Commodore more about his exploits in the Americas to shift attention from himself.

"Tell us about Canada and the polar bear, sir," said Ben. Ben sighed in relief when he had successfully transferred the limelight from himself to the Commodore, who sat there smiling as he related some of his grand exploits.

The trip to Naples was uneventful. Ben learned that the Commodore had acquaintances there, one Lord and Lady Hamilton. The ship was literally speeding over the waves towards the Mediterranean. It was fun to feel the warmer air slide off the sails and run down over his back as he stood on the quarterdeck. The farther south that they went, the warmer it became, but it was still winter and still quite cold at night.

One strange thing happened on the trip to Naples. Six of his men began to complain of stomach cramps. At first two were so bad that they could only double over in agony and could do no work. Then within two hours, three others became terribly sick as well. Finally, the sixth man was admitted to the sick bay. Ben was concerned because that left him short-handed on the port watch. Soon after the first five men were admitted to sick bay, the surgeon, Mr. Wilfred Bowers, came to seek Ben when he was on his dog watch.

"Mr. Rundel, I have a mystery here. Would you be so kind as to come below and examine these men and see if your conclusions match mine?"

Ben agreed readily and was a bit flattered by the request. The surgeon led the way to the sick bay on the orlop deck. Ben could hear moans and groaning from the men even before he could see them.

"These men came in two days ago complaining of stomach cramps. But after awhile the cramps seemed to ease off, so I returned them to duty. Then yesterday they came back, with two others in terrible pain. Now this feller has joined them. I checked them out for appendicitis, but that does not seem to be the problem. I am beginning to wonder if there is not some infection that is starting to hit the entire ship. I'd hate to have over 500 men in their shape," as he pointed to the men in agony.

Have you checked to see what they have been eating outside of their regular mess?" asked Ben as he examined the men for signs of disease.

"Yes, I did that too. Other than an occasional chaw of tobacco, they haven't had anything that the rest of the men on board have not eaten."

"What about mess mates. Are they in different messes?"

"I never thought to check that." The two men turned and went quickly to the deck house where the duty rosters and mess arrangements were posted.

There was a record there of what duty each man aboard ship would have for any specific challenge; fire, man overboard, battle stations, rope handling, sail handling, mess numbers, watches, ships boats, boarding etc. Ben ran his finger down the list.

"What are their names again?" he queried Bowers.

"Let's see. There's Sam Smith, Roger Morris, William Queens, John Silks, Morton Phillips and the last one that came in, his name is Gene Lator." Ben found Lator first, and sure enough, all the other five were in the same mess.

"This could be a conspiracy, Mr. Bowers. Folks on shore don't usually act sick unless they are, but often at sea, especially if the men are not seasoned seamen and are recent recruits from the jails or press gangs, they will pretend to be sick. It's their way of getting out of working and still getting fed. If that is the case with these lads, we can sneak back on them in the sick bay and see if they are still in such great pain. They are bound to ease off after awhile if they are just pretendin'," Ben rationalized.

So the two men moved slowly back to where the sick men were lying on the deck. Sure enough, they were still groaning and all doubled up. One lad looked as if he would not last out the night.

Ben turned to Mr. Bowers. There is a cure for them if they are pretending. I sort of doubt that they are making believe, but we do need to know. If they have some ailment that will be spread to their other shipmates, we need to know that and fast. I had to use this when I first went aboard the *Hawk.* You mix a stiff drink of rum with about 70% fish liver oil and you may have to force them to drink it. You need to promise that there will be another dose in two hours, so they know that they will have more misery in the sick bay than on deck at their duties. It works every time, unless a man is really sick. If they are pretending, the discomfort brought on by the strong physic will send them begging to be put back on duty. If they are really sick, it could purge them of anything bad that they may have eaten," advised Ben.

"I'll try that, but I can't see how they could get sick from the same food that the rest of the men are eating. It all comes from the same coppers."

Ben had to leave to resume his duties on deck, but promised to return again soon. This was not just the surgeon's problem. Ben was affected also.

At the end of the next watch, Ben went below. Several of the men were either asleep or had passed out. One still groaned and rolled on the deck.

"Any change, Mr. Bowers?"

"Only that they have all been completely purged and still seem to be in great pain."

"Hmmm," mused Ben. *I will have to watch that 'Hmmm' stuff. I am beginning to sound like the captains that I have known.*

There was no change early in the next day, but by nightfall, the first two victims had died. Two others, Smith and

Silks, looked as if they would be gone before morning.

Bowers and Ben put their heads together. "Could it be poison, administered, say, after the food is ladled into the messkid?" said Ben.

"Could be. Anything is possible."

I have never seen arsenic poisoning, but the symptoms all seem to fit strychnine quite well too. Arsenic is usually administered slowly over a number of weeks, but suppose the killer wanted to hasten the process. Could he not give a massive dose and kill the men quickly?" reasoned Ben.

"I have never seen arsenic poisoning either. But I have read about it as I suppose you have too. You may have something there."

Ben had to go back to his duties. By the next morning two other men had died and they held one burial for the four men. Commodore Nelson was kept appraised of the situation daily by Mr. Bower's sick room report. He was well aware that something unusual was going on. The Commodore also had been feeling unwell, which added to the concern of both Ben and Mr. Bowers.

After the funeral, Ben approached Captain Miller and requested permission to examine the gear of the two remaining sick men and the dead men. "There might be some clue there as to what has killed these fellows, say perhaps, some tainted or poisoned tobacco, for example."

"You have my permission, Mr. Rundel, but don't let the other sailors see you going through the gear. It is bad for morale you know."

"Aye sir."

His watch was on duty and he asked Tom Murphy to take charge of his crew for a short time. He would explain to Tom tonight. He and Tom had already spoken of the mysterious deaths, and Tom was convinced that it was poison. "That fellow Lator sounds like a Frenchman to me. I'd watch him carefully if I were you."

"But there are lots of Frenchmen who live in England and are loyal to King George III. We can't accuse him of dirty work just because his name is French," said Ben.

Ben wasted no time in going below to examine the canvas duffel bags that most sailors used. He found all six bags hanging against the bulkhead, each with a name scribbled on it with charcoal or with the name embroidered on it. He took down each bag and emptied its contents on the deck. *Nothing unusual there. Same here, razor, some letters, some tobacco, but not opened, shirts, trousers, belt, scarf, a throwing knife, all in order.* Then he replaced the bag with contents intact.

It was not until he reached for the last bag that he found anything of interest. As he poured out the contents of Lator's bag, a small vial tumbled out onto the deck. Ben reached for it. It contained a white powder, but was unlabeled. Could it be powder such as men wore on their wigs? Not likely in the sea bag of a common seaman. He opened the vial and smelled its contents. There was a definite faint smell, but it told him nothing. He decided to take the vial to Mr. Bowers to see if he could identify the contents.

When he arrived at the sick bay, the fifth man had just died in great agony. Ben watched Lator from a distance for awhile. Yes, he could be faking the pain. He was not quite as discomforted as the other men had been. He would bear watching.

Ben showed the vial to Mr. Bowers and later to Commodore Nelson and Captain Miller. No one could identify the odd smell. Ben asked Mr. Bowers to keep a close watch on Lator. If he were not really sick, he might try to harm some of the other men now that he had put his mess mates out of his way.

"But why Mr. Rundel would anyone want to kill off his mess mates? Sure, sometimes there were quarrels among men at sea. That is to be expected. But this is odd." There seemed to be no motive. Ben checked with the Captain's log and muster book. None of these men had ever been in trouble and all were older, seasoned seamen. Lator had joined the ship about two months ago, and was the most recent member to join this mess, but that should not cause any problem. None of the lads who messed nearby had ever heard these men argue or fight. In fact, they seemed to be a laughing, happy lot up until about a week ago. Several of the sailors knew the five older men well and could vouch for their honesty, but no one knew Lator. All they knew was that he always wore a half-sneer on his thin, dark face.

This incident became a mystery that only deepened with time. By the time they had reached Naples, Lator had recovered. Ben went to the captain and explained that he felt the man was some how responsible for the murders of his five ship mates and had faked his own sickness to draw suspicion away from himself. Ben requested that Lator be put in irons and questioned further about his motives.

"That is the best we can do, Mr. Rundel. We cannot prove that the vial contains poison, nor that it was used to murder the five seamen, but it only makes sense to restrain Lator. Perhaps with confinement, a stiff dose of bread and water, he will weaken and we may learn the truth from his own mouth," said Miller.

Ben gave the order to the Corporal of the marines to seize Lator who was still in the sick bay. Ben presented him with the vial and noted that his eyes dilated when he saw the vial. But that did not really prove anything. Ben considered making a drink so that Lator could see him put some of the white powder in the drink and then force him to drink the mixture. But that would have to wait. If it were poison, Ben could be court martialled for murder. They would soon make the port at Naples and there was much to do. Ben went forward with his work comforted only by the fact that no more men had come down sick and that the probable culprit was in irons. Each day out of port, Ben stopped to see Lator.

"Are you ready to tell me what happened to your messmates?"

But the man only shook his head. "I dunno, sir." was all he would say.

Just then the call came for "Clear for action." Ben hastened to his post to see that his men were in place and ready. They performed quite well. Out of the cold winter fog just a few cable lengths away was a French frigate, *La Fleur.* The element of surprise forced the ship to tack quickly to avoid collision. Men raced to the tops to shorten sails and crews on deck prepared to swing the yards on command. Men shouted orders and Ben could hear the bosun's mate crack his cane. The helmsman had already swung his wheel hard to port, and the ship was heeding his command, but slowly, ever so slowly. Surely they would collide. Commodore Nelson gave the command for the guns to fire as they bore. The command rippled down through the leftenants to the midshipmen and a ragged broadside was got off. They were turning just fast enough so that many of the shots raked her from forward. But the French had not been able to fire a single shot. They sent a few cannon balls into her rigging from their port side guns and she dropped her French colours and surrendered. That was one of those fine, rare battles where no one was hurt in the British crew and no damage was done to their rigging or hull. They sent a small crew aboard *La Fleur* to repair her rigging, and they were soon off to Naples. They arrived only ten hours after the battle had ceased.

They decided to clean up *La Fleur* for a cruise back to England. But as soon as repairs were made, Ben was sent to transfer the Commodore's pennant and gear to *La Minerve,* another prize ship. They dropped anchor early in the morning.

Next the British subjects who wished to leave Naples had to be warned and taken on board in a matter of hours. They were put on merchant ships bound for England. All British shipping and supplies that had not been removed earlier were off-loaded and put onto merchant ships so they could be transported to Lisbon in Portugal. There were huge warehouses of ships' supplies belonging to His Majesty and all needing to be transported. The Mediterranean fleet would use the mouth of the Tagus River as its new port because Portugal was still a friendly power. Gibraltar had been abandoned after the Treaty of San Ildefonso in August of 1796 when Spain allied with France against England. With both French and Spanish ships in the Mediterranean as enemies, Britain could no longer protect the bases that it had there, so an orderly retreat was set in motion. They anchored at Elba too. Sailors were running about carrying gear and dunnage to be stowed away on any handy British ship. It was feared that Napoleon would take Naples almost any day now. The Neapolitans would have to manage to get along with the French as best they could. For most of their stay there, the Commodore spent his time on shore occupied with diplomatic matters. Sir William Hamilton was the British Ambassador to Naples and had not received orders from home to abandon his post. He and his wife Emma, would stay on in Naples.

But there were apologies to make to the King and Queen of Naples for abandoning them, and all this took time and great amounts of wine, dining and dancing. Ben did get to see the royal family on one occasion when they came to the wharf to see Lord Nelson off. He was ill impressed by the king, but he thought that the queen made up several times over for his deficiencies. The family seemed frivolous, unaware of the impending dangers and bored with even the concept of war. They seemed to resent the fact that Napoleon with his awful army might intrude on their social life and force them to abandon their false sense of responsibility.

So much of the time, Ben was on his own in setting up the crew and outfitting *La Minerve* for the trip back to the Tagus station. Leftenants Culverhouse and Hardy were hard at work finding space for the extra gear and supervising repairs to some of the other ships in port. It was all like a Chinese fire drill with everyone hurrying around to get this or that essential item to take with them at the last moment.

Finally, they were ready to set sail for the rendezvous

off the coast of Lisbon with Admiral Sir John Jervis. They set sail early on a fine, late January day, the sky clear and the air cool. Ben was glad to be at sea again and away from the land. For some reason, he would never like Italy. He discovered that no first leftenant had come aboard *La Minerve*, so he was made acting first leftenant, and second in command. They were short of officers for this duty because several prizes had to be sailed to England. Tom had sailed away three days earlier in a French prize ship headed for Portsmouth.

The next day after his dog watch, Ben restrung 'laika', his balalaika, with the strings he had bought in Naples and found that it sounded slightly different, but still most pleasant. The afternoon was pleasant, cool, but clear. He sat and played for awhile. Many, including the Commodore, turned appreciative glances in his direction, but they were short handed and there was little time for relaxation. There would be no rousing choruses of 'God Save the King' or 'Britannia Rule The Waves' as there had been aboard the *Agamemnon.* It seemed to calm him to play and the sound of the beautiful music brought assurance that the old carefree life would soon return. But he knew better. He was an officer now.

Before leaving port, Ben checked with Mr. Bowers again concerning Lator. There was no change, but he told the doctor that he had a plan in progress which might resolve the matter. He wished for Lator to be kept in irons. He was becoming surly and unmanageable, but that was all the more reason to keep him in irons. He had refused to drink anything but plain water, and little of that. He was afraid that they might try to poison *him.*

On the sixth night out, Ben had just come off his watch and was about to go below. A cold, dense fog had come over the ship and it would be good to get below to his bunk, even if it did stink of garlic. As he stood by the rail for a second, he thought that he heard something, just a hint of a sound, a far-distant voice perhaps, or maybe a low pitched bellow muffled by the fog?. He strained to listen, but heard nothing more. Even so, the hair on the back of his neck seemed to stand up on its own, leaving him with a prickly feeling and a sense of mystery. Ben's hearing was good, in spite of his service at the guns. Now he was sure that he heard something off in the fog. He told Commodore Nelson of his experience, but he only smiled from one side of his mouth. "There should be no one out here but us. We are bringing up the rear of the retreat. The rest of the ships have all gone on ahead."

Ben had the middle watch that night and came back on deck at 8 bells or midnight. Mr. Wicks was at the wheel. He was doubling as sailing master and helmsman since they were short handed. After checking their course and seeing if Commodore Nelson had remembered to mark the peg board noting our course and speed, Ben paced the quarter deck. At first it was quiet. Then he heard it again. There was a faint sound, ever so faint, but it was really there. He was not imagining things. It was a low human voice. Now he strained harder to hear, riveting his concentration on the murky, cold fog. They had lookouts in the waist, for'ard and aft. They seemed to be awake but when Ben questioned them, they said they had heard nothing. There could be no one aloft at night. It was simply too dangerous.

Ben went back to the quarterdeck and spoke softly to the helmsman. "Let me know if you hear anything unusual." He silenced the ship's bell.

Ben cautioned the other lookouts to remain silent and not to call out for any reason. He stood there perhaps for one glass and then he heard it again. This time it was clear. *"Vamanos"* Ben stiffened at attention. From his pirate days he knew that was Spanish for 'Let's go.' Just then he heard a faint ship's bell, but that was from port and the voice had come from starb'd. They were in the midst of the Spanish fleet. In this dense fog, anything could happen.

Ben turned to the ship's boy who stood by the wheel and whispered.

"Go below and rouse Commodore Nelson at once. Be quiet now, no noise at all. Do you understand? Tell him I need him on deck instantly and *be quiet about it.*" It was awkward summoning the Commodore at night, but there was no Captain aboard *La Minerve.*

"Aye, sir," he whispered.

Within three minutes, the Commodore stood on the deck in his night shirt, shivering and yawning.

"What the deuce is wrong?"

"Keep your voice down, sir. We are sailing through the Spanish fleet. In this fog, we cannot see them, but I can hear them," whispered Ben.

"How do you know that we have not just caught up to our own ships?"

"Not likely, sir, unless British sailors have taken up the Spanish language."

"You do speak Spanish, I understand." This brought the Commodore awake with a jerk. He was now all action. "Good God!" He whispered to Ben.

"Call up the gun crews. Load all guns with double shot, but don't run them out. Have the crews sleep beside their guns. Oh, and also, check the flag locker for a Spanish flag. If they do get a glimpse of us, it would be better that they like what they see. And silence the ship's bell."

"I have already done that, sir. We have been keeping time by *their* bell for the past half hour. I have also doubled the watch up for'ard. There is a chance that we could ram the stern of one of their ships in the dark and fog."

Ben set about getting things in order. The men were awakened by the bosun's mate, one at a time and told that, "We are 'dancin' through the Spanish fleet and if you make a sound, it might be your last. Load the guns double-shotted, but do not run 'em out."

Ben was impressed with the precision and discipline that these men showed. It did take twelve minutes to clear for action with the guns inboard, but he could hardly hear a carriage wheel squeak. The men grabbed oil pots and doused the wooden wheels without being told. They did not put the ship's boats overboard for fear of running foul of another ship, but otherwise, they were ready. As the only leftenant aboard, with only midshipman Bandon on deck to assist Ben, he had plenty to do. Ben sent Mr. Bandon to rouse Midshipman Purdy. They would need him if the Spanish spotted the British ship and opened fire.

Ben stood by the rail for sometime, hearing more discomforting sounds. *That is a door or a hatch, and that a loose block hitting a mast.* Then, he happened to look *up.* He had been looking out at eye level to see the other ship's sails, but suddenly he nearly lost his continence when he saw about twenty feet above him and perhaps thirty yards away, six huge black guns floating by. Most of the rest of the ship was obscured by fog, but the sight of those guns would linger in his memory for a lifetime. These Spanish ships were tall, he knew that, but he had never been so close to one before. *The Spanish build regular castles to put to sea in. If they do decide to fire on us, all they could do is to take out rigging.* Ben doubted that they could depress their guns adequately to come anywhere near their decks, unless from some distance.

The Commodore had gone below to put on his undress uniform and now emerged, shaven and ready for battle. Ben approached him and pointed to the row of guns. The Commodore's eyes bulged out and his mouth fell open.

"That must be the *Santissima Trinidad,* the largest ship afloat. She carries 136 guns. If she decides to open fire, one broadside will put us out of our misery, especially if her captain is smart enough to wear to port a couple of cables," he whispered with an urgency that Ben had never heard in his voice before.

Ben whispered back, "The men are all in place and the guns double-shotted but not run out. Most of the crew is resting on the decks next to their guns. I took the liberty of preparing both the port and starboard batteries because there are Spanish ships on both sides of us, sir. The men may have to run from side to side to man the guns if we run into trouble."

Now came a long period of waiting, a tenseness that made the air thicker than ever. The fog had not lessened, but now and again there would be a small clearing and Ben could see running lights or even yards floating through the air as if attached to nothing substantial. They were just off Cartagena and headed towards the Straits of Gibraltar. Hours dragged by. His watch was up and he should go below, but he could not bring himself to do so. He was fascinated that they had sailed so far through most of the Spanish fleet and had not even been challenged.

Ben was damp and cold and decided to go below for a quick cup of hot chocolate. The order had not been given for dousing the cook fires yet. That might come any minute, and he was thirsty and cold. But something made him linger just a few seconds longer near the taffrail of the quarterdeck. As he looked up, suddenly there appeared the rail of a tall ship, with an officer standing there looking down at him. They were not more than fifty yards apart. Their yards were almost touching. Ben's blood froze in his veins and he suddenly felt deathly cold.

Later Ben did not know what possessed him, but he remembered a phrase from the pirate days that might allay their suspicions of their ship. He had already removed his hat, so that would not give him away. 'Niebla terrible,' he shouted with an ease that startled even him. The Commodore stood nearby and Ben could see him flinch. But he knew as well as Ben that they had been seen. The only thing that might save the day was a friendly call.

The Spanish officer looked for a second at *La Minerve* and then replied, "Y no ayuda en vista."

The Commodore looked to Ben for a translation. The Spaniard then faded back into the fog almost as quickly as he had appeared.

"He said, sir, that there is no lessening of the fog in sight. No, actually he said, 'There is no help in sight'." Ben whispered.

"I wonder what that means? Does he know that we are a lone British frigate caught in the midst of the Spanish fleet and he is biding his time to attack, or does he mean that we are both mired in this terrible fog and there is no *relief* from the fog in sight?"

"I am not at all certain, sir. The words could be taken either way," said Ben. The suspense was killing them both.

As Ben told it, they sailed on for a number of hours. They had one other close encounter with the Spanish that night. Just before dawn, one of the forw'rd lookouts came running to where Ben stood.

"Sir, there's a huge ship jus' ahead, sir, she's a monster an' if we don't do something quickly, we'll collide wi' her." His voice was a harsh whisper made even more grotesque by urgency.

Ben wheeled around and gave the helmsman muffled orders to, "Hard to starboard, *now*." The helmsman whipped the wheel around and they started to turn to pass the huge ship, and she was huge too. *If we collide with that mass of floating wood, we will be kindling ourselves,* thought Ben.

Their jib-boom would not clear her stern by more than a dozen feet, if they were lucky. There was no evidence that her lookouts had seen them, which seemed odd. They were busy staring out to starboard and larboard, with no concern for their stern, while the British ship was about to sail into her captain's cabin. In this fog, that was irresponsible ship handling. *I must remember to always post stern lookouts in a heavy fog.*

Chapter Two

The Battle of Cabo De Sao Vicente (Cape St. Vincent)

Late the next day they made the Admiral's flag ship and news of their wild sail through the Spanish fleet spread through the British fleet like a fire in the hold in a high wind with all the gun ports open. But each one knew that if *La Minerve* could have escaped through twenty odd Spanish ships without being captured, that the Spanish were not going to be too hard to manage. Even with the fog which persisted, everyone expected the Dons to be heaving into view soon.

Admiral Jervis signaled for all captains to come aboard the flag ship. Ben was lucky enough to get to accompany Commodore Nelson. As they entered the ship's boat, Nelson spoke to Ben.

"That was a fine piece of work that you did last night. Especially your little chat with the Spanish leftenant. Your quick action saved all our lives you know. I doubt that the Spaniard even suspected us as British for a minute. Good work, lad, but I must admit you gave me a start there for half a second."

"Having a French-built ship which just happened to have a Spanish flag in her flag locker helped some too, sir," replied Ben.

"I doubt that the officer could see her flag, lad."

Ben had his first view of Admiral Sir John Jervis in the spacious cabin of his flag ship, the *Victory*. He was a tall man, a bit stoop-shouldered. His face was that of someone's fine, old grandfather, kindly and yet there was a sternness there put in place by the burden of command. Ben could imagine soft words as well as stern rebukes from him, all spoken in the same soft, pleasant voice. But he would learn that Jervis, in spite of his gentle exterior, was a stern old war horse, not given to nonsense and a true warrior ready to meet any emergency at sea. He liked the man at once, and sensed that the Commodore respected him greatly.

"Welcome aboard, gentlemen. And I see Captain Nelson that you have brought along that young rascal, Rundel, who saved your ship on a foggy night in the midst of the entire Spanish fleet. Good on both of you for having survived such an ordeal. I should have loved to see it all, from some place else, of course," said the Admiral with a gentle laugh. They exchanged pleasantries and details about the Spanish fleet until the other officers arrived. There would be fifteen British ships to no one knew how many Spanish ships. Ben's estimate was about twenty Spanish ships, but that was too uncertain to be of value.

"Let's get down to business, lads. We are sailing W *b* N and have just cleared Gibraltar. In a couple of hours, we will be off *Cabo do Santa Maria.* The Spanish fleet should be along soon. I intend to confuse them by a swift and direct attack, with our best gunnery and seamanship. Captain Nelson, I would like to have you and Rundel here back in the *Captain* where you have your best gunners. You may leave a skeleton crew aboard *La Minerve,* and she can be sent home as a prize with information of our victory when the battle is over. She may serve well as a messenger ship off to port during the battle as well. There is much that we do not know about this Spanish fleet, but I have heard rumours that they are sailing with a convoy of merchant ships in their midst. I shall endeavour to split their forces by sailing in just here," as he pointed with his finger at the chart before him. If we can divide them, no matter how many of them there are, we should be able to conquer at least her van. We will actually attack and conquer each section, one at a time, rather than taking on the entire fleet. I should hope to be able to engage the van of the fleet here, if all goes well. Each of you shall then engage the nearest ship and work your guns for all they are worth. Is that clear? Any questions?"

There seemed to be complete agreement with the plan, which was not standard ship-of-the-line tactics, but it held promise. Ben thought that the Admiral sensed some reluctance at the use of a new strategy, even though none was voiced. There was a nervous shuffling of feet and some sidelong glances. The Admiral continued.

"If we use the same standard attack plan that has always been used, gentlemen, the Dons will know exactly what we plan to do. If we deviate from that plan, they will not have any idea of our intentions and will have to make instant decisions. That is when instant mistakes are made too. We can benefit from the element of surprise. Watch my signal flags closely."

Ben realized that Admiral Sir John Jervis was a very wise man. He would allow each of his officers enough freedom in their individual attack plans so that each might be able to distinguish himself. And yet, Ben didn't sell him short on discipline. He had a way of pursing his lips that told a man he was determined to keep order at all cost. That was good leadership and the kind that Captain Nelson would fancy. He was impetuous and calculating. He would do whatever he thought would work, and Admiral Jervis knew all too well that he would lose out on some brilliant action if he tried to strap Nelson too tightly into an inflexible plan. Ben was a bit surprised, because he had expected to see some elaborate plan of attack laid out that would dictate their every move like a choreographed dance.

They sailed on, coming about now to face the enemy which they knew was sailing to join the French and Dutch fleets at Brest. The French plan was to muster all the ships that they could at Brest and then proceed to invade their worst and strongest enemy, England.

Ben and now Captain Nelson hastened to switch his pennant from *La Minerve* to *Captain* and to be certain that the men and guns were ready. Mr. Warden was put in charge of *La Minerve.* Captain Miller would serve still as the ship's captain, with Nelson overall in charge.

I am moving yet again. It is doubly good that Tagon is not here. She would be terribly confused by all of this dashing about, Ben thought.

Back on the *Victory,* flag-Captain Sir Robert Calder began to count the Spanish ships as they loomed out of the dense fog. They could see running lights first, fuzzy and distant until they emerged from the fog close enough that they could see the huge ships moving slowly towards them. When he got to twenty-seven, the Admiral stopped him. "Enough, sir, no more of that. The die is cast and even if there are fifty sail-of-the-line, I will go through them." (Nicholas Tracy, Nelson's Battles, 1996). Actually, there appeared to be twenty-seven Spanish ships to British fifteen, but the latter had the advantage of speed and maneuverability, even though one could not count much on speed in such heavy haze. Captain Nelson passed word that he wanted the guns to fire at the rigging and then be prepared to board and conquer.

Ben went down the line of his guns, inspecting each one and talking with the men. He made a point of being sure that they understood that they were to elevate their guns so as to disable the rigging, but should under no circumstances damage the hull. He joked with them and was beginning to know a few of the lads. There were several Cornishmen in his 'Larbowlins,' as they were sometimes called. They had transferred from *La Minerve* to fill out the *Captain's* crew. They were a sturdy lot, prepared to win, but ready to accept death if that was the price of victory. He genuinely liked them and would get to know them better in future. After all, any one of these lads might lie mortally wounded within the hour. He, himself might lie by their sides, his last breath gone from him. The leftenants and midshipmen had all gone to the precaution of preparing wills before the battle, which was customary. Ben supposed that the Captain and Admiral did the same. When they asked Ben why he was not busy with paper and quill preparing his will, he replied, "I have nothing to leave and no one to leave it to."

That was not totally true. He did have a handsome sum in the Bank of London, but it did not seem real. He had never seen it or held it in his hand. And there really was no one. Many of the sailors willed off their meagre belongings before a battle, often agreeing that 'you gets mine if I die an' I gets yours if you die first.'

One sailor on deck was heard to scream, "Why, those are not ships. They're huge castles, high as the Cliffs of Dover," and they did look monstrously large as they loomed out of the fog. Ben could not believe his eyes. At about 11 a.m. the signal came for, 'close haul on the starboard tack.' The *Culloden* aimed for the space between the two divisions as the *Victory* came on a ways behind. The *Captain* was far back in the line. There were two groups of ships, the main Spanish fleet and a convoy. Then they saw a flood of signals from the Spanish flag ship. Ben wished that he could read their signals. Apparently Admiral Cordoba was trying to recall Rear-Admiral Moreno who was conducting the van because it now appeared that the rear was going to be attacked first. It also appeared that he understood that the British planned to split the fleet in two and had ordered his ships to 'close up' to prevent their passage through. Just then Ben saw a masterly bit of seamanship by Captain Troubridge of the *Culloden.* He was aware that Moreno might be called back and he understood John Jervis' plan of attack well enough to execute his move smoothly. Captain Troubridge broke through the Spanish line about 11:35 and split it in two, leaving seventeen ships to windward of the British ships and isolating eight ships to leeward where they could not quickly return to aid the rear. The seventeen ships to windward would get the benefit of all of the smoke from the battle. Ben was too busy to take it all in, but he did see the *Victory* in sharp exchange of gunfire with the *Salvador del Mundo.* 'Savior of the World' seemed a strange name to Ben for a ship that spit only death, but so did 'The

Rights of Man' which had fired the cannon ball that had taken the life of his Tagon. *Focus, you fool or you will not live to see the end of the day.* thought Ben, who was jarred from his reflections by a cannon ball that struck close to home.

By about 12:15 p.m., the *Culloden* had passed through the last Spanish position and Admiral Jervis signaled for all ships to 'tack in succession'. That would bring them all to bear on the enemy ships. Each ship would sail to the point where *Culloden* had tacked and then tack to follow into battle bringing the British ships up one at a time on Cordoba's division. Captain Nelson (for since he was now reassigned to the Mediterranean fleet, his title was no longer 'Commodore', but reverted to that of 'Captain'.) ordered them to prepare for tacking. Just as they were about to tack, *Principe de Asturias (112)* of Moreno's division successfully tacked to port and came to fire on *Captain* as they were tacking, but their rapid and deadly accurate fire quickly drove the Spanish ship off.

When Admiral Jervis ordered Nelson to 'Take suitable stations for mutual support and engage the enemy,' his intention was to cut off the advancing lee division so that it could not come to the assistance of the windward division. But Ben stood there mesmerized as he watched Captain Nelson give the order to 'wear ship', which was in direct disobedience to the Admiral's orders and which put them close beside the *San Nicolas* and *San Josef* in the van of the attack. The *Captain* moved from near the rear of the line to a position far enough forward to prevent the Spaniards from closing the gap and allowed the British ships to engage the Spanish ships. By this action, Captain Nelson prevented any possible reunion of the two parts of the Spanish fleet, thus weakening them. Captain Nelson ordered them to wear ship and caused them to pass between the *Diadem* and *Excellent*, two British ships and to the leeward side of the enemy. Ben perceived that the *Captain* made this move to prevent the Spanish from rejoining its two portions into one fleet and to prevent them from fleeing to land. It was now ten minutes past one o'clock and the guns were firing nonstop. The ship was enshrouded in thick, acrid smoke and men coughed, struggling to draw breath. The *Captain* was hard pressed by no less than seven monstrous Spanish ships and debris was raining from above so rapidly that the sailors could not remove the dead before more debris buried them. Of those seven ships, three were of 100 guns and there was the *Santissima Trinidad* of about 136 guns, the largest ship afloat, which would soon be in position to fire on them. Ben choked with the smoke and men staggered about, trying to serve their guns, but the men did keep firing even during the worst of it.

Ben kept yelling, "Fire, fire!" The deck boards vibrated violently under his feet with each salvo, making his feet sting and burn.

Admiral Jervis saw what Captain Nelson was trying to do and signaled for *Culloden*, *Blenheim*, and the *Prince George* to tack in support of the *Captain*. The Spanish Admiral's ship blossomed out in flags once again, and Ben could see that the Spanish ships were attempting to tack, but it was not well-executed and failed to change the situation. Admiral Jervis then signaled the *Excellent* and *Culloden* to tack across Nelson's wake and support the *Captain,* which they did. The other ships who were coming down on the windward side began to fire on the enemy ships and helped to reduce the pressure on the *Captain,* but they were still under extremely heavy fire. By this time, guns were roaring everywhere and the smoke was so thick that it burned their throats and noses painfully. Thank God there was some wind to clear away the smoke, but it was not enough. Debris rained from above and Ben soon realized that this was the worst battle he had seen so far. He feared not to see sunlight ever again. But he kept to his duty, "Fire." Tom was hard at work supervising a gun crew that had lost most of its men. He turned a smiling, sweaty face towards Ben and at least he was alright for now. The loblolly boys and idlers were busy carrying wounded men below. There were screams and the sound of shot tearing up the ship from all quarters.

Now the *Blenheim* came in close enough to take some of the pressure off the embattled *Captain,* but she was already a total loss.

For every man, there is a time when his heart says that it is best to surrender, and for Ben, that time came about seven minutes before the captain shouted, "Westminster or victory." and ordered the badly crippled *Captain* to be laid along side the *San Nicolas.* The decks of the *Captain* were running with the blood of the dead and wounded and the ship was totally disabled, her fallen rigging having taken away all of her steerage way. Even her wheel had been shot away, two men went with it. Captain Collingwood's ship was severely damaged also.

The guns roared and spat fire and belched smoke, and then came to a halt so they could be cooled, jammed with powder and shot again. Ben's guns were firing at a rate of a bit more than once every minute and a half at dead range, and the *San Nicolas* looked much the worst for his efforts. Two of his guns were out of action and a third was too hot to fire. Seamen poured fresh water into her using the sponge to cool it down, but just then a shot from the *San Nicolas* crashed through the bulkhead and took out the gun and the entire crew. They were dragging most of the rigging overboard, and there was no one free to cut the ship loose. Captain Nelson ordered the ship luffed up to come in contact with the *San Nicolas.* It was all he could do. The *Captain* was no longer able to sail on her own. Just then Ben felt a sharp blow on his brow just above his right eye. He reached up with his hand and felt the blood gushing out. *Just a head wound, always bleeds freely,* thought Ben. Then he fell against the rail and slumped down.

He heard through his pain the order for 'boarding parties to the rail'. Ben opened his eyes and the world spun recklessly. But he could see Captain Nelson standing on the rail, waiting for the ship to luff into position so the grapples could contact the *San Nicolas.* Nelson looked as if he were dancing on the rail through Ben's unfocused eyes. *I am supposed to be there. Captain Nelson should not be leading the boarding party, but it is just like him to do so,* thought Ben. Ben was supposed to lead the second wave of boarders and a group of lads were standing close by with cutlasses and pikes, waiting for his order. Someone spoke, "You alright, sir?" He could hear chopping sounds as they tried to cut some of the trailing rigging loose, but that was not the problem at hand. *He had to focus.*

Yes. I'll be alright in a minute. Ben raised up slowly and wobbled on his legs. He reached for his neck cloth and pulled it loose. With trembling hands he tied it around his forehead to stop the bleeding. Someone lent a hand, but Ben could not see his face.

"Is the boarding crew ready?" asked Ben.

"Aye, aye sir. As soon as you get through doin' your dance." There was a bit of laughter in the voice and Ben knew that Tom Murphy had come to his rescue. He gripped the rail tightly and saw the grapples bite into the Spanish ship's rail. Men heaved to bring the two ships together and the time had come to board. He saw Captain Nelson swing across the gap and land on the other side. Ben saw the Captain motion to his men to follow him as he jumped into the mainchains and onto the deck. A marine broke a window in the main cabin of the *San Nicolas,* and soon Nelson and a number of others slid through the open window and into the captain's cabin. Ben felt better now. He was seeing more clearly and he stood there beside the rail. Apparently the soldiers could not open the cabin door once they were inside the captain's cabin. Spanish soldiers from outside fired at the lock and the door flew open. The Spaniards were met with a volley of shots from British marines who stood close by. The Spaniards fell in a heap, all mortally wounded.

"Follow me, lads," Ben said feebly as he climbed slowly

over the rail and swung a bit uncertainly onto the deck of the *San Nicolas.* Tom was close by and the two young men fought back to back, thrusting with sword and cutlass. Ben had his new sword, the one he had purchased in London on becoming a leftenant and a commissioned officer. *This will be your first taste of blood,* he thought as he parried a thrust from a Spanish officer who had probably spent his boyhood with a sword in his hand and was now well equipped to give Ben, an orphan who had never seen a sword as a child, a very bad time. Ben stepped aside at just the last possible second so that the officer's sword skewered his jacket, but missed him. Ben was still unsteady on his feet and his head stung terribly, but he was able to carry on. He shouted to his men to close ranks and fight back to back. He could see Captain Nelson making his way to the quarter deck, hacking a path through cordage and stepping over dead or dying bodies. Ben aimed a lucky thrust at the Spanish officer and he fell mortally wounded at his feet, but it had taken all of five minutes to bring the enemy officer down. He heard Tom shout over the din, "Keep that up and you will be a master swordsman someday."

But that was farthest from Ben's mind just then. Another sailor had moved into place with a cutlass and was engaging Ben, but a cutlass is no match for a well-handled sword. Ben quickly dispatched the poor fellow. Tom had a man cornered and had whipped his sword from his hand. Then Ben thrust at a fellow who was about to level a pistol at Tom's back. With a steady and decisive thrust, he whipped the pistol out of the man's hand and pinned him against the rail. One of his sailors came to his rescue and tied the hands of the officer and led him off below. But the loss of blood was taking its toll. Ben felt faint and went back to where Tom was standing, sword at his side. Ben could see the battle slowing down. Most of the Spanish officers had already surrendered their swords to Captain Nelson. Some of his lads stood in groups with no one opposing them. To port, many of his men stood encircling the Spanish sailors and were binding their hands. There was a clatter of a sword on the deck, a sporadic gun shot, so it was finally over.

The Spanish Brigadier, who was in the line of fire, fell as he retreated to the quarterdeck, his hand gripping his chest, the grotesque mask that was his face working in agony, and died near the wheel. Ben saw Captain Nelson receive the sword of the Spanish Captain, who bowed on bended knee to offer the sword to Nelson.

"Now, it has just begun," Captain Nelson yelled, "Westminster Abbey or Saint Paul's. Forward men. Captain Miller, send over another boarding party." A group of sailors came streaming after him and Ben could see fierce fighting on the deck of the other enemy ship. He gripped the rail once more and pulled himself full upright. He had a duty to perform.

But for Captain Nelson, it was not over. He yelled, "To me lads! We still have the *San Josef* to take!" and headed for the *San Josef.* The *San Nicolas* was tangled with the rigging of the *San Josef.* Leftenant Berry (later Captain Berry) distinguished himself by taking the brunt of much of the hand to hand fighting. The battle was fierce but brief. Ben's lads could hear screams and clashing of arms and pistol shots even before they were able to engage.

Ben and his group of followers swung across the mainchains just behind Captain Nelson and began to engage the Spaniards. They fought for a short time, fierce, deadly combat that threatened to take a man's life any moment. The marines followed in close to his group and were doing a masterful bit with their bayonets.

Then Captain Nelson made the quarter deck where the commander lay dying and demanded the Spanish Captain's sword. The man looked at him for a second, not quite sure whether to use the sword or surrender it. Finally he bowed deeply and handed the sword to Captain Nelson. The Spanish officers saw their leader dead and one by one they stepped forward, offered their swords in surrender with no further fight. Ben's lads and the marines made fast work of rounding up and disarming the crew. There was no resistance left in them once they saw their leader dead. Had the Spaniards been determined, there were far more of them in the two ships than there were of the British in the 74 and they could easily have taken them all prisoner or dispatched them. Ben felt relieved to see the swords begin to pile up on the deck, but Nelson still could not quite comprehend that the Spanish had given up so easily. He stood with a quizzical smile on his face. "I asked for his sword and he gave it to me," he said incredulously.

As Ben stood there, motionless, contemplating the mess that must be cleaned up after a battle of this magnitude, he noticed that his left arm had a deep gash. It was still bleeding. He had felt the first officer's sword touch his arm, but the sword must have been so sharp that he really did not notice that he had done more than break the skin. He was bleeding profusely again. It was growing dark, near dusk. Darkness comes early in February and this was but the 14th, a day that England would remember in her history books, for sure.

Ben saw the *Santissima Trinidad,* sailing away to the north out of harms way. *Just as well,* he thought. *We could never have fought her and won.* But he looked on in dismay. His beautiful *Captain* was a total loss. The Spaniards had fired into her hold and she was leaking badly as well as being mostly dismasted.

They secured the prisoners below in the Spanish ships and then returned to the *Captain.* The remaining British ships had come together near the flag ship and a ship's boat approached with the Admiral in the stern. He climbed aboard the stricken *Captain,* shaking his head.

"You are a scoundrel, Nelson, but I love you all the same. Best get your men and any gear that you can salvage off the *Captain* and into the *Culloden* for now. I am sure that the stores, powder and shot left aboard the *Captain* could be shared throughout the fleet to replenish their supplies, but you will have to work fast and in the dark.

We'll get you a new ship as soon as one comes out from England. Good work lads!" he called as appreciative heads looked up.

That night was a nightmare. The men were all dead tired. They dragged themselves across the deck of the *Captain* like zombies. Many were wounded and were below on the orlop deck. Ben's first order was to get the wounded and the surgeon to the new ship which stood at sea anchor close by. Ben gave the order to begin moving the wounded to the *Culloden* and a group of seamen staggered in to begin the removal.

As Ben approached the surgeon, he could see that the old man was totally exhausted. Ben had thought to ask him to clean and bind his head wound. But the old man sat in the only chair on the orlop, surrounded by wounded, groaning men spread out across the deck. The British had lost some 400 killed and several hundred wounded, but Ben heard later that the Spanish had lost over 4,000 men. As Ben approached, the old man looked up at him through tired, glassy eyes. His grey hair fell loosely to his shoulders and stuck, plastered to his sweaty skin. Beads of sweat stood on his forehead and ran down his cheeks, even though it was quite cold. One could no longer see the faintest vestage of the London gentleman in him.

"Mind if I dress these wounds myself," said Ben with a weary smile.

"Go ahead, lad. You are probably as competent as I am. He cleaned the arm and it went well. He wrapped it in clean bandages, pulling the severed flesh back together. But as Ben tried to remove the neck cloth from his head, it pulled at the flesh and started to bleed again.

"Leave off that, lad. It is only going to bleed worse. Let me fix it for you." So the old surgeon went to work with shears to remove the cloth and clean the wound. "It is clear to the bone and you will have a scar, but it should heal well. Good thing that you tied it together as swiftly as you did."

As the old surgeon worked, Ben asked about Lator.

"He has not said a civil word to anyone that we know of in days," replied the old man.

"I have a plan to test if the white powder is poisonous," said Ben, "but I will need your help."

Ben thought it was a poor time to ask for the surgeon's help when he was dead on his feet. He had been used to two or three patients a day in his London surgery. Here he had treated over eighty major injuries and a host of minor ones like Ben's in a single afternoon. *He would be justified to refuse to help me,* thought Ben, but he went forward anyway.

"I have a cage that I can easily convert into a trap. All it will take is a few minutes. I do not know how long we will serve together, since the *Captain* is to be abandoned, so I will fix the cage this night. I will bait it with some left over crumbs and catch a rat or two. With a ship about to sink, it should be a cinch to catch a few rats with some food. They will be eager to find their way free. Then we will bring the cage with rats down to the sick bay on the *Culloden* and feed them bread with some of the white powder sprinkled on it. All that you have to do is to watch their reactions. If they get sick quickly and behave as the sailors did earlier, then we know that this is the poison that was used on them. If it's strychnine, they will go through severe tremours of the limbs before they actually die. You will be with the injured day and night and could just glance at the rats from time to time? I will be off on other duty and cannot observe them," concluded Ben.

The old man turned, tired, bloodshot eyes to him and nodded. He would be glad to see that his test was carried out. Ben neglected to say that he would have to appear at the man's trial and testify, but that could wait until later.

Most of the wounded had been removed by the time Ben had finished with Mr. Bowers and prepared the rat trap. Ben gave the order to remove the prisoner who was kept in irons and place him aboard the *Culloden,* under guard and in irons. Ben could hear block's squealing as first the powder was removed and then the stores. These were ferried in waiting ship's boats to the other vessels of the fleet. The British had lost only the *Captain,* which was most lucky. Then he supervised the removal of water casks and casks of beef and pork. Tom was busy cleaning out the bread room. Captain Nelson ordered his things removed from his cabin and put the ship's papers in a weighted canvas bag ready to transfer to the *Culloden.* Ben slipped aft long enough to collect his personal gear and place it in the pile to go to the new ship, along with the captain's gear. Leftenant Hobson had already brought up his gear and Leftenant Warden had just gone below to remove his things. Ben could feel the *Captain* riding dead under his feet. She did not lift to a wave, but sat there solid and let the water fight its way past her.

A sailor approached with a ragged salute.

"Sir, there are about ten casks of beef what is swimmin' in salt water. Should we try to remove 'em, sir or leave 'em behind?"

"Let them be redundant, Mr. Culpepper. They are most likely tainted if they are swimming in bilge water."

"Aye sir."

Ben was exhausted beyond the point of sound judgment, but he did have just enough energy to go below to where he had placed his trap. Sure enough, with the ship about to sink, four rats had taken refuge in his trap where there was food and a solid, dry floor. Ben picked up the cage. They were healthy looking fellows, but disgusting all the same. His nose wrinkled at the familiar smell. He held the lantern to look at his chronometer. It was a bit past two in the morning. He had best make the last boat to the *Culloden* and get settled in. He had been on his feet almost constantly with little to eat since midnight last night. No wonder he was tired.

Ben was given a hammock beside the second leftenant of the *Culloden.* Mr. Hargrove was already snoring sonorously in his bunk and did not even hear Ben come in.

At six in the morning, the crew was roused, even though many had not slept more than a few hours. The men assembled on deck, and the deck was crowded, what with their 420 lads added to their 400 or so regulars. Ben looked over where the *Captain* was at sea anchor and she was riding so low that her gun ports were under water. She was listing a bit to starboard. The *Culloden* had upped anchor during the night so that they would not be too close to her if she sank during the night.

Captain Troubridge appeared on deck and addressed the men briefly, saying that new ships were expected to put out from England shortly. Ben looked at the man carefully. He had a perfectly oval head, the oval completed nicely by his hair which stood up atop his head is if it were a stack of hay. His nose was large with a mouth that tended to turn down ever so slightly at the corners. His left eyebrow seemed to be slightly raised as if in perpetual surprise and he had strong, brown eyes that could bore into a man. He was known as a fine sailor but no grand tactician, no match for Captain Nelson. Breakfast would be served in about half an hour and the Admiral would expect all of the officers of the fleet to attend him in his cabin at 9 o'clock sharp (2 bells). The men were asked to handle the crowding as best they could and to mess wherever they could find space.

Ben collected his gear the night before and had stowed it under his hammock, including his caged rats. These brought many a questioning stare from his fellow leftenants. After breakfast, Ben brought the cage out and headed towards the orlop deck to find the surgeon. But his messmates were not going to let him get away that easily.

"You trying to save a few rats from drowning?" was one fellows comment.

"I have seen many a man get lonely at sea and take up with a cat or a small dog, even potted flowers, but never have I seen a fellow who liked rats for pets." said Leftenant Pilsington, a pudgy fellow with a mischievous smile.

Ben turned and said, "These are caged rats to catch another rat, a murderer." He would explain later and they would not let free of him until he did. Ben took the rats to Mr. Bowers. Fortunately, he had remembered to bring the vial of white powder with him. Ben saved some morsels from breakfast and he sprinkled the powder on the food and then handed it into the cage.

"There, Mr. Bowers. If this is the poison that we think it is, these fellows should begin to feel mighty sickly in about four hours. I have given them a sizable dose. But, here, keep this vial. We may want to send it to England for a definitive analysis when we are through with the rats."

Bowers was busy with his patients and had plenty to look after, but he said that he would check the rats every half hour, 'each bell'.

Ben raced off just making the ship's boat with Captain Nelson already aboard. They were rowed to the *Victory. Good God, I did not take time to shave and I am filthy,* Ben thought. *I will surely live up to my nickname as 'poorest dressed officer in the British Navy' today.* This was the first chance that Ben had taken to look at the fleet carefully since the battle. The British fleet had fared much better than did the Spaniards. There would be a good bit of repair to attend to, but all in all, the ships should be back in seaworthy condition in a day or two. There was a huge pool of man power in the fleet when at sea anchor in close proximity and there were also many places to look for a replacement spar or rudder. Ben could already hear men busy with adzes and saws, clearing rubble and salvaging any usable parts.

The officers filed into the Admiral's cabin and he stepped out of his sleeping cabin to greet them. Ben overheard a bit of conversation as he waited his turn to enter through the door.

"What an act of disobedience and bravado when Captain Nelson crossed the line and attacked the *San Nicolas,* against your orders, sir," said Captain Calder to the Admiral.

"It certainly was so... and if ever you commit such a

breach of your orders, I will forgive you also," said the Admiral. (Nicolas Tracy, *Nelson's Battles, 1996,* Chatham Pub., London). So if that was an example of the Admiral's superb wit, then his grandfatherly face was indeed misleading. Ben liked him all the more. He was a man who could recognize excellence in a Captain and knew how to give him steerage way to use it effectively.

"We are calling his *San Nicolas 112,* Nelson's patent bridge for boarding first rates." Captain Berry chimed in with a hearty laugh. (Nicolas Tracy, *Nelson's Battles,* 1996, Chatham Pub.) The other officers joined in for a mighty laugh too, which released some of the fatigue and tension that they all felt.

The upshot of that brief meeting was to congratulate all the captains on a battle well-fought and won and to convey his thanks to the lads aboard the ships as well. The order was given to repair all but the *Captain.* A decision would be made later if there were any benefit from taking her in tow into port. They were less than a hundred miles from the new station at the Tagus River in Portugal. The ships were to be made seaworthy for the brief journey and final repairs could be made at Lisbon. The sail makers would be busy for days repairing holes in the sails, sewing new gussets and replacing ropes.

"Then there is the matter of the man from the *Captain* who is accused of murdering five of his messmates. Where do we stand on that, Captain Nelson? By the way, it may not be 'Captain' for much longer," Jarvis said with a smile."

Nelson looked at Ben and Ben stood up.

"Sir, we have procured a bit of the white powder that we think is the poison used on the sailors and we have captured some rats who are being fed the powder on bits of food. We should know by the end of the day if this is the poison that was used. The surgeon is watching the rats to see if they respond with the same symptoms shown by the five sailors before they died. We will inform Captain Nelson as soon as we have any results, sir. I am recommending that the vial of powder be sent to London for a more definitive analysis, sir."

"Good. I would like to hold a court martial immediately upon receipt of your results. The fellow has lingered for too long in irons while we were busy fighting the Dons. British justice must be certain and swift. Whose idea was it to use the rats?"

Ben flushed a bit. He was still mighty tired from the exertions of the past two days. "It was my idea, sir. There is no other way to know except to take the powder to England for analysis, and that will take precious time."

"Good thinking, lad."

The Admiral had taken a distinct liking to this promising young leftenant. *He seems to run in deeper waters than most of the young men that I see coming along the chain of command. He will bear watching.*

"I have a good many papers, letters and reports to fill out this day, but I would hope that we could schedule a court martial for the man by, say four bells this afternoon. I should like all of you in attendance who can come. I know that some of you will be busy with repairs to your ships, but come if you can. We'll see to your court martial for the loss of the *Captain* in a day or two when there are fewer vittles on our plate," said the Admiral to Nelson.

"Oh, and I would not worry, Nelson, old chap. This court martial will be a mere formality."

Then he turned to Ben.

"Mr. Rundel, we need to get word of this battle to England as soon as possible. The Admiralty will want full reports which I will prepare today. I would like each captain to prepare his reports to be ready by the end of the day so I can send them all in an envelope with young Mr. Rundel here." He turned to Captain Nelson. "I judge that you will not mind if I send this lad home with papers in the captured *La Fleur?*"

Captain Nelson smiled in approval. "You could do no better, sir."

So it was settled. Ben would once again transfer his

gear to *La Fleur.* Ben was delighted to be going home if only for a short visit. In the ship's boat back to the *Culloden,* Captain Nelson explained that he was willing to let Ben go, but that unless the Admiralty said differently, he would like to have him back here as soon as possible. "And bring me a damned good ship on your way back if you please, Mr. Rundel, one that won't sink so easily."

Ben asked about the supplies on *La Fleur* and if she was seaworthy.

"Well, let's see. There are mostly food stuffs and ordnance, as I recall. We will be in desperate need of those things here at the station. Perhaps you should off-load most of the food stuffs, extra sail cloth and yards and ordnance before you leave. I will send you directions for where to put the goods as soon as I can talk with several of the captains. Some ships did not get any replenishment of their supplies from the wrecked *Captain,* but I am not sure who came up short. You may take the jolly boat and transfer your things to *La Fleur.* She seems to be quite seaworthy. I have a few spare charts and things that you will need. Hasten to London and give the dispatches to the First Lord as soon as you can and then take the next ship headed for the Tagus. We have work to do along the African Coast." When questioned, Nelson would say no more. Surely he had some plan of attack already in mind, with the gun smoke barely cleared from the last battle.

Ben gathered up his gear, checked with Dr. Bowers who insisted on rebandaging his head, and then headed off to his new ship. Before he left, Captain Nelson approached him and handed him a chronometer. "Here, lad. You will need a better chronometer than is aboard *La Fleur.* I checked it the other day and it is not reliable."

Ben selected a crew of twenty able seamen, including Tom Murphy as his midshipman. When he looked over the men assembled before him, he was well-pleased with his selection. *It pays to know one's men,* he thought. *These are all good lads. I can depend on them.*

When Ben heard that he would serve as acting Captain of *La Fleur,* he had uttered a little silent prayer. "Dear God, don't let me lose this ship, not *this* ship. I will sink to the briny bottom with her before I will surrender her." He had lost his first command several years ago and almost his life as well. He could not take a chance on losing this, his second command. The ship was a brig of fine form, a good sailer.

Ben spent the day getting supplies that could be used at the Tagus off-loaded. That required a good bit of book keeping since he had no scribe or purser. He might have enlisted help from another ship, but he decided not to. He would have all of his reports ready for the Admiral by six that night, or die trying. He needed to assign his crew to new duties and watches as well. It took time to fill out a duty roster and when he did find the time, he realized that he was short of topmen. *Well, a few good lads will just have to learn to work the tops,* he thought.

It was late, nearly five thirty when he managed to gather up his things and was rowed back to the *Culloden.* When he walked into the sick bay, he was met by a smiling, but obviously very tired surgeon.

"You were right lad. Those rats ate the food with that powder and in about three hours they became very nervous, raced around the cage and then began to double up as if with abdominal pain. The evidence is quite clear to me. This *is* the poison that killed the men. The rats all died about three this afternoon."

"Good work, man. Can you leave the wounded for half an hour? We need to attend the court martial of Lator on the flagship at six sharp. It is nearly six now. Hurry. I'll pass the word for the marine Corporal and Sergeant at arms to bring the prisoner to the waiting boat at once." Ben did not wait for an answer but was off in a flash. He stopped by the scribes cabin to get a few words added to the end of his report on Lator, and then descended into the boat, to face a belligerent Lator and a sleepy Bowers. The latter sat in the stern of the boat, his head drooped on his chest and snored loudly, to the amusement of the

boat's crew. The old man had not slept in several days and he was unkempt and doddery on his feet, but he bore up well in spite of his affliction.
In the Admiral's cabin there were assembled those officers who were free, Captains Berry, Troubridge, Nelson, Miller and the Admiral. When the preliminaries were completed, Ben was called forward after the reading of the charges to present his account of the treachery of Lator. The man stood there, thin, emaciated, with a wolfish snarl on his face, a man totally rejected by his shipmates. The Admiral read the Article of War pertaining to murder, Article 28. Then Ben read the account of the death of the five men, explaining how they had become sick and showed signs of abdominal discomfort and then after three days, they died. He also explained that they were all in the same mess and the only one to recover was Lator. Lator was the one assigned to bring the food in the messkid for the weeks before the men died. Ben suspected that he was only pretending to be sick. That would mean violation of yet another Article of War concerning dereliction of duty. He told how they had found the vial of white powder in Lator's belongings and how they had trapped rats to test the white powder as a poison. He pulled out the vial with some of the powder still remaining in it. Then he called on Mr. Bowers to explain what he had seen when the rats were given the white powder. The surgeon's testimony pretty well summed up the case. He explained how the rats had showed extreme abdominal discomfort before their death and that all who had received the poison died. He brought out the cage with the dead rats and handed it to Ben to show to the court.

After the presentation, the prisoner was brought forward, a terrible sneer on his ugly face. He was asked if he committed the murders and why. He refused to speak except to say that he was, 'a Frenchman and should be tried in his own country.'

"You have violated English Naval law and must pay

the price. If you were being tried in France today, you would certainly feel the bite of the guillotine. You know that as well as I do," said Captain Berry.

The Admiral asked Ben, "Why do you suppose that this fellow committed the murders?" By this time, every one was convinced that Lator had been the murderer. No other murders or unexplained deaths had occurred since he was imprisoned some weeks ago.

Ben replied, "I think that we have to ask what he was doing as a French national running about the harbour in Portsmouth? England and France have been at war since 1793. Surely he was expecting to be caught by a press gang sooner or later. I suspect that he is a French spy sent to find out what is going on in Portsmouth so that he can report back to Paris. He just happened to run into a press gang and was so angered that he decided to try to murder our lads to make up for his blundering as a spy. You may want to note that his name in the muster book reads, 'Jean Latour', which may or may not be French, as if he were trying to cover up his nationality."

One of the officers added, "He was stone drunk when he came aboard, sir. Must have slipped up and given his true name."

"Beyond these suppositions, sir, we have not been able to get any reasonable confession out of him."

"Humm. That brings up another question here. If he is a spy, then he is guilty of treason as well as murder. Once a man signs onto a British Naval ship, he swears loyalty to King George III and can serve no other. We can try him for murder and hang him if we wish, but if he is guilty of treason on such a large scale as well, we are duty bound to hand him over to the Admiralty for trial for treason. What say you lads? Do you have any further questions concerning the murder charge or the charge of treason?" There was a murmer of approval.

But no one spoke outright, so the Admiral called for a vote and within fifteen minutes of the beginning of the trial, the man was found guilty of murder. Now the Admiral spoke again.

"Since there is good reason to suspect that the man is a spy, we should decide if he will be bound over to the Admiralty to stand trial for treason. If we hang him today, we may never know what his real mission was. What say you?"

"Send him to England," was the unanimous cry.

The Admiral looked at Ben. Mr. Rundel, you have done a superb job in bringing this scoundrel to justice, and we appreciate the work of Mr. Bowers as well. I suggest that you set sail in the morning for Portsmouth with this hoodlum in chains and the vial of powder, and that you turn him over to the port Admiral with a full report of his doings. I will have papers ready for you to carry to London by 6 a.m. tomorrow. Be sure you include your report and that of Mr. Bowers in the papers to go to the Admiralty so they have access to all of the facts. You'll need a second set of those papers to show the port Admiral at Portsmouth so he can take proper action. I will have my scribe copy your reports tonight and all will be ready for you in the morning. I am sending you to Portsmouth since you are most likely to get a ship back to the Tagus from that port. Any questions?"

He continued. "The Admiralty may have other plans for you, but I believe that Captain Nelson has requested your speedy return by the next fastest ship to come this way. We expect to see you and your crew back in record time, lad."

So it was over. He ordered the marine sergeant to take LaTour aboard *La Fleur* and Ben went aboard to wolf down a simple meal of boiled beef and ship's biscuits. He fell quickly asleep. He named one of his men, Giles Conyers, to serve as ship's cook and his steward. (This was when I, Giles Conyers, came officially into Mr. Rundel's life.)

Chapter Three

Horse Capers and The Good Life on Land

Giles shook Ben violently at five o'clock the next morning, trying to awaken him. Ben's head still hurt some and he had to be careful of his injured arm. "It's time to set sail for England, sir," said Giles, a broad smile on his face clearly anticipating time ashore in Portsmouth.

Ben arose and doused his face with cold water. He awoke and bellowed at Giles to, "Bring Mr. Murphy to my cabin at once."

"Sir, these dispatches came aboard just minutes ago, from the Admiral, I believe," said Giles. Ben took the papers and carefully put them in a weighted canvas bag and placed them in his desk drawer and secured the lock. He heard a knock and then footsteps.

"Tom, you ready to sail for England?" said Ben as he tried to shave. His beard had grown coarse and raggy over the past several days and he had no time to see to its proper grooming.

"As ready as I will ever be, sir. If I had me choice, it'd be Ireland."

"What say we try to set a record from Cape St. Vincent to Portsmouth? Or, would you rather play it safe and make a sure, slow passage? *La Fleur* is a very fast ship and she has recently been cleaned of barnacles. We are sailing with only a skeleton crew, so you and I will have to be everywhere at once, but I leave it to you if we try for a record or not. The faster our passage, the more time we will have in London to see the sights," said Ben.

"I don't plan to go to London, sir, unless you need me there," said Tom.

Ben was a bit surprised at that reply. He had noted a change in Tom since the battle at St. Vincent. It could not be physical since Tom came away from the battle without as much as a scratch. "I would enjoy your company for a few days in London, but if you have other plans, that will not be a problem," replied Ben.

"Let's go for a speedy passage. sir, and I will help all that I can," replied Tom, his voice once again animated and cheerful.

"Oh, and did they put La Tour aboard last night?"

"Aye, sir. He's fuming in the hold and still in irons."

So it was decided. Ben had made a firm vow that nothing would happen to this ship and that he would not lose it, but now he felt a bit guilty. *Was he putting the ship in jeopardy by driving her so hard for land?*

No time to think about that. The Admiral had instructed him to make a speedy passage and he would do his best to obey. "Shake out the heads'ls, man the capstan, all hands to handle sails. Up anchor, man the braces, lively there." He stepped to the helm and took the wheel. He had laid a tentative course the night before and would sail away from the fleet in fine shape. Good strong winter winds were blowing from the southwest as they usually did this time of year. All would be well if there were no Atlantic storms to interfere on his way.

The first time that Tom was able to relieve Ben from the helm, Ben went to his cabin and prepared the rest of the duty roster. He had made out only the duties for 'leaving port' the night before, being too sleepy to concentrate on the rest of his work. He noted the figures handed to him by Mr. Ross concerning the last few throws of the log.

"We are making extremely good speed," he told Tom, "We will be in Portsmouth within eight days if this wind holds."

There were no unusual events on the passage to England, no storms, no leaky hull, no adverse winds and no privateers to slow them down. Ben fell into his bunk each night, totally exhausted. He hoped to be able to rest on this passage, but that was not to happen. Tom seemed very tired too. He was not his usual talkative self. Each day wore on like the one before and soon a lookout called to Ben, "Land, ho, sir." They were off the Lizard and gaining fast on Plymouth.

Giles proved to be a fine steward and a fair to middling cook. The men liked him and he did all he could to make the passage easy for all aboard. Only LaTour seemed upset by his being transported to England. He screamed that he wanted to go to France, but they all soon learned to pay no attention to him. "He is a dead man already, no matter where he goes," said Tom.

The harbour at Portsmouth came into view and Ben realized that he had a good bit of planning to do in order to make his arrival a smooth one. Every night as his head hit the pillow, he wanted to lay awake for some time planning what he would do when they made port, but each time sleep had crept in to rob him of his plan. He had not only the chain of orders for coming to anchor to consider, but also the plans for transferring the prisoner, plans to get a jury crew aboard so he could let his men have shore leave. They had been an exemplary crew on the passage home and deserved a few days of shore leave. Most Captains would have hesitated at giving shore leave in an English port during wartime, but Ben knew his men and he was certain that none would desert him. Eight of the twenty lads were married and another eight had sweethearts who waited anxiously for their return. These sixteen would go straight home. With the exception of Wilbur, most of the men lived within twenty or thirty miles of Portsmouth, so they could all make it home in a day. That would give them time to visit and get back.

Then too, he had to arrange for their return passage. He needed to speak with the port Admiral about LaTour and to arrange for his transport to a prison on land. All that would take time and he should be off to London with the dispatches with as much haste as possible.

Ben brought the fine ship to a perfect port landing and gave a sigh of relief. *At least that is over*, he thought.

Mr. Kent spoke to him earlier as spokesman for the

crew and requested permission for their shore leave. Ben said little at the time, but now he had Tom Murphy call, 'All hands'. The men assembled in the waist and Ben spoke to them. It was already ten in the morning.

"Lads, we have made a record fast passage home. You have served the ship and King well. I need your help in getting the prisoner ashore and securing the ship for perhaps an hour or two. Then if I can have your promises to return as planned, I will give you all shore leave. It is my intention to ask the port Admiral for a jury crew to take control of the prize ship at once, so you may want to have your duffels ready to go ashore as soon as we have deposited the prisoner. I will give you a time and place for us to meet after I have seen the port Admiral. You can see the Admiral's purser if you want to draw your pay. Do I have your promise to return as planned?"

The men roared out their approval and followed with, "Three hearty cheers for Cap'n Rundel! Huzzah! Huzzah, Huzzah!"

"Good. We have no marines aboard, so we will remove the prisoner in hand cuffs with leg shackles for safety. Sorenson, Cross, Murdock and Semour, bring the prisoner on deck if you please. The rest of you, port gaskets and hand out the ship's boat."

Ben realized that he had not packed his belongings for going ashore either and headed to his cabin to prepare. In the passageway, he met Tom Murphy. "Sure you don't want to come with me to London, Tom?"

"No. I will stay here in Portsmouth and try to catch up on my sleep," was his reply.

When the ship's boat was ready and all aboard, Ben stepped down, carrying the packet of papers for the port Admiral and those for the Admiralty. He dared not leave them aboard. All were placed in canvas bags with the usual weights in case they needed to be jettisoned overboard.

On shore, Ben ordered the prisoner to be marched to the port Admiral's office and handed the man over to the sentries who stood guard outside.

He addressed the first sentry. "We have a prisoner here to be held for trial for treason and murder. I was instructed to hand him over to your men. I have letters from Admiral Jervis concerning his crimes."

"Mr. Pierson. Take this prisoner to the gaol at once. See that he does not escape." Then turning to Ben, "You may proceed in to see Admiral Mann." The crew stood back, awkwardly, like a bunch of school boys wanting to commit some mischief, but not quite sure if they should.

Ben went into the waiting room and faced a stern clerk. His mind jerked back to the time that he had tried to see the Admiral at London and had been kept waiting for most of two days. Would he face a similar challenge here? There were half a dozen persons waiting to see the Admiral. Ben stepped forward.

"I am Leftenant Benjamin Rundel, acting Captain of *La Fleur.* I need to see Admiral Mann at once. I have urgent messages from Admiral Jervis, information about a recent battle, and a request concerning a prisoner accused of treason and murder." He poured all the urgency and authority into his voice that he could. "There is also a fine prize ship setting in the harbour and the Admiral will want to know about that as well."

The clerk looked up at Ben. He was younger than old Cheevers had been, but he fitted the mould quite well. He sniveled a bit and then said, "Well, it looks as if you have more business with Admiral Mann than all these other folks put together. I'll see what I can do about getting you an audience at once." At that he arose and shuffled to the door, motioning Ben to, "Have a seat, young sir."

The clerk was gone for what seemed an age. When he finally reappeared, he was wringing his hands. "The Admiral will see you in about forty-five minutes."

Well, there was no help for it. He would have to wait. He had put on all that speed to get home, only to be left waiting in the port Admiral's office. Such was life in the Navy. Ben rose and went to the door of the building. He smiled at the sentry and pointed to the little knot of his men who were standing not far off. Then he signaled Tom to come close. "Tom, take the men to the Admiral's purser and give him these records for the lads. They can draw pay against these records and be ready to leave for home as soon as I am through. I will be a while yet, perhaps more than an hour."

But the clerk was true to his word. Forty-five minutes later, he escorted Ben to the Admiral's chambers. It was not as impressive as the Admiralty chambers in London, but it was a fine room, carpeted and with many beautiful paintings of sailing ships as well as ship's plans. The old Admiral sat behind a pile of papers, which he had been shuffling about, apparently in search of some missing document. He looked up through spectacles as Ben approached. Ben saluted, "Acting Captain Benjamin Rundel reporting, sir. I have messages for you from Admiral John Jervis concerning a great victory off Cape St. Vincent. Out in the harbour stands a fine prize ship, the brig, *La Fleur.* I request a prize crew be put aboard her so my men can have a bit of shore leave. There is also the matter of a prisoner accused of treason and murder. And I am to leave for the Admiralty in London as soon as possible. I would also like to request passage for me and my twenty seamen aboard the next ship bound for the Tagus River Station, sir."

"Whoa, drop anchor lad. Let's take one thing at a time." The rise of his eyebrows at Ben's mention of giving his seamen shore leave told Ben that he did not approve, but Ben's general rush of youthful enthusiasm was clearly too much for the old man to absorb.

"You say you are going to give your seamen shore leave? Is that entirely wise?"

"I know these men sir and I am certain that none will desert the service. I have their parole on it."

"I see, and I suppose that they are all gentlemen too?" said the Admiral, clearly thinking that here was another of those soft young officers who would not last long in the Navy.

"Now, what is this about a prize ship?"

"Sir, Captain Nelson captured *La Fleur* just before the battle of Cape St. Vincent and I have been instructed to deposit her here for sale as a prize ship."

"Then you say there was some great battle?"

"Yes, sir. Admiral John Jervis and his Mediterranean fleet met and defeated the Spanish fleet off Cape St. Vincent on 14 Feb. Captain Nelson did a fine job of taking two ships of over 100 guns each, both at once. It is all in this report which I am taking to London today." *Today,* thought Ben, *only if I can get through this infernal red tape and put an end to all these questions. It would all become clear when he read the reports.*

Then, what is this about treason, murder and a prisoner? I see no prisoner."

Ben explained that he was instructed to entrust a prisoner into his hands who had been found guilty of murdering five men at sea, but who was also suspected of being a spy and therefore, guilty of treason. He drew out the vial of poison and asked the Admiral to keep it as evidence of the man's guilt. "This is the vial of poison that was used and it should be analyzed by a chemist at once. Admiral Jervis thought that he should be tried by a higher court than a court martial at sea and so, instructed him to be brought here. He, one Jean La Tour, is presently in the hands of the marines, under guard." Ben handed the reports concerning LaTour to the Admiral.

The old man opened the bag, smoothed out the top papers with his huge hand and began to read. His eyebrows shot up again as he read about the murder of five seamen and the prisoner's behavior. When he had completed the reading, he looked up at Ben. "You did right in bringing this matter to the attention of a higher court. I will see to it that this matter is handled swiftly, be sure. You did a fine job in bringing the man to justice, lad." Ben sensed a new respect from the Admiral.

"Now about the prize ship."

Ben handed the Admiral the reports on *La Fleur,* including her manifests and muster book. The old Admiral scanned them briefly and said, "All seems to be in order here. I will see to the manning of the ship while it is in harbour and her disposal. I will have men aboard within the hour. Now, you say you want to return to the Tagus by the next ship?"

"Yes sir, myself and twenty of my crew."

"The *Theseus* will sail in six days. She will be going to reinforce the Mediterranean Fleet. There should be room aboard her. I would advise that you be on board by 6 p.m. on the first of March. I am not sure of her sailing time, but I will send word to Captain Hawkins of your intended passage. Oh, and a lady, one Betsy Fremantle, will be aboard, so tell your men to be on their best behavior, understand? She's the wife of Captain Fremantle."

"Aye, aye sir."

"But wait a minute, here. These reports from Admiral Jervis are dated 16 Feb., 1797, and this is only the 23 of February. You could not have made a passage from Cape St. Vincent to Portsmouth in such short time."

Ben took the defensive. "I was instructed by Admiral Jervis to bring news of the defeat of the Spanish fleet as soon as possible, which means that I should be off to London at once. We put on all possible sail. With good weather, a strong and favourable wind and a fine sailer like *La Fleur,* such a speedy passage is not only possible but it did happen, or I would not be here, sir."

"I will have to look at the books, but I believe you have broken all previous records, lad."

And so it did prove to be true. Ben, in command of his second ship, had broken all speed records from transport by sail from St. Vincent to Portsmouth and that record would stand for another sixty years, long after he was dead.

"Remind me to look you up whenever I need a message passed from one port to another in a hurry," said the Admiral, all smiles now. "Now tell me more about this battle."

So Ben told what he could remember as quickly as he could. The hand on the large chronometer above the

Admiral's desk was moving rapidly past noon and he knew he must be off. "The rest is all here in this report, sir, which I must speed to the Admiralty."

"Be off with you, young man and see that my regards are given to the Lord Admiral."

Ben found Tom and the men huddled outside. Some had stopped at a pub for some beer and were all smiles. Ben ordered them to hasten to the ship. He could see a small boat load of sailors headed out to the ship from the Admiralty dock, their replacements he was sure. Once aboard, they picked up their gear and were back in the ship's boat within five minutes. *Sailors waste no time when it is shore time,* thought Ben. They passed the port Admiral's replacement crew just as they left the ship. But Ben had departed a bit too hastily. He kept wondering if he had left something valuable on board *La Fleur,* something borrowed and something with sentimental value, but his mind could not focus on what it was, not just now.

As Ben stepped out of the ship's boat, he bade his men farewell, "And be back at the *Lamb Inn* four days from now, by 5 p.m. on the first of March. I will meet you all there and we will go aboard our new ship." He had already arranged with Tom, who was staying in Portsmouth, to take care of his sea chest and 'laika' for him while he was off to London. He did not want to haul all of his gear with him.

Ben hurried off to the stables, but the last carriage for London for the day had already left. Ben was in a furor. That meant that he would have to take a room here in Portsmouth and spend the night. But, he was in a jubilant mood. *After all, am I not bringing good news to the Admiralty and should I not hasten?* He had been in a daring mood, possibly influenced by his recent contacts with one Captain Nelson, ever since he left the Cape.

Ben turned to the livery stable and asked the attendant, "Do you have a good, swift horse that I could ride to London?" Ben should have said, "Do you have a good, slow, dependable horse that will take me surely to London," but such is the innocence and confidence of youth. Ben had never ridden a horse in his life. That was unusual for a country lad, but remember that he scavenged around the country for his food, a cast off orphan, and he had no parents, no landed family to provide him with a horse as he was growing up. In fact, he had grown up mostly at sea.

The man turned a fine, honest face to him and pointed to a fine roan animal. "His *Kingship* here is as fine an animal as you will find in all of Portsmouth, and mebbe in all of England."

Ben reached into his pocket, only to realize in a agonizing instant that he had little money. He had forgotten to draw wages to cover the cost of his trip. And it was getting late, much too late to do anything about it today.

"How much," said Ben.

"Half a pound a day," replied the man.

Ben pulled out his money and counted out several coins. If he were frugal, he could hire the horse for today, have enough left to get a room at an inexpensive inn tonight, with enough left for a most frugal supper and breakfast. After that, he would go to the Bank of London and withdraw enough money to pay for his return trip, pay the livery stable and have some left for emergencies later on. Ben was slowly realizing that his status as an officer meant that he had to have more money on him and that he would have to grow up to his responsibilities. He was no longer a penniless boy. *Now I am a King's officer.*

"I'll take him," said Ben. Rarely would he say words that he would regret so much. The stable boy brought the saddle and Ben watched closely as the beast was fitted with the saddle over a thick blanket. He had never even done that before, let alone seen it done close to. He was well aware that he might have to saddle the animal tomorrow morning by himself. But after all, this was but a trifling detail for a lad who had fought so bravely at Cape St. Vincent. He paid the man his half pound and took the reins.

Ben threw his canvas bag with a clean shirt, a change

of underwear and the Admiral's documents over the horn of the saddle and then raised his leg to mount.

The stable boy came running back to him. "You crazy sailor. Don't you even know how to mount a horse properly. "'E won't let you mount 'im from the starb'rd side. 'E can be mounted only from port."

Ben gulped in embarrassment. He may have heard that somewhere, but it had not been filed away in his memory in a way that it was second nature as it was with almost everyone else living at that time. So Ben switched to the port side and raised his left foot into the stirrup, but the beast would not stand still. He danced sideways, forcing Ben to hop on his right foot to keep up with the beast. This went on for several minutes and Ben was getting angrier by the minute. "Avast there, you beast. All I want to do is come aboard. I'd rather board an enemy ship in the midst of a fierce storm and a full battle than try to get on your back." For a second, Ben toyed with the idea of leading the animal by his reins, at least until he was out of sight of the stable man who was laughing as hard as he could, slapping his thighs, and reeling with laughter. But that seemed like a cowardly plan, so Ben stuck with it. Finally, the stable man came to his rescue. He held his hand against the beasts neck, stroking it gently and talked soothingly to him.

"This 'ere's only a poor sailor man what is not used to the likes o' you. Give 'im a chance. Once you get 'im aboard, you can do with 'im as ye likes." Turning to Ben and by now taking pity on him, he said, "I charge extra for riding lessons ye know. Here put yer left foot in the stirrup and hoist yer right leg over his back." Ben tried it and it worked. He was now aboard. What happened next would sour him on riding horses for the rest of his life.

Ben had hardly gripped the pommel and felt the saddle on his rear when the stable man slapped the rump of the horse and he bolted off like he had been stung by a bee. "Which way to London," called Ben frantically. The stable man, still laughing, pointed to a road to the right and Ben tried to steer the beast in that direction, but this was not at all like taking the wheel of a ship. If he turned the wheel to port, the ship would follow his command perfectly, with only a slight bit of slippage. Not so with this beast. He was off like a shot, going at top speed and Ben could do little more than hold on. He heard the frantic clopping of the animal's shod hooves on the cobbled street and saw mud fly in all directions as the animal literally dove into every mud puddle, spraying innocent bystanders with the filth. Ben gritted his teeth. *Why didn't Tom come with me. He'd know about horses and what to do. If the beast keeps this up for a few hours, I'll make a record trip from Portsmouth to London too,* thought Ben, his mind in a panic. He loved speed, but only when he could be in control if it, and he definitely was not in control of this beast. He decided that he would call the animal, 'Vixen'. It was totally appropriate. 'His Kingship,' hardly fitted an animal like this, except the King had mental problems that left him bereft of his senses for long periods of time. He was given to fits of running about aimlessly, sometimes scantily clad and maybe the name was appropriate after all. The horse raced through the streets of Portsmouth at top speed and did not slow down for over an hour. Ben thought that he would lose his grip and fall under those wild hooves at any moment. He was frankly terrified. He knew that he made the right choice when he stowed away on a British ship. He could have slept in the barn of the King's cavalry instead and that would definitely have been a mistake. *If they had put me in the army or aback a horse, I would have been a total failure. I am sure of that now.*

When the *Beast* did finally slow down, Ben could not believe how it snorted and pranced. *This horse has apparently had a good run stowed up in him for a long time and has not had any chance to exercise it.* He guessed that the stable man sensed Ben's insecurity with horses and wished the beast on him out of jest. Well it was no jest now. While the horse had raced recklessly for the first hour, he now refused to walk at even a calm pace. He dragged each foot, moving ever so slowly. Ben stopped by a brook and tore off a twig to use as a switch, but he dared not apply the switch too firmly lest the beast go into another frantic run and knock him off. But gentle switching did no good. He simply would walk no faster, just dragging along like some old horse headed for the butcher shop. Ben would gladly have consigned him to the butcher shop at that moment, if there had been any available.

It had been coming on for some time now. Ben needed a break. He simply had to get down off that beast and relieve himself. He found a good likely spot at the end of a field behind a hedge row. *Oh, that is so much better,* he thought. He pushed the animal's starboard side up against the hedgerow so he would stand still and let Ben mount. That worked after a fashion, but the prickery bushes annoyed the animal and he gave a great bolt, arched his back upwards and put his head down, stern feet flying high and Ben fell into the hedgerow, much the worse for wear. When Ben recovered his composure, he straightened his battered uniform and tried to mount again, this time away from the hedgerow. It took some doing, but finally he was mounted again. But the animal refused to increase his pace. He simply walked at a very slow pace. Ben got off and tried to lead him, but that did not work. It was while he was on the ground coaxing the beast to move faster that he realized that it was not a 'he' at all. He shook off his foot and tried to clean his boot with some dry grass. *This is a 'she beast' of the worst type. How could they name a female horse, 'His Kingship'?* Ben wondered aloud. The rest of their day together was anything but pleasant.

Finally, at dusk, Ben pulled hard on the reins and the beast stopped by the hitching post of a small inn, *The Guilded Lion.* Ben hitched the beast to the post and when he tried to walk into the inn, he discovered that he was so lame that he could hardly walk. He was dragging the canvas bag and his feet were leaden, like those of some old man. He requested a stable boy to rub down his horse and feed it, although Ben though that the 'Vixen' as he had begun to call her might be easier to handle tomorrow if she had no fuel to burn. He was able to get a room with a view of the stable, "So he could keep an eye on 'is fine horse," said the motherly lady who rented him the room.

The lady who kept the inn was a quiet, grandmotherly person who promised to bring him hot water for a bath and a hot supper soon after, "If the gentleman pleases."

Ben 'pleased' very much. He was famished. He had not eaten since early that morning and he had been knocked about enough that he felt in sore need of food. The woman soon came with a pot of water and Ben stripped and cleaned up in the wash basin. He shaved and put on what little clean clothes he had.

If it had been a trying day, the evening supper made up for it somewhat. Ben dined on juicy roast beef with buttered potatoes, parsnips and carrots washed down with cider in the great room by a roaring fire. He soaked huge chunks of fresh bread in the juice from the meat and thought that he had never eaten a better meal. There seemed to be no other guests at the inn at the moment. Ben went back to his room after supper and tried to repair his uniform. It was not something that he could do without more resources. If only he had brought Giles with him. *He could have this mess ship shape in no time at all,* thought Ben. But soon sleep overtook him and he awoke some hours later slumped in the chair beside his bed. The hearth fire had gone out and he was cold. He scurried under the covers and slept soundly until sounds from below woke him at 6 a.m.

Ben was out early, calling for his horse after a fine breakfast of plaice and eggs with bacon and hot chocolate. But his wallet was completely empty. *I need to make London in time to get to the bank, or I will not eat tonight, that is for sure.*

The 'Vixen' was brought around to Ben, all fitted with her saddle. The stable boy petted her muzzle and commented on what a fine animal she was. Ben said nothing, but thought that the lad might say otherwise if he had to ride her all day. Ben still could not walk normally and his backside hurt even before it hit the saddle. Ben stood for a time stroking the horses smooth neck. *Maybe kindness would win her over,* he thought. He whispered softly in her ear. "Now look, dear lady. I am sorry if I called you a 'he' yesterday and if I used some sailor language on you, but you must realize that this is my first cruise on a horse. I need your help. Please, be a good girl and let me mount."

But either the horse did not understand the King's English, or she just didn't like Ben. She gave him a bad time mounting again and the stable boy had to come to Ben's aid. But once they were finally on the road at a fair trot, Ben felt relieved. He was more than half way to London. They were somewhere near Guildford. If he rode hard, he supposed that he would reach London by sometime in the late afternoon. But in the first hour, 'Vixen' threw him twice. Ben let lose a string of expletives that would have blistered any sailor's ears as he pulled himself up out of the February mud and made a lunge for the horse again. Once on board, all went well for awhile, except the horse seemed to want to travel at its own pace, regardless of what Ben wanted. Once when he was busy reading a series of signs on a post, the beast took the wrong turn and headed off down a lane towards a handsome stallion who reared and waited for her with great expectation. Ben had to act fast. He never supposed that landsmen had to react to emergencies the way he did at sea, but this was an emergency. If she came any closer to that stallion, Ben would never get her away. He pulled the reins hard enough to injure the animal's mouth and headed her back where she belonged. *What will this wiley beast pull on me next,* he thought.

It was three in the afternoon when Ben and 'Vixen' pulled into Whitehall Street where the Admiralty building stood. There were other horses tied there to posts, each calm as could be. His mount seemed intent on taking him right by for a scenic tour of London. "No you don't, you hairy bastard. Stop right here or I'll beat you to glue as you stand," said Ben.

The Admiralty was a strange building. In front were a series of low arches held in place by two flat-topped columns. Atop each column was a sea horse so that the two mythical animals faced each other. Fanning out on either side of the arch were walkways with lower arches, something like the railing and supports of a ship's deck, but higher. Far back down a long path stood the Admiralty building itself, with its high, polished wooden doors and great brass hinges. Atop a mast on a tower there was a wind gage, the same one that sent the wind direction to the compass on the wall of the Admiral's chambers. Ben remembered it all. He was here not many months earlier, but he had been so overwrought at the time because of the pending leftenant's exam, that he had hardly noticed any of the finer details. He took up his canvas bag with the Admiral's document inside and walked somewhat lamely to the sentry at the door.

"Acting Captain Benjamin Rundel, with urgent dispatches for the Lord Admiral, sir."

"Acting Captain of what, sir? Your horse just untied its reins and is galloping away," said the marine sergeant with a trace of a smile on his face. Ben turned around to see 'Vixen' hard bent for someplace far off.

"All the better to be rid of her. She is nothing but a nuisance anyway," growled Ben.

The sergeant straightened and looked quite formal again. "You may pass, sir, into the waiting room to the left, if you please."

Ben walked into the gloomy room. He half expected to see old Cheevers sitting like a vulture on his high stool, but he was not there. *Either Cheevers has gone redundant or it is his day off,* thought Ben. The man who sat atop the tall stool was perhaps thirty, with a gruff look about him and a fair head of curly brown hair. Ben repeated his name and request and was told to, 'take a seat'.

Ben complied. At least there were only three others ahead of him, but the hour was late and he might not get to see the Admiral today. And who was Admiral now? He would be surprised if Admiral Hood were still here. He was supposed to be in charge of the Channel Fleet.

After about half an hour, the huge doors of the Admiralty chambers opened and the sentry called, Captain Benjamin Rundel, looking about for some handsomely dressed gentleman, but there was no one there except Ben, and he was anything but handsomely dressed. After several days on an obstinate horse, his uniform was a mess. Perhaps he should have ignored his orders and found an inn, taken a bath, shaved, eaten dinner and then approached the Admiral, but that was not what he thought that Admiral Jervis would have wanted him to do. He strode forward as if he were dressed in his very best. As he passed the sentry, he whispered, "Who sits as First Lord of the Admiralty?"

Through closed teeth, the man answered, "Lord Spencer, lad."

Ben advanced and saluted. His eye caught the large wind dial on the wall over the mantle, the one that registered wind direction continuously so that the Lord Admiral would know if the fleet really could sail from Portsmouth or not. It looked like a huge chronometer but had only one hand which seemed to fidget and move continuously.

"Leftenant and Acting Captain Benjamin Rundel, sir, with news from Rear Admiral John Jervis of a great victory for England off the Cape of St. Vincent. We have defeated the Spanish fleet before she could join up with the French and Dutch fleets at Brest."

"Let's see here," as Lord Spencer reached for the packet of letters. He slipped back in his chair and motioned for Ben to have a seat. He examined each letter summarily over his glasses which seemed to serve no purpose, riding as they did on the end of his nose.

"Hmmm. This bears some careful reading. There is beef here." said Lord Spencer as he looked at Ben.

"You must have come here by horse from Portsmouth,

and in some haste I would judge," said Lord Spencer. Ben realized that he was referring to his untidy uniform and unshaven face.

"I was told to make all haste to see you, sir."

"I see that you are living up to your reputation as the most poorly dressed officer in His Majesty's Navy, but never mind. I would have groused if you had run off to clean up and kept this juicy news from me until tomorrow. Nevertheless, I should like to have you stand by for a time in case there are questions. This is very important information that you have brought me. You had any dinner, lad?"

Ben was surprised by the sudden change of topic.

"Why, no sir. I came straight away here."

"Mr. Montgomery. Bring us tea and some scones, if you please."

So Ben sat back and watched the Lord Admiral read the dispatches. More than once did his eyebrows shoot up and several times he looked at Ben with a slight smile at the corner of his mouth, as if he knew some secret that he refused to share with Ben. Ben thought that his name might be there once as the leftenant to bring home *La Fleur,* but doubted it would appear elsewhere.

When the Lord reached the part about LaTour, he asked, "And where is this fellow LaTour now?"

"I left him in the care of the port Admiral at Portsmouth, with the marines, in irons, sir. I had no way to bring him here with me."

"Well, you did right in bringing him home for a trial by a higher court. We will try him alright and make such a spectacle of him that no Frenchman will ever want to set foot on English soil again, let alone think of spying on us. His name will be plastered in all our papers and we will make a sacrificial pigeon of him, to be sure."

Ben reached for another scone. He had already finished off three and was still famished. He found that he was extremely thirsty too and he finished off his third cup of tea. The Lord Admiral smiled as he watched the youth devour his tea. He had been there once himself, a long, long time ago.

The Lord Admiral read on. Then he looked up. "Where did you learn to speak Spanish, lad?"

Ben slacked off on the scone that he was about to stuff in his mouth and explained that he had once been kidnapped at gun point and forced to serve on a Spanish pirate ship several years ago."

"Hmmm. Good for a lad to have several language in his magazine. Could come in handy sometime, as it did with you and that Spanish ship you passed in the fog. Fine job, fine job."

"Do you know how you plan to return to the Tagus?"

"Yes, sir. I have reserved births for myself and my men aboard the *Theseus*. She sails in four days from Portsmouth."

"Too bad. I should have liked to break you in here for a few days. Much a promising young lad like yourself can learn in this place." Ben looked at the wainscotted walls with their paintings of ships and the soft carpet. Service here for a few days might be alright, but he had a feeling that he would soon long for the gentle lift of a deck beneath his feet.

"I have read these document once, but will want to study them further. I will have a packet of orders for you to carry back to Rear Admiral Jervis. Don't be surprised if you do not have to address him as 'Admiral' soon, and as for that disobedient scoundrel Nelson, he may be headed for a rear Admiral's title, if not more. Quite a stroke of genius, his pulling out of line and engaging seven ships on his own, then boarding one and bridging over to the next without even getting his feet wet. Congratulations to you all. I can sleep the better tonight knowing that France cannot now float a full invasion. I will send my compliments to the crews of the fleet as well. They are a fine lot of sailors. Stop by here tomorrow, no perhaps morning after tomorrow and I will have all the documents ready for you."

He rose and held his hand out to shake Ben's. Ben could remember when he did not know what a hand shake meant, but he knew now what this one meant. The Lord Admiral had been much impressed with his work, but perhaps not with his dress.

Ben walked down the Admiralty steps, thinking that he would have to spend the rest of that day looking for that cursed 'Vixen'. So he was surprised when he came to the arch and saw her standing there comfortably nibbling on a bag of oats. The young horse sergeant spread a broad smile and said that he figured Ben would have his hands full trying to retrieve his horse, especially after a session with old Lord Spencer. "Any time I bring out the oats, any horse within hearing distance will come arunnin', and sure enough she did." Ben thanked the man, but did not have the umph to climb back aboard. Frankly, his derriere hurt so badly that he was pleased to walk, even if it was a long way to the inn where he had planned to spend the night. He took her reins and they stumbled off down the street together towards the Bridge where he would spend the night. Ben drew out his chronometer. *Good God! It is too late to get into the bank. I will have to do some fast talking to get a place to sleep this night. I have not a ha'penney on me.*

It took over an hour to find the right street. Ben asked several times and finally found the *Royal Arms.* Perhaps Gilda or someone else there would remember him and he could get credit for just one night. *Too bad I look so much the part of a tramp,* he thought. *They might not even let me in, let alone give me a meal and bed for the night.*

But Ben need not have worried. The stable boy took his horse readily and disappeared behind the inn with it. When he went inside, Gilda spotted him at once and came over, smiling up at him. She remembered!

"How could I forget anyone who could eat so much custard, sir," she said in her deep, husky voice.

Ben welcomed her and asked for a room for two nights and a hot bath. No one questioned him about money, so he was contented that he could get into the Bank of London tomorrow early and pay off his debt to the inn. He sat down in the great room to rest while Gilda found him a room and sent a boy to fetch warm water. *Is that not Admiral Robinson over there at that table, the Admiral whom I met in the Caribbean, the one with the winsome daughter?* The more Ben looked, the more he was certain that it was Robinson, a bit more fleshy, but otherwise the same fellow. Should he interfere and introduce himself, or sit quietly by the fire and enjoy its warmth? It was a fiercely cold February day and had started to rain quite hard.

Ben decided that it would be in his best interests to clean up first and then perhaps, if he could get the mud from his uniform, to approach the old Admiral after supper. A warm fire awaited him in his tiny room and he went to stand by it, rubbing his hands together for warmth. Soon a fine bath was laid and he stripped and crawled into the tub with a feeling of ecstasy. Contrary to the opinion of many of his betters, he did not like to appear unclean or his uniform unkempt. It was just that he managed to get into some of the worse messes at the wrong times. He had always liked to be clean since he was a child at the Broken Bridge.

Ben did what he could with a brush on his uniform and then came down for supper. He dined on roast lamb with applesauce, potatoes dripping with gravy and buttered carrots with cabbage on the side. *Their cider is especially good here,* he thought. As he ate, he tried to plan his next day.

It would be his only free day since the rest of his time would be spent trying to get that ornery beast to take him back to Portsmouth. His first stop would be the bank. No question about that. Then it hit him. What day was tomorrow? He looked at Gilda and the urgency in his eyes made her come to him at once.

"What day is tomorrow? I must get into the bank," whispered Ben urgently.

"Why it is Friday. The bank will be open as usual," she said, running her finger playfully over the polished surface of the table. She seemed to be baiting him. Did he want to be baited? The truth was after so long at sea and such a traumatic ride to London, he was ready for anything. She would be as good as any other to teach him what he needed to know. But if she expected an experienced lover, she would be in for a surprise. True. He was over six feet tall, with great broad shoulders and by now he should have seen considerable action in the bedroom, but that was not the case. But she did attract him, leaving a most pleasant uneasiness in his loins that demanded attention. The very smell of her as she bent to serve his meal was disturbing.

Ben ate his meal in silence, all thought of the Admiral now lost, at least for the moment. *How should I ask her? I mean, what does a man say when he wants a woman? He does not just come right out and ask for it.* Ben was sure of that. There must be some proper, polite words that he was supposed to know. If only Tom were here. He had been initiated and he would know what to say. But sleep overtook him. He was bone weary after the events of the past weeks and no amount of longing could keep him from his bed that night. After his meal, he went promptly to bed and slept like a babe.

For all his worrying, he had no trouble getting into the bank and collecting sixty pounds to meet his immediate needs and for future emergencies. He was pleased to see that the interest had built up many pounds in his account and that when he withdrew sixty pounds, he still had more than he had owned when last he visited the bank. Soon there would be some pay added and some prize money as well. He was slowly becoming rich.

Ben spent the next hour visiting Dobson's where he had bought clothes before. His best uniform could be cleaned and made to look decent again. Since he had no other clothes with him, he convinced the clothier to do the cleaning and repair while he waited. Soon, he emerged with a small bundle of stockings and shirts under his arm and a smart looking uniform that would pass inspection.

What now? One sight that had haunted him while he was at sea night after night was that of the beautiful diva that he and Tom had watched rehearse at Covent Garden. He longed for just a glimpse of her. She was so ravishingly beautiful, surrounded by her many admirers. He could not hope to even get close enough to her to speak, but he longed for just a glimpse, or perhaps the sound of her beautiful contralto voice. So his steps led him off to the north to the Gardens. But when he arrived, he found the doors closed. There was no rehearsal today. The billboard announced that there would be an opera performed tonight at 7 p.m. It listed the singers, but since he did not know her name, he could not tell if she would sing or not. Ben felt foolish walking such great distances when he had a horse at his disposal, but he could not bear the thought of mounting that ornery beast until he absolutely had to. He would walk back to the opera tonight, after supper.

At supper, he flirted with Gilda again. So far he had not seen the dark man that had seemed to shadow her when he knew her on his previous stay at the inn. He suspected that she had a regular lover if not a husband.

After supper, Ben left and walked the several miles to the opera. It was cold and he was glad of his warm greatcoat. He was able to get a balcony seat and he watched with great expectation as the curtain rose and first beautiful strains of music floated to his seat. The opera was *Don Giovanni* by one Wolfgang Amadeus Mozart. Now Ben had never heard a symphony orchestra and never heard great choruses such as these. But music was the essence of his existence ever since he had been a boy at the Broken Bridge. He sat there enthralled by the beauty of the music. Each act unfolded with more surprises. They had given him a translation of the libretto and he was able to follow what was happening. He absorbed the action with every pore of his eager young mind. He would be sure to attend an opera any time he was in London. He was sure of that. But this Don Giovanni was certainly not a very nice fellow. He would be glad to get him on the business end of his sword someday. Ben sat on the edge of his seat throughout the long performance. But there was no lovely lady of his dreams. *Alas, she is not singing tonight.*

Although his soul longed for a glimpse of his favourite lady singer, still he could not but thrill at the beauty and artistry that was there before him. He was like a small child beholding the most beautiful thing it had ever seen and heard. When it was over, Ben walked stiffly out of the gallery. He had no longing to walk the miles back to the inn, so he hired a chaise to take him home. Just as he was about to get in and close the door, there she was, just a few feet away. She was talking with some young people and there was a bandy rooster of a fellow strutting around her as if he were herding a flock of chickens into a coop. He clucked over her with such effeminate gestures that it made Ben sick. He turned to the driver of the chaise.

"Do you know who that lady is there," as he pointed to her.

"Why, yes, sir. Every one knows our Annie. She has the finest voice in all England."

That was all Ben could learn, but it was enough. 'Annie' ran through his mind all the way home, mixed with strains from the opera, beautiful cascading sounds that would travel through his mind and put it at ease on many a stormy night. All the way home, he hummed the fine phrases from the opera. It was turning colder and it was snowing lightly. It would be good to get back to the inn. He had spent more of his money than he intended, but he felt the experiences of that night were worth many times more to him than those few cold coins.

At the inn, Gilda was clearing the tables. He looked at her in that special way and asked if he might have a cup of tea. She smiled her knowing smile.

"You are leaving tomorrow, sir?"

"Yes," said Ben. He wanted so to share the beauty that he had experienced that night with her, it surged through his veins and he knew that he could make her happy, if only for a few seconds. In the end he said nothing, but his eyes said all that his tongue could not say. In a little while, when the inn was quiet, Gilda came to him as his first woman, a cup of tea in her hands. It was a grand sensation, but somehow when it was over, Ben felt that it would be far grander if the woman were someone that he truly loved and had waited for, longed for some time, not just an attractive tavern girl. She had been gentle, coaxing, understanding. He was most appreciative. They spoke little, but Ben knew that she understood that this was his first time. She was talented far beyond that of the average woman. Ben was sure of that. He did get her to agree to give him an extra serving of custard at supper the next time he came by.

The next morning, Ben arose stiffly still hurting from his long ride, and ordered a quick breakfast and then his horse. The other serving girl was there, so he imagined Gilda curled up in her warm bed somewhere. What a comforting thought that was. He would ride to the Admiralty, if it killed him, and it nearly did. But he wanted to be there bright and early so that he could be off to Portsmouth with his packet of orders. 'Vixen' seemed to have mellowed out for the first several miles. She behaved most admirably. He remembered something that Gilda had told him when he complained of the bruises that the beast had given his backsides.

'I'll stop by the stables on my way home and give her a gypsy whisper. That will make her tame and she will obey you most dutifully.' *Maybe she had and maybe it worked?*

The clerk at the Admiralty informed Ben that the orders were not ready yet and that he might have to wait an hour or two. There was naught for him to do but take a seat and wait. But after a few minutes, he decided to take a walk and see more of this part of London. He excused himself and told the clerk that he would return in an hour. The time was spent in pointless wandering, on foot, of course. 'Vixen' stood at the hitching post with her reins double-tied, eying him suspiciously as he walked past her down the street. *Your turn will come, and soon, old girl,* he thought. Ben managed to pick up some steaming hot pasties to eat on the way to Portsmouth. An hour's delay would not cause any problem, but he should be on the road soon since he needed to be at the *Lamb* by 5 p.m. tomorrow. While that seemed like enough time to make the trip, still, he had that worthless horse to consider.

Ben returned to the Admiralty about an hour later, but the clerk merely shook his head. "There is some problem, sir, with the issuing of the orders."

Ben looked at the man. He was small, by Ben's standards, slight waist like a girl's, thin shoulders, his arms just skin over bones with a meagre allotment of muscle. His curly blond head was odd-shaped, like a pear with an extremely pointed chin, a nose that sniveled all the time and eyes that were sunken and small. *Where does the Admiralty find these fellows to serve as clerks,* he thought.

Ben could not stand the confinement of the waiting room any longer. He had to get some fresh air. The sky had grown dark and it was threatening to rain. At sea he would have given appropriate orders for 'shortening sails, and reefs all around' and possibly changed course slightly to meet the wind on his starboard quarter. But here he was helpless. He could only wait until the Admirals had completed the packet of orders that he was to carry. He wondered if any of those orders were for him? But most of the time, he stood back out of the rain and thought about Annie. She had seen him and their eyes had met, for an embarrassingly long time in fact. Would she wonder about him? Would she be repulsed by the gash on his forehead and the injury above his ear? And why did she take up with that silly fop who wore a dainty baby blue coat and trousers, with dark blue trimmings? He pranced about like a pet poodle on a leash. Ben could never believe that she would choose to marry a man like that or that she would prefer him over a naval officer like himself. And there was that other nagging question. Was she married? He had no way of knowing.

The rain began in earnest now and Ben sought shelter in the waiting room. By the time that his papers were ready, it was after 11 a.m. and the rain was falling in torrents. 'Vixen' looked a pitiful sight as he approached her. The saddle was dripping and water poured off her back in rivulets. There was no help for it. He would have to ride her, wet as she was and wet as he would soon be in spite of his great coat.

The orders were safely stowed away inside his greatcoat and Ben headed 'Vixen' out of London at a gentle canter. All went well for the first two hours. Oh she tried to dart down the lane where the white stallion stood, awaiting her, but Ben grabbed the reins so forcefully that she had to obey. He headed her back to the main road saying to her, "Not today, my lady. It is too wet for that nonsense. Besides, he is just an old work horse anyway. You want none of that." But Ben did not really believe what he was saying. He would have lain with his Annie in a mud mire if he had to. He knew that. He and the horse suffered the same torments.

Then there was a slight pause in the rain and the sun tried to shine. It was during those few minutes of warming sun that it happened. Ben had been riding along at a good pace, day dreaming of 'his Annie' as he had come to call her. Then suddenly a bird decided to fly close to 'Vixen's' head. 'Vixen' shook her head and let out a snort, and in a flash, she was after the bird who had intruded on her territory. Her hooves hit the mud with such force as she bolted forward at a maddening pace that Ben, who had come to believe that she was a reformed horse, was jolted out of the saddle, his head hanging down and one foot caught in the stirrup. He was lucky because he did not fall completely from the saddle. He still had hold of the saddle horn and after a minute or two, was able to pull himself upright again, but no amount of pressure on the reins could dissuade 'Vixen' from her insane dash down the muddy road. It seems that someone had used the reins so frequently and heavily on her mouth that there was now no feeling there at all. Ben gave a tug at the reins that would have stopped any normal horse dead in its tracks, but 'Vixen' dove straight on. She slipped and slid, careening madly back and forth across the road, all at speeds that would place her in the lead at any horse race. Ben could do little more than hang on. As he swayed with her erratic motion, he realized that he might have lost his packet of orders when he fell headfirst to port. Frantically he let go the reins with one hand and felt his breast pocket. *Thank God the packet of orders is still there. At this mad pace, I would have no idea where to look for them if they had slipped from my inner pocket.* The canvas bag with his clothes hung from the pommel of the saddle and was spattered with mud, but it still gyrated wildly in the air as the horse bolted onward.

As Ben swayed and bounced in the saddle, his heels digging into the animal's sides to hold on, thoughts came to him of his childhood days by the Channel. He had a rocking horse that he called, 'orsey'. He had loved the little wooden horse dearly and would rock for hours on it while his Auntie Jo sewed to support them. His enthusiasm had cooled only when, after a fit of furious rocking, he had rocked across the cat's tail, to the great consternation of the old tom who let out a howling scream. But there was one big difference. That horse was a mindless piece of wood and could be controlled. This one could not.

'Vixen' carried on for a little over an hour. Then, as quickly as she had taken off, she stopped dead in the road, shook herself, and began a funeral procession pace. *This is just what she did to me on the way out, the beast.* thought Ben. But since she had decided to slow down, Ben decided to dismount for a bit of relief. It had started to rain fiercely again and he would make it a short stop indeed. He stood for just a second contemplating the horses back. *Every time I have tried to mount her, she has given me the old merry-go-round treatment. There must be a better way to board her.* Ben had watched men mount horses when he was in town, and on several occasions in the Caribbean. He thought that they tended to take a little run at the horse from about twenty feet away, quickly hiked the left foot into the stirrup and in almost one continuous motion, hoisted the right leg over the animal's back. That took the horse by surprise. *Maybe I am too gentle and determined,* he thought. *It is worth a try.* He had to get off down the road. There were many miles to ride yet that day. So Ben backed off as 'Vixen' watched him from the corner of her eye. He made a frantic run at the animal, aimed his left foot for the stirrup, and started to raise his right leg to mount. At just the right instant, 'Vixen' stepped sideways, just about a foot. It was just enough that Ben missed her altogether and fell on his bottom in the mud. He lay there for a second, the rain pelting down on his head. *If I had a pistol this minute, you would be a dead horse,* he thought. But fortunately for them both, he did not carry a pistol, just a sword. Ben rose up out of the muck and stood up, dripping mud, sore in every muscle and joint. There was an evergreen tree near by and he kicked the horse, tugging at her reins to bring her near the tree. At least he could run her aground against the tree and then he might be able to board her. But just then he remembered the pasty in his lower pocket. Ben slid his hand into the pocket. The pasty had been wrapped in a piece of newsprint. He felt something warm and mushy. The pasty was smeared all over the inside of his coat pocket. "Ick!" He would have no dinner that day and a deuce of a job cleaning up the coat. But 'Vixen' would get no dinner either. He would see to that. This time he rammed the poor horse against the tree, mounted her and kicked her flanks until she was moving at a satisfactory pace. Ben was sure that he could see a satisfied sneer on her long, stupid face. *Someone rented me a trick horse that no one can ride,* thought Ben. But when he finally arrived at the stable the next day, the stable boy mounted her with no trouble and she went off tamely to her stall.

That night he stopped at a small inn at Hasselmere. He was drenched and famished and he ached so that he could not sit upright on the beast another minute. As he dismounted, he felt something thrust into his pocket. *That ornery horse is trying to eat my mushed pasty.* he thought. He grabbed her by the ear and pulled her muzzle from his pocket. "Horses don't like beef and gravy, carrots maybe, but definitely not pasties." He stomped off to the inn door, *The Iron Cockerel* and faced the sullen little man who rented him a room for the night. He cleaned his coat as best he could and then cleaned up. After a quick supper, he spread his clothes about the room to dry them, stoked the fire in the fireplace and slid into bed.

The next day he was off early. He could not guess what trouble 'Vixen' would give him this day, but he wanted plenty of time to deal with it. But it was not 'Vixen' who troubled Ben that day. It was his own laxness. As he rode down the narrow, muddy track to Portsmouth, he suddenly remembered Captain Nelson's chronometer. He had left it aboard *La Fleur.* What would happen to it? Worse yet, what would happen to him if he could not retrieve it? Captain Nelson was a congenial fellow, but he would certainly not take the loss of a valuable chronometer lightly. Would *La Fleur* still be there, or was she sold by now? If she were sold, he might have to try to buy the chronometer back, or find another one. But he would not arrive in Portsmouth harbour much before 4 p.m., if all went well. With 'Vixen', all could be depended on not to go well. Ben needed this distraction. He had been unable to think of anything but Annie all the way from London. It was time to recall himself to his duty.

He swatted 'Vixen' several times and succeeded in picking up her pace a knot or two. Haste was important now. Now, when he needed her, she would not do one of those famous high speed gallops of hers. Why could horses never be trusted?

About quarter to four that afternoon, Ben came in sight of the stable. He jumped off into the mud and handed the man two pounds. "That is more than enough for this ornery beast," he said.

Ben grabbed his duffel bag and headed for the inn where Tom was staying.

He might need Tom's help in retrieving the chronometer. Ben raced up the stairs to the loft at the *Inn of the Gables* and pounded on Tom's door. He must have been asleep because he answered in a sleepy voice. "Open up Tom. I need your help."

Tom opened the door and a look of astonishment passed across his broad Irish face. He looked as if he had seen a ghost.

"Well, what 'ave ye been doing, lad, a ridin' a sow all the way from London? Ye 'ave mud on you from rail to keel."

"I'll explain all of that later. I need to get aboard La *Fleur.* Is she still in the harbour?"

"I guess so. At least she was this noon."

"I forgot to collect Captain Nelson's chronometer when I left the ship. I must get it back. If I don't, Tom, my career in the Navy may be at an end."

"I'll come with ya," said Tom, his face now deadly serious.

So the two men set out to find a boat. Two young girls rowed over to where they stood beckoning. "Where ya' wants to go, young gentlemen?" said the smaller one.

"To *La Fleur,* there," pointed Ben, and be fast about it.

As the boat with Ben and Tom approached the ship, an officer standing by the rail challenged them. Ben was first to climb the battens and had just set foot aboard the ship.

"No one's allowed aboard here, sir. Admiral's orders," said the officer.

"I am acting Captain Benjamin Rundel and I have come to reclaim some gear that was left behind."

A sentry stepped up to where Ben stood. "Sorry, sir. The Admiral has ordered that no one board this ship until the purser has completed his inventory. She goes up for sale tomorrow."

"But I must recover Captain Nelson's gear, sir," putting

all the urgency and authority in his voice that he could.

The sentry moved forward to bar him from advancing with his gun, and there was no choice for Ben but to back down the battens and leave the ship. Once back in the small boat, Ben sat thinking. *I must not fail Captain Nelson. I must get that chronometer. There is no excuse that I could offer for losing it.* The girls rowed them back to the quay. The two men sat silent, their faces grim. Ben handed them some coins and asked them if they would be willing to row he and his twenty men to the *Theseus in* about half an hour.

"It'll take about four trips, sir, but we can surely do it," replied the older woman. Ben told her to wait and he and Tom raced to Tom's room to collect their gear. On the way, Ben breathless from the mad dash, whispered to Tom, "I am going aboard tonight to get that chronometer."

Tom stopped dead in his tracks, the creases in his forehead more prominent than usual as he squinted to look at Ben. "You aren't going to risk a flogging or much worse for that, are you?"

"I must get it back and I know no other way. You need not come, unless you want to."

Tom knew that Ben wanted him to agree to come along and he would have to fight down his reluctance. He knew that Ben would need him. Nothing more was said. The two young men raced to the *Lamb* with their gear. It was quarter past five when they arrived. "There is no one here." said Ben. "The crew has either left or is not coming aboard. Ben knew how a few days freedom on land could affect a man and he might lose the whole lot. He doubted that they could get a warrant on a Sunday to track down some replacements.

"Hold your horses. They may be along yet. We still have time to get aboard the *Theseus."* saidTom.

"I hope you are right. Tom, I plan to hire the girl's boat and row out to *La Fleur.* I noticed that there is a rope dangling from the stern when we were there. And you remember there is a window in the Captain's quarters that will not shut tightly. I will climb up and squeeze through the window, secure the chronometer and climb back down. It should be quite easy."

"It would be a lot easier to buy another chronometer, wouldn't it," said Tom.

"Not on a Sunday, it wouldn't." Besides, Ben finally had a few pounds in his wallet and he wanted to keep them for emergencies. If he could find a chronometer, it would take everything that he had. He hated going to sea broke again. Just then the door opened and Mr. Sorensen thrust his smiling face through.

"We'll say no more of this in front of the men," said Ben.

"Bet you thought we wasn't goin' to show, eh, sir? Our wives didn't want to let go o' us." said Cross who came behind. Ben's handsome face lit in a broad smile. He was happy to see the lads again, not just because he would not have to press some replacements, but because he genuinely liked them. He counted as they filed in, each with a full duffel bag over his shoulder. Some carried bags or boxes with special treats prepared by their wives or sweethearts. Murdock had a huge cake that he carried most gingerly.

"For 'ard times at sea, sir," he explained. Smitty had a couple of huge tubs of jams that this wife had made and others carried scones or other treats.

Ben counted, "One...two...three... twenty-one? That last fellow is a stranger. Is he with you?"

"Aye, sir. 'E is Trainor's younger brother what wants to go to sea. Thought you wouldn't mind takin' him on, sir," said Sorensen. Ben stood up and walked towards the lad. He had a light complexion and was slender and almost frail looking, but then he had been no Goliath when he first come aboard either. But this fellow had something strange about him, which Ben could not quite place. "What's your name and where are you from, Lad?" asked Ben.

"Laslo Trainor from Wiltshire, sir," answered the youth

in a raspy voice. Ben shook his head. He would have sworn that Trainor came from Kent, but there was not time to worry about that now.

"Let's get aboard, lads. I have a boat waiting for us at the quay. It seems that the Captain of the *Theseus* has forgotten that we are to come aboard today at six. They have sent no boat for us."

Ben and Tom hurried the lads along to the quay where the two women sat at their oars. The girls ferried the men out to the ship and Ben sent Tom ahead to request permission to board. Ben stayed behind. He paid the two women well for their ferry service. Then he leaned over and whispered to them.

"I want to hire your boat for a little row around the harbour tonight. Be here at 12 mid night. I shall be right where I am now. Don't be late and don't make a sound, do you hear?"

At that he held up a coin that made the two women's eyes pop open. They nodded to him that they would be there, for sure. As they rowed away, Ben heard one of them say, "Bet those two youngsters is goin' to smuggle a couple of hussies aboard," followed by girlish giggles.

Ben made the deck and there met for the first time Captain Fremantle. "You know Thomas Hardy, First Leftenant." He saluted a heavy set but tall, broad-shouldered gentleman with close cropped brown hair. He wore no wig. Ben could not understand why men wanted to hide their hair beneath a wig. It looked awful. Besides, wigs were expensive. He knew that he would never wear a wig, even if he became totally bald and a Captain to boot. Hardy's hair was thinning in the center and he had a most pleasant broad face. He tended to appear stern, but there was usually a hint of a smile around his mouth and eyes. Ben liked him almost at once. Ben explained that they had orders to rejoin the fleet at the Tagus. He was told by the Lord Admiral to return at once.

"We sail at dawn, Mr. Rundel. You can bunk with the other leftenants. Mr. Murphy is seeing to space for your crewmen. You will sail with us as passengers, unless, of course, one of my sailors or leftenants happens to get sick. We have a full crew for once and I will not need you to serve your watch. I understand from what I have heard about Cape St. Vincent that you might be able to do with a bit of rest," said Tom Fremantle.

"Thank you, sir. May I entrust these orders to you to be put away in the safe?" Ben was relieved as he drew out the orders in their canvas cover and handed them to Captain Fremantle. His scheme to retrieve the chronometer depended on his not having watch duty for at least that night. Tom would be free too. *Maybe now I can convince Tom to come with me. There is no rest for the wicked and the forgetful,* thought Ben.

Ben handed his gear to a sailor who led the way to his quarters. He would bunk in tight quarters indeed. As soon as his things were stowed, he attended mess with the other leftenants.

Then Ben sought out Tom. "Have you given any further thought to my problem?"

"Yes, lad, and I can see us both flogged round the fleet or worse yet, hung from a yardarm if we get caught."

"We will not be caught. And if we do get caught, my defense will be that I was simply recovering Captain Nelson's gear. I did not tell the marine who was on guard duty what type of gear I needed to retrieve. Chances are it will never be missed. The original chronometer will still be there, even if it does not work."

"An' we could be set on the beach too. Laddie, can you think what two sailors like ourselves would do for the rest of our lives stranded on the beach? I have no landsman's skills, nor have you."

"There is not time to think of that now. I'll meet you on the port side at exactly 8 bells. That will give us time to get the deed done."

Ben did not go to bed. He was certain that he could not get out of bed in the close confines of their sleeping quarters without waking the other leftenants. If he were missed for several hours from his bunk, that might raise some questions. But if he had never been seen in that bunk, they would think that he had decided to sleep the night on deck. Besides, he had some serious uniform repairs to make.

At exactly eight bells, Ben stepped quietly onto the battens and slipped down the side of the ship. Sure enough, the girls were there. They came so silently that he had not heard them, and he had been standing by the rail just above. He saw Tom slip out of the darkness and descend to the waiting boat.

Ben whispered and pointed. "Row us to the quay where we were this afternoon." Not another word was said. The girls rowed as silently as a boat crew with frapped oars. A heavy, cold fog had settled in over the harbour and it was damp and chill. Ben shivered as he looked at Tom.

At the quay, Ben ordered the girls to leave the boat. "We are going to row for ourselves around the bay for a little while. Be back here in an hour," whispered Ben. He tossed them a coin to buy some hot grog with at one of the local pubs. Then he motioned for Tom to take an oar and they headed off into the dense fog.

"This is a deuce of a wild plan of yours. What if they open fire on us from the ship? We'll be blown out of the water, or worse yet, killed on the spot. Ben, I'm too young to die," pleaded Tom.

"Keep your voice down. Sound travels unbelievable distances in the fog," begged Ben. Tom clearly had no stomach for stealing a Captain's chronometer from an impounded King's ship.

"But I have no choice, do I. That chronometer was given to Captain Nelson by his wife, Frances. He would never forgive me if I lost it. I have to think of my career in the Navy. I suppose, if this fails, neither of us will have careers in the Navy."

"Right you are, lad. What if the purser has already inventoried the chronometer? What happens if it comes up missing?"

"All I can say is that we should be well on our way down the Channel by then and it should not concern us."

"But the poor devils who are guarding the ship will be charged with the theft. What then?"

That stopped Ben short in his tracks. He had no answer for that one. He was the last man that would want to cause another man undeserved pain.

"Pray, Tom. Pray that he has not looked into the cabin yet."

Ben was thankful for the dense fog as they approached *La Fleur.* If it had been a clear night, they would not have stood a chance. He had purposely rowed far astern and then come in straight at the stern, so as to be as invisible to the watch as possible. Ben felt the small boat bump gently against the rudder. Tom grabbed the ship and tied the bow line loosely to a pintle. Ben stood up to reach for the rope, but it was too high up. He could never reach it from this level. It would be hard to climb the rudder in the dark, near impossible. Tom stood up and the boat threatened to tip over with their two swaying bodies standing there. Tom grabbed Ben and heavy though he was, he lifted him up and held him as high as he could. Ben grabbed for the rope and caught just the end of it. Tom, thinking that Ben was on the rope, let go and Ben fell back into the boat with a thud. Ben looked at Tom, "Higher," he whispered. "And don't let go until I start to wiggle." This time it worked and Ben began to climb up the rope. It was only about sixteen feet, but old 'Vixen' had left her mark on his young body and he was extremely sore. Each time that he reached up for more rope, his muscles screamed and complained. But there was no help for that. He was almost there.

But as luck would have it, the stuck window was somewhat to port of the point where Ben reached the transom. He would have to climb across to try to reach the window. It was not open either, but Ben was pretty sure it would yield to a little pressure. With his feet dangling in air, he walked his hands across the stern until he was below the window. Then he held on with one hand and pushed hard on the window with the other. The window opened and he swung his sore body up onto the edge of the window. It was dark inside. That was good. He let his eyes adjust. No one was sitting there. Ben crept in quietly. *Let's see. The chronometer should be in this drawer here,* as he approached the desk. Quietly he opened the desk drawer and reached his hand inside, but the chronometer was not there. He was sure he had left it there, certain, almost. He opened another drawer and then another. There, he could feel the smooth surface of the instrument. He could only hope that it was the right one and not the old one that did not work. He opened the cover and ran his fingers over the inside of the cover. If there was engraving there, it was the right one. Just then he heard someone outside the door and a voice called,

"I thought I heard sommat in the cap'n's cabin. I'll take a look see."

Ben bolted to a position behind the door. As he moved, he grabbed the night glass which lay on the desk. The door opened and a curly head popped through. *Not too hard, now,* thought Ben. He swung the night glass at the back of the man's head and saw him fall to the deck. *He should have a sore skull tomorrow, but I am sure that I did not hit him too hard,* thought Ben.

He retreated to the window, slid the chronometer into the front of his trousers and slipped his legs through the opening, but getting back to the rope was going to be a challenge. He contemplated dropping the twenty feet into the water, but that would get the chronometer wet and ruin it. That would never do. He reached for the rail, but his hands were damp and he could not hold on. For a second, he hung suspended by only one hand. Frantically, he grabbed at the transom with his free hand and managed to get a hold. Slowly, with frighteningly painstaking moves, he made his way to the rope. Then he grabbed it and slid down to its end. Where was Tom? He could not see the tiny boat or Tom at all. Had Tom heard the altercation in the cabin and rowed off to safety? That was not like Tom. He'd never run from any battle, no matter how bad the odds. Ben swung helplessly for several seconds on the end of the rope. Then he felt Tom's hand on his legs. "Ease off there an' I'll catch you," said Tom. When Ben let go of the rope, he was certain that they both would end up in the cold water. The little boat rocked crazily, but Tom let him down slowly and then bolted to the oars and began to row. Ben joined him and neither lad was sorry to see the dark form of *La Fleur* fade into the mist.

When they were several hundred yards away, Tom whispered, "Did ye get it?"

"Aye, I think so."

"You think so? What kind of talk is that?"

The boys rowed back to the quay and picked up the two women. They rowed them to the ship, with not a word said. Ben rose and grabbed a batten as he let the silver coin fall into the hand of the older woman. She almost cried aloud. But Ben cautioned her to silence with his finger to his mouth and motioned for them to shove off. When the two men were aboard, Ben went to the binnacle light and examined the chronometer. *It is the correct one. I am saved, at least for now until it is missed.* Years later Ben would learn that a then Midshipman Burns was officer of the watch that night. When he had found Carson, one of his sailors lying on the floor of the captain's cabin, he turned in a report that said that, 'Apprentice seaman Carson had hit his head on a beam in the Captain's cabin and was found unconscious.' Apparently he had not noticed the cabin window which Ben had been unable to shut. Maybe he preferred not to notice it. Also, the purser came aboard at six bells the next morning to inventory the Captain's cabin, so the chronometer was never missed. That was a great stroke of luck and in their older years, Ben and Tom would reminisce happily about their adventure of that foggy night at Portsmouth.

Chapter Four

Willing But Unwilling - The Rescue

Nothing much unusual happened on the passage out to the Tagus River. Ben, Giles, Tom and several of the seamen took turns at trying to patch up Ben's uniform. By the time they arrived off the Tagus, Ben appeared like a proper young gentleman in his uniform, as if he had never met a horse named, 'Vixen' at all. He vowed never to hire a horse again as long as he lived, but circumstances would make it hard to keep that vow.

Ben found great comfort in having time to relax. He needed it. His life had been nothing but endless work since he had stowed away aboard the *Faithful* some nine years ago. For awhile his men were happy just to lark about with no responsibilities to force them to duty. But by the time they reached the Tagus, all of them, including Ben, were ready to get back to work. They were becoming bored with simply eating and sleeping. The average tar has to keep his hands busy or he will start to get cranky. They had heard each others stories about their shore leave many times over, and played cards, sang and played other games until they were tired of it all. But all of the men liked to hear about 'Vixen' any time that Ben would care to speak of her. That animal was not his favourite topic of conversation. He told only Tom about Annie.

"I was pretty sure you would look her up," Tom said.

"And I am almost sorry that I did. I need to know if she is married, Tom. It is eating at me, especially with being so idle with nothing to occupy my mind. I think of her every hour. I wonder if she read in my eyes what I saw in hers?"

Captain Fremantle entertained his officers and guests several times on the voyage out. Betsy Fremantle sat with them and sometimes they played whist, which Ben could not seem to enjoy. He did like Betsy, though. She was a fresh, pretty lady with many opinions of her own and was not shy about sharing those opinions. She told stories of her days as a young girl at home which interested Ben considerably. He had never really had a childhood and it was fine to hear what it should all have been like. She was bringing a small spinet piano with her and she often played and sang for the officers. Ben joined in happily, sometimes playing 'laika' at her elbow.

The only strange occurrence was about seven days out of Portsmouth. One of Ben's men came to him with a strange look on his face, a cross between a sneer and a smile, if you can imagine that.

"I hates to be a squealer, sir, but I think that that new recruit, Laslo, is a woman!"

You could have knocked Ben over with a gentle south-westerly breeze. But as he stood there and thought about it, he realized that was his suspicion back at the *Lamb's Inn* too. That was what was so strange about him. Not only was he slender, but he had a woman's build. Now came the challenge. How could he find out the truth? That would be tricky. If it were a woman, she would have trouble in the head with all those men about. Ben started to watch when she went to the head. It was always after the men had left. She was sneaking in after watching to see that all of the men were clear. Sometimes Trainor waited outside for her. He was probably her husband. Ben shadowed her quietly the next day and when he entered the head, he knew the truth instantly.

He asked to see Captain Fremantle. Fremantle was a very proper man from a good family. He was so beside himself that Ben was afraid he would throw Trainor and the girl overboard on the spot.

"This is an outrage," he stormed. "I know that some captains allow women aboard while at sea, but it bodes for no good, no good at all. In fact it is bad for the men. They can't keep their attention on their duty. I will have to put her ashore at Lisbon. There is no other choice.

You may go now, but don't pick up any more female recruits."

Ben sighed in relief. He had weathered that storm, but for a time he felt that he might be dismasted. The trip out to the station had taken twice as long as it had on the way to Portsmouth, but March was a troubled time of year and the winds were not favourable. Some of the sailors blamed the slow passage on one Willy Kink. It seemd that Willy liked to whistle and whistling on board ship gave rise to the superstition that the ship would come to trouble somewhere on her voyage. Worse yet was the superstitoin about women aboard. "When a woman is in her time, something awful always happens to a ship," said one old fellow through blackened teeth. Ben put little faith in superstitions.

Betsy Fremantle exclaimed with a loud, "Oh lordy! A woman sailor on board, and my poor husband with the whole mess dumped in his lap. What ever would possess a woman to go to sea anyway? Why, these sailors are the rowdiest, roughest, most mutinous lot that I have ever seen."

Tom took a decided disliking to the woman. "Too outspoken for a lady," he would say to Ben.

The two young men retained all formality in their friendship when they were on duty, but in private, either was pleased to let down his hair and talk freely with the other. Such was their understanding of each other that they could be true friends, even though Ben was the superior officer. But Tom was nine years his elder and still a midshipman, and it should have rankled. If it did, Ben never heard a word about it. Tom was moving slowly in mastering the science of navigation. Ben drilled him with the types of questions that he knew he would get in a leftenant's exam, but Tom seemed to forget from one time to the next. When Ben questioned him more closely, he was now more committed than ever. "All I want is to make first leftenant before I die. I care not a twig for anything further. I have seen too much of the hair pulling that goes with command, mind you."

Back at the Tagus station, the very first thing that happened was that Ben sought Captain Nelson and returned his chronometer to him. The Captain (now Rear Admiral) seemed distracted and paid little heed to the fact that his chronometer had come back. He had no notion what trouble Ben had gone to secure it for him. Then Ben delivered the packet of orders to Rear Admiral Jervis.

"Sit down, Mr. Rundel, while I scan these. There may be questions," said the Admiral.

So Ben watched the face of the Rear Admiral as he read the orders.

"I see that I have been promoted from rear to Admiral and will bear the title, Lord Saint Vincent. Quite an honour, I am sure. I will have to report back to London before long. Oh, and here, Nelson is being promoted to Rear Admiral. I knew that would happen too. He should be in for some title or other, if I am not mistaken, fine man, that. Oh, the least that he can get is the order of the Knight of the Bath. That carries some pretty gaudy jewelry which he will like, much better than being made a baronet."

"There are some orders here for you, Mr. Rundel, but I should like to speak with captain, er, excuse me, Rear Admiral Nelson before I send you off on this expedition. Come back later this afternoon and I will speak with you then. You can keep your things aboard the *Theseus* for the time being. Oh, and have Rear Admiral Nelson report to me at once, if you will."

"Aye, sir."

So Ben left the flag ship. He found Nelson with Captain Hardy, sharing a glass of sherry and warm memories of earlier times. They were apparently close friends. Ben asked to be admitted.

"I have a message for Rear Admiral Nelson, sir," he said to Captain Hardy, a bit of a smile whipping across his handsome face. Nelson looked at Hardy and a broad smile passed between the two.

"I knew it, old chap. I knew you would be promoted for

that gallant move at Cape St. Vincent," said Hardy as Ben stood by to catch every word.

"Surely you do not jest, lad," said Nelson.

"No sir. Admiral, Lord St. Vincent sent me to request that you attend him in his cabin aboard the flag ship at once."

The two men looked at each other again and Hardy reached a hand out to Nelson. "By God, you have both got your just desserts, sir!"

When Nelson returned from the flag ship, he gave orders for his things to be moved to the *Theseus*. He was to take command of the fleet and the *Theseus* would be his flag ship. Admiral Jervis was being called home, but not soon. "And it is time. The fellow is getting on in years," said Hardy.

Ben returned to the flag ship late that afternoon. Lord Jervis was seated at his desk and he had a grim look about him. Ben wondered if he was upset about being called home. He would not enjoy time spent on the beach, even at full pay. No officer enjoyed being redundant.

"Mr. Rundel, I have orders here to send you off on a fool's errand. I hate to do this and I had to twist Nelson's arm near off to get him to agree to this duty for you, but here it is. You know that we started to withdraw our ships from the Mediterranean after the treaty of San Ildefonso in '96. We drew off some more ships and supplies just recently in January before the Battle of Cape St. Vincent. It seems that the *Livorno* Consul to His Majesty, one Alfonso Bendotti, has a daughter who lives in a little village of *Piana* on the east coast of Corsica. She moved there a few years back when she married an Italian soldier. Corsica became French back in '69 when the French invaded the tiny isle." He pointed to the small bay on his chart north of *Piana*. "The French are all about the area and even though there has been no fighting there lately, Signora Belinda Gardini has lost her husband in fighting in Austria or North Italy, I forget which. The Consul fears for her safety and wishes that we should bring her and her two children to England at once. The rub comes in that the lady does not want to leave Corsica and may have to be taken by force. But the Consul is adamant that she be brought to him as soon as possible and that no violence be done to her or her children."

Ben thought for a second. *A woman and two children. They should not be too much trouble.* Ben was young and still had a great deal to learn.

"You shall be given a shallow draft schooner to rescue the signora and a small crew to man her. I expect you can select your own crew and I would hope that you would be off to Corsica tomorrow at dawn?

"I understand that it is the largest house in *Piana*. That is all that I know. You should return these people here to Rear Admiral Nelson as soon as you can." At that, he smiled and rose to shake Ben's hand. "Good luck lad, and I hope you can make *Piana* on your first try. There is a sizable bay just to the north of it. That is a treacherous, rocky coast, so beware."

As Ben was rowed back to the ship, he ran through his mind what he would need. Tom was a must and there was a fellow who spoke some Italian, one Alberto Mondazzi, who might be most useful. Ben carried orders to Captain Fremantle that he could have the pick of his crew, within reason, and that they were to be transferred to the *Witch* that night. There was a world of things to see to and Ben, ever the planner, had little time to prepare. At least, he would not have time to think about Annie.

Making Piana straight on will be a good test of my navigational skills, he thought. This might not be such a bad duty after all. Ben went to work with frantic preparations. He selected his crew carefully, all seasoned British sailors who would be unlikely to desert him on a shore held by the French. Then he assigned his men to watches and made up a duty roster. He decided that they should appear on shore as fishermen, so he sent Tom below to scout out some common seaman's clothes that might pass for the clothes of Italian fishermen. He needed at least four outfits. Let's see. He would need pistols, cutlasses, glass, flint and steel, several small mirrors for signaling, rope and food for men on shore for several days. They scouted out small backpacks from the marines which would hold enough food for a man for at least three days and a light blanket. Then he had to survey the *Witch* for compass, charts, chronometer and other essentials. She seemed seaworthy enough, but she was small. He sent Tom below to check out their supplies to see if there was enough food and water aboard. The ship had only two pop guns, small swivel guns that would be next to useless if he ran into trouble, but there seemed to be plenty of powder and shot aboard.

When Ben was preparing his gear, Rear Admiral Nelson stopped by to see how he was doing. "I suggest that you land by night using the ship's boat in the small bay to the north and then make your way under cover of darkness to the town. I think there is a road that skirts the coast at that point. Finding the right house in the dark might be a challenge, but you will have to do it. Most houses of any consequence have gilded names over the front door.

"I have already made plans for that, sir. We will masquerade as fishermen since the local village is a fishing village."

In all of the excitement, he nearly forgot to select his five marines. He did not know these fellows very well, but in the end he selected five men who were all from Cornwall. He could trust a Cornishman over anyone else. He was sure of that. Mr. Pierce would be in charge of the marines, who would cover his retreat from the town, if needed. That night he tumbled into his bunk aboard the *Witch* too tired to pay much attention to the smell of garlic. His men were stowed aboard and they had adequate food and ammunition for the passage. All he needed now was a plan, but his brain was too tired to focus any more. He must sleep and sleep he did.

They weighed anchor at a little past six in the morning. It was cold and foggy and he would have trouble getting a good noontime reading if the sun did not burn off the fog. He was keen to make a good landfall and not have to sail up and down the coast looking for *Piana*. The trip out was uneventful. On the second day, the fog cleared and he was able to get a good noon siting. The ship's log showed that they were making good time, somewhere near six knots. Ben had borrowed charts from Rear Admiral Nelson and would make a point this time of seeing that they were not left behind. Ben had to take the wheel for one watch each day and she was a beauty to sail, especially when it turned warm and sunny. She scudded along with all the ease of a ballerina on a smooth dance floor. Ben tried to focus on a plan for the rescue of the woman and her children, but it was hard to formulate a plan when he had never seen the surrounding area. Was there cover? How much and how effective was it? Was there a place he could hide his marines?

All that became clear on the eleventh day when they hove to in sight of land. Ben studied the charts for sometime until he was convinced that the peak to starb'd was *Cabo Rosso.* The entrance led into a wide bay with high rocky cliffs most of the way around. There was a narrow beach and a trail to the starboard side of the bay. No ships were in sight, so Ben ordered out the boat and took a quick tour of the bay, making soundings as he did. There were some problem spots. He would be best off to leave the ship near the entrance and row in to shore that night. He ordered his man to row back to the ship. Then he called a meeting of all the persons who would be going ashore, and of Midshipman Bandon who would be in charge of the ship while he was on shore. He wanted to leave Tom in charge of the ship, but he felt that he needed Tom's wise advice on how to smuggle the people from this place. Besides, Robert Bandon had passed the leftenant's exam, but was not yet twenty years of age, so he could not officially hold the rank of leftenant for another half year. As Ben thought about that, he realized that he had been commissioned leftenant in His Majesty's Navy at only eighteen, but no one knew his true age.

Ben had the cook, Giles Conyers, prepare packets of ship's biscuits and some cold meat and cheese for the five marines and the four who would come with him to the house. Mr. Pierce issued guns and cutlasses to the crew and saw that his marines were well provisioned. Ben wished that they were not going on shore as 'lobster backs'. Those colourful uniforms were of no use in a plan like this in enemy territory. He had tried to convince Mr. Pierce that they should don grey coats over their uniforms that would hide them when they were on shore. If their positions were discovered, Ben might be left stranded on shore with no means of escape. Finally, he prevailed and the marines agreed to wear blue great coats. That would keep them warm since they might have to spend several nights on shore and it would help disguise them from the enemy.

"Here is the plan," Ben began, although he did not have a clear plan yet in his head. "We will frappe the oars of the ship's boat and row into the beach that we saw this afternoon, about here," as he pointed on the map. "There is a good growth or gorse and brush there so we can hide the marines there. The four of us," he pointed to himself, Tom, Mondazzi and a sailor who had been a pick lock, Sly Pitten, "will walk under cover of darkness to the town. We must find the right house that night and locate places to hide so we can observe the comings and goings at the house. Sly will be the runner. If we need help, he would run back down to the beach for the marines. The marines are equipped with signaling devices, including rockets, so they could direct the *Witch* to come in close to pick us up if things get hot."

Ben judged that it would be about eight miles to the village, maybe a little more. "And we have to cross a river, just here, as he pointed to the map. I assume that there is a bridge, but if we have trouble crossing, we will rely on the marines to build a small raft to get us across. Our plan is to observe the house for a day or two if needed so that we can time our entry when there will be the least interference. We need to know how many servants there are at different times of day, where they sleep and where the signora and her children sleep. Each of you will have to fend for yourselves. You have food for three days, but you will have to find places to drink. The river may be potable, but take care. Any questions?"

"Do we await your return here on the beach sir?" spoke Mr. Pierce.

"Yes, but you must remain out of sight at all times. Stay away from any French patrols. And Mr. Bandon, you should stay just close enough to land so you can see our signal. You can expect it at any time in the next few days. We may be successful in locating the lady quickly and be back by tomorrow night, or we may run into a French patrol and have to run for our lives. Whichever occurs, we will need the ship's boat close by and quickly."

"Aye, sir."

So they set off. Ben would have liked to leave the ship's boat hidden by the beach, but since it was the only one that they had, it was too risky. He left Mr. Sherwood and a crew of six sailors to row her back to the *Witch.* Ben sent the marines off to their hiding place in the dense brush and then started up the hill with his band of kidnappers. Unfortunately, it was a lovely moonlit night in March, well past midnight. The road was dusty so it had not rained for sometime. They walked on cautiously, Ben leading the way. Suddenly he raised his hand. The men stopped. "Scatter to cover," he whispered. "Someone is coming."

Within seconds of his warning, a patrol of French troops rounded the bend in the road and marched on past them. The men had taken cover in a grove of small Corsican pine trees beside the road.

When the patrol had passed, Ben came out, motioning his men to advance. "That was a close call, sir," said Tom. They pushed on until they crossed a small footbridge. It was none too sturdy, but it would serve. Ben thought that their boots made too much noise on the bridge, but there was no way to muffle them.

After about two and a half hours, a small village lay before them. It was colourful even in the moonlight with the church steeple and the houses huddled in neat rows. Ben ran his eye over the village. *Where is the largest house?* he wondered. *There, no perhaps that one over there. It has more land and gardens. It should be the one.*

"Come lads, we must move on. It will be sunup in about two hours. We must find the right house."

They made for the house with the fine gardens, but when Ben crept up to the door, it said, 'DiGiorno,' not 'Gardini'. He returned to his men saying that must be the mayor's house. The other large house was on the opposite side of the village and some distance away. As they approached it, Ben could see that it too had considerable gardens and much land. This time, he made a direct hit. The name over the door in bold green letters was, 'Gardini'.

Now Ben looked about for a hiding place. The rear of the house had the most protection. There was an orchard there and he and Tom could easily see the house from the fruit trees. Mondazzi and Sly were stationed a bit farther away, near the road so that they could head for the marines if needed. This house was on the north edge of the town so it would be easy to retreat from there. These fellows were to keep watch for French patrols and would use a low whistle to alert Ben of danger.

"Get some sleep lads. We are likely to be awake most all day tomorrow." whispered Ben.

By day the house was more imposing than it had been at night. It had a fine porch on three sides and was draped with vines, which did not improve their chances of determining who was coming and going. All morning Ben and Tom watched, but nothing happened. Early, about six, two serving women entered the back of the house but no one had come or gone since. Then one of the serving women came out the back and headed down towards the town. She returned later with a large basket of produce, *far too much for one lady and her children,* thought Ben. After a time, Ben decided that they needed someone to watch from the front of the house. Persons could come and go without their being able to spot them from the fruit trees. So Tom offered to place himself in the row of tall poplars that lined the lane to the house. He would signal Ben using mirrors by day and a small candle shielded by night. Two flashes meant that someone was approaching.

All afternoon was peaceful. Birds sang and Ben grew tired of his perch in the trees and slipped down to the ground. He could still remain well-hidden here because there was a small patch of gorse to one side of the orchard. He trained his glass on the windows of the house and had decided that the signora slept on the second floor, on the starb'd side. He thought that he saw children in a room on the same side but on the first floor.

By nightfall, business picked up. There started a steady stream of French soldiers to the front door. First there was a plain soldier. He stayed for perhaps three quarters of an hour and then left by the back door. No sooner had he left than an officer appeared and was admitted to the front door. He stayed an hour. Then another officer and another. Each stayed about an hour and left by the back door. Then about ten o'clock, an officer of obvious high rank appeared. He was let in and Ben could see his shiny gold trim sporting about in the upstairs bedroom. *So that is it. Madam does not care to leave Corsica because she is having too much fun here.*

Ben signaled for Tom to rejoin him, using his candle and a brief flash of light. It would be easier to keep watch with two of them there. Ben was getting sleepy and he needed to know when the officer left. This officer stayed until four a.m. and then, apparently dressed hurriedly and left on his horse for some garrison that must be close by.

"That puts us in a fine mess," said Ben. If this goes on every night, we will not be able to get to the woman until sometime after four a.m. That will give us only about two hours to get her to the bay and to the ship."

"Impossible," said Tom.

"I know, but what do we do about it? It would be foolish to try to take her during the day when all four servants are there. At night there appear to be only two on hand and that makes it easier. I don't want to have to kill anyone."

They observed three French patrols that passed through town that day. One came at about 8 a.m., a second three in the afternoon and the third was the midnight patrol that had nearly caught them the night before. That might be why the general, as they assumed he was, left at four a.m. He would not meet any of his own men and have to explain where he had been at that hour. Ben and Tom slept soundly on the damp ground until nearly seven the next morning. The sun shone in Ben's eyes and awakened him from a troubled sleep. Part of his problem was that Tom snored loudly and he was afraid that some of the servants from the house would hear him and come to investigate. He might have to move Tom a bit farther away from the house for the next night.

The two men hurriedly ate some bread and cheese and drank a bit of small beer. Neither dared to take his eyes from the house for more than a few seconds, so they took turns eating.

That day, there were no comings and goings to speak of. The signora slept until nearly two in the afternoon. They did get a glimpse of two small children playing by the door sometime around noon.

But when night came, it was a whole new situation. Groups of soldiers, all French, started to appear at the front door about seven p.m. Ben could hear their garbled speech and was just able to recognize it as French rather than the more distinct, clear Italian. Some women appeared too. "Not the type that one would take home to me mother," said Tom. Ben counted sixteen and Tom thought that there were thirteen. "All four of last nights visitors are there too, sir"

It would be just like a woman to throw a party on just

the night when they had planned to abduct her. With so many enemy soldiers in the house, they would have to keep a very careful watch to be certain that they had all left. Surely some one, at least the general, would be staying after the party. And party it was too. Ben and Tom could hear gay music, see people dancing and hear cheerful laughter until close to 2 p.m. In fact, it was an uproarious party. The noise was so loud that the two men could talk normally under their favourite tree with no concern for being heard. They could see couples racing up the stairs and candle lights shining in all of the bedrooms, then flash off as someone snuffed out a candle.

"How are we ever going to know if these people have all left," said Ben in despair.

"Beats me. I think we may have to wait another day."

And so, in the end, they decided to wait another day, hoping that it would be more predictable than the one just passed had been. They counted nearly thirty people leaving the house that night between two a.m. and four, but only twenty-five had gone in. This was simply too risky to try a rescue with such unknown odds. "We are sailin' in shallow, treacherous waters, sir," said Tom.

The next day was quiet all day. Ben rendezvoused with Mondazzi and Sly and said that they would enter the house tonight sometime after midnight, if possible. He would need Sly and possibly Alberto as well. Ben reasoned that with all that partying, the general might be a bit overtired and might take himself home early. "At least we can hope," whispered Tom.

So they waited. Ben was tired of ship's biscuits and he was thirsty. There was a little brook nearby, but the water did not look clean to him and he drank only when forced to by his thirst.

That night, the plan of the first night unfolded again. First the common soldier, then three officers and then the general.

"She must be a pretty sight by the time the general gets to her, sir," said Tom with a twitter. Neither of them had been able to get a good look at the woman. She seemed to be heavy set, but they could not see her face, especially with the candle light shining from within at night. On occasion they heard a high-pitched voice from the second floor, but Ben thought that it must be one of the maids scolding the children.

Ben sat up with a start. It was barely past one in the morning when the rear door of the house opened and there stood the general in the moonlight, his medals and gold lace shining. Ben awoke Tom. "Run for Sly and Mondazzi. The general has just left and I doubt that any woman could handle yet another man tonight. We will make our move within the half hour."

The three men came puffing up to where Ben stood. "There seems to be total quiet in the house. The children's nurse seems to be asleep. At least her light is out. No movement in the bedroom above and no suitors at the front door. Time for us to move in. Sly, I will need you to open the back door. Think you can do it?"

"Aye, sir. Never did find a lock could keep me out if I 'ad me tools 'andy." They approached the back door cautiously. Ben whispered to Tom to take charge of the children. Mondazzi could go with him and explain in Italian that they were about to take a nice trip on a pretty ship. He would see to the woman.

Sly had the lock disarmed in nothing flat. The beautiful, carved wooden door slid open and Ben lit a candle for himself and Tom. Ben made for the stairs and ascended slowly, feeling his way. But as one might expect, the stairs squeaked. His heart pounded in his chest and he had to stop. Had he joined the British Navy for this? When he heard no doors opened and no sound, he went forward again. He could see out of the corner of his eye that Tom and Alberto were advancing on the nursery. At the top of the stairs, Ben though that he should turn to port, but as it happened, he was wrong. The first door he opened looked in on an empty bed, the covers thrown aside in disarray. So he moved down to the next and then the next. *This is taking too long,* he thought. *I will have all of the servants awake if I am not more careful.*

The next door that he opened he saw a woman lying in the bed. How could he be sure that she was not some servant? That had not occurred to him before. He advanced carefully and whispered, "Signora Gardini?" He could not think of her first name for the life of him. The face that he looked down into would not have suggested her name either. She was called, 'Belinda', but that face was anything but beautiful. Ben thought that he had never seen an uglier woman. She had a series of double chins and a round, petulant face that even in sleep seemed to be disapproving of something, perhaps everything. Her skin was a pallid white and she had a ring on each finger, save her thumbs. Her body was flabby and there was certainly a good bit of woman there. She reminded him of Angelina, Fergo the pirate's wife, but she was about six stone lighter.

The woman opened her eyes and looked at him. "Go way. Don' want any more man tonight," she hissed at him, partly in Italian, partly in French.

Then her eyes opened again and grew large and round in her round face.

She let out a string of Italian words that would have filled a ship's log from cover to cover. Ben stepped back so as not to be bruised by the torrent of strange words that she was tossing at him. Obviously, she had realized by now that he was not one of her lovers come back for a second helping. She must have recognized him as an Englishman right off as she cringed and slid away from him, spewing Italian blasphemies that would blister the eardrums of any shore hand or fisherman in the village. Ben did not know what to do. There were no books that a midshipman could study to tell him how to handle a big Italian woman who was acting like a lose cannon.. Then he realized that his only hope of getting out of here without rousing the whole house was to tie a gag around her mouth. But of all the things that he had remembered to bring, a gag was not among them. He grabbed a part of the bed sheet and ripped off a large chunk and stuffed it into the woman's mouth. The Consul may have said 'No violence', but he would have to understand that a sailor has to do what a sailor has to do.

Then he tied her hands so that she could not swat him any more. He said in slow English, "I come to take you to your father, at his orders." The woman's eyes blazed. There was no question that she wanted no part of her father or his help. Frankly, she was doing mighty well all by herself. Ben looked around for clothes. She would need clothes for the trip, warm clothes. He searched her closet and came out with a sturdy garment that he threw over her shoulders. Then he went to her dresser and brought out underwear, which he picked up gingerly with his thumb and forefinger and dropped into a wooden box. Then he found a hat, some shawls and other clothing and threw them in a bundle of bed linen. He found a gown or two also and put them in with the other clothes. Then he lifted the mumbling woman to her feet, her eyes darting about for any weapon that she could use against him. He pushed her not too gently towards the door, but she tried to run. Ben felt in his pack for rope. He would have to shackle her so she could walk but could not run. Or, he could take her shoes off? He placed good shoes for walking on her feet, but perhaps that had been a mistake.

They made it downstairs somehow, agonizing step by step, with muffled complaints at each step. Ben saw a light flickering two doors down the hall and stepped in, the woman on a leash as it were behind him. Ben could not believe what he saw. A small boy in his night shirt was riding on Tom's back, playing 'piggy back'. Tom looked up sheepishly, a grin that nearly cut his face in two, displaying those perfect white teeth lined up like a picket fence. Alberto stood by, beaming. He had the little girl partly dressed and almost ready to travel. Their nurse was trussed up like a turkey and sat leaning against the nursery wall, a formidable scowl on her face.

Ben sized up the situation in an instant. "Mr. Murphy, let drop the play if you please and find some clothes for this child. We are in dire need to flee for our lives," he whispered most urgently.

Ben could see that this was not going to be an easy duty. He hated to wipe the grin of sheer joy off Tom's face, but it had to be done. He was clearly enjoying playing with the little boy and had forgotten how desperate was their plight. Here they were well into French territory, and they, two British officers about to steal a French citizen from her home. But Tom had done a good thing too. He had won the trust of the children. Belissima cried when Ben refused to let her ride the nice sailor man. Although he could not understand a word that the child spoke, he was sure that she was fretting because she had been cheated at her turn on Tom's back. But that was just like Tom. He would make a fine father. He loved children and could not help himself.

"Mr. Mondazzi, would you tell this fine lady that we are here at the command of her father and that we are to take her to him in England for her own safety. No harm will come to either her or her children. And ask her to please be quiet and cooperate."

Ben handed Belinda's leash to Mondazzi and scurried around to find clothes for the little boy. He and Tom dressed the children warmly and then put together a packet of clothes for them for the trip. Sly had disappeared and Ben wondered where he was. Many years later Ben learned that Sly retired a rich man on the loot that he had lifted from that house in Corsica.

It was half past two when the party started out down the road. The children were fully awake now. Tom carried one under each arm. They were just a comfortable load for him, for about the first mile, but they began to chatter loudly and Ben called a halt so he could put gags on them both. After that, the children walked or dragged behind the adults. Ben sent Sly ahead to scout for French patrols, but to keep within sight at all times. They did well until Belinda managed to spit out her gag. Then a terrible torrent of Italian words flowed from the woman as if she were possessed, or had been a storehouse for words whose door had not been opened for a long time. Ben looked at Alberto. "What is she saying, man?"

"You don' want to know, sir," he said as he shook his head.

Ben grabbed the gag out of the dust and fitted it so that she could not remove it so easily, tying it behind her head. While he was busy with her, the boy spotted a rabbit or some such creature and headed off up the hills after it. Belissima was just behind him. They were four and five and quite able to get around in this hilly country. There were clumps of stunted trees and shrubs, large clumps of grass and plenty of rocks to hide behind. By the time Ben had finished with the mother, the children were no where in sight.

"Come on. We'll have to round them up. I don't dare return to the Tagus without the children. Quiet now, but let's spread out over this hillside, as he pointed to starboard. The port side led straight down to the sea. He tied the woman to a small tree and set Mondazzi to watch over her and to keep an eye out for the French patrols.

Alberto offered his opinion. "They are just playing hide an' seek with ol' Tom 'ere. They'll come out in a few minutes."

Tom looked at Ben. "If you hadn't muzzled them, we could call to them and they might answer us," he said accusingly.

"Yes, and bring the French patrols down on us and end the whole mess," said Ben. They walked cautiously. It was dark. The moon slid behind a cloud and like a shy lady refused to come back out. They walked and looked, poking here and there, but there was no sign of the children. Ben doubted that such small children would walk very far. He expected them to be nearby in some depression or behind a rock. But after two hours, he was at his wit's end. No one could find any trace of the two small children. Ben headed back up the slope and stood there for sometime, listening. One of them would sniffle or make some noise. He had little experience with children, but he knew that they could not be silent for long. He motioned for the others to stay behind. But there was not so much as a mouse squeak. Now totally frustrated, Ben stood up and roared at the top of his voice, "I did not study navigation and seamanship all of my life so I could play hide and seek with two imbecile children on a Corsican hillside." His outburst was so unexpected, so boiling with anger and authority that the children who had been hiding behind a rock near by, ran out and headed up the hill in fear of their lives. But Ben saw them, strode forward with his long legs at top speed and caught each by the waist. He hoisted them up under his arms and called for Tom to get rope to hobble them NOW! With that incident over, they could now proceed, but there was already a tinge of light in the sky to the east and they had two hours more of walking. And walking with hobbled captives was no easy matter, requiring constant prodding and cajoling.

"Wish we had horses," whispered Tom.

"No you don't," countered Ben. "We have enough trouble as it is."

They were off again. But with two small children, now quite tired from all the excitement, their progress was slow. Ben decided to send Sly for the marines. They could signal the ship and have the ship's boat there waiting when he arrived with his caravan of disgruntled souls. Sly slipped off, only to return within an hour.

"The marines ain't there, sir. They 'as left." Were the discomforting words the wretched man had for Ben.

"Gone! Where to?" There was no place for them to *go*. "They were to stay there until we arrived with the prisoners, er, passengers. Something must have gone wrong. Maybe the French patrols found them." There was nothing for him to do but to forge on to the thicket where he had left them. Perhaps there would be evidence of a struggle there. He could hardly signal the ship with only a candle, but perhaps they had hidden the rockets in a safe place and he could launch one of them. It was cold and damp and he felt terribly tired. Her was hungry too. He had not eaten a decent meal in three days, just some cheese and ship's biscuits.

Two hours later, at near dawn, they arrived at the thicket where he had left the marines. There stood Mr. Pierce in his full uniform for the whole world to see.

"What mean you man,? You are endangering us all. There may be a patrol along at any minute. Get your great coat on this minute." Ben could take command when he felt threatened and he felt that way now.

"Where were you when Sly came for you several hours ago?"

"Dunno, sir. We jus' stepped over the hill there to a house where there are some nice ladies with 'refreshments'. It was mighty cold 'ere sir an' we thought to get us some fine French wine."

So that was it. He might have known that five marines could not stay on shore for three days without finding some women. Well, no harm had been done, yet. He ordered all of the lobster backs to put on their great coats to hide their uniforms and to stay out of sight. Then he found the rockets and sent one up over the bay. Wherever the *Witch* was, she should see that signal. They waited, hungry and tired. Ben knew in the name of humanity that he should remove the woman's gag, but he dared not. If a patrol did come into sight, she would be the first to give them away.

The sun rose, a brilliant golden red orb in the east. The warmth was welcome, but it would be harder than ever to hide now. What must they do now? It was over an hour since he had sent up the rocket and the *Witch* was no where in sight. Ben wished that he had left the ship's boat hidden on shore. At least they could avoid any patrols that way, but it was already full sunup and a patrol should come along within the hour. Ben fished for the last biscuit in his small pack and then lay back. There was good water at a spring close by and he made frequent trips to refresh his thirst.

Where was that accursed ship's boat? They should have been here hours ago.

Just then Ben heard the grating of gravel. He looked up and there were the tops of the hats of the patrol dancing just over the brow of the hill to the south. "Down, everyone and no noise." whispered Ben. He forced Belinda down with a firm hand that her father might not have identified with, 'no violence'. They were huddled in the thicket beside the road where he left the marines. There was hardly room enough for all of them, but it would have to do. He eased his pistol out of his waistband and cocked it. He heard Tom do the same. The marines lay on their backs. *Good god! One of them has forgotten to put on his great coat. There he lays in our midst like a huge red lobster out of water. He'll have the whole French patrol down on us.* Ben rarely panicked, but he did now. He slid over next to the marine and threw his coat over the man to hide the brilliant red of his jacket. He would be disciplined later on. By now the patrol was abreast of their hiding place. Ben could hear them breathing and see the whites of their eyes. He held his breath. But he happened to catch a glimpse of something off on the horizon. There was the ship's boat, slowly rounding the point and heading their way. Hopefully, the patrol would not spot the boat too. If they did see it, they must have thought it was a fishing boat, because they never broke pace.

Once the patrol had passed, Ben rolled over on his back and let out a great sigh of relief. The children were restless, not having had much sleep that night. Tom put their heads under his arms when the patrol came by so they could not accidentally slip out and give them away. Typical of him, he made a game of the whole thing and the children were most happy. He let them free now. The boat would be ashore soon. The patrol had disappeared over the hill and was gone. *Thank God!*

Half an hour later, the ship's boat landed and Ben

hurried his party from hiding towards the boat. Just then a rattle of musket fire broke lose from the cliff above them. Bits of sand flew in the air as the shots missed their targets. There was a zinging sound as a second set of shots were got off.

"Hurry, lads, hurry. Those French are not as dumb as we thought. They must have seen the ship's boat approaching and thought that something was up. We have to shove off *now*." With that, Ben gave a great shove and the boat slid into the water. Just as he was about to jump into the boat, a musket ball hit his lower leg and he fell into the water. But Tom's hand shot out to grab him and he and Mondazzi pulled Ben aboard. "Row, you bastards, row," called Ben, still in pain. Tom pulled up Ben's trouser leg and examined the wound. They were out of musket range now, but the French still fired at them, considering them to be fish in a barrel. *Good thing they are such poor shots,* thought Ben. No one else was hit.

"It's not serious. Just a flesh wound, sir. Too bad an' its your good leg for mountin' horses too," said Tom with a broad smile.

They pulled out of the bay and boarded the *Witch.* Ben's first words to Mr. Bandon, who was in charge, "What took you so long to answer our rocket?"

"Sorry, sir, but we have been hounded the past two days by an armed brig. She keeps coming after us and I have had to sail into very shallow waters to avoid her. She must be some sort of French shore patrol."

"Well, you made it just in time, and we are mighty glad of that. We came out under musket fire."

After the ship was underway, Ben saw to his leg. The wound was only superficial and did not damage the bone. He was lucky.

They took the gags and hobbles off the woman and children as soon as they reached the ship. But then all hell broke loose. The children were totally undisciplined. Their mother had appeared little concerned about them all the way from the house to the ship. Even Mondazzi remarked that she seemed to care little for her children. Most Italian mothers would have been in tears over her poor infants, but this one seemed to care only about herself. She did not know where they were or what they were doing and did not care. Ben wished now that they had brought the nurse along. *She must have some control of the children.*

Ben gave Belinda his cabin, which was adequate for three people. But the woman carried on a constant barrage of Italian, which beat on the ear drums mercilessly. Ben told Mondazzi to explain what was happening to her again and to tell her to be quiet. He did and he said that she understood perfectly well, but was determined to make his life as miserable as she could. Mondazzi gave a little smile and said, "And you would never guess what she will do to you if she gets you alone, Tall an' Skinny." Apparently she had started to refer to Ben as 'Signor Tall and Skinny' in her long tirades against him. Ben directed Mondazzi to keep an eye on her and to report, 'only if she has something significant to say'.

"Oh what she is sayin' is mighty significant, sir, but I doubt that you would like to hear the translation," said Mondazzi with a snicker.

"There, Luigi is climbing the rigging. He'll fall and get killed," shouted a sailor.

"Hey, who's ringing the ship's bell?" said another. It was Belissima. Ben learned that Belissima meant the most beautiful, but he failed to find any beauty in this child at all. She was pure, distilled devil.

In the midst of all the confusion, Ben managed to get the cook's attention and called for food for all those who had just come aboard. He had a few eggs saved and some bacon and now savoured visions of sizzling bacon and fried eggs. The bacon did sizzle and the eggs were fried, but as soon as Belinda smelled them, she commandeered them for herself. She approached the steward, Giles, with such overbearing authority and presence that he could not withstand her. He reported to Ben, crestfallen, that he had failed him on the eggs and bacon. Ben had to eat mush and ship's biscuits with a bite of cheese. He was beginning the think that if ever he got her alone, there were some unpleasant things that he would like to do to that woman too. He had dreamed about those eggs all the time he was waiting to storm the house, on the track to the coast and all the way out in the ship's boat.

Then Ben spotted Belissima playing with the sand glass. She was turning it this way and that, watching the pretty sand grains slip through the little hole. Ben raced to the child and took the glass from her. He took the glass from her gently, but once the glass was safe, he was anything but gentle to her derriere. He wondered how long she had played with it, and how far off their ship's bells would be? The only thing that he could do was to use his chronometer to reset the sand glass at the next half hour. Then the children went racing around the hold, bumping into things and raising general cane with the ship's rats. Even they ran in fear of their lives as the children approached. Only Tom could handle the little brats. He would play with them and keep them absorbed for as much as two hours at a time, but he was short handed and Ben needed Tom at the conn.

The mother was a constant irritation. Ben gave her a chamber pot, but she complained that it was too small. Ben countered that it was good enough for him, it should be good enough for her. Whenever she had the time and energy, she would crank up her Italian attack on Ben and the ship. Ben soon realized that she was trying to lure his sailors to her cabin, (hell, it was really *his* cabin) for a tryst. It takes very little to distract a sailor at sea and a woman is just the thing that will do it, and after long enough at sea, even an ugly woman will do. Ben came near to flogging one fellow who was all too willing.

"She is a guest of King George's and we must treat her with respect," he said. He forbade his men from making any approach to the woman. All day long he could hear her mumbling in Italian or sometimes shouting. Never did she seem to worry about her children. Not once did she ask for them, or ask after their health.

Their first night at sea, a heavy fog settled in and it was impossible to see any distance at all. During the night, Ben was on watch. Then about 8 p.m., he heard a ship's bell not more than fifty yards to port. He slipped from his post and cautioned all of his men to remain quiet. He ordered the men to tie gags on the woman and her children. He could not trust them to obey any orders, no matter what the language.

Back on deck, Ben caught a few words of French. He was quite certain that this was the armed brig that Mr. Bandon had seen earlier. Ben could not be sure that they knew he was so close by. Once Ben caught sight of a gun port through a thin place in the fog. That did it. He had to do something to protect his ship and his men. Ben thought for awhile. They had only a pop gun, a tiny swivel gun on the deck, but it would be useless against a full-sized, armed brig. The other swivel gun was found to be faulty and could not be fired. It would do little good against a full sized ship anyway. They were as good as sunk and dead already if he could not think of a way out. There was almost no wind, so they lay close to the enemy ship, both becalmed.

Maybe that pop gun is of no use, but its powder might come in handy. Ben knew that there were about five barrels of powder in the hold for use in the guns. He was hatching a plan, but as was his nature, he needed some encouragement. He sought out Tom and whispered his plan to him.

"Should work, sir. It is the only hope that we have. There are probably at least ninety of them to only twenty of us plus the marines. She probably has at least twenty guns, ten of 'em aimed point blank at us."

"Get the powder barrels up and drop the ship's boat from starboard as quietly as you can. Load in the barrels, lash them down, and put two men at the oars, two who can swim. Give them a goodly length of rope to tie on with. I'll handle the rest."

"Aye, sir."

It was all done in fifteen minutes. Ben helped tie the rockets to the barrels of gun powder. A shot anywhere near those rockets would set them off and detonate the powder. That would blow her stern clean off and sink her. Swanson and Ames were the rowers. They were good men. Ben gave them their last minute instructions, "and don't let them see you or hear you or it is all over for you. We will watch for you to swim back. It is only perhaps sixty yards," said Ben. Then Ben sent for Mr. Pierce who was not on duty.

"I need four marksmen in the tops to aim at the bomb that I have set for the French ship that is shadowing us. The powder and detonators are in the ship's boat which is being attached to the rudder of the enemy ship. When I give the word, your men are to shoot for the rockets. I have tied red flags on them so they will be easily visible. Is that clear? Send up your best men, if you please, and we will replace them every four hours. Sometime this fog will lift and when it does they can blow us out of the water with a single broadside. We have to beat them to it."

"Aye, aye sir."

They spent the night taking turns watching the enemy ship. The ship's bell was silenced by tying a rag on the clapper. Ames and Swanson returned, happy that "the ship's boat would blow 'em to kingdom come, sir." Ben took the precaution of locking his cabin door from the outside and barring all of the cabin windows so the 'black widow,' as he had begun to call her, could do no harm.

Ben desperately wanted to sleep. His head bobbed down onto his chest and he was almost asleep on his feet. *I can trust Tom.* He had slept more on land than Ben had, that is if Tom's snoring was any measure of sleep. Ben curled up on the deck with a blanket. The cold and dampness soon got to him, but sleep overtook his consciousness before the cold became unbearable. Tom was to awaken him in two hours or as soon as the fog lifted enough that he could see the enemy ship.

They went through the night changing guard every two hours, but by dawn the fog was still with them. Ben could still hear deck noises, so he was certain that the French ship was still close by. They had breakfast and Ben resumed his vigilance. Now and again he could see a dull white orb that must be the sun trying to burn off the fog. *It must come soon,* he thought.

This would be a supreme challenge of his ability to bluff his way to safety. If the Frenchman even had a few minutes to think about it, he would know how helpless Ben and his ship really were.

Then suddenly, as if some huge hand had swept the fog aside, the enemy ship stood in the clear of daylight. Ben scanned her decks quickly. She had not run out her guns yet. She apparently thought that she had already captured the small schooner. She was not large, but was a well-built ship, faster than most brig sloops he had seen.

There appeared an officer at her rail.

Drat. He could not speak French. If ever he needed command of that barbaric language, it was now. None of his crew spoke French, and the 'black widow,' could not be depended on to convey his message.

Ben could hear movement behind the bulwarks as if guns were being leveraged into place. It would come any second now, the blinding broadside that would send them all to their deaths. He had to do something, fast.

He spoke slowly, purposefully. "Ahoy there. I would not run out your guns or open your gun ports if I were you. We have placed a bomb boat under your stern." He pointed meaningfully toward the ship's stern. "I have four marksmen placed in the tops ready to detonate that bomb at the instant that you fire a shot, put a boat in the water, or open a gun port. One step towards the stern to cut the boat free and we will fire her. There is enough gun powder there to blow you all to kingdom come. We can blow your stern off with one shot, long before your men could reach the bomb boat. I have you at a disadvantage, sir. I ask for your surrender at once," said Ben, all very slowly and carefully.

He was in luck, because the first leftenant of the French ship spoke English and had heard every word. Men raced to the stern and heads craned over the taffrail of the French ship to view the ship-bomb that Ben had planted close to their stern. Ben watched as the Captain and his mate talked in French, wild frantic gestures of their hands and arms punctuating each sentence. Ben heard arguments, words spitted at each other as if they had eaten something distasteful and were about to spit it at each other. He thought, *At least Italians pronounce all of the vowels. I can guess what they might be saying, but I have not a clue what is being said over there.*

Time dragged on. A good three minutes elapsed since Ben had made his challenge. Any longer and they will be able to send a man down over the stern to chop the ropes lose. The two Frenchmen continued to argue on deck, now joined by two others.

"I want an answer now, or I shoot," shouted Ben. He glanced at his riflemen. Good thing he had thought to use four marksmen. Any fewer and the French could pick them off with one volley from their tops.

There was no answer from the French ship. Ben looked at the marines and signalled for them to get off a shot, to miss. "Zing!" as a shot hit dangerously close to the French ship. Ben realized that with no wind, they could not just sail away out of range of his musket.

Then it came as unexpected and halting as had been his challenge. "We surrender. Here.. is... my... sword."

Now Ben had a real problem. He had not really expected the Frenchman to surrender. Ben had no ship's boat with which to receive the sword. He could hardly swim over there to pick up the sword. Speed was essential. These Frenchies might change their mind at any moment and open fire. All they had to do was to kill him and it was over for the *Witch.*

"Put your boat in the water. I will receive your sword here aboard the *Witch,"* called Ben. That was a long shot. The Captain could well refuse to come to him. Indeed, it went against all practice in war. A man had won a battle only if he could stand above the bent head of his foe and receive his sword on the enemy's territory. Ben took a deep breath.

"All right, English. We come, but don' you shoot."

"I will hold my fire. Come swiftly," ordered Ben. The Frenchman did not apparently realize that the schooner had only one ship's boat and that with it out of commission, Ben was helpless to take his prize.

Seven minutes later the French captain stood by the rail on the *Witch* and handed Ben his sword. His scowling first leftenant and second and third leftenants offered their swords too, but Ben sensed that if he had turned his back for a seconds, they would have knifed him in the back. The younger men wanted to fight, thinking that Ben was bluffing, but the captain did not want to take the chance. *Does he possibly have valuable cargo aboard? Does he hope to get aboard and then overpower our small crew and take our ship and his own back to his home port?* Ben would have to be extremely careful.

"Take these men below and put them in irons, and place a marine guard over them night and day. Also, the 'black widow's' door is to be kept locked and the children confined for the rest of the voyage. I will see that food and water are taken in to her," Ben ordered Tom and Mr. Bandon.

Then he sent twenty sailors and two marines across to confine the French sailors using the Frenchman's own ship's boat.

"Mr. Bandon, I am giving you temporary command of the French brig. You may have ten seamen and two marines of your choice. I want a complete report of the stores on board her by late tomorrow, if possible."

On their return trip Ben gave orders to retrieve his ship's boat using the French ship's boat. That would leave no ship's boat aboard the Frenchman, except a small dingy. No matter. The two ships would sail in close proximity. There were ninety one men aboard the French ship. Ben left Mr. Bandon in charge of sailing the ship, giving him sailing orders and bearings. He was to stay close by for the trip to the Tagus. He ordered the French cook to prepare a meal for his own men under guard. That left Ben with ten men to sail his ship, with him in command, and two marines to guard the captured officers.

But the weather turned fair and they could expect a quick passage. After all the details of getting the two ships under weigh were taken care of, Ben collapsed in a sound sleep and slept on deck until after five o'clock that evening. He awoke, feeling most guilty at leaving Tom at the conn all those eight or nine hours. Ben hopped to his feet, made his excuses, and then returned to take over the sailing of the ship. He looked to port and there was the *Curieux* scudding along handily about a hundred yards off. *Bandon is doing a good job handling the ship,* he thought. He would have to remember to put that in his log, when and if he could get time to write in the log again. He had it removed to Tom's quarters so that the 'black widow' and her children could not damage it. He had already found awkward scribbles in the log where the children had decided to make their entries. If he survived this cruise, he would be able to face almost anything. He knew that he would plead for mercy if they were to send him on any more rescue missions of unwilling patriots.

At four in the afternoon, the *Curieux* signalled that they should stop for a gam. Ben wondered what was up. He saw Bandon lower the ship's boat and he was rowed swiftly to the *Witch.*

Bandon climbed up onto the deck breathlessly. "Here, sir, are the lists of supplies as close as we can make them, mostly barrels of beef and grains. But, the real surprise is that she is appartently a payroll ship. She is carrying over 4,000 pounds in silver."

"Thank you, Mr. Bandon. You have done a fine job. We are not long out of home port now, so keep a close eye on the prisoners, if you please."

The whole time that Ben was awake that night, the

'black widow' wailed and carried on. Ben hadn't a clue what was bothering her and he doubted if she did either. He was simply going to ignore her. What else could he do? When it came time to sleep, he shut her out of his mind. The men said that she quieted down at night, but you could not prove it by Ben. He went to sleep with the sound of her hoarse voice ringing in his ears. The children behaved badly for the entire voyage. Mondazzi said that one thing the woman wanted was for us to take these beastly children from her. She did not want them under foot. That Ben would never do. There had already been enough damage done to his ship by these little demons. And he was shorter on men now than ever. His men were having to stand watch for four hours and then sleep for sometimes only two hours. The winds were fresh and rascally and they had to alter sails and tack often. *There are barely enough of us to do the work.* Ben saw that they had the best food he could provide and no one seemed distraught, except at the constant wailing of the Italian woman. Everyone lent a hand to speed the trip back to the Tagus where they could discharge the cargo.

Ben stopped by Tom as he stood near the taffrail that evening. "I am sorry that I could not give the *Curieux* to you, lad, but I need you here. I was too spent to sail this ship by myself after our tour on land. You understand?"

"Aye, sir. I expected as much," was all he said. Ben knew that he would make it up to Tom as soon as he could. Tom could handle the French ship every bit as well as Mr. Bandon, and Ben knew it. Since Bandon had passed the leftenant's exam, Ben had to give him a chance at command. Tom was still a midshipman, but with skills far beyond his station.

Ben was so busy and tired the day before that he neglected to order the unloading of his ship's boat which was still in tow some considerable distance behind the *Witch.* He made a point of letting the French officers see his men carrying the barrels of powder with the rockets still attached into the hold to be stowed. They disassembled the explosives once they were below, but the eyes of the French first leftenant fairly bulged out when he saw the barrels of powder being brought below. Now he knew that Ben had not been bluffing, but he would never know that Ben would have been reluctant to give the order to fire into the barrels. *Le Curieux* was a beautiful ship and he would have hated to blow her out of the water. She would make a fine prize. So what did it matter that his orders did not include capturing a full-sized armed brig with a small schooner. He was sure there would be no reprimand.

When Ben took the food to the cabin for Belinda and the children he also had to remove the pot. That was anything but enjoyable and he was glad to hand it over to Giles to dispose of. But he could not believe his eyes when he surveyed the inside of his cabin. For days the children had been noisy, but seemed not to be causing any other problems. Now he looked in on a scene of total chaos. The bedding had been torn, scattered all over the floor, the desk ransacked. There was little of value in it, but it was a fine old desk, now not so artfully carved by the two villainous children who had held back a knife from their last meal. The wall was smeared with graffiti, words Ben could not recognize and did not want to know. Even the windows, which had been shuttered from outside had scribbling on them. The children had found some chalk from the desk. Their mother sat in the midst of this chaos, on the deck, her head hung down on her fat chest, her eyes blazing hatred at Ben as he stood over her, anger building in him until he thought he would explode. But reason prevailed and he remembered that these were 'guests of King George III's' and their behaviour would have to be tolerated, no matter how bad it might be. Ben locked Giles in the cabin, bucket, cloth and scrubbing powder in hand, with the woman and children for a morning, with instructions to, 'clean up this mess'. He apologized to Mr. Giles afterwards, making him feel like a hero, which, if he had survived that place for four hours, he truly was.

So when the next day the River Tagus and the British fleet came into view, Ben was relieved. He had done his duty and then some. To Ben's surprise, Admiral Jervis had not sailed yet. The flag ship blossomed out with orders as Ben's ship approached. Ben did not have a signal book aboard. There was not one to spare when he left. But he recognized the order, "Captain repair aboard the flagship at once," and that he would do. His uniform had not fared well on this passage either, but it would have to do.

I don't know how His Majesty can expect any officer to do his duty and still stay clean in white trousers in time of war, thought Ben.

The Admiral met him at the tumblehome. "What the devil is that French brig doing following you? I thought I sent you to bring back Signora Gardini?"

"So you did , sir and so I did. It's a long story. I have it all outlined here in this report, but if you would like the details, I would beg for a day to catch up on my report writing. With two ships to sail the length of the Mediterranean, we were a bit short-handed, sir," replied Ben.

"Well, come to my cabin and we will see what you have here."

The Admiral read the brief report, his eyebrows flying out of control more than once like a lose sail in a windstorm. "Yes, lad, I want every last detail you can give me of this remarkable voyage. I can't believe my eyes. And if that brig were not out there riding at anchor, I would not believe it, not one word of it."

"I will need to transfer the Gardini family to another ship, sir, and also to transfer the prisoners of war, some ninety one, to a prison ship."

"That's why I am still here, trying to get this blasted station to function properly so that Rear Admiral Nelson can take over. We just finished setting up a hulk as a prison ship yesterday. She sets off there towards the port bank. We still have some warehousing problems to solve, you know. Oh, and the Gardini family can stay aboard for another day until I decide what to do with them. I'll have Captain Miller send some crewmen to transfer your prisoners. My, ninety-one prisoners and a twenty-gun brig taken by twenty men and four marines in an unarmed schooner. Unheard of, lad, unheard of."

Ben went back to his ship. He longed for his own cabin where he could concentrate and write his report, but that was not to be. Signora Gardini was at it still. She could be heard all over the station with her howls and complaints. It made report writing for the Admiralty most difficult. Ben sat with the pen in his hands for awhile, thinking. *I am handsome, seventeen, almost eighteen and a successful King's officer. It is time for some romance in my life. Why could not this lonely widow that I have just rescued against her will have been a beautiful maiden, blooming with joy, one that I could fall in love with on the spot? Why does she have to be a harridan? What will ever become of me? I sense a need to belong to someone, anyone who is good and sweet.*

The children were let out. It was Tom's idea. They had been cooped up in that tiny cabin for two weeks and that was just plain inhumane. Tom was at his ease now that they were in port. So he had time to chase the children around and play 'hide 'n seek' with them. He seemed happier than Ben had ever seen him, but when he was on duty, they could expect almost any calamity to break loose. The children had spent two weeks thinking about what they *would* do if they *could* do anything, and now they *did* it, all of it. The cook found a dead rat in the meat broth that he was preparing, there was an unspeakable mess in the hold where the crew tried to dry their clothes, and they found lines cut in the running rigging. Belaying pins disappeared into the briny deep. Ben told all his officers and men to keep a close watch on the little devils, but it seemed to do no good. They were extremely crafty in picking their times and their crimes.

It was amidst this type of chaos that Ben finally completed his report to the Admiral. He asked to be rowed over to the flag ship late that day, feeling like he was a sail that had been through a severe storm with all its gussets blown out and tears and tatters all around.

Ben left the report for the Admiral and retired to his ship for a good night's sleep. But not before he spotted a pretty tiger cat curled up in a coil of rope just outside the Admiral's cabin. He stopped to pet her, or he assumed that anything so pretty must be a 'her'. The animal looked up at him with loving eyes and began to purr. *Someday, lady, ...someday I will own and love the likes of you again.*

Chapter Five

The Tragedy At Tenerife - 'I Will Bow To Your Stump Tomorrow'

The next morning as Ben sat eating his breakfast, his signal officer came to him saying. "They are flying our number sir, and asking for the captain to repair aboard the flagship at once."

"Thank you Mr. Riggs." But Ben was not about to be rushed through his breakfast. The cook who served all the men in so small a ship, had sent ashore for some fresh eggs and had fried up a big batch for Ben. Nothing was going to deter him from executing his duty towards those delicious eggs. He had fond memories of living off eggs when he was a runaway orphan at the Broken Bridge. But they never tasted better than they did today. *I could even almost tolerate the signora if I can get a good plate of eggs in my stomach,* he thought.

Ben arrived at the flag ship half an hour later. He asked to be announced, and the sergeant of marines who guarded the door pronounced in an artificially formal voice, "Third Leftenant Benjamin Rundel to see you ,sir." He was apparently teasing Ben for his capturing a twenty-gun armed vessel with his tiny pop gun. That story had spread all thought the fleet by then. *Well, at least it gives bored men something to think about,* thought Ben.

"Well, lad, you have had quite an adventure. I never intended for your trip to Corsica to be such a challenge. You not only seem to invite challenges, but you can also overcome them. Captain Miller and I sat over a glass of claret last night and howled over the audacity and foolhardy bravery in your report. I am having it copied now and will send it on to London with the next ship. Oh, mind you. Tom Hardy has just been promoted to commander for his daring cutting out of *La Mutine* under the nose of her French captain. Which brings to mind another topic. You have done such a fine job in capturing that brig that I am asking you to take her on to London with our honoured guests, Signora Gardini and her two children."

The alarm that registered in Ben's face must have read like a book in large, bold print. Ben stood there, not sure what to say. The words of the old sailors at Saltash came back to him. "Always do your duty, no matter how hard it might be, an' you'll manage right well in the Navy." Ben knew that this was true and he also knew that his nerves could not stand three weeks or so of the brats and their mother. *No, no,* ***No!*** *Let someone else do it for a change. He had had enough. He needed some rest.*

Ben snapped out of his self-examination. "Sir, I do believe that Rear Admiral Nelson has asked me to return to his command as soon as possible. Also, sir, what you ask is incredibly painful for me. These people have nearly driven me and my crew mad." Ben decided to be honest. Honesty could do no harm, as long as there was enough honey with it. He knew that John Jervis valued straight out honesty. He need not play games with him.

At that, the old Admiral let out a loud laugh and slapped his ample knee. "I was wondering what you were going to say, lad. She has been in port only a day and I have had a complaint from darned near every British ship here about her constant loud babbling. I don't know how you put up with it for two weeks. I was just teasing you, lad. No offense, I hope."

"None intended, none taken, sir," but Ben would always think of that moment as one of his worst. He had to tell his superior officer that he did not have the guts to take on an odious duty. *Admirals have to have some fun too,* he thought. He knew that from his first encounter with Admiral Spencer.

"No, I have a young leftenant just out of London who is a bit oversized for his britches. He will get the job of taking this fine lady home, and mind you, he has earned it, every bit of it. Ben would learn later of the agonies of that short passage to London. "The ship was the *Narcissus* and her young acting captain one, Leftenant Harvey Boggs. Ben had known him aboard the *Hawk* many years before. He did not dislike Harvey, at least not enough to wish this on him, but old Boggs could be a bit overbearing at times, a bit pompous. Ben could see how Boggs might get on the wrong side of an Admiral without hardly trying. Boggs would now assume the temporary command of *Le Curieux.*

"Rear Admiral Nelson is out on patrol off Cadiz and should return here in about six days. I imagine that you can occupy your crew in cleaning and repairing your ship during that time. We took her straight from the Frenchies with no time to clean her up. She will be sent home as a prize sometime soon, although I have a notion to keep her here as a messanger. She is a good fast sailer."

So Ben returned to the *Witch* and set his crew to work putting her in top shape. Signora Gardini and the two Gardini devils were put aboard *Le Curieux* late that afternoon for transport to London. Ben spent a few minutes with Harvey Boggs and exchanged some notes. Ben had a chance to catch up on the fate of his former shipmates. A few were dead, some had made leftenant, actually all but Cunningham had passed. Lakeham had a deuce of a time, but did finally pass. Boggs figured that he would never make it to post captain. Robby Stewart, their ensign, had married and left the service. Hewlett had been tried and the surgeons had found him unfit for duty. He was put on the beach with no pay for the rest of his life. He could never set foot in a British ship again. Cookson had gone on to become a Captain and had some ship in the Caribbean. Ben spent a pleasant hour reminiscing over 'old times' with his former shipmate.

Boggs was quite aghast at the things that Ben had done during his year since the *Hawk*. "If I had not been here when you brought in that brig with your little schooner, I would never have believed the story. You are in the *Naval Chronicle* and sometimes the London papers, even in the *Gazette* quite often these days. I suppose that this recent caper will make the papers also."

Was there a hint of envy in Boggs' voice? Ben could not be certain.

Ben returned to his ship to find an invitation to dine with the Admiral. *That would be a pleasure,* thought Ben. He liked the old Admiral and even if he had played a cruel joke on him today by making him think that he would have to sail the Gardini family home, he was still a fine old fellow. That was one of the most pleasant evenings Ben had spent in a long time. The Admiral planned a fine meal and invited the other captains who were in port to join him. Ben was the only leftenant present. The other Captains, James Saumarez, Ed Berry, Davidge Gould, Alexander Ball and Tom Foley all made a congenial group with whom to dine. Ben was cornered as the port and cheese were served. He had to tell about rescuing the signora and capturing *Le Curieux.* There was no escaping it. He hated to be in the limelight and now there was no Nelson there to whom he could shift the attention, so he had to knuckle down and tell his story. They all laughed at his bravado in asking the French captain to 'surrender, or I will blow you to bits'. Foley said that an act like that took just shear courage and guts, what with ten loaded guns pointed straight blank at his ship. They drank to his health and Ben turned in for the first night of truly good sleep in over a month. Signora Gardini and the Gardini Devils were gone and it was *quiet.* But when he awoke in the morning, he imagined what kind of sleep Harvey Boggs had enjoyed, and a sly smile lit across his face. Slowly, he thought, *I am making friends in higher places. Maybe someday, maybe, I will get my wish ... my own ship and my own command.*

Later that day, Ben happened to speak with the Admiral. As might be expected, the subject of rescuing the unwilling Gardini's came up. The Admiral smiled a sly smile. "You know lad, no one ever expected you to be able to bring those people out of Corsica. We all thought it a waste of time because the lady was too willing in some departments, but unwilling to go to England. I must commend you on completion of an impossible mission."

On the way back to his own ship Ben began to think. *Why didn't I think of that earlier. I was sent to get Signora Gardini because I am a nobody. No noble family will have to languish in the displeasure of the King because it was their young kinsman who failed to rescue the Consul's daughter. I was used as a scapegoat. I can expect some more darned-fooled expeditions like that. The Navy was always looking for a scapegoat. If the mission failed, they can lay it on the fact that I am a young nobody. If it succeeded, then so much the better for the Admiral who chose me for the duty.* But as Ben thought more, he realized through all the hurt and anger that he had really won. The Admiral liked winners and Ben had saved him from having to make an embarrassing excuse for the failure of a delicate diplomatic mission. He would think favourably towards Ben in the future. It was a start on a long journey to a captain's commission, he hoped.

It was early April and the surrounding hillsides were flowered out and the grass was green. Ben had his men hard at work. Rear Admiral Nelson was due here in a few days. Everything would be at its best for his return.

When the Rear Admiral returned, he went immediately aboard the flagship. When he emerged from the Admiral's cabin some hours later, he was still smiling. One sailor overheard Nelson say, "Why that young rascal could steal a grandmother's slippers right off her feet and she none the wiser. No one ever has captured a brig with an unarmed schooner. No one!"

It would have made an even greater impression on the Rear Admiral if *Le Curieux* still sat at anchor there, but there was only the tiny, unimpressive *Witch.* Rear Admiral Nelson invited Ben to dine with him that night. It was an intimate supper with only himself, the rear Admiral and Tom Hardy, but it was great fun. Ben had to tell the story all over again and he had to guard against embellishments, for that comes quite natural with all of us.

"Come now, lad. You did not really ask the French captain to surrender his fine brig with twenty guns to your tiny schooner with just one pop gun, did you?" taunted Nelson.

"Well, of course he did, Horatio. He has as much gall as you do but you are not willing to admit it," said Hardy.

During their rambling, Nelson touched on Ben's love life. "We might as well discuss his love life, Tom as yours. You rarely have anything to say on that subject," teased Nelson.

Ben had little to offer that would interest a veteran like Nelson, and he was bold enough to say so.

Ben was told to come aboard with his pick of the crew the next morning. He need leave only four men behind for duty on the Station. Ben did not want to part with any of them. But as soon as he came aboard, he passed word for his sixteen chosen men to be prepared to board the *Theseus* under Captain Miller the next day.

Their duty was to patrol from the station to Cadiz keeping an eye on the Spanish who were largely holed up at Cadiz and could not get out. It was boring blockade duty and Ben sensed that Admiral Nelson would tolerate it for only so long. It was important for the British to keep the enemy there. A navy that cannot get to sea will soon rot. Men desert and it becomes increasingly hard to get supplies. In one way Ben welcomed a few months at sea with no immediate action and nothing but his regular duty. He had been through an intense time since the first of the year and had faced a host of challenges. He and his men could use a bit of relaxation. On the other hand, blockade duty was extremely dull, most of the time. He would soon grow restless and long for some wild assignment where he could use his planning skills and once again feel alive. But for awhile, it was good to just do his daily duty and have some free time. His thoughts went back often to his Annie. How was she? Was she still singing? Would he ever be lucky enough to hear her sing again, and would he ever meet her?

It was fine being aboard the Rear Admiral's ship. If there was one talent that Ben was learning, it was how to rally men all around so they will give their very best. He had seen Nelson heap praises on a common seaman for a common job well-done, and he saw the same thing when his officers were at their best. Nelson drew men to him, made them want to fight for him, if not for King George. He was an inspiration. He never simply laid out the plans for a battle, not without enlisting the ideas and support of all of his officers. And now and again something new and useful came of these conferences with his men. They often ate together and shared much companionship. In all, Ben would look back on his time in blockading Cadiz with Rear Admiral Nelson as some of his very best.

One day Ben approached Tom Murphy. "I have been most negligent in your education in navigation. I plan to rectify that here and now. Get your books, Mr. Murphy. We are going to get this navigation thing settled once and for all. It really isn't all that hard. You just have to focus on the figures and it will come easily." So the two men went to work. Ben wanted to see Tom advance from midshipman to leftenant, even if he did not want to go any further. He was a good lad and Ben hoped that if he ever became captain, he might be able to persuade Tom to serve as his first leftenant, but that was a long ways off yet.

They were hard at his studies when one day a call came for' "Sail Ho to port." Ben and Tom looked up and saw a fast cutter heading straight towards them.

"Looks like a cutter by her single mast and note how the bowsprit is steeved at near-horizontal. Strange looking vessel and she is certainly in a great hurry," said Ben.

The way she is traveling, she'll catch up with us within the hour. I wonder why all the rush?" The young men went back to Tom's studies, but soon were distracted by the arrival of the new ship. Why, she's the *Witch of Endor*, by golly, said one older sailor who had seen her before. No ship sails quite like her. She is a gem, she is."

Soon flags were bent on the flag ship's signal halyards and a boat was hoisted out of the *Endor.* A young leftenant climbed aboard and saluted smartly.

"I must see the Rear Admiral at once, sir."

Ben was the officer of the watch, which had just changed at 2 bells.

"This way, sir."

Ben lead the young officer to Rear Admiral Nelson's cabin. The young man had an annoying habit of sailing with his nose high in the air, perhaps to emphasize his importance. Ben did not particularly like him. The sergeant of marines announced the officer. "Acting Captain William Murray of the *Witch of Endor* requests an audience, sir."

"Show him in, Mr. Pierce."

Murray was closeted with the rear Admiral for only about fifteen minutes. As he left, Ben heard a call for, "Mr. Rundel, if you please." Soon he heard the call going out for Mr. Ames and Mr. Sherwood, the first and second leftenants of the *Theseus.*

"Gentlemen, we have grave news from Spithead. The crews of the ships of Admiral Bridport's fleet at anchor there have mutinied and they have thrown most of the officers off their ships. They have drawn up a series of demands, more shore leave, better food, especially when in port, higher pay, that sort of thing, and are refusing to set sail. Apparently they have several spokesmen who are quite articulate and they are giving the Admiralty serious trouble. It seems as if the Admiralty will give in to all but their demands for shore leave. One Richard Parker at the Nore, has not been as adamant in his demands, but he still has brought down the anger of Lord Bridport's fleet on the heads at the Admiralty. Things are not good, gentlemen. Murray does not think that all of the sailors are really behind the insurrection, but they have strong leaders. This fellow Murray was sent out in the dead of night by the Admiralty to avoid being seen by the ships of the fleet. He is to call at the Channel fleet, the Mediterranean fleet, which is what we are still, and the Caribbean fleet. That is why such great haste. He would not even stop for a glass of claret," said Lord Nelson.

Everyone stood there, their mouths open in disbelief. Ben was the first to recover.

"So we must keep this from the men at all costs, sir."

"Yes, and I am afraid that mail has come out from the mutineers that will spread the news to our crews all too rapidly. We may have to do something of which I heartily disapprove. We may have to screen the mail," as he lifted the mail bag from the deck, "and search not for the content of the letters as much as for dates. Anything written after 14 April should not be disbursed to the men until sometime later when this whole thing is settled. Maybe we should make it 1 April. There must have been talk of the mutiny and planning long before the fifteenth when it actually occurred. Gentlemen, I will need your help. No one must know what we are doing, but the Lord Admiral thinks that it is best. Even Murray has orders to speak to no one except me."

"Sir, we cannot take the chance of a mutiny out here on the high seas. We do not have the Admiralty nearby to support us. We would be helpless to negotiate with the men," said Mr. Ames.

"Worse still would be if the French got word of a mutiny in the British fleet. That would give them an ideal time to attack or even invade England with a much reduced fleet," said Ben.

"You are correct, Mr. Rundel. You all understand that you are not to mention a word of this to anyone. Is that clear?" Heads nodded a strong affirmative.

"I'll help with the mail, sir, on my off-watch, volunteered Ben."

"I am free right now," said Mr. Ames. I'll help get started."

"You can call on me after my watch sir, or I can put Mr. Murphy in charge if you wish."

"Also, there is word that the upstart by the name of

Napoleon Bonaparte is residing in Paris and giving strong support to The Directory. There is much to fear from this man. I believe that he has scarcely ever lost a battle."

As they worked, the Admiral told them more of what was in the dispatches from the Admiralty. "On 18 April, the French and Austrians signed the Peace of Leoben. It is effectively a cease fire between the two countries. That means that England now has another enemy, Austria, although she has no navy to threaten us here at sea. She can still put a goodly number of soldiers in the field against whomsoever Napoleon decides to attack next."

"Best that we all pitch into this mountain of mail and do what we can as fast as we can. The sailors would have reason to complain if they saw a mail bag arrive today and did not get their mail until tomorrow afternoon."

Ben found Mr. Purdy and asked him to take over for him for a few hours, then he and the others began sorting the mail. They were most often able to lift the edge of the page and examine the date without opening the letter. That made it much faster, but some of the writers had omitted a date. Ben found several letters that spoke of the mutiny and encouraged the men to join in. They would have to be held back. In all, they were at it for four hours, well into supper time. The Admiral could not conceive of so tiring a task without proper libations, so they were given ample glasses of port every two hours. Ben had to refuse, but asked the steward for some lime juice instead. He had acquired a taste for lime in water with a touch of honey. The others ribbed him mercilessly because to them it seemed an awful concoction, but it suited Ben well.

"You'll never become a proper captain if you don't learn to take your spirits," chided Nelson as Ben looked the other way.

Ben was concerned about the Admiral. He looked very tired and showed severe signs of ill-health. His face was drawn, his complexion yellow and there were dark circles around his eyes as if he might have some bilious troubles.

Ben suspected that he was weakened by slight recurring attacks of fever contracted in the Caribbean much earlier and he also suspected that he might suffer from a hernia.

"You should rest, sir, coaxed Ben. "You look very tired."

"I am, Mr. Rundel, but it will take more than sleep to heal this old carcass."

There was one letter in the lot that was for Ben. It was from his friend Torrance Bailey, son of the Captain who had taken him under his wing so many years ago and had seen to his education. Ben fingered the letter, thinking that he would not be standing here now amid this pile of letters if it had not been for kindly Captain Bailey. He would be one of the crew at Spithead, angry and defiant, mutineers. Ben decided not to open the letter then. They had too much work to do. The fleet was running sixteen ships or somewhere in excess of nine thousand men. There were a lot of letters coming out for them. This had been the first shipment since Christmas. His letter would have to wait. He looked at the Admiral. "Sir, this is a letter written around Christmas by my friend Torrance Bailey. May I keep it?"

"Why yes. It should be no problem. That's Captain Bailey's son, isn't it?'

"Yes, sir."

A few minutes later, the Admiral's steward served a fine meal for them. They were down to the last small mountain of letters and expected to be finished in another hour or two. Ben excused himself and went to see how his division was doing under Mr. Purdy, but all was going well. As he returned to his fellow officers, he thought back to the days with Captain Bailey. *He knew how to treat men right. He had even purchased fresh fruits and vegetables with his own money, when there was none available from the purser. He was reasonable with shore leave too, but the one thing that he could not do was to increase the common seaman's pay. He did lead us to some fat prizes which would help to set even a common seaman up handsomely in retirement, if he survived the sea and its battles.*

Ben went back to their work. He hated snooping like this, but none of the letters were being read. Just the dates were being scrutinized.

When the work was completed, Ben retired to his bunk and pulled out Torrances' letter.

"Dear Ben: 8 July, 1797

I have been very neglectful of my adventuring friend. I have not written in a long time, but I too, have had some adventures. You must know that my dear father died shortly after he was put on the beach. I think that his heart was broken when he saw me here with mother. (at least 'mother' had now been dignified from 'mummy'.) He seemed ill at ease and longed to go back to sea, but the Admiralty would hear none of it. When he received his last letter from the Lord Admiral, refusing positively to let a sick man back to sea in charge of a King's ship, he seemed to go down hill fast. His parting words to me were, 'To go, leave your mother, find a nice girl and marry and never come back to see this woman again.' I know that they fought constantly and that they could not agree on anything. Father would emerge from breakfast pale and haggard looking, my mother's words hounding him, thundering from behind him to 'Get out and earn a respectable living for your family like any decent man would'. He could never seem to bring home enough money to keep her happy. Lord knows, father did try, but he could not bear up under her constant strumming at him. Finally, his weak heart gave out and we lost him. I am devastated.

After he died, I did leave home. I have found me a fine young lady whose name is 'Alice' and I plan to marry her. I am apprenticed to a Mr. Philpott as a clerk and hope someday to have my own business.

I hope that this finds you well, dear friend.

Your Servant Always, Torrance Bailey."

Ben folded the letter and put it in his sea chest. This was the most informative letter that Torrance had ever written to him. Ben felt good that his childhood friend was finally growing up and might be getting on with his life. But he had fears for him too. As an only child, his father's death left his mother all alone. She would most likely begin to feel that loneliness and hound Torrance until he returned home to her. It would take a good bit of strength, something that Torrance never seemed to have, to stand up against her.

But there was something else there in his innocent, still childish hand that was disquieting to Ben. He would not admit it to himself for several days, but poor little Torrance had found a girl, a mate, and he, tall, handsome Ben the adventurer, had none. That was what was eating at him when Tom teased him the next day.

"Why are you so quiet and pensive? You look like you swallowed a frog," teased Tom. Ben had a problem with Tom. He had never kept a secret from him before, and they had sworn true friendship. Neither would ever think of keeping anything from the other, but now Ben *must* keep this business at Spithead a secret. True, Tom was on his way to being an officer, but Lord Nelson had cautioned his officers to share this secret with no one. Besides, Tom was not the best one to keep a secret. The very safety of the ship and the fleet depended on his refusing to tell Tom about the mutiny. But he could share Torrances' letter with him, at least in part.

Finally Ben answered slowly, "I guess that I feel like life is leaving me behind. I should be courting some beautiful girl right now and preparing to ask her to marry me, but here I stand on the quarterdeck, holding my hands behind my back. I feel helpless, useless, Tom."

"And so do we all. Eighty percent of the lads aboard are single and sixty percent of 'em would like to be married right now. But that isn't practical in war. I'd be the first to lead a girl down the aisle, I can assure you of that, if I were free to marry, but I am a King's officer or almost one anyway," said Tom. Ben was relieved. Tom was finally getting to understand percentages.

"There's got to be more to it than that. Something in that letter upset you, didn't it?"

"Well, not really. Torrance is planning to get married next year, and I wish him all the well, but that is not helping my case any."

But one can keep news of a mutiny under tarps only so long. It was not more than four days and words began to be whispered. "Did you hear about the lads at Spithead?" And, "I heard that the men at the Nore are not going along with those at Spithead. Quite an argument goin' on, there is."

"They're tryin' to get us more pay and shore leave, an' some good fresh food when in port. I says, all the best to 'em," said one old sailor who had only about six teeth left.

Ben heard grumblings among the sailors of his division, and he was wary. Now he could discuss the mutiny with Tom. It was no longer a secret. "Some one of those letters must have had a word or two in them about what was happening in port," offered Tom.

"We best be careful and look for signs of unrest in the crew. I will speak with the Admiral. I think we can quell some unrest with good treatment of the men, as much fresh food as we can cram on board," suggested Ben.

Just then a lookout called "Sail Ho," and the two men went about their duties.

We were headed back to the Tagus when Rear Admiral Nelson called us to his cabin. Nelson was now Commander of the Mediterranean In-Shore Squadron. That meant that they were more or less independent of the Commander-In-Chief and that they were focused on blockading Cadiz.

"John Jervis hopes to bottle up the Spanish in Cadiz and deny them all supplies from outside. That way, we may be able to force them to sail out and fight," said the Rear Admiral.

"I am tired of sitting here like ducks in a pond waiting

for someone to shoot at me. I plan to take the ship back to Elba and assist General de Burgh who is still trying to complete the evacuation there. With that completed, we return to the eastern fleet on or about 24 May, 1797. I think that hard work, strict discipline and improved living conditions will quell the discontent that I see in the faces of this crew. St. Vincent quite agrees with me. I hear rumblings from the men everywhere. Gentlemen, we are sitting in the midst of a mutiny about to happen. If we do not keep the men occupied, there certainly will be trouble," said the Admiral.

One measure that Admiral Nelson used which quieted down some of the mutinous talk was to forbid the speaking of Gaelic. The Irish, who were not insignificant in numbers, liked to gather often in groups and speak Gaelic so that the English sailors could not understand them. This aroused suspicions that the Irish were planning a mutiny, when, most likely, they were probably just talking about home and their women. Another measure which seemed to work wonders was to segregate the marines from the sailors. There was an unexplained hatred between these types of men and keeping them apart resulted in much less friction.

They kept the men busy by frequent bombardment of Cadiz. It was often ineffective, but it kept the men busy. The Admiral also saw to providing better food and took time to walk among the men and speak with them. He often teased a bit, and dropped a joke here and there. The common sailor is not stupid and these fellows soon realized that Nelson sympathized with them, although he might be the first to turn a gun on them if they disobeyed him. They found the fine line between friendship and command and the sailors were content to stay in place.

On one attack, the bomb vessel *Thunderer* was sent in close to bombard the fort. The Spanish under Don Miguel Tyrason sent out a launch with twenty-six men to attack the bomb vessel, but Nelson sent his barge with himself, Fremantle and fifteen men to defend it. The fighting was fierce and close. Foley in the *Goliath* was to cover their retreat.

So they went out to meet the enemy. Soon the battle deteriorated into a hand to hand fight from boats. Ben went in the barge with Admiral Nelson and Captain Fremantle. They were ten to the twenty-six in the Spanish barge. Ben was amazed when the Admiral climbed into the barge and took charge. *I thought that Admirals were supposed to stay aboard ship and direct an attack led by leftenants, not pile into a barge with sailors and engage in hand-to-hand combat,* thought Ben. He had ample time to use his sword, but not near space enough. The fighting was fierce. Ben was in the stern with the other officers, but began to move over bodies to the bow where there was the most action. Suddenly, Ben saw John Sykes, the coxswain, reach out and shield Nelson's body with his bare hand. One Spaniard had aimed his handsome silver and gold sword directly at Nelson's head while Nelson was engaged with another swordsman. Only the swift movement of Sykes saved Nelson from being killed, but *Sykes must have suffered a severe cut,* thought Ben. But he was too busy just then fending off some grandee who also wielded a beautiful sword. Ben was suddenly gripped with an overwhelming desire to seize that sword and keep it for himself. He lunged viciously in a second when the other barge was tipping his opponent off balance. It worked. Ben had killed the man and managed to reach for the sword just before it fell into the water. Then another man turned on him and Ben was able to dispatch him quickly. A swell sent the barge sliding sideways and Ben, who was several yards away, saw a sword about to sever Nelson's hand from his arm, but again Sykes moved swiftly, interposing his own body to shield the Admiral. Sykes had one other chance to defend the Admiral's back when they were nearly through fighting. One injured Spanish sailor made a sudden lunge at Nelson, but Sykes, who seemed to be at Nelson's side continually, interposed his sword and brought his opponent down for good. Ben took out one more Spanish sailor and then it was over.

Only two of their men were badly wounded, but eighteen of the Spaniards lay dead and several more were wounded. Admiral Nelson received the sword of their Commander and the battle was finished. They rowed back to the ship. They had made little progress in subduing the Spanish fleet. They were simply not willing to come out and fight. Then under Nelson's orders, they withdrew the attack and went back to a steady blockade.

Day after dreary day of blockade went on. The Admiral was getting impatient with the absence of real fighting. He despised men who would not come out and engage in a good honest fight. He was boiling for action.

Then one day Leftenant Hardy was walking the quarterdeck. He spotted a piece of paper on the deck. "What the... what careless fellow has left paper lying around." He picked up the paper and read,

"Success attend Admiral Nelson. God bless Captain Miller. We thank them for the officers they have placed over us. We are happy and comfortable and will shed every drop of blood in our veins to support them, and the name of *Theseus* shall be immortalized as high as the *Captain's* .

SHIPS COMPANY."

The words were written in a bold hand. *Whoever wrote this is clearly their leader, and we have done right by him,* thought Hardy. He raced off to hand the letter to Admiral Nelson, knowing that it would cheer him up. That night the Admiral wrote home to his wife Fanny, telling her what the men had written, and how clearly pleased he was that his medicine for a sick ship had worked so well. Betsy Fremantle was amazed when she heard about the note. "It just goes to show that some men have that special touch that can get through to almost any hardened soul. Horatio Nelson should have been a preacher like his father, he surely should have."

But Captain Fremantle disagreed with her. "He is much too valuable to us as a leader and an Admiral. Leave the preaching to lesser men who lack the courage and spirit of Horatio. I fancy he will lead us off on some glorious chase any day now. He is clearly tired of this meaningless bombardment and the citizen's of Cadiz are sick of having their town blown up just to protect the Spanish fleet. Something has to give soon."

It was during this period that Ben became aware that Lord Nelson had a sense of his destiny, that he was expecting to do something beyond the dreams of ordinary men to benefit his country. He often seemed to dwell on death and sensed that his end would be a glorious one, where he would die because he had done a duty beyond the reach of other men.

Ben longed as a younger man to learn the social graces and politics of Navy life. He bemoaned the fact that he could not learn these things from some book. He now had a chance to learn by doing, but found that he was a slow learner. Once Betsy and Tom Fremantle returned to the Station, the social life on the Station picked up noticeably. Betsy was a bright lady, smart, witty and a bit outspoken by Ben's standards. She even had a harpsichord put in her cabin so she could entertain and sing. Everyone liked her and she was always the center of attention.

The Captains and Admirals dined together frequently to relieve the monotony of blockade. Their stewards vied for first position by preparing elaborate meals. As a leftenant, Ben was frequently invited to attend these suppers. It was here that he tried to learn the proper address, how to greet a lady, dancing and other social graces that he lacked. He was often the source of amusement to his fellow leftenants who considered him to be a 'handsome goose with all of the grace of a hog in pen'. Betsy took him in hand, sensing his uncertainty around women, and led him through yet another stage of his education in the graces of society. Ben would always be awkward in polite society, but he would also be ever grateful to Betsy Fremantle for her patience and teachings. Betsy put him on the right tack and he soon could steer clear of trouble on the dance floor, most of the time.

One startling discovery was that although Captain Foley had been much in love with Betsy before she married Tom Fremantle, he still attended her suppers aboard the *Seahorse* and seemed quite at ease as her friend. Ben could not imagine how a man could love a woman, lose her and then remain her close friend. His mind was still that of a juvenile where the world is black and white and such strange things cannot happen.

But the blockade went on. Nelson had twenty ships under him, ready to fight. Another ten were shuttling back and forth to the Station for provisioning and watering. Ten more were expected to sail out of the Mediterranean any time now. Then he would have a force large enough to soundly whip the Spanish, if only something would happen.

It was not Lord Nelson's way to wait forever for things to happen. He was given to *making* them happen. So there was jubilation among the officers of the *Theseus* and the other ships when Admiral St. Vincent (John Jervis) gave the order for a major bombardment of Cadiz on the night of 3 July. The plan was to force the fleet to sail to meet the British in open battle. Local pressures on the Spanish Navy were becoming unbearable because the townspeople were tired of having the fleet docked at their door step. They were exhausted by the constant bombings and the destruction of their homes and businesses.

Not all Captains took the precautions against mutiny that Admiral Nelson and Captain Miller had. There were strains of mutiny in the air during the battle on 3 July. By 5 July, during the heat of the bombardment, four mutinous sailors aboard the *St. George* were tried, convicted and sentenced to death. The mutineers asked for five days to prepare themselves for death, but St. Vincent would have none of that. He figured that they would foment more mutinies in their five days and more men would have to be hanged as a result. They were to die on the following morning. But their commander, pious Vice Admiral Thompson, requested that the hanging be postponed because it was the Sabbath. He wrote a letter about the ungodly practice of hanging men on the Sabbath, which stirred the firey St. Vincent and Admiral Nelson as well. Ben was there when St. Vincent's orders came demanding the immediate removal of Vice Admiral Thompson from the fleet. The hanging went forward on Sunday as planned.

Later, Nelson wrote a letter to St. Vincent in which he said, "Had it been Christmas Day instead of Sunday, I would have executed them {still}." (Roy Hattersley, *Nelson* 1974).

After the mutiny had subsided, it was clear that nothing that the British tried could smoke the Spanish out of their stronghold at Cadiz. Ben kept hoping that the citizens of the town would drive the fleet off their shores, but that did not happen. There were no reports of victories to send home and when that happens, field Admirals become uneasy and the Admiralty looks down its long nose at the list of supplies and the cost of ships that are being employed in a pointless duty.

So when St. Vincent heard a rumour that a treasure ship, *El Principe de Asturias* was about to anchor at Tenerife in the Atlantic, he had the solution he needed. "Let that daredevil Nelson tear off after that treasure ship. Then I can have something to report to the Admiralty that they will want to read."

Recently, before the bombardment of Cadiz, Nelson's step son, Josiah Nisbet, had joined the crew. He was the son of Nelson's wife, Frances Nisbet by her first marriage. He seemed a fair lad, not overly heroic, but was meeting his obligations as a leftenant reasonably well. Nelson seemed to care about him, but he did not give him easy service or spare him odious duty.

Accordingly, Ben received notice during his tour as officer of the watch from Admiral Nelson that they were setting sail immediately for Tenerife. Ben knew where Santa Cruz de Tenerife was in the Canary Islands. He was relieved as were others to be facing some new duty away from the staring senoras who watched them daily with scorn from the town walls of Cadiz, and off to action suitable for real men. Lord Nelson appeared on deck, looking still as tired as usual, Ben thought. He had received a letter from his wife Fanny, decrying his going into battle in a small boat like a common sailor. She preferred that he leave that for the captains. He told Ben about the letter and his wife's fears. Nelson seemed not to be as sure of himself as he had been in the past. Earlier Ben noticed that he was burning the letters from his wife, a sign that he felt that this might be his end. He also called for Mr. Josiah Nisbet and seemed to be in earnest conversation with the lad, as if he might not have a chance to tell him something at a later date. He fretted about the possibility of death and his concerns for the possible loss of his step son as well.

"We are off to a glorious victory or an ignoble defeat, lad. We shall see what fate has in store for us, soon enough."

During the short passage to Tenerife, the Admiral called his officers to his cabin. "You probably know that we are headed for Santa Cruz de Tenerife. That is where Tom Hardy won his laurels, you know. He was sent in by Captain Hollowell in late May of this year. Hollowell had spotted a French ship, a brig-of-war, there on a previous mission. Hardy and several others succeeded in cutting out the *Mutine* under heavy fire from the shore batteries. Captain Xavier Pommier was ashore when Hardy came after his ship and was apparently in a red rage over the whole thing. St. Vincent, bless his heart, was so pleased that he made Tom a commander and gave him the ship to command. He commissioned the ship with 14 guns as a runner and forwarding vessel." The men could plainly see that Admiral Nelson was most pleased with Hardy's 'desperate enterprise,' and that he held the young man in high regard.

The Admiral continued. "We are going to try to take the treasure ship that is harboured at Santa Cruz. I want frequent gun drills and we should prepare all boats with frapped oars. Mr. Pierce, have your marines ready and in top condition, if you will. We will need your help most urgently."

They met frequently in the Admiral's cabin, Fremantle from the *Seahorse,* Troubridge from the *Culloden,* Sam Hood from the *Zealous,* Thompson from the *Leander,* Waller from the frigate *Emerald,* Bowen from the *Terpischore,* and the captains from the cutter *Fox* and the mortar-boat *Cacafuego.* St. Vincent gave Nelson his choice of captains, and the Admiral chose his best. There were talks about the plan of attack. Nelson was open to suggestions, but he clearly had a good plan and few found reason to dispute it. "We are a team and we have to work together to succeed, like a group of men playing at a sport, except this is a deadly life and death sport." Ben was learning. He was now his own teacher and he liked that too.

Ben thought about his career. He was happy for Hardy with his new command. He had known Tom Hardy now for several months and he liked him. He was much older than Ben, nearly 26, but he was a straight-faced, serious young officer, just the stuff that Ben liked. But he, Ben Rundel, had done some spectacular things as a young officer too. He would surely be in line for a ship of his own in a few years. His record exceeded that of any young man that he knew or had heard of in the Navy. Ben began reading the *Naval Chronicle* so that he could follow the careers of men in the Navy and the progress of the war in general. He was growing in responsibility and he had to grow with it. He also sought out any London newspapers that came their way to learn all that he could about the events in France and other parts of the embattled world. They all had bearing on his life and any of them could trigger a train of events that might take his life sometime in the future. When reports came of fighting in Italy and the battle at Lodi in which General Bonaparte defeated the Austrians, Ben took note. *This is where history really comes from,* he thought.

As they approached Tenerife, they planned to move close inshore at night and wipe out the batteries on one side. This was to be a cutting out exercise using the ship's boats and large numbers of men as well as an attack on the fort. The men were told to spare the town at all cost. Nelson planned to land a good sized party of marines and sailors between the fort on the northeast headlands and the town. With the fort in his hands, he would demand that the Governor surrender the treasure ship, and more if he felt justified.

Tenerife has a high mountain peak near the shore. It has a nasty habit of creating strong downdrafts that whip up high seas in the harbour and strong currents. It was similar to conditions that Ben had seen in the Mediterranean, the 'Levanter winds'. But unfortunately, this July night was one when the mountain chose to show her strength and dominance of the sea. There was an exceptionally strong current and sharp winds near the shore and the boats could not draw near. It was 25 July, 1797 and quite warm. They laboured to work the boats off shore and regroup for a second assault, but by dawn, they were still a mile from shore. They had only needed to row some three miles, but the winds erased their best efforts. The lads were exhausted from trying to row against the fierce currents that were whipped up by the down winds coming off the mountain. Now the element of surprise was lost for good. The *Principe* , the treasure ship, clung in close to the shore batteries which would protect her.

Captain Troubridge, who was in charge of the landing party, noticed a small beach to the north of the Fort where they might be able to land and storm the fort from the rear, but he preferred to confer with Admiral Nelson before leading such a wild attack. Ben noted a strong intelligence in Troubridge, but a general reluctance to act without higher authority. Ben realized that he would have to learn the delicate balance between taking the initiative when conditions demanded it and simply following orders. That would be a grand challenge that would plague him all of his life.

In Troubridge's case, delay proved a fatal mistake. True, the men were exhausted and in need of rest and refreshment, but the three hour's delay that resulted from the return to the *Theseus* was more than enough to allow the Spaniards to prepare. Nelson agreed to Troubridge's plan immediately and after a short respite when the men were given something to eat and drink, they rowed back to the small beach. Ben was in the launch with Captain Troubridge. The landing succeeded this time at about 9 a.m. and they climbed up the first low hill, thinking that they could look down on the fort. What they saw instead, was alarming. There were actually two hills with a valley between. Lined up on the opposite hill were several thousand Spaniards, armed and ready to fight. In order to attack the fort, they would have to descend the first hill, cross the narrow valley and climb the second hill, overtake about ten times as many men as they had in their force. It was an impossible task. Had they arrived three or four hours earlier, before the Spaniards had time to figure out their plan, it might have been easy. But now, they would be good targets as they descended the hill, fish in a barrel once they made it to the bottom, and sure targets as they climbed up the second hill towards the Spaniards. After hours of staring at the Spaniards, Captain Troubridge gave the order to retreat and return to the ships.

As the day wore on, the weather grew ugly, black storm clouds formed overhead and the wind picked up. That relieved the heat, but promised a stormy night.

The next day Nelson ordered another assault, with the ships pouring shot over the heads of the sailors in the boats. Ben was in one of those boats and never felt more insecure or scared than when one of those huge cannon balls sailed over his head. Their four frigates were firing at top speed to divert attention from the landing party. He much preferred to be back on the deck of the ship directing his division in the firing than to be huddled out here in an open boat, hoping that some gunner who had indulged in a bit too much rum had not misjudged his elevation and would presently lob a ball right into the boat which would sink her instantly. He would have to give Tom a lecture for letting his gunners come so close that Ben kept getting his uniform wet from the spray flying up in the air as the balls bounced off the water and skidded in towards shore. The fire coming from the fort was accurate and non-stop. Ben was certain that they would be blown out of the water any second now. He felt almost sick, but carried on the best he could. Nelson's courage was infectious even from the far off *Theseus*. Ben would never be the martyr. He was too modest for that. He knew he was scared and he would not hide it from anyone.

After several hours, one thing was certain. They were not going to get in close enough to cut out the *Principe* and the fort was well-manned with men able to fight most efficiently. Concentrated fire came from the Mole and even from the town. That made their assignment to bring back the *Principe* almost impossible to complete. Ben was ready to give up when the signals came from the ship for 'boats to return to their ships'.

Just as the boats were about to head back, a lone soldier swam to Ben's boat and grabbed the gunnels. They pulled him aboard and found that he spoke some guttural tongue which no one could understand. Ben ordered his men to row back to the ship, their dead heaped down the middle and wounded piled in the bow, groaning and flailing in desperate attempts to sooth their aching bodies. Ben took the foreigner to the Admiral and the two were closeted with marine guards for about ten minutes. A German-speaking sailor was summoned and the Admiral learned that the garrison was poorly manned and that morale was low.

By the time Ben made the ship, the storm had begun to break. The waves were running high and the wind began to howl about their ears. It had turned deathly dark and compared to the heat of the day, it was now cold. The ships drew out to sea, as if they had given up any idea of attacking again. The Admiral called his officers to his cabin and laid out plans for a larger assault that night under the cover of darkness. He would use all of the free men and available ship's boats in a concerted effort to silence the cannon at the Mole. Ben was aghast when the Admiral announced that he would lead the assault himself. He called for his barge and for a good crew. Weapons were refurbished in the hours left before dark and they readied themselves for yet another major attack. The grinding stone was not silent for two full hours as each weapon was honed to a razor's edge. The men were exhausted from all of the rowing against the current and then in the violent seas that had worked up later in the day. Some sat together in small groups and made out their wills. Even the officers repaired below deck to write wills. Ben just watched it all. He had no one.

The cook served a good meal and ample grog was served to each man just before dark. The men would need the extra heat if they were to fight these high waves. The men began to pile into the boats about eleven p.m. Ben was put in charge of the cutter. His crew was made up largely of the lads who had come to know him from the Italian rescue days, his hand-picked crew that he trusted. When the Admiral was in his barge, he looked up suddenly to see his step son climbing down the battens to join him.

"I'll not leave you, sir. Mother would never hear of it. She would want me close to your side," the young man cried over the roar of the sea.

"And if we should both fall, Josiah, what would become of your poor mother?" replied Nelson (Hattersley, 1974, *Nelson)*. He was heard to say earlier that he wrote to St. Vincent that, 'by tomorrow I will either be crowned by laurel or cypress'. But there was no time now to think of that. Glorious battle was calling, and Nelson was anxious to be off. His fatalistic thoughts had to be swept aside and the high winds and crashing waves were more than enough to do that. The lad knew about the danger that Nelson had faced at Cadiz when he escaped sword wounds three times only because Mr. Sykes, his coxswain, had been there to shield him. He knew that his step father was a frail man, and he apparently admired his courage.

As they approached the town, the waves lifted the boats high in the air, fine targets for the musket and cannon fire from the town. Then as swiftly, the waves would drop them out of sight into a trough and Ben's boat would be swamped with water. The wind was fierce and made the men feel cold. Ben wished for once that he liked rum, but he had gone off with no spirits in him at all, so he felt the cold all through his tall, lean frame as he handled the tiller. He told of the events in his own words:

"There was not a dry inch in the entire barge. Even pistols jammed into waist bands became soaked. The frigates were sent to one side of the bay to make it look like our attack was to be centered there, but it was the ship's boats that would carry the attack under the cover of darkness and a raging storm to silence the mortars on the Mole. As we drew near to shore, a constant and intense musket and cannon fire was directed at us from the Mole and the town. I was in a boat just behind Admiral Nelson. Captain Fremantle directed a boat to our port side, and Captain Bowen came close behind him. In all, we formed a small group of about five ship's boats. A large number of our boats from other ships were struggling to stay afloat in the pounding surf and high waves. Many were being carried off to port of the Mole by the wind. Most of our boats were never able to come to action on the Mole. They were swept by the violent storm onto the shore to port and there stove up by an incredibly fierce surf. Many men died from drowning. A few escaped to shore only to be taken prisoners.

Then a lucky shot from one of the mortars hit the cutter *Fox* dead center and she sank within minutes with all hands lost, some 97 men and their Captain.

It was 1:30 a.m. and suddenly, above the wind of the storm, we heard a peal of church bells, signaling the alarm that we were close to the Mole. That brought heavy fire from 30 to 40 mortars close by, with a constant rain of musket fire directed towards us. Men began to drop into the boat and some fell overboard into the angry sea. We were able to land our boat only by a strange running tactic. The second the bow touched rock, everyone who was able jumped out into the water and ran with the boat up onto the rock breakwater to a safe point. Most of us were unable to fire our muskets for the powder was damp. I left mine in my waist band and went to work with my sword. It had seen considerable duty now and my hand was well-accustomed to its feel. Tom was close by my side, his cutlass gripped in his huge fist. We, some one hundred half-drowned souls were pressed by perhaps 400 to 500 enemy soldiers, but the shear gall of our attack under such inclement conditions seemed to weaken them. After a hard hour of close combat, the Spaniards fell back and fled back into the town.

As the Admiral's boat approached the Mole, he began to step ashore. It was then that Admiral Nelson let out a loud scream, although none of us remember hearing him above the raging storm. There were screams everywhere and one sounded much like the other in this storm. I saw his step son, Josiah Nisbet, find the Admiral lying in a pool of blood. A shout went out from Mr. Nisbet that,"the Admiral is hit bad." He had been hit in the right arm and lay back, falling onto the seat of the barge. His body lay limp as if he were dead. Nisbet told me of the tragedy later after the battle. His step son was one of the first to attend him and he was appalled at what he saw. The Admiral's right forearm was totally shattered. The lad quickly made a tourniquet from his neck scarf and tried to ease the pain. When Nelson groaned and complained that the sight of his bloody arm made him faint, the lad put his hat over it to shield it from the Admiral's eyes. They took him speedily back in the barge from the *Seahorse.* They moved him carefully to the long boat and made to row back to the nearest ship. The men plied the oars frantically to escape the fire from the battery which was now raining down upon them. Several rowers were killed and others stepped bravely into thier places to row to safety.

As they rowed back to the ship, Nelson, now conscious, demanded that they pick up survivors of other boats which had been holed by the fire from the battery. He noted bitterly that the *Fox* was holed below the water line and appeared to be sinking. He already considered himself to be a dead man and had told his step son as much.

One interesting incident occurred on the way to the *Theseus.* A sailor of my division told me about it later. Nisbet and others decided to take Admiral Nelson to the *Seahorse*, where Betsy Fremantle was aboard. They all agreed that he might bleed to death if more time was wasted in taking him to his own ship. He needed immediate medical attention. Nelson, when he saw the name of the ship, declined to be taken aboard there, no matter how badly he was bleeding. He complained that he did not want to alarm the good Mrs. Fremantle, especially since he had no idea of the safety or whereabouts of her husband. He demanded to be rowed to the *Theseus* instead of to the *Seahorse.* "If I must, then I will die," said the distraught Admiral. At the side of the *Theseus,* the Admiral declined any assistance in climbing the battens. He railed that he still had two good feet and one good arm left and could manage on his own. But he called loudly for the surgeon to ready his tools. He would have the shattered arm off at once.

They made the *Theseus* safely, but the entire crew was exhausted, some unable to pull themselves up the battens to the deck unaided. It had been a long, hard three days.

When the order came from Captain Troubridge who was still on shore to advance on the town, we found that it was impossible. Every street was guarded by field pieces and men swarmed all over. There were more than eight thousand troops on Tenerife and by now they were ready for us. Such rapid fire from muskets from the Citadel and from the houses above the Mole pinned us down. Any man who tried to advance in the driving rain was instantly shot.

Rogers, one of Ben's men had been sent to the ship for treatment of an ugly wound. He told Ben about the happenings aboard ship. "Back aboard the *Theseus,* the Admiral had regained full consciousness and was calling for the surgeon to remove his lower right arm. He knew that it had been shattered and could never be of use to him again. Mr. Bowers gave the Admiral a stout drink and then placed a strip of leather in the Admiral's mouth and told him to scream all he wanted to, but bite on the leather. He gave him some laudanum to dull the pain. Then, swiftly, he removed the arm just above the elbow, severed the flesh and then sawed off the bone. He noted in his report to the Admiralty that the artery had been split in two and could never heal. The bones were shattered beyond any repair. The pain must have been awful, but no worse than hundreds of other wounded common sailors would suffer in the hours that lay ahead. Nelson bore up most manfully. They attached the ligatures which would help the arm to heal and bandaged the stump so that the Admiral could get about when he was able. Mr. Bowers administered more laudanum to the Admiral after the amputation to calm his severed nerves."

It was now that Ben decided to make a move on the cannon that were only forty yards from them. If he could only put them out of commission, then they would have some power with which to bargain. He dropped onto the soggy ground and began to crawl. Without a word, his men followed suit. All eight of them wormed their way towards the cannon emplacements. The rain pelted Ben's back and rivulets of muddy water ran over his back and down his sides and neck.

"Our dead lay all about, but we summoned up the strength to advance to where we could spike the guns."

The crew that had been assigned the duty of spiking the cannon had perished in a boat to port that had been holed early in the attack. As his men moved close to the first gun, George Amber, a tall, strong seaman suddenly stood up and grabbed the gunner by the neck and strangled him. In a flash, we were at his side, slashing at the gun crew, which was speedily dispatched. The musket fire from the houses above the Mole was unbelievably rapid and deadly. They were shooting at faint, moving forms in a dark rain, and yet they were hitting us with deadly accuracy. They hit some of their own men as well. They could not help it. Conyers went down and then Silvers. It was sometime during that frantic struggle on the Mole that Captain Fremantle was hit in the right arm and was taken to a local hospital.

Ben had no tools with which to disable the guns. He had to improvise. He pointed to the blocks and tackles that held the guns. The men removed the pins that held them together and with rocks, rammed these into the touch holes solidly. Once the first gun was spiked, Ben and his crew, crouching low now, moved to the second and on down the line, under a constant rain of musket balls. It was at the sixth gun that Ben heard a scream and saw Tom clutch his leg and double up in pain. One of the musket balls had hit his leg. He was down. Ben went to him and looked at the injury. "It seems to be a flesh wound. I think the bone is intact. Can you walk?"

"Aye, sir, if ye'll give me a lift." Ben helped Tom to his feet, but they needed to move fast and Tom was riveted to the spot, his legs would not move. He was a hefty chap, weighing several stones more than Ben, but there was nothing else to do. Ben hefted Tom on to his shoulder like a sack of grain and ran as fast as he could, slipping over the wet ground that ran with a strange mixture of blood and mud. The last long boat was just pulling away. "Here, can you take one more? This man is wounded in the leg." shouted Ben.

"Heave 'im aboard, there." called a voice. Ben helped Tom into the boat. "Don't worry, lad. I'll be not far behind. You are in a longboat and you will be cared for." Someone reached for Tom and tied a cloth around his injured leg to stop the bleeding. The last Ben saw of Tom, he was huddled against the thwarts of the boat, a strange mask of pain playing across his normal smiling face. Everything seemed so macabre in the faint light from the town which was all that lighted the drab darkness of that stormy night. He did not even know to which ship Tom was being taken.

Now, Captain Troubridge moved in to take over command. No one knew where Captain Fremantle had gone, but he was supposed to be dead with the many sailors and marines. Troubridge could see that the raid was a disaster and that they could never cut out the treasure ship. He had watched Ben's crew as they spiked the guns and was much impressed by the swiftness of their action. But he forged on, with as few as 80 marines, 80 pikemen and perhaps 180 common seamen with small arms. Ben and his men followed. Their boat had been taken earlier to transport wounded men back to the ships, so they were stranded there on the shore. He was propelled forward more by courage and guts than by any logic. Troubridge sent a leftenant accompanied by two gentlemen of the town off to contact the Governor. But when the leftenant was not heard from again, he assumed that he had been shot. Now he contacted the Spanish Governor directly and threatened to burn the town, but the Governor knew that Troubridge could not make good his claim in this stiff wind and rain. He had too few men standing. Finally, unable to advance and unable to retreat, Troubridge hoisted a flag of truce as he was faced with insurmountable odds.

The Spanish Governor proved to be a fine gentleman. Always an admirer of courage, he invited Troubridge, Hood and a few others to dine with him and he sent down food for the troops. He also arranged for boats to take the men back to their ships the next day.

In the end, Troubridge was faced with getting a safe conduct for his men back to their ships if he promised not to attack the Canaries again. The Spanish Governor proved his value as a fine gentleman. Ben was impressed with the courtesy afforded Captain Troubridge by the Spaniards, who apparently, admired the courage of men who would attack so strong a fort in such a violent storm, and then threaten to burn the town to the ground. These were strong men, men to be admired, even if they were British. But the German soldier had not been truthful. There were thousands of militiamen there in port and the handful of British could never prevail against them. Moreover, their morale was high. They were winning and they knew it. The British withdrew swiftly, to disappear into the dark stormy night, thankful that the Spaniards had been so magnanimous. This may have been a turning point in the relations between France and Spain. The Spanish were coming to honour the courage and fighting spirit of the British far above that of the French. *Perhaps this will turn Spanish sentiment in favour of the British someday,* thought Ben.

Once back aboard the *Theseus,* Ben took the time to enquire about Tom. He was not aboard his ship, so he must have been taken aboard one of the other two surviving frigates. Eventually Ben found him on the *Culloden* and was told that he was doing well. Ben would visit his friend the first chance he had, but that would have to wait until they made the Mediterranean fleet again.

Four days later, the Admiral had mastered writing left handed well enough to complete his report to St. Vincent and had written a letter to his wife in which he praised his step son as having saved his life. He was sure that his mother would be proud of her boy. As soon as he was able, he wrote to Don Antonio Guttierrez, the Commandant General of the Canary Islands, thanking him for his noble and humane treatment of his men in their time of extreme need. But his letter to St. Vincent, which he shared with his officers, was most grim. 'I am become a burden to my friends and useless to my country...you will perceive my anxiety for the promotion of my son-in-law, Josiah Nisbet. When I leave your command, I become dead to the World; I go hence and am no more seen ... the Boy is under obligation to me, but he repaid me by bringing me from the Mole of Santa Cruz. I hope you will be able to give me a frigate to convey my carcass to England.' (Hattersley, 1974, *Nelson*).

The surgeon's report on his amputated arm was good. The sore no longer bled and was healing over nicely. One ligature was about to slip out, meaning that the healing process was going forward well, but the other stubbornly refused to come lose. The surgeon pronounced Nelson to be in excellent health, but that proved not to be true. Even Ben could see that. Nelson was greatly relieved when he learned that Captain Fremantle had suffered only a minor wound and was happily reunited aboard the *Seahorse* with his wife.

The fleet sailed back to Cadiz. Ben was busy with his duties, but had frequent contact with the Admiral, which he did not enjoy. The man was in an evil mood and thought so little of himself that Ben could hardly bear to be around him. He happened to see a letter on 16 August written to St. Vincent in which Nelson complained that 'A left handed Admiral will never again be considered as useful, therefore, the sooner I get a very humble cottage the better.' (Hattersley, 1974, *Nelson*). The Admiral wrote in reply, something to the order of, '... he could not blame himself for not having shown a great degree of heroism and that men cannot command their own success, but must be contented that they have done their duty as best they can and must settle with what fate deals them.' St Vincent went on to send his love to Mrs. Fremantle and 'I will salute her and bow to your stump tomorrow.'

Ben followed the fortunes of his hero, Nelson, through his steward, one John Frisbe who was constantly at Nelson's side during his recovery. Admiral Nelson was sent home to England with the Fremantles aboard the *Seahorse.* The Admiral spoke of that voyage often as 'one wrought with pain'. Fremantle was in great agony with the wound in his right arm that refused to heal. Nelson, himself, was in great pain with his recently amputated right arm. The two could only look at one another and exchange groans. Even Betsy Fremantle was discomforted. It was bad enough to have to listen to all of the agonies of her men friends, but it was close to the end of her pregnancy and a lurching ship was anything but comfortable. Then, the hold was full of men injured during the recent battle and they could not keep from calling out from severe pain. Many of them were beyond any help, but they still lived. They would be taken to hospital ships and cared for as long as needed.

Nelson arrived at Spithead on 1 September and spent some time in Bath where Fanny had taken up residency to begin his healing. It was often thought of as a disgrace for a captain to be invalided home and Nelson was such a one to take the return home that way. He was in a deep depression. The truth was that he longed for the sea and his ship, his men about him and the camaraderie that they shared. It was his life that he had lost, not just his forearm. He was ill at ease here on the land, even though Fanny tried to amuse him with all manner of schemes and social gatherings. His wife, Fanny tried her best to comfort him. At first she was so repelled by the sight of his stump, which was not healing as Dr. Bowers had predicted, but continued to be inflamed, hot and cantankerous, that she could not bear to handle the dressings. But soon she realized that it must be done and it was, after all, a wifely duty to tend to her husbands wounds. Nelson spent some time with his father, whom he still considered to be a stern sort.

Tom Murphy was on the mend and would be put back aboard the *Theseus* soon. Ben was glad of that news. He missed his best friend.

Nelson went to London frequently to visit a surgeon there who was doctoring his stump and to make his appearance at the Admiralty to remind them that he was still alive and would welcome any assignment that would take him back to sea. He longed for the time when he could stand the deck of a ship again. That was what made a man alive. He also had to spend time at the Admiralty trying to arrange for his pension. He had been beached at half pay. While in London, he attended the formalities at St. Paul's Cathedral where he was awarded the order of the Knight of the Bath. There he was told that he might be needed by his country once again someday. That pleased him much and raised his spirits for at least a few days. But he could not hide the fact that he was in a great deal of pain. The last ligature still had not come lose and the swelling and puss were most annoying.

But the people of England loved him and Nelson thrived on public acclaim. He was invited to Norwich where he was awarded the 'Freedom of the City'. Then he went to the Guildhall where he received a golden casket, which was a protection should a second operation on his arm be needed. It was while he was there that he learned that the *Foudroyant* of 86 guns was to be launched in January. He had hopes that he might get the command of her. With a new ship under him, his indominable spirit led him to believe that he could overcome any physical disability. Here, finally, was hope. And sometimes hope is the most powerful of all medicines. The prospects of returning to sea seemed to magically free Nelson from his melancholy and his arm began to heal. The ligature came lose a few days later and the swelling subsided. Now the true healing could occur and soon he was feeling much relief. He was finally able to sleep without drugs or pain. Nelson gave thanks for his recovery to Almighty God through the Vicar of St. George, Hanover Square.

But by 21 December, 1797, the *Foudroyant* was no where ready to sail. So, the Admiralty sent word to Nelson that he would sail in command of the *Vanguard* which would be his flagship. Nelson was elated and ready to rejoin the Mediterranean fleet. No tonic could have healed more surely than a sturdy ship beneath his feet. He sailed in sight of the Mediterranean fleet four months later, a man ready for any challenge once again. He was now sure that his God had spared him for some better work, of which he was yet ignorant. Strangely enough, about the same time, a Corsican now residing in Paris by the name of Napoleon Bonaparte had similar visions of his own greatness.

Chapter Six

Camperdown, Their Tails Between Their Legs

Ben returned to Cadiz with the *Theseus,* but soon learned that several of the officers of other ships had been killed in the action. Soon orders came for Ben to transfer to the *Venerable* 74 which was headed for the North Sea. Once again, he left the ship that he had come to love to join Admiral Adam Duncan who had lost his third leftenant in a skirmish in the North Sea. Tom Murphy would be left behind. His leg was not fully healed and he could not leave his ship for action. Ben was to board a small brig, the *Flying Fish.* She was sailing directly to the North Sea with orders for Admiral Duncan. Ben was received aboard the *Venerable* with a good welcome and he soon felt at home.

For a time their duty was to patrol the area near the Texel to blockade the Batavian Fleet of Vice Admiral Jan de Winter. Their fourth leftenant, Robert Keen, told Ben of the happenings in the North Sea. It seems that the Dutch had joined the French who established a puppet state called, 'The Batavian Republic'. These Dutchmen now wished to join up with the French Navy to clear the English Channel for a third invasion attempt on England. The British fleet under Duncan was set against allowing the French and Dutch navies to join forces. Many of the ships in Duncan's command had taken part in the great mutiny only months earlier and there were raw feelings among the crew members. Some felt that they did not get a fair deal from the Admiralty. Ben would have to keep a close watch on his men for signs of unrest.

The North Sea in October was quite different from the western Mediterranean in summer. Ben found it hard to adjust and wished that he could have found time to go ashore and procure a new great coat for comfort on stormy days. The *Venerable* called at Yarmouth Roads to revictual and make repairs. Ben was fortunate to catch her before she sailed again. He thought often of Tom and wondered how he was getting along. He could not forget the huge question that spread across Tom's handsome face as he lay in his hammock. He was concerned that he might be put on the beach with no pay. What would his family do? They were still most dependent on him for partial support, especially with the girl's seeking dowries now. Ben knew how he must feel and wished he could help. But Tom was only a midshipman, and that rubbed Ben harder than anything else. He should have completed his training by now so that he would have the courage to face the leftenant's exam. Now with Ben off to the North Sea, there was no telling when he could resume Tom's training in navigation. He would have to fare on his own, but Ben knew that he would just give up. He was not motivated to great accomplishments or martyrdom, not Tom Murphy. He was made of the simpler stuff that makes good husbands and fathers, that gets the world's work done with no special thanks. Ben felt that he had failed in his duty to his friend.

They completed their refit swiftly because word came that the Dutch might be out and about. That was what Duncan feared. He had to keep the Dutch from joining with the French ships at all cost. Ben settled in as third leftenant. He would find some interesting fellows on this ship and he would long remember his time on the *Venerable.* Mr. Michael Kinkade was the first leftenant, a fine fellow who had a pleasant face and loved to tease and play tricks on his fellow officers. His easy-going nature endeared him to Ben almost immediately, but he was thought by the officers to be a bit too soft to ever make a good captain. Then there was the second leftenant, Mr. Hugh Worson. He was quiet, the exact opposite of Kinkade, but also considered to be a poor candidate for post captain because he seemed indecisive and withdrawn. He did not know his men and was a strange fellow at mess, quiet, sullen. Ben sensed that he had been sent to sea against his wishes and was doing his best to see it through. Ben had a small bunk on the port side and found his position quite suitable. He played 'laika' on the first Sunday below decks and the crew counted him as a fine replacement for their former third leftenant who could neither play nor sing. He had not played for sometime now.

They left port on 9 October to a brisk, cold wind and headed for the Texel. Ben had not been given time to get to know his crew, but he did ask permission to run them through gun exercise just once on Monday, the tenth. It was then that Ben met Melvin Hixson. He was a tall lad of perhaps twenty. He was the best gunner that Ben had ever met. His ability to handle his men came from the fact that he was so large and strong. He had the strength of two men and the stature of one and a half. He seemed to have incredible power over men and they looked up to him, worshiped him. *Too bad that he can never rise to the position of captain. He has the powers of leadership and is surely able to lead men. But by virtue of his humble birth, he will likely never be anything but a gunner,* thought Ben.

When he thought about it, he was in the same situation. He wondered how long he would serve as a leftenant and if he would ever get a shot at a post captain's cabin. Oh, he knew he was not ready yet. He was only seventeen. There was so much more to learn, and here was a master from whom he might learn a good bit. Adam Duncan was a shrewd Scott with a fine record. He was Admiral of the Blue, and when Ben came aboard, he welcomed him with a broad Scottish brogue and a firm handshake. "I expect that you will settle in swiftly, Mr. Rundel. We seek the Dutch and may beat to quarters almost anytime now. I am glad to have you aboard. I have read some of your exploits from the *Chronicle* and *Gazette*. You should serve us well, indeed." Ben was finding that serving on a variety of ships brought him in contact with a great many people, all quite different and some more interesting than others. He now knew how to sail almost any type of ship, although he lacked hands on experience with the larger and some of the smallest ships.

One captain that he met made a distinctly bad impression on Ben. He was Captain John Williamson. He dined with the Admiral and Ben and some of the other officers on their first night out of port. Williamson was nothing short of a braggart, an outspoken fellow who knew little about his trade. Ben wondered how he could ever have made leftenant, let alone captain. Most of the young officers that he met had come along the standard route. They were sent to sea by wealthy families with only a landsman's education. Greek literature did little to help one sail a ship through a storm or to fight off a lee shore. Most of these young officers had come by their training as midshipmen aboard ship from the sailing master and understood navigation reasonably well, but they knew little of the real workings of a ship or of the weaknesses of men. Few had ridden in the tops, furled sail, swabbed decks in the boiling heat or performed any of the more odious duties that were expected of seamen. Ben watched them make serious mistakes, asking a man to do some duty that made no sense or which could not be safely performed. He was becoming resentful of the young officers with whom he had to compete, who went around with their noses high in the air and would barely lower themselves to speak to a common seaman at all. Ben, on the other hand, won the loyalty of his men quickly by his superior knowledge of the duties of seamen, and their limitations, and by his open friendly manner. His balalaika probably won him more friends than anything else. He loved to play it and men loved to listen to its tinkling sounds and even to sing heartily to it. Ben now realized that he was one of them, one with the common sailor in his heart. He was not in any way sympathetic to the young men of noble birth who made their way in the Navy by being related to someone important. So when Williamson started his conversation with, "My great uncle is an MP, you know and my cousin is the King's horseman," Ben retaliated with, "And who are you, may I ask?"

That made him an instant enemy of Williamson and the young noble instantly challenged Ben to a duel.

Ben stood there looking at the fellows yellow head, his thin frame and nervous hands that clutched at his belt. He had a hawk nose and thin, tight lips. He was pretty too, like a girl. He was not one that Ben would particularly want to fight.

"I would not dirty my sword on the likes of you. We will be in action soon with the Dutch and I would preserve my arm to do the King's service there instead of wasting it on idle play here. You would do well to do the same, sir. Admiral Duncan may well need us both in fine health come tomorrow. I should not disappoint him by appearing minus a limb or a life," said Ben. Here again, Ben knew that he had received his training in the handling of a sword from tough sailors who had seen many battles and who knew how to dispense an enemy swiftly so as to preserve their own lives. He felt that he would have a fine chance to win over this fellow, "but that is not what war is about, killing one's fellow officers, is it," said Ben. "I thought that the French were the real enemies." Ben turned and walked away from the enraged captain. The man surged forward and threw a glove at Ben's face. Again, Ben picked up the glove and handed it to the lout. "Here, you have lost your glove, I believe, sir." Ben was not to be provoked to a duel. He did not feel the urges of some nonexistent honour that would force him to battle needlessly. That was the meat and drink of the aristocracy. Admiral Duncan, unbeknownst to Ben or Williamson, stood not far away and heard and saw all that went on. Ben had surely won the admiration of Duncan that night. The latter considered Ben to be a man who could hold his temper and who would be a great asset in any battle. He did not read cowardice in any of Ben's actions, while some of the other young gentlemen did.

Later when Admiral Duncan questioned Ben about his

unwillingness to fight, Ben replied. "I could see no use to His Majesty in reducing the men in his fleet by either one leftenant or one captain, sir." Ben neglected to say anything about the Articles of War prohibiting him from striking a superior officer, or about the offense of fighting, but Admiral Duncan knew that Ben understood his ground and had defended it most admirably.

"You are a smart lad, indeed, but I have some bad news for you, I am afraid. It seems that Captain Williamson is short one leftenant. The man we expected to put aboard failed to show up before we sailed. As you know, we have four leftenants aboard the *Venerable.* As a temporary measure, I am putting you aboard the *Bellona* as acting first leftenant. The other two officers on board are not only young, but have never seen action. They are young gentlemen and quite inexperienced. While you are younger still, you seem to have had a great deal more experience than either of them have had. I would watch Captain Williamson carefully if I were you. I have some reservations about his ability. I will be signaling *Bellona* 'to hove to' any minute now, so be off with you, and good luck, lad."

Ben stood for a second and looked at the man who had just handed him the second position of command in a third rate. Adam Duncan at perhaps fifty, was not overly tall, a bit heavy midships, with a definite hawk nose, small eyes with huge circles under them. His complexion was that of a sailing man and his mouth had a decided downturn in the corners. He was known as a fine tactician and a brave fighter. Ben saluted and was on his way. His only regret was that he would not be aboard to see what orders the Admiral gave and to watch the battle through his eyes. But no matter. He had his duty to carry out. Moving had become a way of life with him now. No more clothes thrown over a chair or scattered about. They were either on his back, in the drying room, or in his sea chest. He could up and move at a seconds notice.

Ben was received somewhat coolly aboard the *Bellona.*

That was not surprising. Williamson had probably told them about the coward on the *Venerable* who refused to fight him. If they had any sense, they would realize why he had refused to fight. Such an aside remark should not be reason for any man to kill another, let alone all of the other good reasons there might be for not fighting just before a major battle. But Ben had begun to wonder about himself. He knew that he loved beautiful things, beautiful music that touched him clear to his soul, beautiful women like his Annie. Was he really getting too soft to be a good officer?

On 11 October, they were headed towards Camperdown when they met the patrol ship which signaled, "Enemy sighted to leeward." Ben knew that de Winter had ships of shallower draft than the British had and that he could take advantage of the shoal areas to draw his fleet out of harms way and perhaps run the British fleet aground to boot.

Admiral Duncan pointed out that they would be outgunned the first time when he briefed his officers in his cabin. "We have seven 74's, seven 64's, and two 50's against the Dutch four 74's, seven 64's and five 50's. Our biggest worry is to keep the Dutch from moving to leeward so they can escape us. And our second worry is that we may be led aground by the shallower draft Dutch ships. This will be a tight fought battle, gentlemen. I expect each of you to do all in your power to bring the enemy to task. Watch my flags closely. I will be giving you frequent cues to bring the battle to a quick conclusion. My plan is to form us a line here, as he pointed, and then penetrate the Dutch line at three or four points. Aim for the hulls. We want to disable and sink the enemy ships so they cannot return to port or join the French. It is particularly important that those in our rear pierce the line to cut off the last three Dutch ships. Otherwise, they will feel free to come into the shallower water to starboard and rake us from both sides."

Admiral Duncan gave the order for a general chase and the ships went off in search of the enemy. Captain Williamson called for general alert. Soon the drums rolled and the bosun's whistle shrilled its' call. Men flew to action, to their stations. All of the many details that must be seen to before battle and that require the diligence of the common seamen were being seen to. Ben was concerned because he was afraid that the mutinous mood from the Nore might still be with the fleet and that they might be faced with a morale problem. Duncan, he knew, was most concerned about the same problem. Ben noticed a little sulkiness among his men when he exercised them at the guns on the *Venerable* earlier. They had not used powder, but simply went through the motions so that Ben had a feel for how well his men would perform. Now he had a new ship, the *Bellona,* and a different crew to deal with. He knew nothing about these lads at all except that they had been at the Nore and had mutinied. He must be satisfied with what he had, and he was satisfied now as he saw this new division move swiftly into the assigned duties at the call of, "All hands to action." The bosun's pipes shrilled and the drums rolled, calling the men to instant alert at their duty stations.

By 11 a.m., they located the enemy ships just about nine miles off Camperdown. Ben using his glass saw a line of ships to the northeast, with five frigates and four corvettes forming an inner line. Admiral Duncan signaled his ships into two divisions for the chase, but now he sent up signals for the two divisions of ships to form a line each, headed straight towards the enemy line to engage the enemy as soon as each ship came to bear. Duncan's ships began to move straight at the enemy line in a manner which would dissect it at four or five points. That would allow the British ships to cut out sections of the enemy fleet and destroy each in turn. *The divide and conquer principle is becoming more sophisticated,* thought Ben. From the quarterdeck of the *Bellona* Ben could see ships in the van already engaged with the enemy. *The plan is superb,* he thought. Each British ship passed between two Dutch ships, firing full broadsides at the stern of one and the bow of the other. Before the enemy could get off a single shot, the British ships had inflicted considerable damage on the Dutch ships that they had engaged. Ben saw the mainmast of one Dutch ship topple and yards came crashing down on other ships. He knew that many had already died aboard the Dutch ships and many of their guns were already useless. *But why aren't we tacking?* The order had come sometime earlier to pass through and tack in order.

Ben looked at Captain Williamson, who stood near by. His face was as white as a sheet. They were still headed to pass between the *Alkmaar* and *Haarlem.* Suddenly Captain Williamson knocked the men at the wheel aside took the helm and put it hard to starb'rd which would carry the ship swiftly down the Batavian coast and *away from the battle.* Ben's mind was in a panic. They were cutting and running from their duty. They would all be court martialled. Ben could not endure that, nor the stigma of being labeled a coward. "No, No!" he shouted as he ran for the helm. He struggled with Williamson for several minutes. The ship was turning. Soon it would be too late to undo the damage. There was no way that he could have misread Captain Williamson's intentions. He *was* running.

There was no other solution. It might mean a court martial for himself, but he had to take over the command of the ship. To remove a captain at sea is treason and mutiny and punishable by death, but to run from one's duty was even worse. Ben swung around swiftly and grabbed the captain in a strangle hold. He nodded to the two helmsmen. "Carry on lads on the bearing that you were following originally. The cap'n is not well." Ben kept his strangle hold on Williamson and shoved him down the companionway. He grabbed a belaying pin and hit the captain hard on the back of the head and the poor wretch fell forward, unconscious. Then he carried him to his cabin.

"Cap'n's fainted," said Ben to the sentry at the captain's

door. "I'll put him in his berth." Ben left Williamson in a soggy heap on his bunk and swiftly left, locking the door behind him. *I must get back on deck. We must be almost ready to engage the enemy.* The other two officers stood idly by as Ben had dispatched the captain. He hardly knew them, one James Shook and the other Henry Freeman. They looked at him disapprovingly, but they did not flinch when he gave the orders to, ' prepare to fire'. "Aim for the hulls, lads."

They were back on course and were just about close enough to engage both Dutch ships. A flurry of signals came from the flagship while Ben had been busy with Williamson. The ensign was following Ben around like a new born puppy with messages that he had translated in his hand.

"Sir, 'e says, what in blazes is going on there,' to our ship number. Then 'e says, '*Bellona* come about and cut the line as ordered.' then there is some stuff that I don't understand sir. 'Stand to and do your duty,' and then 'That's what I meant.' Oh, an he also said to, 'pass through and engage on the leeward side to prevent the Dutch from escaping to shallow water.'

"Thank you, Mr. Sorenson. I am now the acting captain of the *Bellona.* You may signal the flag ship and say that all in well and that Leftenant Rundel has taken charge."

With that, Ben glanced at the two Dutch ships. *We are on them.* "Fire as you bear," he shouted at the top of his lungs. The order was passed from midshipman to midshipman, like a ripple.

The ship shivered violently as both broadsides were fired at once. The guns fired in succession, rippling down the side of his ship with a precision that he could not have imagined possible, each gun firing half a second after the last. He saw the mizzen mast of the *Alkmaar* crash and the bow of the *Haarlem* had been smashed to kindling. The men at the nearest guns turned smudged, blackened faces towards Ben and there were smiles of approval. Ben realized that the agony of the mutiny had pretty much passed. Whatever history would decide that he had done, it met with the approval of the men. There was no question about that. If they had persisted on the course set by the captain, they would be left out of all prize money. The promise of prize money, even though it would be meagre, was strong incentive for a seaman to put his life on the line for His Majesty. A ship that was lucky enough to capture three or four fat prizes and a sailor who survived all of these battles might do quite well. Many eventually retired ashore and bought pubs or small farms.

"Hard a port," roared Ben. He needed to stay close to the *Jupiter* to engage her. He had not yet realized that he was commanding a 74, but the power of his guns did remind him that he was now engaged in a full battle with a large ship of equal size. "Fire as you bear," Ben shouted. The sailors were in good command of their guns and as soon as the *Bellona* began to swing towards the *Alkmaar* they roared out at close range. Ben saw more masts and yards fall. The *Alkmaar* now began to return fire. Ben ducked as a bit of rigging swung down to deck near his head. Then a gun nearby was upended. Men screamed and the deck was slippery with blood, in spite of the sand. "Return fire, repair that cannon," shouted Ben. The other leftenants and midshipmen were following his orders surprisingly well. Some probably did not yet know what had happened to the captain. If they did, they might not be as willing to follow Ben's orders. A cannon ball crashed through the bulkhead just beside Ben, missing him by only inches. But a sliver pierced his leg. It was small, so he pulled it lose and put his neck cloth over it. They continued to pour shot into the *Alkmaar* for another half hour, and then it was over. Through the choking smoke, Ben could see a white flag being held by someone on deck. Was it an officer? If it were not, it might be just a sailor who had grown tired of battle and was waving his shirt to get out of the mess. The deck of the Dutchman was strewn with debris and there was hardly a man standing. Ben looked more closely. Mr. Singleton stepped up to Ben. "Sir, they are signaling a surrender, I think. And , sir, Mr. Shook has been killed."

"Thank you, Mr. Singleton. Carry on."

Then Ben looked again. Yes, there was an officer's hat on the man who was weaving the flag. They hardly had anything left fit to fly a flag of surrender from. These Dutch had given the British a brave fight.

Now Ben realized what he must do. "Cease fire! Boarding parties ready to port. Bring her in close, helmsman. Grapples ready."

Within five minutes they were boarding the Dutch ship. It was a total shambles. The dead lay in heaps. There had been no time to throw them overboard. Ben stepped forward, towards the man who held the white flag, "Benjamin Rundel Acting Captain of His Majesty's ship *Bellona*.

"Hans Wentz," Captain of the *Alkmaar*. At that, he handed Ben his sword. There was no hand to hand fighting. The Dutch were thoroughly defeated and there was no fight left in them. Ben left thirty of his men aboard to try to rescue the mess of the *Alkmaar* and directed the rest of his crew back to their own ship.

"Shove off, Mr. Freeman," called Ben. We are off to find another opponent. Men were scurrying about cutting away rigging, but the *Bellona* was still sea worthy. She had one hole in her hull, but it was above the water line and she had all three masts intact, albeit, missing a good bit of rigging and yards. As the lines were cut and the ship came adrift, she went towards the shoal water and Ben became nervous. They had passed through to the leeward side as ordered. Now it was becoming hazardous. He had no good charts of this section of coast. He guessed that this ship would need a good thirty feet of water to be safe. He ordered the helmsman to steer a course that would carry them close up to the next ship, the *Delft*. She had been in action briefly with the *Veteran,* but the latter ship had worn away to deeper waters. The crew worked frantically to clear the deck of the *Bellona* . Two guns that had been put out of action were now restored. They cut loose a bit of their rigging which was dragging in the water and had made it difficult to steer the ship. Ben could breathe easier. They were out of the shallows, but it would require constant vigilance to fight a battle on the lee side and still manage to keep from being crowded into shallow water by his opponent. Ben ordered Mr. Brown, the sailing master, the keep a close eye on the water depth and to make course corrections if needed without command from him. Ben wanted to concentrate on his handling of the ship and conducting the battle. Now all but one of his guns were restored to service. "Fire as you bear!"

Ben felt the deck rock under his feet and the cloud of smoke that engulfed him left him temporarily blind and choking. He reeled and just as he started to step further aft to get out of the smoke, a yard crashed down, hitting his left foot. Ben fell to the deck, screaming in pain. His foot was crushed. Two sailors came swiftly to his aid. They lifted him up from the debris and set him where he could stretch out his leg. Ben felt the leg. It was injured, but not broken. He could hardly feel his foot, but otherwise, he was functional. The two sailors started to lift him to take him to the orlop sick bay, but Ben nodded his head. "No lads. I am alright. I can still perch here on this skylight and conduct the battle from here. Go to those who really need you."

The battle went on for sometime. They were at close quarters so that each shot told, but the enemy ship was getting off about four cannon every six or seven minutes. His men had reduced their rate of fire too. The smoke was too thick to see to get shot and cartridges to the guns for rapid fire. Each man could bring up only two cartridges in his pack at a time. Many of the young men serving the guns had been injured or killed. Ben sat there in the dense smoke, wishing that he had not taken control of the ship. He had been too busy up until now to give it much thought, but surely there would be a court martial and he would be hanged or at least beached for his efforts. And he had heard that Graves, the man who had given him such a bad time at his first court martial was here with the Baltic Fleet. He might even sit at his court martial again. Ben felt faint, not from his injury, but more from dread of the near future.

But the immediate future suddenly looked bright. The *Delft* was hauling down her colours. He could see the flag in bits and pieces through the dense smoke, coming down from the mizzen mast. Yes, they were bending on a white flag.

"Cease fire," yelled Ben. "Boarding parties ready!"

The lads were eager enough to close off action. They had been in a hard -fought battle for many hours now and the repairs of the ship would take days. Ben jumped gingerly down on his good foot as the ships came together.

He wanted to lead the boarding party, as he had done with the first ship, but his foot was quite swollen and painful. He could not walk unaided. Off to the north he could see that most of the firing had ceased and the British were making efforts to regroup and repair. The Dutch ships sat there in the water, like a bunch of lambs rounded up and ready to be hauled to market.

"Mr. Freeman. You will lead the boarding party, and receive the sword of the Dutch Captain," called Ben. "Also, leave about twenty men aboard after you have confined all of the Dutchmen below under arrest. Give orders to begin to clean up the ship for towing back to England."

"Aye, sir."

Ben hobbled to the rail. His foot hurt, but it would mend, he was sure of that. It would be a temporary annoyance, nothing more. He looked off at the other ships. It was a sad scene, for anyone who loves ships. The remains of the Dutch fleet was now huddled in a small circle, all flying white flags. A few had escaped to the shallower water, but those that were still at sea were little more than hulks. Some of the Dutch ship's captains realized that they were outgunned early in the battle and headed off north towards the Texel. The water was full of floating debris, dead bodies, and bits of cargo. At one point, de Winter was the only one left alive on the deck of the *Vrijheid,* his flag ship. He escaped without injury, a shear miracle.

The British ships were badly damaged too, but they were drawing close to the circle of Dutch ships, boxing them in. Ensign Singleton came with word that the battle was over. "The Admiral has signaled that we are victorious and asks for all captains to report aboard the flag ship at once."

Now that presented a problem for Ben. Should he take Captain Williamson with him as captain or as a man in chains? Ben decided that he would have to stand by his action as necessary for the safety of the ship and the fleet and so, he ordered the corporal of marines to prepare the captain for removal in chains and under guard. Ben had not thought about Williamson for the past three hours or more. He now must make his way to the captain's cabin and unlock it. Slowly, with painful steps, he made his way to the captain's cabin. Williamson lay in his bunk, curled up like a sick puppy, shaking uncontrollably, his face stained with tears and red. *So this is the man who would have put a musket ball in me just hours ago,* thought Ben.

The trip to the flagship was painful in more than one way. Ben's foot throbbed with pain. He would have the surgeon set the bones later, when the other more seriously wounded men had been attended to. Right now, he was faced with the most challenging task of his life. He would have to justify his actions in taking over the *Bellona.* That might not be easy. Admirals looked mighty hard at anyone who would take over the command of a ship from its rightful captain, especially after the recent rash of mutinies.

The second point of pain was Williamson. Ben hated to see any man reduced to such a blubbering mass of insecure flesh. He hated to do what he knew he must do, and he could see in the man's eyes that Williamson would hate him for the rest of his life.

The third point of pain was to see those beautiful ships reduced to rubble and debris, some anchored by their fallen masts, some floating aimlessly, mere hulks that might never be redeemed. The water, too, was floating with debris and Ben longed for a fresh breath of air. The yellow, acrid smoke of battle hung in the air and bit at his lungs, making him feel dizzy.

Ben had to be helped onto the deck of the flagship. He remembered Admiral Nelson after he had lost an arm. He refused help up the side of his ship. *I am not made of quite the same material as the Admiral,* thought Ben.

In the cabin of Admiral Duncan, Ben was pleased to see that the old gentleman was in good shape and had not suffered personal injury during the battle. He saw the captains file in, one by one. Some he knew, some not. He motioned for the marine corporal and his aide to set Williamson down on a chair next to him.

Admiral Duncan stepped forward. Rundel, you are injured man. Couldn't you have that attended to before you came aboard?"

"Sir, it is not serious I have training as a surgeon and the foot will need to have the bones set within the next few hours, but there are other men with far graver injuries. They must be seen to first," said Ben.

The Admiral called for his aide and asked him to send the surgeon as soon as he could be spared.

"Aye sir."

The captains stood in a group gathered in the opposite corner of the cabin, talking excitedly. "Now, Mr. Rundel, tell me just what all that fancy ship handling was about out there."

"Well, you see sir, Captain Williamson was in command. He appeared not to want to engage the nearest ships and had taken the helm himself, pointing us off down the Batavian coast, away from the battle. I sensed that that was the opposite of your command and so, I took the helm and put us back on course to cut the line between the *Alkmaar* and the *Haarlem.* I saw that the captain had lost control of himself, sir, so I took him below to his cabin where I confined him for the duration of the battle. As acting first leftenant, I was forced to assume command sir."

"And you took the "*Alkmaar* and the *Delft?"*

"Aye, sir, and both ships have men aboard preparing them for transport home. Their crews have been confined, sir."

The Admiral turned away without a word. Ben now had a most uncomfortable feeling. He did not know if the Admiral approved of his actions, or if his silence meant that he was angry with him. In fact, Ben did not really know Admiral Duncan at all. He had sailed with him only five days. Surely he had stepped over the line. He would be the first to admit that. And certainly he did not want to take over the ship, there was no conspiracy, but there was no other alternative either. They needed every ship that they had. The Dutch are formidable enemies.

The Admiral called his captains to be seated. He thanked them all for their brave action during the battle. Ben heard a slight whimper from Williamson. "If you will each call out the name of the ship that you have taken, we may be able to get an idea of the extent of our victory. Let's start with you, Vice-Admiral Onslow."

"*Vrijheid,* sir and she will be fit to tow in about a day."

"*Jupiter* , sir and she will be seaworthy in about two days."

"*Haarlem* , and she is in poor shape, sir, give her several days of hard work."

"*Alkmaar* and *Delft,* sir. They are being prepared to sail, but it may take several days to bring them into seaworthy condition," said Ben. He noticed a look of surprise and admiration on the faces of the captains. Well, he was only a very young third leftenant, and this was his first command of a large ship. To have taken two prizes was no small feat, especially with a totally strange crew and two officers who were estranged, to say the least. Ben felt their eyes closing in on him. He added, somewhat defensively, "But the *Delft* had already been in combat with the *Veteran,* sir."

The Admiral looked at him hard, for a few seconds. "How old are you, son?"

That same old question again. What does it matter how old I am. Ben hated to lie, but he had to keep up the pretense.

"Nineteen, sir." The truth was closer to seventeen, but no one knew the truth except Captain Bailey and he was now dead.

"*Monnikendam,* sir and she is totaled."

"*Hercules*, sir, and she is being refitted."

"*Gel-ijk-heid,* 68, sir, or however you might pronounce the name. She is in fair condition and should be ready to sail in a day or so." Everyone laughed at his bizarre pronunciation. Ben was glad that he had the luck of capturing ships whose name he could pronounce, if only just.

"*T. H. de Vries,* 68, sir. She can sail in a day, with luck.

The Admiral looked to the last man, a stalwart seaman of considerable proportions. "The *Wassernaar* , sir, and she is sunk. The *Embuscade* may be made seaworthy, but we have not had time to evaluate her condition yet. The guns have not yet cooled, sir."

"Let's see, that makes at least eleven ships if you count the *Vrijheid,* that was taken by the *Venerable.* I know that it is soon to count the dead and wounded, but can you give me some estimates, lads?"

They each went through the list. Some said that they had not had time to do any accounting. They listed the officers dead and wounded. These were pretty well known. Then they estimated their losses of men. The Admiral totaled his list and looked up, addressing the captains. "It looks like some 244 killed and 796 wounded, plus one here. Mr. Rundel has not been put on the injured list." Just then the surgeon entered the cabin and bent to look at Ben's foot.

"Not too bad, sir. If you will come below, I can set the bones and bandage it now. Here, I'll help you."

Ben looked to the Admiral for permission, who nodded his head. "Take the lad below and take good care of him, Mr. Seward."

Later Captain Burke, who was present, told Ben of the things that happened in the Admiral's cabin after he had left.

After Ben had left, the Admiral's face turned grim. We have a problem here, lads. That youngster there, as he pointed through the door where Ben had just left, was forced to take over the command of a 74 from this incompetent sitting here," as he pointed to Williamson. Williamson slid even farther down into his seat, his eyes still red and his face tear-stained. His face had a livid scar on it from some childhood nonsense and it was now a brilliant red, making him look even more pitiable.

"I know we will have to hold a court martial for Williamson, but it seems that he had an attack of panic just as we were about to go into battle. He started to take his ship out of action. Rundel, there, seized the captain and put him in confinement in his own cabin and then took over command. He went on the capture two ships. Not bad for a lad that looks barely more than sixteen. What do you say to that?" The Admiral was fishing to see how strongly the officers would condemn Ben's taking control for the wheel. They might go either way. But how did they feel about an officer taking the control of a ship from his captain, who chose to disobey orders?

There was a general murmur in the cabin. Then Captain Mead looked up and said, "I can't fault the leftenant for taking the command from his captain, given the circumstances. He only did his duty. However, he should be made to understand that he should never attempt such a darned fool thing in the future."

"Do the rest of you agree with Captain Mead?" There was a shaking of heads and a general murmur of approval.

"Then it is settled. I do not have to hold a court martial for young Rundel as well. He can be allowed to testify concerning his behavior aboard the *Bellona.* I know that you all have much to do to get your ships in order, so I will send you off with my blessings. It looks as if we may be able to sail for the Nore the day after tomorrow. If anyone has problems, send word aboard and I will see what can be done. We'll plan for the court martial at the Nore," said the Admiral. "Congratulations, gentlemen, on a job well-done. We'll hoist a glass in friendship in a few days when things are in better shape."

Then the Admiral turned to the marines who were guarding Williamson. "Take this man below and put him in irons. Normally he would be put in his cabin on honours arrest, but I do not think that he deserves such fine treatment."

Meanwhile, the surgeon had helped Ben to the orlop deck and there, amidst a welter of wounded and dying men, he began to cleanse Ben's foot and set the bones. Ben knew how small and frail these bones were and he could only hope that the man, John Seward, was a good surgeon. He could tell little about him from his operating table. No surgeon can hope to have a clean table after a butcher battle like this one had been. Ben watched carefully as the man felt his foot and tried to put the bones back in their proper place. It felt like only two of the bones were broken. He was bandaging the foot tightly when the Admiral stepped through the door. He suffered an involuntary wrinkling of his nose at the stench and the warmth of blood that met him. He moved to where the surgeon was working on Ben.

"How is he, Mr. Seward?"

"It's not serious, sir, just a few broken bones. He should be up and about in about a week, maybe two. He should stay off this foot for at least a week, though, and then he should be on crutches."

"Good. Mr. Rundel, the captains have agreed with me that you are in no way to be held criminal for your seizing the ship from Captain Williamson. There will be no court martial for you, *per se,* but I hope that you will be well enough to testify against Mr. Williamson back at the Nore. We will sail in about two days, God willing. And I am relieving you of duty for a week. You can rest and let that foot heal. That was a darned fool thing that you did, taking over the helm from Williamson, but I am sure glad that you did. If you had vacated your position along the line, the Dutch rear would have come along beside our ships and poured shot into us from leeward as well as from windward. We would have been lost, lad, lost." His voice trailed off. "We lost only about 244 lads, with 796 wounded, but our estimates of the Dutch losses are much higher, 540 dead to 620 injured. I am pleased at the work that you did. You will make a fine captain someday, and I hope it won't be too long."

Those words made Ben feel good, but he knew that it might be a long time. It might be forever for an orphan boy with no family and no influence in the right places.

"Oh, and I am putting Leftenant Briggs and Captain Horace Wilson on board to take care of the *Bellona,* so you need not fret about your ship.

Ben returned to his ship. In the several hours that he had been gone, the seamen had cleared the deck and were busy repairing yards and rigging. The deck was a welter of the tools of activity. It would soon be supper and they would rest for the night, but clearly, all was well with 'his ship'.

Later, in conversation with the Admiral, Ben expressed his thanks that the sailors had forgotten the mutiny and were now solidly behind King and Country. He had already made a speech to his men aboard the *Bellona,* thanking them for their support during a very difficult time and commending them for their bravery. He would never spend enough time with these men to really get to know them, but they, one and all, admired that youngster who had led them to fame and victory. Some would retire with enough prize money to live comfortably, but unfortunately, some would lose their prize money right before their eyes and stand helplessly by as it vanished under the waves. He was satisfied that he might someday be able to do the work of a captain, even if he might never hold the title. The men cheered loudly when he finished his speech. Ben felt his face flush and he thought that he might begin to understand what Lord Nelson felt when he was cheered by the masses. There was a certain elation in success, lifting a man far above where his feet should stand, every bit as driving as the bitterness of defeat. He had yet to try that vintage, but he knew he would and he knew it would leave a bitter taste indeed.

The next few days were full of frantic activity to get the ships ready to sail back to England. Ben wanted to take part, but his foot was quite swollen and painful. He did go on deck daily and supervised men at some of the carpenter tasks with which he was familiar.

That evening they dined with the Admiral in his cabin. It was a congenial meal, served most ably by the Admiral's steward. They dined on boiled duck smothered with onions, roast goose, potatoes, roast mutton, carrots, beans and apple dumplings for dessert. The Admiral served a fine wine, but Ben settled for cider, which was excellent. The captains showed considerable interest in Ben. Each man took time during the long evening to speak with him. Most asked about his family and home. That was always difficult for Ben. It was interminably hard to have to reply that he had no family and no home. He tried to change the subject, or to use evasive answers like, 'Cornwall,' but he was not good at faking anything. They must have all guessed that he was an orphan. In spite of his humble beginnings, Ben did feel that he had the respect of these men, and that was a good feeling.

After another day of frantic repairs, they had the most seriously damaged vessels in tow and the rest ready to put to sea. It was a short voyage to the Nore, some 120 miles or so. It should have been a short passage. The night before they set sail, the sky turned a mean, dark colour and the wind began to whip up the waves. By morning, the storm was breaking and they began to realize that they would have to limp back to port in a howling gale.

They set limited sails, just enough to keep the ships stable, and headed off to the southwest, but the winds were coming from that quarter, and they could not make any progress. They tacked and tried to handle their ships as best they could, but the waves were now of epic proportions, pounding down on their decks and slamming into the bows as if they were toy ships in a real sea. Ben could do little. He was still under surgeon's orders to stay off his foot, but he felt like he might need to use his feet to swim soon, if the force of the storm did not abate. The storm was so fierce that it drove the ships apart. They soon lost sight of one another and so, could be of no help or comfort to one another. Ben spent as much time on deck as he could stand. With an injured foot, he could hardly manage the great gyrations of a ship working its way through a pounding sea, but he felt safer on deck, lashed down, than below where he could not see anything. As he sat, lashed to a mast, he could see through the rail, the *Veteran* with the *Delft* in tow. Ben focused on the smaller ship. The *Delft* was having a deuce of a time staying afloat. Each wave seemed to push her farther into the dark, angry water. But again she would bob back to the surface, still afloat. Ben watched fascinated for a time. The rain poured over his face, obscuring his vision. He sat at times in water over his head, sometimes tilted at a sickening angle as the ship pitched to rid herself of the unwanted water. He would emerge from one of these drownings, gasping for breath and sputtering like a whale. Big mouthfuls of ocean were spit back onto the deck. He seriously doubted that any of them would ever see land again. And he fretted because more than anything he wanted to see his Annie again. He knew now in his heart that she had read his eyes and he knew what his eyes had said. He had to live, if only to see her once again. And he had his other wish too, to return to the Broken Bridge where he had grown up, if for only an hour. He longed to see Kateleen again and to see the familiar sights of the best days of his childhood. That was it. When someone asked him where he was from, he would say, 'Broken Bridge'. No one would know where that was since it was his name for the place, but he could then follow up with, 'Cornwall'. That would quell the curious and put an end to some of his misery. His mind wandered on with bits of this and that nonsense, as will happen when a man is afraid for his life and does not want to focus on some problem about which he can do nothing.

Then it happened. The *Delft* was lifted high out of the sea by a huge wave. She came crashing back down, so hard that it must have breached her hull. She began to sink, bow first, going ever deeper with each sea. The waves beat on her deck and she seemed to lie there like a lifeless thing, dead, no fight left in her, and now at the mercy of the cold sea. Ben watched as she disappeared beneath the waves, but only her bowsprit reappeared. He could see frantic action aboard the *Veteran* to cut her hawser with axes before she could drag them down into the deep with her. Ben thought of all the men who had planned on prize money from that ship, and he realized that in a way, it was his ship. He had captured her. It was painful to see her now, sinking helplessly beneath the waves. Ben caught a glimpse of her for just a second more, and then she was gone. Huge bubbles drifted to the surface of the water, barrels, debris of all kinds, and yes, dead men too, floated up out of her as she settled into her final grave. Over the howl of the wind, Ben could hear a strange moaning, a sighing sound. Then there was silence except for the storm. Ben thought that there was nothing quite as sad as the death of a ship. It was almost worse than the death of a human. *A ship is so helpless in a sea like this.* He prayed as he had not done before that his ship would make it to port. He was not ready to die, not the way those poor seamen had died aboard the Dutch ship. There must have been over five hundred Dutchmen and some sixty Englishmen aboard.

But just then a huge wave broke across the *Bellona* and Ben nearly lost consciousness before the water could all unload and run back into the sea. He shook his head, made gargling sounds, spit up a substantial amount of sea and gasped for breath. *Will this never end,* he thought. Out of the corner of his eye, he saw another ship that appeared to be in trouble. She had been driven far off to port and was now headed for the Ressen Sands. Ben watched, terrified, as she drove at a great rate of speed directly onto the sand banks. When she hit there was a loud crashing sound that drowned out the storm for just a frightening second. Her masts flew from her decks as if they were but small sticks of wood. Her entire deck was swept clean of all structures and life in a matter of seconds. *The poor devils below deck must all be drowned by now.* There was nothing that anybody could do for them. And there went another six or seven hundred lives as well as the prize money that her crews would have received. Ben felt such pain in his mind that he closed his eyes for a time, to try to ease his troubled soul. *If I can't see it, maybe it will not be so bad,* he thought. But it did not work. When he did open his eyes again, he saw that their deckhouse had washed away. Later he would learn that many men below decks were mauled by moving lumber, barrels shifting and other objects that are normally tied down properly, but which must inevitably come adrift in so severe a storm. He had fared well enough above decks. His mast had held and his rope ties did not part. He was drenched and had swallowed so much water that his stomach felt stretched and sick.

But the storm was not over. It held them there, in the approach to the Channel, for four days. The Nore must be not much over fifty or sixty miles away, but they could not free themselves of this devil wind to make port. Ben watched as ship after ship was dismasted. Some of the Dutch ships were old and some broken up. One, the

Embuscade 36, broke up as she went ashore on the Dutch coast. Ben wondered how much change this storm would make in the butcher's list that Admiral Duncan would have to present to the Admiralty.

But when it finally was over and they limped into port, the British had lost only a few men, mostly the prize crews aboard the captured Dutch ships. Even some of them survived to become Dutch prisoners of war. The sad part was that when the damages to all of the captured ships had been assessed some week later, none were found to be suitable for repair and use by the British Navy. They would be sold and most would become prison hulks or hospital ships. Their hulls suffered too much damage from the battle and from the storm to make them seaworthy again. Ben would remember that aiming cannon at the hulls of enemy ships carries a price with it that may be too much to bear. It was a bitter victory, but at least it was a victory and they need not slink home with their tails between their legs as the few surviving Dutchmen had done. But the memory of the dead Dutchmen would haunt them for years to come and many men felt beaten in spite of their victory. The Dutch had been soundly beaten, but it was a ferocious fight between two nearly equal opponents. Ben was certain that the balance of power lay with the British seamen and their mastery of gunnery. They had maintained a rapid rate of fire that ships of no other country could match. Her gun captains were second to none and they had won the day. Ben was proud of the service.

But did the British Navy really win that day? Ben thought that the real victor was the angry sea and the unrelenting storm that had wrested victory from them by sinking many of their prizes. It was the storm that sent them home, their tails between their legs.

Ben felt strongly that Admiral Nelson's approach of making all of his men feel as if they were part of a team was the best possible way to manage a group of fighting men. He saw problems during this battle which would not have occurred if Nelson had been in charge, but there was no fault to be found with Admiral Duncan either. Ben knew that Nelson was home at Burnham Thorpe recovering from the amputation of his arm.

To Ben's surprise, there was a letter from Tom Murphy awaiting him. Tom had a childish scrawl, not the bold hand of a scholar, but the words put hope back into Ben's heart. He missed his friend and would so like to see him. It seems that Tom's wound to the leg was mainly a flesh wound, although the bullet had nicked the bone. It was healing well, but there was a small lump deep in his leg which seemed hot and did not change. Ben knew that Tom was writing to him as a friend and as a surgeon to see if there was any advice that he could get to ease his pain. Tom was back on duty as midshipman, but he was still quite uncomfortable. Ben thought. *He must have a pocket of infection deep in the muscle, possibly near the bone. His body should be able to conquer that infection, if he can be patient. It might be necessary for the surgeon to open the wound and drain it, especially if there seemed to be a build up of pressure.* Ben resolved the day that they anchored off the Nore that he would write to Tom and tell him what he must do. He would write to Torrance Bailey too and tell him of the battle. He would be sure to include his congratulations on his pending marriage. That was the least that he could do for his friends. He had no idea if he and Tom would meet soon again or not. He did not know what the future held for him. No sailing man ever knows that or most likely they would never dare to set foot aboard ship.

The court martial was set for 22 October, 1797. Ben was kept busy with preparing his presentation for the court martial. The Admiral said that he would need to speak clearly and frankly about the conditions that he found aboard the ship when he came aboard, and that the defense would probably question his ability to judge if the captain was incompetent or not. Williamson sent word to shore as soon as they dropped anchor. Dicking said that he wrote to his family, which was most influential at court and in the House of Lords, and asked for a good lawyer to defend him, 'and I hope you will send your blessings on to your poor son who is so vilely slandered by those around me.'

Ben knew that he had a task ahead of him. Could he remember anything about the condition of the ship, her rigging, sail handling, cleanliness? Was there good order in the cabin, papers in proper order and officers neat and trustworthy? All of these things would bear on the condition of the captain's mind just before the battle. But Ben had been aboard only hours before the action began. He had little way of remembering the conditions that were there. Any evidence of poor management had been blown away by gunfire from the Dutch ships. There was not a single scrap of evidence that would indicate that Williamson had been guilty of acting incompetently in the past. The only thing that he could say with truthfulness was that the man froze, his face pale as snow and then went into a panic, seizing the wheel and setting them off course. Could a man suddenly lose all of his senses? Could he have been so scared of the pending action that he lost his reason? That would have to be Ben's position. Had he known the man a bit longer, maybe there were other indications of his weakness, but he had known him scarcely three days. But... there was the incident of his challenge to Ben when Ben had asked him who he was. Would that hold some power? Ben could not be sure. He knew that many of the officers of His Majesty's ships were tired of the whole idea of settling quarrels with duels. It cost them too many good young officers. It was still common to hear of a ship having to sail without one of her officers because he had been killed in a duel.

Ben's foot healed quickly, although he would always favour his left foot a bit when he walked. He was clumsy with it, for some reason that he could not understand. But slowly, the bones were knitting together and the pain was less. He would always get a twinging pain in that foot when it was going to rain or when a major storm was brewing.

A week later, the Admiral called the captains who were in port to sit for the court martial of John Williamson. Ben made some new acquisitions of clothes and was able to appear, for once, quite properly dressed. Even the Admiral remarked on his fine appearance. Ben knew that he had to appear as professional as he could. Most of these men were new to him. He was familiar with only the officers of the Mediterranean Fleet. He was met by stern faces, men who had seen much and whose experience far outmatched his. Among them was Captain Bligh, a most able navigator. Williamson stood, or rather slouched, before the long table with the captains seated behind it.

The Admiral read the charges against Williamson. Then he nodded to Ben to step forward and present his case. Ben had written down his testimony. He could not help but smile at the odd curly wigs that the captains chose to wear as symbols of their judicial duties. He prayed never to have to serve on a court martial and never to be forced to wear one of those contraptions, all smelly with powder. He was extremely nervous with all this testimony and was afraid that he would omit some critical point. As he stood, a half foot taller than Williamson and much more handsome, he cleared his voice and addressed the court.

"Sirs,..." He went on to tell the court about the events of the 11 th day of October when he came aboard the *Bellona.* Ben mentioned that she had been in the command of Captain Thompson until a week before the battle. He described Captain Williamson and the state of mind in which he found him. He told about sending the captain below to his cabin, but omitted the coercive use of a belaying pin on the captain's head. If that had been noted, he would have to answer for it, but he felt that there was no other way to subdue the man and take him from his agony. How could those seated here in this quiet room judge that?

"When Ben had finished, he bowed to the court and

stepped back. He could see the fire in Williamson's eyes as he turned to take his seat. He knew that he would have a life-long enemy here, but there was no helping that. He had his duty to perform.

Next, the captains questioned Ben. "Was there evidence of the *Bellona* being a poorly kempt ship?" asked Captain Bligh.

Ben had to answer honestly. "Sir, I had been aboard less that three hours before the battle began. I had little time to assess the condition of the ship. The men in my division seemed proficient at their guns and I saw no deficiencies in sail handling. The ship had been in Captain Williamson's control for only about a week. Much of the ship's condition would be attributable to the diligence of the former captain, sir."

"Was Captain Williamson congenial towards you?"

Now that was a difficult question. He would have to explain the happenings aboard the flagship. Certainly most of these captains had heard about it. "When I was introduced to Captain Williamson aboard the flagship, he took offense at a question which I asked him and challenged me to a duel. I ignored his challenge. His majesty does not need two injured or dead officers just before a major battle, and dueling is forbidden by the Articles of War. I am certain that Captain Williamson was upset with me for refusing to fight, but I felt that abstention was in the best interest of the Navy, sir."

"And did he seem to carry that grudge over when you boarded the *Bellona* under his command?"

"I had so little contact with him because we were so busy preparing for battle that it would be hard to say. I sensed that his attitude towards me was, at best, a bit cool, sir."

"Were you, ...did you have trouble getting the captain into his cabin?" asked Captain Foley.

Whoa! Ben had to tread carefully here. "I am a strong man, sir, as you can see. I had to use some force, yes, but I did nothing that would harm him permanently, sir," replied Ben.

"I see. No more questions."

"Any more questions for Mr. Rundel?"

"There being none, I will invite the council for Captain Williamson to examine Mr. Rundel."

The solicitor representing Williamson had a grand reputation in London, but Ben quickly sensed that he knew nothing of the sea or naval law and could do Williamson more harm than good.

"Now, what exactly happened that convinced you that Captain Williamson was unfit for duty?"

"He seized the helm, threw it sharply to starb'rd, carrying us away from the battle and our opponents, sir, against orders from the flag ship."

"And why did he not simply give the helmsman orders to change course?"

"You will have to ask him that yourself, sir. I believe that he was seized by panic. I saw terror in his eyes as he watched one of our ships which was already engaged lose her mainmast. I believe it was the *Goliath, 74* under Captain Foley, sir."

"And by what authority do you consider yourself competent to judge if an officer, especially your captain, is fit for duty, young sir?"

The question was insolent, but Ben suddenly realized that he had a strong defense in his previous medical training. "I served aboard the *Hawk* for several years as acting surgeon and was surgeon's assistant to Jim Ledyard aboard the *Faithful* for two years." Ben saw some heads nod in approval and a few eye brows shot up in surprise. "On board the *Hawk* I had to deal with a leftenant who had a severe problem with alcohol, and an officer who was facing the advanced stages of syphilis which rendered him poorly suited for duty. I also had to deal with other unpleasant mental disturbances while serving as surgeon. Captain Williamson's actions were in direct disobedience to our orders to, 'come to grips with our opponents,' sir. He was clearly reacting out of panic and a troubled mind. I had no other choice, sir."

Then the solicitor leveled the fatal blow. "And how old are you, son. How old are you really?"

Ben felt his face flush a brilliant red. He knew he was going to have to lie before a court martial, but there was no one alive who could prove him wrong. Hopefully the captains would interpret his embarrassment to the fact that he was a bit young to serve as a first leftenant, even in 'acting' capacity.

"Ben looked squarely at the solicitor. "Seventeen, sir, er sorry sir. I just turned eighteen."

"Hmmmm. No more questions."

Then a parade of officers and seamen from the ship were brought forward. Each were asked questions, usually different. It seemed that they were trying to ascertain whether Ben might have had some buddies aboard ship and whether they had planned to overtake the ship and relieve the captain of his command. But each man asserted that he had only met Ben that day and all seemed contented with his handling of the ship and with his treatment of the men.

One old fellow spoke up after he had answered his question, his cap in his hand, tanned, lined face abeaming and his one or two black teeth showing through the smile. "An 'e was a mighty fine cap'n sirs, that 'e was. 'E led us to two fine prizes, 'e did."

So, finally it was time for the captains to debate. All bystanders were led from the room and the captains each debated. Ben learned later from Captain Bligh that he had handled himself most properly and that the captains were pleased with his ability and intelligence.

"He'll make a fine captain someday, I reckon," said Captain Foley. "We need more young men like him. I didn't realize who he was when he began to speak, but now I remember reading about him in the *Chronicle*. He's the one who saved his shipmates when they were stranded on a French beach near that semaphore, and he swam the Caribbean to get away from a slaver. Then he took three pirate ships and sailed them into Bridgetown Harbour with only ten men. This is no ordinary young leftenant, whatever his age may be."

After two hours, they had completed their deliberations. The sentence was pronounced. It seems that there was some reluctance to beach a man with such social prominence, but in the end, the captains did the right thing. Captain Williamson would lose his commission and would be put on the beach without pay. Ben thought that was a light sentence, at best. But he was connected to an influential family and Ben knew that they would see that he was not hanged or flogged around the fleet. Ben had no idea what they might do to retaliate against those who were responsible for Williamson's loss of his commission.

When Admiral Nelson heard about the court martial, he railed against the lenient sentence given by the court martial. "Upon the general question, that if a man does not do his utmost in time of action, I think but one punishment ought to be inflicted...I would have every man believe, I shall only take my chance of being shot by the Enemy, but if I do not take that chance, I am certain of being shot by my friends." (Hattersley, 1974, *Nelson.*) Ben took these word to heart. He believed firmly in Lord Nelson's strength and righteousness. No one could ever tell him that Nelson spoke more strongly than he would have acted. Ben would not listen.

Shortly after the court martial, Ben wrote to Tom Murphy.

'Dear Tom:

I have just survived an extreme test of my conscience and fortitude, and I have emerged unscathed. We tried Captain John Williamson for cowardice at the Battle of Camperdown today before a panel of the best captains in His Majesty's Navy. Williamson ran from his duty when we were about to engage the enemy. I was put aboard as acting first leftenant, his other two leftenants never having seen action before. I was forced to take control of the ship. You remember how we used to kill fish that we had caught from the quay in Gibraltar? Well, I was a bit more gentle. I believe that the sentence was too lenient. He was stripped of his commission and beached for life with no pay. The only hurt is to his pride since I have learned that he comes from a wealthy family.

The stripping process was impressive. They lined up the entire ship's company on mid decks and paraded the former captain before the men. The Admiral stripped each symbol of leadership from him, his sword, his braid, epaulet, bicorn, gold buttons, the whole bit. We stood by amazed. I told you earlier about how he challenged me to a senseless duel and how I ignored him. I am sure I have a lifelong enemy in the man, but there was no other choice for me.

And dear friend, how is your leg progressing? You should have relief from the swelling by now. If you do not, see the surgeon at once. He may have to drain it. If he does, I expect to hear your screams clear to the Nore. I will sail in a few days on the *Monarch* with Rear-Admiral Onslow. I expect to rejoin the Mediterranean fleet, there being no pressing duty here now that the Dutch fleet has been dispatched. I look forward to spending Christmas Day in your company.

Your Friend Ever

Benjamin Rundel"

Ben did sail with Captain Onslow, but just before the anchor was weighed, he received an order from the Admiralty.

There were the usual long formalities telling about Lord Spencer's heredity and his duties and then the order read,"

'Leftenant Benjamin Rundel is directed to ship on the *Monarch* to the Tagus River Station. There he is directed to go aboard the *Hermione* 32 under Captain Hugh Pigot. He will serve as third leftenant until further notice."

Lord Admiral Spencer'

Ben had heard a little about the *Hermione*, but it would be an interesting tour, he thought. He was to learn differently.

Chapter Seven

Hermione - Hell Ship

The voyage out to the Tagus was peaceful. The men were constantly busy completing repairs of damages from the battle at Camperdown, but she was in all, quite seaworthy. It was early December and most cold. The damp air seemed to penetrate Ben's body, clear to the bone and his foot ached constantly. But he served to relieve Mr. Masterson, the other third leftenant. They got along well and it was an interesting voyage, in spite of adverse south-westerly winds which seemed fickle, not wanting to blow consistently from any quarter.

Ben did not observe his birthday since he did not know the exact date, but sometime in September before the battle he turned eighteen. He had been too busy to even give the matter any thought until now. It would have been different if Tom were there. He always made a lot of Ben's birthdays.

They arrived at the Tagus the day before Christmas. The *Hermione* signaled for Ben to come aboard at once. He picked up his gear and was rowed to the ship. His first impression was that she was not in particularly good condition. She was a frigate used mostly as a courier, traveling often from Portsmouth to the Caribbean.

As Ben stepped through the tumble home, his left foot caught on a carelessly placed rope causing him to trip. His foot was still not fully healed and not as strong as it should be. Ben was embarrassed, but picked himself up and saluted.

"Leftenant Benjamin Rundel reporting for duty, sir," he said to the captain who stood there before him, his face contorted into an unfeeling sneer. The first leftenant, Mr. James Cogson stood close by, his face as blank as a piece of unused parchment.

“Good God! Can’t those idiots at Whitehall send me a decent leftenant for a change. I am sick of these dandy boys who have never been to sea and are in need of their mother’s nursing. An’ this one can’t even stand up. An’ he just fresh out of a court martial to boot.” At that the captain turned away, leaving Ben spluttering and about to explode. He had as strong a record at sea as any man his age and he resented being called a ‘dandy boy’. But leftenant Cogson grabbed him by the lapels, pulled him close and looked at him with fish eyes, his breath foul.

“He ain’t like other captains. Ye best learn right now to accept his abuses or you’ll have the hide burned off of you in no time at all. He’s a mean one, an’ bosun’s mate Collins is a corker with the cat. Be sure of that. Walk carefully, young mister Rundel.” and he threw Ben backwards.

Ben stood back and looked at the officer. His uniform was not clean or neat. Well, Ben could not fault him for that. His own was rarely in acceptable condition. It was a bit rumpled now from being in the boat and from the rain. But Cogson had a strange, flat, cold face. Ben never did see any emotion on his face, not love or hate or pity, that was sure. He seemed incapable of registering emotion. His blond stringy hair hung down from beneath his bicorn and his sallow, white face was unshaven. He spoke to Ben through an unusually small mouth and his eyes were grey, deep set and expressionless.

Ben stepped away, nodding and saluting the man. He was his superior officer, but never had Ben disliked someone so instantly as this fellow. That dislike would grow into pity. He was as helpless as a baby against the captain and he had lost all of his self respect. Ben would come to know why too.

“Mr. Gildersleeve. Take Rundel here below and see that his gear is stowed. We set sail in five minutes.”

“Five minutes, said Ben aloud. I had hoped to get permission to go aboard the *Theseus* to visit with a friend who has been wounded.”

"That'll have to wait. Get to your duty." Then he called, "Man your braces, up anchor, clew up the heads'ls, unfurl the topsl's, the mains'ls." His voice was raspy as if he had been up drinking all night.

Ben was thrown instantly into the tortured life of this new ship. He could not even get a note off to Tom to explain why he had not come to visit. Ben was told that they were off to the Caribbean and would not celebrate Christmas Day.

Failure to celebrate Christmas came as a hard blow to Ben. He had been through a trying ordeal lately, and he felt the need of a bit of Christmas cheer. Even if they did have orders to sail, the steward could cook up something special to bolster the morale of the men, but Ben soon learned that these men had no morale. They walked about the deck like zombies, attending to their duties as best they could, but there was never an enthusiastic, 'Aye, aye, sir,' or a smile. Ben could not understand this ship. He had been aboard happy ships and unhappy ones, but nothing like this one. *Every ship has some handsome young sailor who is full of spirit and loves to sing, dance or just horse around, but there is none of that here.* Within his first two hours, he saw a man stripped to the waist and flogged during a blinding snow storm for not coiling a rope correctly. Ben could see nothing wrong with the way the rope was coiled. When he asked Mr. Gildersleeve why the man had been flogged, he replied, "It's just the captain's way. He will flog a man for nothing at all. He's a hellion, he is."

Gildersleeve was a fat, no, pudgy fellow who would naturally have a smiling face, but his face had become set in a stern grin, his pale complexion suggesting that he had never been to the Caribbean before. He had a short, fat nose, a pouty mouth and curly, unruly brown hair that was greying. *Yet he must be a young man still,* thought Ben.

Christmas day was like any other aboard ship, except that this was not like any other ship. They had some tough salt beef, no gravy, and ship's biscuits. Late in the afternoon, Ben decided to try something. This was by far the saddest group of men that he had ever seen. He knew that a good song had cheered up his lads many times before on other ships, and so, he brought out his balalaika and began to play Christmas carols and sing. Below decks was a tangle of human bodies on any day at sea, especially during the dog watches. Men sat and talked, read letters from home or played games. Mostly these men just sat and rested. Ben began softly with , 'Silent Night'. He loved that carol and it made him lonely for England as he sang it. He had stood outside the tiny church at Saltash and sang that song with the choir. It had been a good time in his life.

By the time he began the strains of 'Deck the Halls' and 'Oh Holy Night,' several lads had joined him and they were singing well together. He smiled at them and they offered timid smiles back. After the third song, when Ben was just warming up, one of the sailors whispered quietly, "I wouldn't sing too loudly, sir. The cap'n don't like singin'."

"But, lads, it's Christmas. Surely he won't deny us a bit of singing on such a festive day. Too bad that we did not have any special victuals today, but they can't take away our song, can they now."

Ben started off on 'The Wassail Song,' when there was a commotion at the companionway. "Let me through, you lubbers. Can't you see that I have my duty to do."

The captain strode over to where Ben was sitting. Ben smiled up at him, full of the joy of the season that he was bringing into the hearts of his men. All of the sailors had gathered around by now, and later Ben would think that the captain had waited until he knew that all of the men would be listening so that he could make his assault all the more painful.

"Good evening, sir and a Merry Christmas to you," said Ben.

"Stop this nonsense at once. The men are not allowed

to sing unless they are at the capstan, do you understand that, Mr. Rundel? Put away whatever that thing is that you have there that makes that plinking sound and see to your duties. I'll have no one singing below decks or, next time, Mr. Rundel, it will be you what spreads his carcass over the grating." At that, the captain started to turn to leave, but Ben was not satisfied. If he could not play laika for the entire voyage, he would be most unhappy. He felt the men would too.

"May we not just sing a chorus or two of 'Heart of Oak, sir?'"

"Did you not hear me, Mr. Rundel! You are not to sing or play anything! His Majesty does not hire the likes of you as an entertainer, a trained seal. Now let that be all that is said." The captain stormed out of the lower deck, black lines tightening in his face making it a horrid mask and his hands working as if he would like to strangle someone.

Ben stood up and stared after the captain. He was not terribly old, perhaps late forties. His stooped shoulders gave him a rounded, defeated look, but his face was lined and grey. *No place there for a smile to sneak in between the hard lines,* thought Ben. His hair had been black or dark brown but was now infused with grey and he limped when he walked, probably an old injury. But the face of the man was that of a stern old man who had never felt warmth or love, quite the opposite to that of Lord Nelson's. While Nelson could not be considered handsome, there was always that lingering hint of a smile on the port side of his mouth that Ben had come to know. And his voice had a pleasantness, an intimacy to it that was most endearing. But Captain Pigot spoke with a harsh growl, the voice of a man who had hawked fish for too long on the streets of London. He would never stir men to love of King and Country, while Nelson affected nearly every man that he met that way. Ben turned to his audience.

"Sorry, lads. I guess we cannot carry on with our celebration. Perhaps some other time."

Little did Ben know that he had unwittingly sewed the seeds of mutiny. Several of the sailors walked away speaking softly. "What did 'e mean by,'Perhaps some other day?'"

"E means that we must get rid of the captain, or we will never be able to sing again like good seamen should."

"Here, here, Jack. That's the talk of mutiny. Ye'll get us all hanged." chided Bill Simms.

"No, lads, I am serious. We 'ave had quite enough of this high-handed Cap'n Pigot. He is not fit to command good sailors like us."

As those things will do, they simmered in the men's minds for sometime, but almost every day there was some incident that would lend strength to their complaints. The men were becoming restless and Ben was well aware of it. When he mentioned it to Captain Pigot as his duty required, Pigot simply pushed him aside.

"No man would dare try to take this ship from me. He knows I'd have 'im drawn and quartered."

And so it went on. There was a flogging at least every other day and the cruelty to the men made Ben certain that the lads at Spithead had been right to complain. He wondered how many captains there were like Pigot in His Majesty's Navy?

One day a fellow stood looking at a frayed line in the standing rigging. The Captain thought that he was staring at him. "I'm not a freak to be stared at, I'll have you know," he shouted, waving his fist at the sailor. He had the man flogged. The fellow, one Peter Muller, died. He had been flogged several times before and he had a bad heart. Ben knew about his heart condition and asked the captain for leniency, but Pigot had him flogged the full twenty lashes any way. When they cut him down, he was already dead. Ben approached him in his hammock the night before and said that he would try to get the captain to forego the punishment. It was then, with seven witnesses standing by, silhouetted against the bulkhead by the light of the single candle, that Peter told them that he was watching a frayed line in the shrouds. "I thought I saw it comin' undone, I did. I weren't lookin' at the cap'n at all." When Ben inspected the shrouds the next day, sure enough, the line had parted and the shrouds were unsafe. The entire structure of the ship depended on the strength of the shrouds. Ben ordered a crew to replace the line, a devil of a task to have to perform at sea.

When the surgeon, one Wendell Morrison, pronounced Muller as 'dead,' Ben ordered that he be laced into his hammock and prepared for burial at sea. The captain saw them on the deck and said, "Throw the lubber over board. The sharks won't even bother with him." But Ben went ahead with the funeral. Old Muller had been aboard that ship most of his fifteen years in the Navy and he had a lot of friends. There would have been mutiny on the spot if he had refused the man a funeral. And through his death, he had alerted the men to a danger aboard the ship, the captain.

Ben was given a lecture the next day for disobeying the captain's order and allowing the funeral to go forward. "And what did you mean by the words, 'and with his death he has alerted us all to a deadly danger on this ship?" Ben explained about the parted line and that he was having it repaired at this moment. The captain said no more, but slowly, day after day, Ben grew in the respect of his men. He could see that the other two leftenants were totally unconcerned with the plight of the men. They were having too much trouble trying to keep their own selves free from the wrath of the captain.

The food aboard was the worst that Ben had ever experienced. The men ate the same thing every day. As the ship's biscuits began to go stale, it was almost impossible to get the food down. Even the leftenant's mess was unacceptable. None of the officers wanted to lay out any money for special food, so the steward simply dished their food right out of the coppers with that of the crew. Ben had eaten better as an apprentice seaman aboard the *Faithful.* He was ordered aboard ship in such haste at the Tagus that he had no chance to procure any special treats.

There were no exquisite suppers with the captain either. He preferred to dine alone.

They were well into the warmer seas now and were headed for the Caribbean. The only joy in Ben's life was the fresh, warm air, the feel of the sun on his back and the wind in his face. In every ship he had ever served in he had found some special friend, someone that he enjoyed talking to, but that was not to be so on the *Hermione*. It seemed that every man was so steeped in hatred and misery that he closed himself off from all others and withdrew to some inner, private place where he could live in his own comfortable fantasy. Ben was never lonelier in his life. He longed for Tagon. At least she would keep him company and warm his hammock at night. Tom was the one he could talk to about all that was going on aboard ship, but he dared not commit much to paper for fear that the captain would find it and have him hung. But gradually, Ben realized that this was truly a mad man and that there had to be some clear record of his misdeeds. It was not his job, but he was certain that neither Gildersleeve nor Cogson had kept any records. So Ben took out a sheaf of paper and began with his first day aboard ship. He was able to recall most of the events of the past two weeks all too vividly. He made careful notes on the death of Muller and several other men. He commented on the quality of food. When the sample of the food to be fed to the crew was brought to him by the cook's mate for approval, his usual comment was, 'inedible or barely palatable'. Ben took great pains to conceal his notes. He had found a lose board in the bulkhead and he was able to slip the paper in such a way that it could not be seen from either side. One side of the paper was quickly filled, then another. Then Ben borrowed another piece from the surgeon, who as usual, was drunk. His excuse was that he wanted to write home. So secret were these men that Ben had not confided in anyone.

On the 12 January, they were sailing along in a good wind. Ben began to see strange fish, especially the sail fish that he remembered from his previous trip across the Atlantic. They were into the Trade Winds now and moving swiftly towards their destination. It was Sunday and usually there was no religious service, in spite of the fact that the muster book listed a 'William Goodwin' as clergyman. Ben had never seen the man and wondered if he had succumbed to a flogging early in the trip for trying to practice his profession. Later he learned that the Reverend Goodwin had been flogged and died for holding services on Sunday.

"The Articles of War specify that they are the only document to be read on Sunday. There is nothing said there about preachin' the gospel. I don't know why Whitehall insists on shipping a clergyman in my ship," was what Pigot said.

The next day four men were flogged for trying to catch fish with baited lines. They were hungry for some fresh food and these waters abounded with fish. Ben could not blame them at all. But the captain took their fishing as an insult and ordered four floggings. That took all of the energy of the three bosun's mates. When they were cut down, Ben went below with them to the sick bay. He began that practice soon after coming aboard. The surgeon was not only unclean, but much of the time unfit to minister to sick or injured men. The crewmen knew that Ben was trained as a surgeon and they welcomed his visits. He cleaned many a cut back, some cuts were clear to the bone where a man had been flogged twice. Ben saw to it that the men were properly treated and commanded several of the loblolly boys to clean up the sick bay. When he had the chance, he joked with the men and tried to win their confidence. He might need them someday. Things were going mighty poorly aboard the *Hermione,* mighty badly indeed. He passed the word to the captain again that the crew was restless and mutinous, but it did no good.

His efforts to comfort the crew and to ease their pain did not go unnoticed. The day the men were flogged for fishing during their off watch, he was heard to remark, 'Is there no freedom that a man can count on aboard this ship?' Most captains would have welcomed the efforts of the crew to provide some fresh fish, but not Captain Pigot.

Now the weather turned warm and they were able to dress lightly. Pigot refused to spread a tarp to shade the quarter deck, so the officers must carry on their duties in uniforms and sweltering heat. Pigot was on deck. Cogson called, 'All hands aloft to reef sails." Pigot turned on his heel and yelled, "And I'll flog the last man off the mizzen topsail yard." The men raced through their duties and two, Ames and Crooks, who were out on the farthest ends of the yards and had the farthest distance to go, jumped over the closer men, but missed their footings and slipped to the deck, to lie limp and dead. Both had been flogged for minor offenses before and both knew that they could not endure another flogging. Yet, theirs was the most dangerous and difficult task that men had to perform aboard ship. The captain's actions were so cruel and unfair that the lads gathered around the two dead men on the deck and a great wail went up from them, these two fellows had been universally liked. Now, they were dead and gone, all for a bit of nonsense, some bravado of the captain. Ben went to console the men, but they were in an ugly mood.

"The least that we can do for these two poor lads is to prepare them a fine burial," suggested Ben. But Pigot overheard him. "Throw the lubbers overboard. {No one will miss 'em!}" (Blake and Lawrence, *Nelson's Navy*)

Ben went ahead with burial preparations and made certain that they each had the proper service read over them. He took charge of the burial services, in the absence of Goodwin. Someone had to do it and it was a cinch that the captain would not be bothered to read the burial service for two unfortunate seamen, dead because of his foolishness.

That night, as Ben went to his tiny cabin to sleep, he was suddenly accosted by two dark figures who stepped out of the shadows. They grabbed his arms and pinned them to his back, none too gently either.

"Hey, what?" exclaimed Ben. "What do you want with me? You know it is against the Articles to manhandle an officer." The men remained silent and pressed Ben into his cabin. They drew the curtain and then held the candle to his face where they could see him.

"It's 'im, alright," said Finch. Ben could see that Jack Tarkington was the first man and Bill Simms was close behind.

"We want a word with ye, that's all. We are not goin' to harm ye," said Finch.

"We wants to thank ye for takin' such good care of our mates today. But there's more. We want to take this ship and make you our captain. Ye 're the only officer what's got much in the way of sense," said Tarkington.

Ben had to blink several times. The light was blinding him and he had dreamed of such an encounter, but never thought that it would happen. But then, as he thought about the events of the past month at sea, he knew that these men had been stressed to their limit. Something was bound to happen, and now it had.

Ben struggled a bit, "Unhand me," he complained.

"Let 'im lose, lads. He ain't goin' ta give us any trouble," said Simms.

Ben was thankful that he had given the problem some thought. "Lads, this is mutiny. It will only get you all hanged. There is a better way."

"What better way can there be? We can't stand any more floggin's and we are dead tired of the rotten food," said Tarkington.

"Ben thought fast. "Well, this is a rather short cruise. I understand that we will call at Barbados and then pick up messages to carry back to the Admiralty. In all, that should take not more than three months, maybe less. And we are almost there so that leaves us with less than two months left. When you lads arrive home, you can apply for hardship discharges. Henry, your mother is sick and

Jack, your father needs you. Bill must go to help a sick sister, and so on. At least that will get you into new ships."

"They'll never buy that for 260 men. We all need to find a new ship an' mighty quick. Some of us have families to return to and they want to see us alive again."

"I understand, lads. But here is something else to consider. We need to put Pigot out of action. You and I know that he is not fit to command a ship, even a small one like this. Can any of you read?"

Simms turned his face up to Ben's. "I can, a little, sir." Ben knew that he was taking a dangerous chance by showing any one but the port Admiral his notes on the events of the cruise, but he must do all that he could to stop a mutiny. If they mutinied, they would probably kill all of the officers, including him. If he lived, he might be able to get these damning notes to the proper authorities. "Here," he turned to his hiding place and pulled out his notes. Hold the candle close so Simms can see what is written."

Simms looked at the notes. Ben had written small so that he could keep the notes condensed, but they were complete enough that if he were to die before they were delivered, they could be read and understood. Simms wrinkled his nose and squinted as he stared at the paper.

"Why it's all 'ere, it is. All the floggin's and even the things that Pigot said. He's got it all."

The other two men looked on approvingly.

"As soon as we make port, I will hand this to the port Admiral. In light of some of the events here, which can only be interpreted as cold blooded murder, he will be forced to detain this ship and to hold a court martial. That will solve your problem for good. The next time you sail, it will be with a new captain."

"That don't mean nothin'. I've sailed with several cap'n's what 's almost as bad as he is." The men looked at one another and shook their heads in agreement. Now Ben knew all was lost. He could not convince them to hold off until he could get help from the port Admiral. *These men have been pushed too far, too long,* thought Ben.

"We needs someone what can navigate the ship, sir. An' the other two officers seem not to know that we exist. The midshipmen too, are so scarred that they scurry about like leetle mice rather than men. They are no good to us, "said Tarkington.

"All right. I will agree to serve as your captain, but not willingly and I will not join the mutiny. I have a fine career ahead of me and if I take part in the mutiny, I will end up dangling by my neck from a rope. You will have to agree to spare the lives of any innocent officers. Cogson and Gildersleeve and the midshipmen, and Morrison have done you no harm."

"They ain't done us no good, either, sir."

Ben noted the 'sir'. They still respected him and he was glad for the little effort that he had made to win their friendship. It could save his life in the dark hours to come. "If you take all of the officers as captives, I will turn them over to the port authorities when we make land."

"We aren't goin' to Barbados. We are tired of the British Navy. We want the Spanish Main. There's gold to be had there."

"Well, I will navigate for you and give orders so you can make the Main, but you will have to keep an armed man with a gun by me at all times when I am on duty. I will do so only under duress," said Ben.

At that the men filed out of the cabin. Ben half-hoped that he had convinced them to forego the mutiny, but late that night he heard a musket fire, then two and several more. They were taking the ship and he was powerless to stop them. He would document the events of the day in his notes, but what else could he do?

By the time that Ben reached the deck, Pigot lay on his back, his cold grey eyes staring unseeing at the night sky. Cogson and Gildersleeve lay beside him. Morrison and several midshipmen had been put to the sword. The sailors hated Pigot so much that they dare not torture him. They were afraid he would recover and come after them with a starter or cat. One sailor picked up his feet and said, "Here mate, give a hand. We'll throw 'im over board to the sharks. No one will miss im." At that there was a great cheer, as if they had done something mighty fine.

Jus' be sure the sharks don't throw 'im back to us as garbage," said another. But they left the other men lying there where they had fallen, along with the bosun and all of his mates. They were hated almost as much as Pigot.

"You good to your word, sir?" said Simms to Ben.

If they only knew how hard it was for me to do this. "Yes. I'll take over as Captain, but for all to hear, I do so not as a mutineer, but as a man who has a gun at his head. You know that I sympathize with your cause, but I cannot accept your methods."

The crew quickly routed out a few more weak bodies, but they left the gunner, cook and sailing master alive. Ben secretly believed that the sailing master did not side with them, but he was never able to coax anything form the old gentleman. He was an old Dutchman and very secretive. He rarely spoke to anyone, including the midshipmen. As a result, their studies languished and few if any had ever passed the leftenant's exam from this ship. That reminded Ben of Tom whom he had promised to assist with his studies. He would too, if the Navy would ever let the two of them stay on the same ship for a little time. He seemed to be constantly flitting about, from ship to ship. And then it came to him. *The Williamson family probably knows about the bad reputation of the Hermione and have probably worked some influence with the Lord Admiral to have me transferred at the last minute from the Theseus to the Hermione. It is their way of getting even with me for having testified against their son at the court martial after Camperdown.* Ben would learn later that this was what really happened, but for now, even without proof, he was certain that they were taking their revenge. The Williamson family thought that he might not survive the cruise, and well he might not too.

The men were in a surly mood. He went immediately to the liquor cabinet and then took all of the keys from the dead purser. He opened the liquor cabinet and managed to stove in most of the barrels before the men caught him. But the smell of wine in the bilges was more than they could endure. They had regularly been denied their daily tot of rum and most of them planned to make up for those deficiencies all at once. There was little Ben could do. He set sea anchor and prayed for fair weather. There was no way he could coax those drunken men into the tops to set or reef sails. He stood by and watched, and planned his next move. He owed some duty to the dead officers. He gave them all burial, but only three sailors stopped by to watch. They were too drunk to know what they were mourning, so Ben let it pass.

Ben's first move, after the liquor cabinet, was to complete his notes on the events that had occurred on this ship since they left port on Christmas day. He could write them out fully now, fit for an Admiral to read, but he wondered if he would ever find an Admiral to read them. Ben sat in the captain's cabin and went to work. He stopped about half way to raid the captain's stores, which were quite complete. He found edible biscuits, some fine cheese, and a bit of jam. Then he returned to his writing. He bolted the door, but outside he could hear the lads raving about the deck. He would give them two days to sober up. Then he would come down hard on them. There was no use trying to sober them now. They were in the heat of a successful mutiny and Ben knew he would have little control of them. But in two days, when they were hungry and the grog had run out, he could get their attention. Ben saw that the cook had joined in with the revelries, and he knew there would be no food served for at least a day. That would be enough. He found some rum stored in the captain's cabin. It would last a few days at standard rations and could be doled out once they were under weigh again.

Ben struggled with the wording of his report. He must be certain that the Admiralty understood the cruelty under which these men had lived, and also the brutality they had used when they made up their minds to take over the ship. There was no justification for making the mutiny sound less serious than it was.

When Ben had finished his reports, he sat back in the chair, stretched his legs and thought for a long time. Had he done the right thing? By staying alive and agreeing to navigate the ship, he might be able to save His Majesty's ship and get her to a British port. But would a group of stuffy captains at a court martial who had never faced a mutiny see it that way? Should he not be better off lying at the bottom of the ocean, cold and dead like the rest? At least he would be free of any guilt. He would probably be accused of mutiny, no matter what he did, as long as he was alive. He would have to do the best that he could. No man could ask more.

Ben went below to check the stores of food for the crew, locking the captain's cabin behind him. There was actually plenty there and he breached a barrel of unusually good quality beef. He found some carrots and cabbage, too. They would not last much longer. He'd see that the men had a good meal when their revelries were over. That should make them easier to handle. He also found some spirits that they did not know about. He would get those moved to the liquor cabinet after this was all over and resume regular rations of grog. That would help morale too.

Then for a time, Ben watched the men. For lads who had been quiet and sullen as a bunch of prisoners a day earlier, they now had turned into a bunch of rowdy, noisy, crazy fools. Men danced on the yards, larked in the rigging and they were singing loudly and terribly off key. One fellow shouted, "I wonder if ol' Pigot can hear that where he is now."

Another replied, "'E can't hear anything down there. "E's a burnin' up. Hot as Hades, 'e is."

There was much talk and some arguing about where they would go and what they would do. The ship was theirs now, and Ben their prisoner. They were free to go wherever they wished.

"Let's go to America. I always wanted to see that country," said one.

"Naw, they'd jus' put us in irons. They don' hold with mutiny any better than our folks do."

"Shut up, you fools. We will sail for the Spanish Main. There's lots of gold to be had there. We'll outfit this old lady as a pirate and we will go find some o' that fine gold fer ourselves," said another.

All that talk about where they would go made Ben wonder where he *could* or *should* go. No matter what happened, he would have to try to escape. It was only a matter of time before they killed him too. Ben could not help but wonder why they had spared him. They had the sailing master and he could navigate and take them anywhere they pleased to go. He knew how to handle a ship. Perhaps they were not too certain of his loyalties. He was a most quiet, stubborn man. He would not take orders from anyone, except the captain.

That night he cooked some of the beef for himself, with carrots and some cabbage. He had a good meal and, in spite of the infernal noise, was soon asleep. The revelers began to quiet down about midnight.

The next day, Ben found that there were still some spirits left in the barrels, but not much. He let the men go about their fun for the rest of the day, but spent many hours in his cabin trying to figure out where he would escape to if they made the Spanish Main. It now seemed that he had no choice but to take them to the coast. They were mostly experienced seamen and any attempt on his part to steer north instead of west would not go unnoticed. He figured that he would take them to La Guaira, a small town on the Spanish Main. He could abandon them almost any place on the coast, but that would afford no opportunity for him to escape. He was pretty certain that once on land, they would hold him prisoner so they could benefit from his navigational skills. He had to find a way to escape. Ben sat and thought for a long time.

But there were other duties too. He made an inventory of all of the captain's belongings and took the liberty to read the two personal letters that he found. After all, if the man had a widow, she should be notified of his death. But the letters were both from fellow captains. There was no mention of a wife or marriage, or even children in any of the documents that he found. Then he procured several large canvas bags from the sail maker, who was a more moderate man than the rest. He was still partly sober. He put the captain's small personal possessions into one of them. The furniture was probably mostly his, but it was most austere, not worth much at all. There was a small chest, a chamber pot, a sword and several uniforms, but no wine or extensive stores of the 'comforts' that most captains took to sea with them. The Admiralty would have to see to finding relatives, if there were any and to the dispersal of his belongings.

Next, he put the belongings of the first mate in a bag and labeled it. He too, seemed to be single and without any immediate evidence of a family. But Mr. Gildersleeve did have a mother and father of some prominent position in Dorset, so he put his things away in another labeled bag. None of the midshipmen had been old enough to be married. One appeared to have had a girl friend, but nothing more than that. He secured all of their belongings so that the crew could not pilfer from the dead men. In their present mood, almost anything could happen.

Lastly, he went to the purser's cabin and found that Mr. Skinner had also apparently been single. His belongings proved most interesting. He carried with him chunks of gold, silver, precious stones, and art work from around the world. There was a crystal ink well and several fine boxes that he assumed were made of teak. Some carved boxes were hidden away. His clothes, too, suggested that he was a wealthy man, although Ben doubted that he was over forty years old. The deck of his cabin had a carpet that might have come from India, with many colours and shades artfully blended together. He preserved as much of the men's belongings as he could and secured them in the captain's cabin.

Next, he decided to move into the captain's cabin permanently. He gathered up his belongings. A plan was beginning to form in his mind. It was vague as yet, but occasionally it took a firm shape. One thing that he knew for certain was that he would try to escape. If at all possible, he would take his most important belongings with him, 'laika,' cutchie, cuppa, flint and steel, sheepie and at least one change of clothes. Books and other clothes might have to stay behind. *Oh, I cannot leave this behind.* His hands came to the fine little book that Captain Bailey had given him sometime ago. It was leather bound and his prize procession. *If nothing else goes with me, this must go.* He placed the important belongings in yet another bag which he did not label and hid it in the captain's cabin. Finally, he put his notes on the events of the voyage, rolled tightly into the lining of his shirt and sewed them there. No matter where he went, the shirt would probably go with him. It was hard to conceal them, but he managed finally. He cursed his lack of sewing skills.

Ben sat back. Had he forgotten anything? He let his head droop forward and he dreamed of Annie there in London, singing her heart out, and dressed as she always was in a pale green gown with dark green ribbons and gold lace. He could see her auburn hair trailing down to her shoulders in lovely, graceful curls and her smiling, oval face glowing with health and youth. How he had loved to watch her every movement, the litheness of her body as the brilliance of her voice soothed his soul. He might never see her again. How could he even hope to get back to England, and if he did, she might have nothing to do with an ex-pirate captain, masquerading as a King's officer. That was where he found himself just then. He had never been more unhappy. He wondered, too, why the crew had spared him? They had the sailing master, Mr. Wendt. They did not really need him. Wendt was old, but he was a fine sailing master and could handle this ship better than anyone else. He was all they really needed. But, did they really trust his loyalty? The sailing master was, after all, a warrant officer, and the very word 'officer,' carried with it the threat of authority. Perhaps they thought that Ben would be easier to handle because he was young and less experienced. He would have to assert his authority and soon, before things got too far out of hand. Ben was aware of talking outside the cabin door and had been half listening to the conversation of the crewmen for the past half hour.

Then a knock came to the door. "Come in. The door is open."

"Pardon, sir, but we are goin' after the money in the ship's safe." The man was reasonably sober and seemed most determined. A press of half drunk, smelly and dirty men waited just behind him. Ben could smell the liquor on their breaths.

"Come on in, Jack. I can't stop you, I suppose," said Ben. They had taken his service sword and his pistols, but they did not know that he still had the sword that he had taken from a pirate some years ago in his sea chest. But a sword would be of little use against so many men. Ben thought of using the cannon against the men, loaded with grape, similar to what he had done aboard the pirate ship, but then he would have no crew and he could not man a cannon or sail the ship alone. He might as well go along with whatever they planned, for the time being. *I need to build their confidence.*

The men rushed in, pushing things aside. They went directly to the safe. Apparently they had been arguing about what to do with the ship. Ben overheard some of their conversation. Every time the discussion came around to turning pirate or even privateer, someone would bring up the fact that they had no money. The men grubbed through their own things in search of money and could come up with barely sixty-two pounds. "How much does it cost to provision a ship like this," asked Simms?

"Dunno," was all the answer he could get.

"I'm sure that sixty-two pounds would not go far to filling our bellies, let alone purchasing shot and powder.

We got a small amount of both aboard, but it won't last long. The gunner, Mr. Hawkins, says that we would spend most of our shot in one good battle. Powder's scarce too."

"So what do we do?"

"Well," said, Tarkington. "A big ship like this must have some money on board, shouldn't it?"

"Should," said several of the men.

"But we killed the purser. 'E's dead an' gone."

"Well, let's go see what is in his cabin." At that the men had rushed off to rifle the purser's cabin, but they found nothing that would do them any good. One man opened his ledgers and looked mystified at the numbers.

"Here, Jack, let me see that." He ran his fingers down the columns. "Hmm." "Looks like we are carrying about 4,000 pounds of goods on board. That means that we need that much to keep her afloat."

"There's nothin' here. Let's try the Captains cabin." said Henry Arnold.

"Yea! Why didn't we think o' that before," shouted several of the men."

"Because the Navy didn't hire us fer our brains, stupid," said Jack.

That was when Ben knew that they would be at the safe. He did not have the key for the safe. He had already tried all that he had. If he had the key, he would have thrown it overboard to keep the sailors from getting at it, but he could not find a key anywhere in the Captain's cabin. He had said as much in his report. Like as not the key was somewhere at the bottom of the ocean with the captain.

The men jostled the safe trying to open it. Ben could not imagine how much money might be there. Four fellows stood there and lifted the safe up and crashed it to the deck, but it did not open.

"That'll never do, Jack. I'll get a pry and we can open it that way."

When the man returned, he was carrying a long pry bar, and soon the men had the safe open. Ben was amazed at how quickly they had opened the safe. *Too bad these fellows have mutinied. They are mighty cleaver. Just the kind of men His Majesty needs for the Navy in the hard years of war ahead.* But he knew that most certainly they would all hang. And he might be forced to join their company as well.

As the safe belched out its papers and coins, the sailors scrambled to sweep them up in their hands.

"This will never do, lads, called Ben. You must appoint someone to count out the money and then divide it into 260 parts so each man has his share. Avast there," he said with such authority that the men instinctively stepped back and let him advance. He looked at Henry Arnold. "You can cipher, can't you?" Ben had noticed that he was often reading from a book and assumed that he had some education.

"Aye, sir."

"Well, we'll all set right here and let you count out the coins into piles of tens and then we'll total them up and divide them equally," said Ben. He swept the desk clear and set the man to his task. Sailors hung on the door and some sat on the floor. Many craned their necks from outside on the deck to watch the process.

"Give here," said Ben as he noticed a few coins in one man's hands. The sailor gave him the coins with the look of a naughty child. "I'm your captain now."

The men were unshaven and were in need of food. They had not eaten in two days. Ben singled out the cook, Mr. Howard Fish. He wondered why the men had not killed him. He was a scurvy sort and was barely worth the powder it would take to kill him.

"Here, Mr. Fish. I have found some good beef in the hold. It's set aside. Rustle up your helpers and get the food up here and feed these men. There's carrots, still good and some sauerkraut and some good ship's biscuits. I want these men fed well. Oh, and a figgy dowdy would go well after a couple days of drinking. Get to it, man."

"The rums all gone anyway," he said under his breath.

"Nothin' else to do but to eat, I suppose," muttered the cook.

Ben went back to the cabin and made his way through the crowd of men. He saw the captain's desk piled high with coins. "We got some 899 pounds here, sir," said Arnold.

"Hmmm... Let's see. 260 men and 899 pounds, that would be...3.49 pounds each," said Ben. He thought. *Monthly pay for an able bodied seaman was only 24s. This would amount to about 14 month's pay for each man. The Hermione has been to sea for over a year. More than likely King George owes these lads 3 pound 49 pence anyway. I should not get into trouble for paying them what is already owed, under the circumstances.*

"Pardon, sir, but we're only 254 men now that the last men have departed this life," said Simms.

"Right," said Ben. "That will be 3.5 pounds each. You parcel it out, Mr. Arnold, if you will. Here, take the muster book and put a dot by each man's name as he collects his money."

"But we will need that for outfitting an' provisioning the ship when we gets to shore," said Tarkington.

"It's fair that each man should get his share, and then each one can contribute his share or whatever he wishes to whatever project you might want to undertake," said Ben.

Ben was amazed when an hour later, the distribution of money had all been seen to and Arnold handed him 3 pounds, 50 pence. At first, he thought to decline the tainted money, but something made him reconsider. "Thank you, Mr. Arnold," he said. He suddenly realized that he would probably have to fend for himself for many weeks, possibly even months before he could find a ship back to England. A little money would come in handy. He had a few pounds left from his last London visit, but it seemed to find ways of being needed in unexpected places and he could definitely use the money. He pocketed the coins and set about completing his business with the men.

Ben was being devious. He wanted the men to have some money in their hands when they reached shore. If they did have money, they would head for the first tavern or cantina they could find. In a night or two, the money would all be gone. Then they would not be able to take the King's ship back out to sea. If the *Hermione* were stranded there at La Guaira long enough, he might be able to get in touch with a British port and have the ship and the men seized. It was a long shot, but it was better than getting himself shot trying to defend the King's money.

"Now, you men are not fit to serve on a pirate ship. Look here, your shirt is filthy," as he slapped one chap on the back. "And look at that moth-eaten beard. I want you men cleaned up for supper. It will be served in about an hour. Then we will turn in for the night. I will arrange sailing orders and we will resume watches tomorrow at 6 a.m. We sail for La Guaira tomorrow, unless you tell me otherwise." A cheer went up from the crew. They were already bored with a life of revelry and idleness. It suited them well to get back to their duties. They brought out the pumps and began to wash.

The ship's bell and watches had all ceased to exist since the mutiny began. Ben took care of the chronometers, but that was all that was necessary. There was a bit of grumbling, but the men were tired and the thought of food and sleep was a pleasant thought just then. Ben realized that he was tired and needed some food too. He would have to put up with Fish's cooking for a few days. He figured that they were 1800 miles east of La Guaira. They should make it, with luck, in about ten to twelve days. But the winds had been fickle, blowing lightly when they blew at all. It might take longer.

The next morning Ben arose early. He met his men on the deck milling about. *This will never do,* he thought. "Mr. Arnold, I am appointing you as acting first leftenant." Arnold was a good lad and Ben felt that he could depend on him. But he also knew that Tarkington would be angered by not getting the second position of command.

Tarkington was the son of a minister in Lancashire, one of twelve sons, and he showed such little interest in his studies that his father, in despair, sent him off to sea as a midshipman aboard the ship of one of his parisioners. Tarkington lasted less than a week as midshipman and was promptly demoted to apprentice sailor. His career progressed no further in ten years and he was still a poor sailor and definitely not to be trusted as an officer. But Ben had to do something with him.

"Mr. Tarkington, you will be the main spokesman for the mutineers. You will consult with me whenever there are problems. Is that clear?"

"Aye sir." Tarkington appeared to be contented with his new duties. Ben was pleased because as spokesman, he had no authority or responsibilities, yet he could bask in the limelight and accept his fellow's approbations. "Mr. Simms, you will act as second leftenant. Basically, you will forward my orders to the crew and will stand watch when I cannot be on deck. Any questions."

"No sir."

"Have Mr. Hawkins pipe the men to order on deck by division as usual, Mr. Arnold, if you please." The *Hermione* was too small to rate any marines during war time, so Ben had no police force to aid him.

Night still gripped the ocean, but the sun was trying to intrude as a thin sliver of reddish light on the eastern horizon. Ben looked at his men lined up in the waist. They looked clean, reasonably well-shaven and ready for duty. He addressed them.

"Gentlemen. I have been asked to serve as your captain. I do so under protest for I cannot join your mutiny, although I understand and sympathize with your griefs and complaints. We will proceed from here to La Guaira as you have requested. We will maintain British Admiralty standards and conduct until such time as you take over the ship at La Guaira. There must be order aboard any ship, and a well-run British ship should cause none of you grief. We will operate on watches as usual, eat at the usual times and observe the proper address when speaking to an officer. You may set up your own rules when you organize yourselves later on. Also, I have taken over the captain's cabin and it is off limits to all seamen, except by my permission to enter. I warn each and every one of you, I will flog a man who violates ship's rules. You know what they are and have heard them read many times. I will be fair, but I will punish any man who presumes to step over the line. Is that clear?" Ben had put all the depth and authority he could into his young voice. After all, he was only eighteen. Most of these men were old enough to be his father. It was awkward for him to assume command, but he must do so, if only to save his own life.

No one seemed to object to his maintaining British discipline aboard, as long as he did not go too far, was what Mr. Simms told him later. But Ben knew that the next few days would be some of the most difficult of his life. He would be walking on a bed of eggs, trying to break none. There were many men aboard who would like to challenge his authority and some who would try anything to get him into trouble with the rest of the crew. Some would step out of line just to try him. Would he really order a flogging? Tarkington was the first that Ben watched. He would like to be captain, but had not enough knowledge to know where to begin. He saw Tarkington watching his every move, studying him, as it were. He knew that sometime in the future, Tarkington would try to dispose of Ben and take over his position as captain. Simms had hinted as much.

Calm seas were a blessing. Ben went to considerable trouble to find decent food aboard ship for the men. He even contributed large amounts of food from the captain's meagre store to help make the men happy. It was just too bad that Captain Pigot had no wife and was not predisposed to maintain a good larder aboard ship.

The first day passed with no incident. Ben rearranged the watches so that certain trouble makers would come in less frequent contact with one another. *So far, so good.*

Ben set course for La Guaira and let the two officers, mutineers, know that he was sincere in taking them to their destination. But he spent as much time as he could looking at the charts. If he left them at La Guaira, he would have to make his escape from there. British ships did not call at the Spanish Main and he could see no way of getting free of the mutineers. The nearest British ports were some great distance from the Main and he could not see how he could get to even Barbados, which was one of the closest. The more that he studied the maps the more he felt trapped. If he took a small boat, he would certainly be smashed to pieces by the surf off the coast of South America. He could not hope to go on foot north up through Central America. It was too far. He would have to row or walk, as the case might be, all the way to America. And where would he find a British ship there? Certainly not until he had gained the Louisiana Territory, and then not likely. His only hope was to walk east, along the coast of Venezuela to a point near Trinidad. But he had no idea what type of ground he would have to cover. Were there mountains or was it jungle or swamp? He could not tell. He had never sailed off the coast of the Main. The closest he had ever been was Curacao, but it was an island and not likely to resemble what was on the mainland. He was certain that he would have trouble handling a small boat on the coast. He would have to come in and out through the surf and that could be impossible for one man alone. His only hope was to walk east to a point where he could get a fishing boat to Trinidad. From there he could island hop to Barbados.

With that decided, he looked for the presence of settlements along the Venezuelan coast, but the charts were for ocean going vessels and told almost nothing of the coastal towns, unless they were of considerable size. East of La Guaira was San Jose de Rio Chico. That posed another problem. He might have to get across rivers where there were no bridges. The maps showed no rivers at all, not even the larger ones. There was another place called Puerto La Cruz and just before it Barcelona, but both looked to be tiny villages. Beyond that was Cumana and Carupano which was on a long peninsula. It pointed directly at Port of Spain, Trinidad. At the tip of the point was a small village of Macuro on the Golfo de Paria. There must be fishing boats that would go out from there. He had a little money and that should suffice to buy him supplies. Certainly he could get passage on a fishing boat to Trinidad. It looked like the end of the peninsula and Port of Spain might be 40 or 50 sea miles apart. Getting from Cumana to Curupano would require walking inland some distance since there was a peninsula there and he would have to walk many miles to go around it. Once he reached Rio Caribe he would be in good shape. Ben looked at the meagre charts daily and tried to find a better way to escape, but none was apparent. He memorized the location of the few towns that were mapped there and steeled himself for a tough walk of perhaps 360 to 400 miles. *That should take me about 20 to 25 days,* he thought. But the unknown far outweighed the known, and he was prepared to do whatever was needed to win his freedom.

The second day went well. They were sailing slowly because the winds were light and they had to tack frequently. The next day Ben spotted some sailors working on a skull and cross bones flag, a pirate flag. "You don't intend to fly that out here, do you?" he asked.

"Why, sir, we 'as taken the name of the 'Bloody Brits,'" an' we sure do plans to fly our flag, jus' as soon as we get 'er stitched up."

Ben went directly to Tarkington. "You surely do not want to fly a pirate flag until the ship is ready for service. Out here we may spot a British ship any day, headed for Barbados. If they see a pirate ensign at the tops, they'll not hesitate to open fire. We'll be blown out of the water. We are the smallest frigate that His Majesty has. We cannot fight. Our only hope is speed to run away from an overwhelming enemy. And, Mr. Tarkington, our bottom is badly fowled. We could never outrun a British ship."

"We got powder an' shot, don't we?"

"Yes, but powder is in short supply. You would not last more than half an hour and your guns would be out of powder. Old Pigot was not one for taking care of details," said Ben.

"All right. We'll stow the plans to fly our flag until we reach La Guaira, but you jus' watch us then."

The next day was as fine a sailing day as a man could wish for. But early in the afternoon, the lookout shouted, "Deck there, Sail ho to the nor'west."

Ben shouted back, "can you make her out?"

"I think she's a British frigate, sir."

That was all Ben needed. If they were questioned by a British frigate captain, he would have to tell the truth, with the certain loss of his life. Tarkington and several others carried guns in their belts constantly. One improper word from him and he would lie bleeding on the deck. He went to the cabin to look up their challenge and answer for the day. It might be best if he issued the challenge. With the midshipmen gone, there was no ensign to bend on the flags. Ben would have to do it himself. He prepared to fly the ship's number and the challenge for the day. It took him some time since he had not worked with signal flags for awhile. Simms stood by, eager to see what he was doing. The British ship was drawing closer. "She may be one of those ships sent out to catch the pirates that are damaging British shipping. If we do not respond, she will become suspicious and think we are a French ship or a pirate hiding from them. This way, if I fly the challenge for the day, they will answer and all will be well. We don't want them to come nosing aboard now, do we," said Ben. Simms shook his head, content that Ben knew what he was doing.

The British ship hoisted the correct answer, but still came on, heading to meet them in about an hour. Ben was worried. What if their captain had dispatches for Pigot and wanted to come aboard. He could not produce a Captain Pigot from the grave and he had no idea how to proceed. The other British captain would be in peril for his life and would certainly be killed if he came aboard. Ben would die too. There was no way to warn the ship of the impending disaster. Many of the sailors knew some of the signals, enough that he dare not fly, 'ship in distress'. They had seen the signal for 'mutiny' many times at Spithead during that mutiny. Ben did not dare to fly a flag signal that would warn the approaching ship of the mutiny aboard. There was nothing to do but to wait. If the captain insisted on coming aboard, Ben would try to get a boat in the water ahead of him and would try to meet him on his own deck, but that would put him in danger. The British ship would not be cleared for action, not while approaching another British ship. Ben was glad that he had convinced Tarkington not to fly the pirate flag or they would surely be in for trouble. The ship's guns had never been deshotted since the beginning of the mutiny and Ben realized too late, that he had made a mistake. He should have ordered them deshotted at once as a precaution against such an encounter with a British ship. Now, the men would not follow his order to disarm the guns. They felt threatened and he could see in their eyes, a solemn resolve to stand and fight rather than be hanged for offenses that they felt were not justly deserved under Pigot. He must avoid an encounter at all cost. If these men really saw themselves as pirates, they would not hesitate to take the British ship, even if she was of 50 guns and if they were outnumbered by four to one. *They must not fire a gun.*

Ben watched, a great lump in his throat as the ship grew nearer. Then quite to his surprise, a man on the deck picked up a speaking trumpet and shouted, "Give my regards to my brother, Tom Parsons,"

Ben shouted back, "That I will, sir." Tarkington stood two feet behind him with his musket cocked and hidden under his shirt. Ben knew that there were several other muskets trained on him too.

At that, the British ship veered off to the northwest again and went on its way. She was the *Widow.* The last recorded captain was a Captain Wilbur Parsons. Ben breathed a sigh of relief and stood by the rail, his head in his hands. That had been too close for comfort.

On Sunday, Ben refrained from reading the Articles. It could only rouse resentment and start trouble again. But in the afternoon, he did order the cook, Mr. Fish, to make a figgy dowdy as a dessert and he brought out the last of the preserved plums for the feast. He also brought out 'laika,' his balalaika, and sat on the deck for several hours. Soon the men came by, all smiles now, and sat beside him. Some sang. He started with the Russian songs that he loved so well, but the men did not know these. He soon switched to good old English and Irish aires that they knew and loved. It was hard to think that he was sitting here singing and smiling at a group of men who only a few days earlier had found no problem with killing the captain and officers of this ship. But, music soothes the soul and Ben thought that the men were happier and more willing after they had spent this time together.

He had to have their confidence for a little while longer, until he could make his escape.

The next day went well, but the day after, the men were getting restless. About midday, a fight broke out midships. It seems that Mr. Simms gave an order to Wally Fleece, one of the men that Ben distrusted from the start. He was unreliable and likely to cause trouble. Fleece was one of those lads who always had a marlin spike handy and would quarrel with anyone who would give him the time of day. He would stick the spike in a man's eye until he screamed and then stand back with a laugh. Most of the men were on to him by now, but his new watch had not figured him out yet.

He mistreated Hugo French and called him a, 'meddling Frenchman'. But French was not of that country and he took exception to being mislabeled. When Mr.

Simms came up to stop the ruckus, he ordered Fleece to get back to his duty where he belonged. But Fleece refused, saying that, "Smart Mr. Simms 'ere. You can't go giving me orders. You're a common sailor man just like myself."

He snapped his suspenders and strutted about. Then he belted Simms a good one beside the head with his marlin spike. Simms went down and there was a little blood, but no harm done. The real harm was in the breach of discipline. About then Ben came on deck and spotted the trouble. He walked up to the party and asked what was the trouble, reaching his hand out to help Simms back to his feet.

"It seems that Mr. Fleece has been fightin' with Mr. French and refused to go to his duty when I told him to, sir."

Simms omitted the part about hitting him behind the ear with a marlin spike. "Thank goodness it was not a belaying pin, Mr. Simms, or you might have been seriously hurt," said Ben. Ben had no choice but to call for some of the hands to take Fleece below and put him in irons. He did not have a clue if they would do it or not. After all, he was their shipmate and they were a ship technically in mutiny. But several of the lads had seen what happened and, feeling that Fleece had overstepped his bounds, grabbed him and hustled him below. As the surly face went past Ben, he got a strong whiff of rum. The man must have hoarded rum from the period after the mutiny and was now mostly drunk. Drunkenness was against the Articles, also. But Ben seriously doubted that he could use the Articles to punish the man. They were technically no longer British seamen but mutineers. On the other hand, he had to show some discipline and fighting among themselves was not permitted even on the worst of pirate ships. Certainly attacking an officer would never be tolerated even by pirates.

Ben thanked Simms for his courage. "You did the right thing, lad," said Ben. He examined the wound. It will not give you any trouble, Mr. Simms. Carry on. Then he turned to go below to check on Fleece. The men put him in irons properly and Ben held the only key that would set him free. He had threatened a flogging if any man stepped out of line. Was he going to have to live up to his boast? He walked up to Fleece and smelled his breath. There was no doubt. The man had been drinking. Ben had reinstated their daily tot of rum and the men had seemed amazed that he could do so when they believed that they had drained every drop of liquor aboard the ship. They considered him somewhat of a magician when he produced the first cog of rum and added some lime juice to it. But this man smelled of *wine.* The men had drunk all of the wine that was aboard ship right after the mutiny.

"Did you save up some wine to drink after the ship sailed?" said Ben.

The man looked at his feet, somewhat confused and said nothing. "You know it's against ship's rules to hoard spirits," said Ben. He had to be careful not to push ship's rules too hard because it was the harsh interpretation of those rules that had caused the mutiny in the first place.

"Yes, sir," answered the surly youth. The fact that he had been put in irons seemed to have quieted him down a good bit. Ben wondered if he had caused the ruckus just to test whether he would give the man a flogging or not.

"You have anything to say in your own defense," queried Ben.

"No sir."

"You will be flogged tomorrow at noon. You understand why you are being flogged?"

"Aye." His voice was hollow and sounded tired.

So now, there was no bosun's mate and who would make a cat ? Ben did not have an idea whom to ask. He finally decided on using a length of knotted rope. It would work as well. He could not do the work of twelve officers, bosun's mate and still sail the ship. Ben never felt more alone in his life. He missed having other men in command to talk to. There was no one who could sound out the mood of the men. Were they going to shoot him if he ordered a flogging as he had promised he would? Ben decided to talk with Tarkington.

"Jack, you know that even a pirate ship has rules. One of those is that there is to be no fighting among the men while at sea. I know. I served on a pirate ship once. You know that I'll have to flog Fleece for his striking Mr. Simms."

"We wuz talking about that a while ago, sir. 'E deserves a floggin' and I am surprised that Pigot had not killed him long ago." Then he added, smiling a bit as he shuffled his feet. "We choose you fer cap'n 'cause we knowed you had served on a pirate ship before. You'll make a fine pirate cap'n, you will, sir."

So that is it. They had spared me because they want me to lead them in piracy. That would never do. Ben had the heart of a stout British subject, no matter how humble his birth. He could not bring himself to lead this rabble to piracy and get them all hanged for his efforts. He was more determined than ever to pull away from the mutineers as soon as he could. He worked on his plan of escape that night, trying to foresee every hurdle just as he had when he was a small boy at the orphanage, trying to escape to avoid the work house. He had made that escape work and he had to do the same this time. He reduced the rum allotment the next few days, saying that supplies were running low. No one had the keys to the rum closet but him, and no one seemed to question it when he pretended that there was a nearly exhausted supply of spirits. If his idea worked, the men would head for the nearest cantina when they dropped anchor at La Guaira and would soon be stoned drunk.

He thought about the execution of a flogging. There were no marines, no surgeon, no captain as such. He was duty bound to refuse to flog if there was not a surgeon aboard. They had foolishly killed the surgeon. Even though he was not of much use, he could have helped them in future when men were wounded. But Ben could not use that excuse. It would look like a weak way to avoid his duty. Besides, he had served as a surgeon's mate for sometime and then as acting surgeon. Some of these men knew that. He was as well qualified, perhaps better qualified, than old Morrison was to administer to these men.

The next day at noon, Ben called for, "all hands to witness punishment." The absence of a bosun was a continual nuisance. He had to give the order to Simms and then hope that he could get the men to comply. Ben threw the starters overboard when they sailed after the mutiny as a sign that he intended not to use unnecessary punishment. When the men assembled in the waist, he spoke to them.

"You know that on board any ship there must be a certain amount of order. You want to be pirates. Well, I can speak as having served in a pirate ship. Strict discipline is maintained at all times at sea. Fighting among the men is forbidden, except on land. I must warn you that fighting aboard ship can lead to total loss of the ship and all hands."

Ben stretched the truth considerably there. The discipline aboard a British ship was far more stern than aboard a pirate ship, but they did not know that. He needed to justify his punishment of Fleece.

"I will read the articles which apply during war time to all British ships. This is still a British ship, gentlemen," he said.

Ben read Articles 22, 23 and 33, all of which bore on maintaining the discipline aboard ship. Ben was sure that his reading of the Articles would result in a great outcry against him, but none came. He stepped back and looked Fleece straight in the eye. "Do you admit to being drunk, fighting and hitting a fellow officer?"

The man hung his tousled, yellow head and muttered, "Yes sir," through tight lips. His face was heavily pockmarked and he had pale skin, not like a seaman.

"Do you understand why you are being flogged," asked Ben.

"Aye, sir. Jus' do it an' get it over wifh."

But Ben was not through with him yet. He turned to the men. "Do any of you think that this punishment is undeserved? If so, speak up now."

There was a slow rumble among the men, but no one stood forth and spoke for Fleece. He was hated and the men would be glad to see him flogged.

At that, Ben turned to Fleece who was tied spread eagle onto the grating and leveled 24 stout blows at his skinny back. Ben flinched with the first blow. He had never ordered a flogging before, let alone administered the blows. It brought back the agony of his pain when he was flogged as a boy aboard the *Faithful* for neglecting his duty when he was first learning to read. The adventure story had so gripped his young fancy that he had been unable to put it down. Now, he was inflicting pain on another man, but for a just cause.

When the flogging was over, he cut the man down and administered to his wounds. He could only pray that nothing more would happen to occasion a flogging because the men were not in any mood to stand for a flogging each day as they had with old Pigot. But no one complained about what he had done. They knew justice when they saw it.

The rest of the voyage went without incident, except on the eleventh day they spotted a sail on the horizon. Ben watched it for sometime and concluded that she was Spanish. *Not surprising for these waters,* he thought. Ben saw Jack Tarkington stride confidently to the signal lanyard and run up the skull and cross bones. It was appropriate now. There was little he could do to stop it. With the British flag in these waters, the pirates would blow them out of the water.

On the fourteenth day they sighted the port of La Guaira. Ben was delighted at his luck in making the landfall just as he had predicted. Those days drifting at sea could have put him off by a good bit, but he was lucky. As soon as the land was sighted, he went to his cabin and locked the door. He pulled out the canvas bag which held the belongings that he wanted to take with him. He went through the items one by one. He did not really need 'laika,'" but he could not bring himself to jettison it or leave it for the mutineers. He had a good flint and steel which had not rusted, and several shirts, socks, a small coat and 'cuppa, cutchie,' the knife that he had found aboard a derelict fishing boat when he was a boy, and 'sheepy'. *That is too much, too heavy,* he thought. He set the bag down. It was not really heavy, but if he were to drag it with him for twenty days or more, it would soon become a burden. He bolted onto the deck and found a piece of stray rope. *A good ship would never have rope lying around that is not in use,* he thought.

He took the rope below and cut two pieces long enough to go completely around his canvas bag, with some extra left over. That made a sort of back pack of the bag. He checked the rolled documents telling of the event that led up to the mutiny and made his last entries, explaining that he intended to flee from the mutineers late that night. He found some oiled cloth that he could wrap the notes in to keep them from getting wet. He sewed the documents back into the lining of his shirt, although they were quite bulky by now and could be easily found. Then he wrapped the shirt in the oiled cloth and put the bag away. He was about to pull the strings tight to fasten the bag when he realized that he had no food, He made for the pantry and found a couple of handfuls of ship's biscuits, some cheese and a small jar of jam. They were all he could find that would fit in the sack. He had made certain that his money, some twenty pounds, was securely put away as well, leaving a few pounds in his pocket to pay for his dinner that night.

Then, just before he gave the order to drop anchor, and furl all sails, he strode over to the ship's boat and put the sack in the cuddy, well out of sight of the men. He could only hope that they would decide to use this boat for going ashore. He would have to make certain that they did. As always, Tarkington was watching him, but Ben was certain that he had not seen the canvas bag that he had slipped into the boat. Fleece was lurking a ways off, as if he wished to say something to Ben, but he had too much to attend to with making port and securing the ship.

Once they had come to anchor, Ben ordered the port gaskets to be put in place and the ship to be guarded by two men. He chose two older men who were not much for drinking and offered them each a bottle of the captain's wine, if they would agree to guard the ship while the rest went ashore. He figured that they would both drink just enough to pass out by the time he chose to make his exit. They were the least likely to side with the mutineers and Ben thought that they would serve his needs best, if worse came to worse.

Ben ordered the boats lowered. It was already growing dark and there was a sprinkling of lights on the shore from houses. The men were like children let out to play. They could not get things done fast enough to be on their way. *Rationing their rum may have had some effect,* he thought. They vied with one another for hold of the ropes to lower the boats in the water and they clambered in like a bunch of rowdy boys off on a picnic, often overloading the boats. One boat did capsize, but they managed to right her and get ashore, minus an oar. Ben's earlier concerns were unwarranted. The jolly boat was hoisted out for shore duty, along with every boat there was aboard. Several men would be kept busy for half an hour ferrying men to the shore. Ben left early. There was nothing left for him here and he was hungry. He followed the straggling line of men to the nearest cantina. Tarkington was right behind him. He knew that his loaded pistol was there too. He would have to take care.

At the cantina, *The Sea Breeze,* the men lined up at the bar and were ordering drinks. Ben decided to take a table near the back door. That might afford him a chance to slip out later on when the men were drunk. He hailed a dark-skinned girl who was serving and asked her to bring him something good to eat. He was famished.

About half an hour later, she reappeared, balancing a tray of wonderful smelling food on her hand held high above her head to make it possible to move through the writhing sea of smelly bodies. There was already a goodly group of men there who looked to be pirates. Ben had removed any proof of his naval command and looked like a well-dressed sailor. *Not a man here would not gladly slit my throat if he knew who I really am,* thought Ben. He could only hope that none of his shipmates would give him away. That was always a possibility, even innocently as they related how he had brought them to the Spanish Main. He would be shot on the spot if they knew who he really was. One of His Majesty's leftenants just does not drop into a pirate port and sit down casually in a pirate bar, not one with a name like, '*The Gold Coast*' or the '*Skull and Crossbones*' which he had seen further down the road.

The food was unbelievably good. He was glad not to be a drinking man, for once, although he did order a bottle of beer. He had to keep up the pretense of drinking in order to lull the mutineers into ignoring him. He would nurse one bottle all night long. But then there was the food. He ate pieces of chicken cooked in a fine sauce with pine-apple chunks and a bowl of a strange dark rice with raisins that tasted wonderful. Then there was a soup with turtle in it and dark bread that made him more hungry the more that he ate. He could not guess when his next good meal might show up, so he ate heartily, ordering a second of the banana flan that the girl brought him.

Ben ate ravenously at first, for he was hungry from the exertions of the day. But he soon realized that this would be a long night and that he would benefit from eating more slowly. So, he sat back and ate more leisurely, savouring every bite. When he had finished the meal, he leaned back in his chair to watch what was happening in the cantina. More sailors from another ship had come in.

The little cantina rang with a babble of loud Spanish and English. *It will not be long before a good fight brakes out.* He had seen many a fight at the cantina on La Isla when he had been forced to serve in a pirate ship. Already small knots of men were arguing furiously, fists shaking and heads bobbing vehemently. He would try to escape as soon as a good fight broke out.

Meantime, he rethought his strategy concerning drink. He did not like to drink and he certainly would not try to escape if he had been drinking too much. But, he did not see many streams on the map that he had of the local coast. He might have trouble finding water to drink. Often in these countries the water was not fit to drink anyway. He could get nothing at the cantina except *cerveza.* Perhaps he would try to pick up some empty bottles from other tables to make it look like he had drunk a good deal. If he pretended to be drunk, the mutineers would ignore him.

In the midst of his planning, a fight suddenly broke out. It was on the far side of the room, but Ben could see Wally Fleece in the midst of it. He was not surprised. He waited a few seconds to see if it would develop into a real fight, and it seemed like there would be a general free-for-all between the Spaniards and English. Ben looked at Jack Tarkington. He was standing on the sidelines, watching the fight. He did not seem to be watching Ben. *This is it,* he thought. He got up, carrying his bottle of beer with him and went slowly towards the head. He was just about to pass by the door and strike out on his own when he felt a cool piece of steel against his cheek. Jack was there, his beady eyes condemning Ben.

"I was just planning to pay a visit to the head, Jack. Come now, you would not deny a lad that, would you?"

Jack said nothing but followed him into the head to assure that he would return. On his way back to the table, Ben picked up two mostly empty bottles of beer and set them on his table. He would play the part of a drunkard anyway, even if he was too smart to overindulge.

For the rest of the evening, Ben sat there and watched Jack. Jack sat at a table on the other side of the room with some of his ship mates and watched Ben. He looked towards Ben every five minutes, sometimes more often. That meant that the most Ben could hope for was a five-minute lead. That was not enough. He needed time to retrieve his gear from the jolly boat. If worst came to worst, he could pretend to leave and hide behind the head and hit Jack over the head with a bottle as he passed by in search of him. He had to think clearly. There were so many factors to consider. If all of the ship's crew came running after him, he would not have a chance. He had to wait until most of the crew, including Jack Tarkington, were dead drunk. They were making good progress, but he must be patient yet awhile. Ben wished that whomsoever his parents had been, they had allotted him a greater portion of patience. He seemed sorely lacking in that particular virtue.

He leaned back further, tipping his chair on its two hind legs. A pirate came by about that time and thought to have some fun. He kicked the two back legs of Ben's chair out from under him so that he came crashing to the floor. With most men, that would have started a fight, but Ben had a bigger agenda and would not be baited so easily. He lay there mumbling for a minute or two. Then he got up, acting as if he had been so drunk that he had fallen out of his chair. He put a silly grin on his face and set his chair back up, regaining the seat with some difficulty. The evening wore on. The noise was getting louder. The men were quite drunk by midnight, but not yet drunk enough.

Some men began to disappear up the hill with some of the women from the cantina. Ben could hear some strains of Caribbean music away in the distance. It sounded beautiful and inviting, almost romantic. But he must endure this mess a bit longer. Just before 2 a.m., when the cantina closed, another fight broke out. Two men wanted to accompany the same woman home. One drew a knife and the fight was on between two pirates. Ben surveyed the room. Jack was well into his cups, his head sunken down onto his chest. The other crewmen were either drunk and snoring on the floor or so bleary eyed that he doubted that they could even see him. Ben had not seen Jack glance his way for almost twenty minutes. Some of the men were too far gone to even pay any attention to the fight. Well, this had to be it. He was certain that they would confine him to the ship tomorrow when they sobered up and he would have no means of escape.

Ben arose slowly, walked cautiously towards the door, still carrying a half-full beer bottle. He had purchased two full bottles earlier that evening, thinking to take them with him for drinking as he made his escape to the east. They were tucked into the front of his shirt, along with two loaves of fine French bread. The room was smoky, stinking of sweat, beer, wine and urine. A terrible mixture of odors assailed him, rising up from the heat of so many bodies. He could not wait to get out of there. He stepped cautiously towards the door, his eyes ever on Jack. The fight was getting well under way. He saw all eyes that still could focus riveted on the two men who were circling each other with knives drawn. Ben was not about to wait to see which one won the fight. As soon as he reached the outside, he breathed deeply and began to walk briskly towards the quay. The bottles clinked lightly in his shirt. He put one in back to stop the noise. He did not want to draw attention to himself.

As he approached the quay, he looked back to see if anyone was following him. There were only two love birds rolling beside the road. *So far, so good.* As he approached the quay, he noticed that there was a sailor in the jolly boat. *It looks like old Pat T. Brown.* By the looks of the bottles in the water and lying on the deck of the boat, he had been kept well-supplied by his buddies that night. The old man was sound asleep, dead drunk slumped over in the stern , his upper body resting on the tiller. Ben saw something shiny lying on the bench before him. It was a ship's pistol, with the bag of shot and a flask of powder. The old man was prepared for any trouble, but had not been able to stay awake. Ben climbed cautiously into the boat, trying not to cause it to rock. He reached into the cuddy and pulled out his bag. Thank heavens it was still there. Then he stood looking for a minute at the sleeping figure. If ever there was not a mutineer or a pirate, this was the man. He had the look of a whiskered cherub as he lay there, his hands clasped together. Ben debated. He would have to take two steps to get to the pistol and powder. He knew he could not do that without rocking the boat some. If the old man awoke and was startled, he would surely reach for the pistol and shoot Ben. Ben somehow doubted that he would kill anyone if he had time to think about it. He was too gentle and kind a soul. It was a big risk, but a pistol might help him out of some scrapes in the days to come. It could be useful for obtaining food too. But he was wasting time. He reached into his shirt and withdrew the two beer bottles, setting them on the quay with his canvas bag. Then, balancing as carefullly as he could, he stepped over one bench and set his foot on the bottom of the boat. He looked back towards the cantina. The lights still shone and the place was exploding with sound, shouts, screams, blasphemies, suggesting that the fight was still going on. No one was approaching the quay. Ben lifted his other leg over the next bench, setting it down so that there was only a gentle rocking of the boat. He reached for the gun with his right hand, and swept up the powder flask and balls with his left. *So far, so good.* Now he had to back up. That was going to be harder than moving forward had been. He swiveled on one foot, balanced for a second and gave a leap onto the quay. As he landed, he looked at the old man. He still slept peacefully, totally oblivious to what was happening. "Good bye, old friend," Ben whispered. He had liked the old man and would do nothing to harm him. He tucked the pistol into his trousers and put the powder and shot, with the bottles into the bulging sack. Then he swung the sack onto his back and headed off down the beach, east, ever east.

Chapter Eight

The Long Voyage Home, One Foot After The Other

The events of the next several months so touched Ben Rundel that he told it to me in his own words, often stopping to hold back tears of remembrance.

"I walked on slowly at first so as not to draw attention to myself. The night was clear and cool, birds and crickets sang and there was a smell of fragrant flowers in the air, a pleasant release from the stench of the cantina. I looked out to the bay, to where the *Hermione* was anchored. There was *my* ship. If things had been different, she would have become my ship too. I did not dislike the men all that much. They had suffered severely and were not really themselves. How I longed to take that ship and sail it to Barbados, some four hundred miles away. But I alone could not even weigh anchor, or set sails and man the lifts and helm. One man could not sail a 32 gun ship. Even if I could convince the two older men who were aboard to help me, which I doubted, the three of us could not handle so large a ship. Sailing a three master was clearly the job of a full crew, a team effort as Lord Nelson would say, not the work for one boy. I could not be blamed for abandoning King George's ship under the circumstances. All that I could do was to get word to the port Admiral at Barbados that she was close by and hope he would send a ship to capture her. I watched her, a thing of beauty with the full moon shining down though her yards. She rode lightly in the water, sparkling ripples passing by her hull, shining from the moonlight striking the water.

Good bye, old girl, I thought. I did like the ship, even if it would always hold bitter memories for me. I turned to look behind me, but there was no one there. I picked up the pace now and began to walk briskly down the beach. The strand stretched on ahead, inviting because it promised freedom. But it seemed to end quite a ways off where the waves were reaching for high headlands, their foamy crests bright in the moonlight. The high hills to my right were grassy, with a few scrawny shrubs. I walked, wondering, *How many foot steps between here and home? How many steps needed to take me home to my Annie?* I thought of her now as only *my Annie.* I could not conceive that she could truly belong to anyone else. I needed her now more than ever. It was she who would bring me back home, back to life. When I closed my eyes, I could see her dancing before me, an enticing smile on her face, moving ever back from me, arms outstretched, luring me onward. I walked for sometime this way, so wrapped in my memory of that beautiful diva that I paid little attention to where I was. Suddenly a sneaker wave came crashing in and pulled at my feet, sucking the sand from beneath them. I fell and was in danger for a few minutes of going to sea without a ship under me. But, with luck, I managed to roll on my side and frantically clawed my way back to shore until I was upright again. *I will have to be more careful. This is no Sunday School picnic. I am running for my life.*

I walked on until dawn. By then, I was exhausted. The slopes above me were mostly grasslands with here and there a tree. I decided to lie down for a few hours, off the beach and out of sight. There were no boats or ships in sight and no one on the beach. Possibly I had been able to escape unnoticed. I learned many years later that an escaped felon had been seen heading west from La Guaira that night. When word reached the mutineers, they thought that it was I. The man had procured a pistol and they assumed that it was the pistol that had belonged to Patty T., but it was not so. The time they spent chasing to the west gave me ample time to make many miles to the east. Travel that night was too difficult, but at times the sand was soft and I seemed to take two steps backwards for every step forward. There were boggy areas and I had to struggle through mud knee deep, trying to keep my boots on and still make time. I doubted that I had traveled even ten miles that night. I took the cork from one of the beer bottles and drank thirstily. I was very thirsty, but hunger could wait. The heat drove me on to try to find some shade. Water poured from my body as if it were a fountain.

Finally, I found a log close up on shore and decided to lie down behind it. There were no signs of life here. It seemed safe enough. Within minutes the sand crabs and sand fleas had found me and I began to itch and crawl with 'bitchos,' the Spanish word for mosquitoes. I slept little and swatted much, wondering how people who lived here could survive. Then I remembered the small piece of netting that Niles Durban had given me on board the *Celeste* when we were after slaves in Africa. I rummaged in my sack and found it. The netting discouraged insects from biting my face, but they were still eager to crawl up my trouser legs and shirt sleeves.

I awoke about nine with the searing sun shining in my eyes. It was time to be on my way. I had decided to eat only at night when exhausted and to use the daylight hours for travel, until it became too hot. The day was scorching, but it did not last for long. By 2 p.m., it began to rain, not normal rain, but the skies grew black as if it were night and the heavens opened up and flung rain to the earth so violently that it hurt my head to stand in the rain without a hat. My bicorn came out of the pack and was promptly put on my head, but I immediately perceived that it would be an excellent vehicle to catch rain water in for drinking. Cuppa would help too. I pulled it out and within about five minutes, it was full. I drank thirstily and set the cup down for more. It filled again and I drank. By the third time, the storm was abating and I was only able to collect three fourths of a cup. Still, it was refreshing. As soon as the rain stopped, the sky became bright as if someone had lit a celestial lantern and the sun began to dry off everything. I was soaked and it felt good to have the warm sun back, causing vapour to rise from my wet clothes and everything around me. In an hour, everything was dry again. The grasslands still flanked my right side. I decided to capitalize on each storm, filling the one empty bottle from the brim of my hat and cuppa.

I had expected to see fishing huts along the coast, but none were evident. Now the strand disappeared into the surf and I was forced to climb labouriously up the headlands to find safe footing. It was slow, tedious work. I would be lucky to make ten miles today instead of the twenty that I had planned. At least here, there was a sea breeze that cut the scorching heat some, making it easier to breathe and live.

That night I stopped at dark to eat. I made one of the loaves of bread do for my supper and drank part of another bottle of beer. I was about to throw away the first empty bottle, but decided to keep it. I could always store rain water in it. It weighed little. Sleeping would be a problem this night too. I was on a high headland with mostly grass. Here and there was a strange looking tree. I decided to sleep under a tree, for no real reason. This must be the llanos that I had heard about.

That night I slept fitfully. Something seemed to be biting me, but I could not find the offender. It was not mosquitoes and the netting did no good to protect me from the critters. By dawn, I knew what was wrong. I had lain down near an ant nest. The ants made a meal of me all night long, but I was so tired that I could do little but stir and squirm. I had angry red welts all over my body.

I headed out that morning with a drink of beer and no food. I would walk the day before I would eat. The next day was much the same, except that I picked my bed more carefully. Still, I was attacked by insects.

The next day brought me down into some broad-leaved forests. The heat was intense, seemingly bottled up and saved by the dense forest. I was still close to the ocean, but could not find strand that was continuous at all tides, so I stayed inland a bit. All went well until I went to step over a log. Suddenly, the log wrinkled and moved beneath my body. The thing was alive. It was not a dead tree trunk at all. It was a giant snake, perhaps fifteen feet long, stretched out across the forest floor. Where I had chosen to climb over, it had ingested some large animal and its body was swollen with a meal. The creature that had been eaten must have been about the size of one of the baby wild boars that I had seen earlier. I was glad to have my pistol because the sharp tusks on the boar would cut a man to pieces if he could not defend himself. I backed off from the snake, not wanting to cross so large a beast. I watched fascinated as the muscles of the body rippled, forcing the food parcel towards the end. What a magnificent beast this was. I had no desire to shoot it. Anything that could live long enough to get to that size deserved to live on undisturbed. I was contented with this plan as long as the snake would let me alone. I stood there and gradually the animal wiggled away, leaving my path once again clear. I sighed in relief when I could no longer see the snake, but resolved to watch more carefully for his brothers. The jungle in which I found myself was fascinating. I was slowed by my insatiable curiosity. There were strange flowers blooming from the boles of large trees and odd ant structures plastered against the bark of some trees. Then I found the bases of leaves of shrubs swollen with whole colonies of ants living inside. Stranger still were the huge ant fortresses built of mud in the trees. I wondered if these might be termites, but could not be certain. These fortresses were molded around branches in some way by the worker ants and had what resembled a thatch type roof. When it rained, which it did again promptly at 2 p.m., the water ran freely off the thatches. This was a strange world indeed. One could not live here, evidenced by the fact that I had not seen a single soul since I left La Guaira, but still I hardly wanted to leave the place for the fascination that it held. I happened to cut open a jointed stalked plant only to find each cell of the stalk filled with ants living as a colony. Ants rule this jungle for certain. It was hot.

Then the rain came. At least I had the protection of the broad-leaved canopy, but still the rain came through the leaves so violently that I sought shelter. But there was none. I stood under a tree and felt the water as if from a waterfall cruise down my backside. Well, no matter. I needed a bath anyway. I stripped off my clothes and stood under the tree, my back pressed against the bark. Water poured freely over me and strange as it may seem, the water was *soapy* , making ample suds as I scrubbed my body. When I was clean and a good bit cooled down, I picked up my clothes and began to use the free water to scrub them too. Cuppa was set by another tree, but later I would wish that I had collected more water. I was soon thirsty. The beer was all gone and still I had not seen running water that I thought might be suitable for drinking. I went to sleep thirsty that night, but clean. I still had a few ship's biscuits and a bit of cheese, but hoped to find a village soon where I could buy some food. I wished that I had come up with a plan to take the chart with me, but it had been needed in the chart house right up to the time we came to anchor, and I could see no way of getting it out without arousing suspicion. I wondered what the men of the *Hermione* thought had happened to me. They may well think that I was holed up in one of the local shacks with some native woman and was simply too busy to come down to see them.

That night I found a bit of high ground that seemed dry. I laid down to sleep and slept well, for once. But when I awoke in the morning, I was covered in large welts, particularly around my ankles and waist. It seemed that the Capoeira has many litter insects that will also feast on human flesh, or any protein that they can get. My ankles were so swollen that I could not put my boots on. I had to put them in my sack and I pulled out a shirt. I tore it in two and made rags to cover both feet. I was in some pain and when I stood up, my ankles felt as if they had great wheels of fat around them, filled with water. I felt the swollen tissues drag at my every step. It was most painful and slowed me considerably, but I was determined to travel on.

But my throat was dry and for the first time, I succumbed and drank from the tiny pools of black water that I found on the forest floor. I had the sensation of drinking more than just 'water'. The heat seemed never to relent, following me everywhere that I went, sapping my strength and taking away my vital fluids.

I continued to be fascinated by what I saw as I walked on. Often I heard the groan of trees as they rubbed together, moved slightly by the gentle winds form the Caribbean. Sometimes those breezes found me and cooled me. Others, it was steaming hot, without a seeming breath of air to be found. I struggled on, walking ever so slowly. Suddenly, just ahead of me, there stepped into my path the largest cat I had ever seen. She was huge, shining black, with bright yellow eyes turned curiously towards me. I froze where I stood. Never had I seen such a fine beast. I was certain that she was the queen of this jungle and had been watching me with those sharp eyes. It had to be a 'she', because all of the cats in my life were females. She must have ambled down to look me over more closely. I stood frozen, fascinated and unable to speak or even to think clearly. Here was a panther, an animal that most humans never see or even read about, and she was there only ten yards from me. I wondered if I should be ready to grip my pistol and cock it, but my heart would not let me move. If one of us had to die to feed the other, I would almost rather it be me than her. She was so beautiful and I was, well, just a plain sailor. We stared at each other for perhaps three minutes. Then she flared her nostrils, smelling me out. She opened her mouth and showed me a fair set of fangs and gleaming white teeth. In a wink she was gone. I could not even see where she went. But I knew she was about to leave when I saw the great muscles flex under her silky black coat. I was suddenly thankful to be alive, and gave God my thanks for having seen such beauty. It made the swarms of mosquitoes and the heat almost bearable, for a few minutes, at least.

The afternoon rain came on suddenly, but I was prepared. I was able to get enough to drink to last the rest of the day and into tomorrow. It seemed that San Jose de Rio Chico should be somewhere close ahead, but the reality was that it was still almost four days distant. I was traveling much more slowly than I thought. I ate the last of my food that night. I had been on the beach some seven days.

That night, I was tired of sleeping on the ground. I found a bit of strand and decided to curl up there. The sand crabs and fleas were far preferable to the litter insects. I went to sleep sometime after eleven o'clock, totally exhausted. But about three in the morning, I had the strange sensation of rocking, being moved about. I awoke with difficulty, just as a huge sneaker wave landed full force on me. It pulled me down into the surf, sucking at my prone body. I scrambled up the strand, gripping my canvas bag tightly. I had developed the habit of sleeping with one arm through the strap of the pack, so that I could move rapidly if needed. This time it paid off.

But the damage to my pistol was considerable. The powder was wet and the barrel full of sand. I sat by moonlight and cleaned up the pistol, using strange stems that had a variegated pattern on them as cleaning rods. They were a bit abrasive and so, worked well as cleaners. I scoured some of the rust from my flint. I would need it soon. The rest of the night was spent sitting, head tilted back, against a tree. I did sleep a little, fitfully.

The next day, I walked suddenly into a strange, new forest. It was still broad-leaved, hot as Hell, but the trees had their roots surrounded by brackish water. I stood at sea level and when the tide came in, the tree roots were inundated. I thought that this must be mangrove forest. It was memorable because it was a grove of trees that a man could hardly penetrate. I stumbled, crawled, fell and climbed through the tangle of roots and knees, often losing my sense of direction. My mind forced me to find the easiest way to advance, but that way was often not to the east or to my advantage. I was forced to put my boots back on. The swollen ankles had shrunk just enough that I could get them on, but it would be awhile before I could take them off again. I threw the rags from my feet. They had ceased to do much good after the first two miles. My feet were now masses of sores and cuts. I had no stockings left at all.

Finding a place to sleep that night was a nightmare. Everything that I tried had problems. I now knew why no one lived in this area. It was just too forbidding. There was no food or water and not a place to lay one's head. I longed for a hammock. It could be strung from tree to tree and one could rest comfortably under the netting. I considered making a hammock out of lianas, but it would take precious time and I was already far behind what I had planned. Besides, it would be too hard to carry a hammock and the grasslands had too few trees to make a hammock useful.

So, I tried to climb a tree. That should be possible, but it was much harder than it looked. The lower twenty feet of the tree trunks was covered with a slimy growth of algae and mosses that prevented me from getting a good grip on the bole. Every time I would get eight to ten feet off the ground, I would lose my grip and come crashing back to the ground. My feet were constantly wet now in the water around the trees. There was no helping that. The energy needed to climb a tree in this heat was immense and I was already becoming weakened from lack of food and drink. A small tree finally solved the problem for that night. I was able to climb its rough bark and lay myself out on the branches until I was reasonably comfortable. The only problem was that I had to leave the sack on the ground. I could not climb with it on my back. I fell promptly off to sleep.

The next morning, I noted that many of the leaves were cupped and that there was a good bit of fresh rain water caught in especially the dry leaves that were hung up in the crown. I drank freely from the little pools of water, until I found one with small larvae wriggling violently, always keeping their heads to the surface. I could not stomach that, but I did need food and soon. I had not eaten for a day and a half.

That problem was soon to be solved. As I lay there, watching the amber rays of the first sunrise, I saw a large snake working its way across the tree tops in a most magical way. He seemed to be able to extend the third forward portion of his body, sense where there was a secure branch and slide forward, all in one rapid, smooth motion. He was headed directly for me. I lay, my eyes pinned on his sleek, rapidly moving body. Suddenly I realized that he would be upon me in a matter of a couple of seconds. I had to either fend him off or shoot him. I drew my pistol from my trouser band, cocked it, and aimed for his body just behind the head. He had a tiny head. I could not see how he could harm me, unless he had a strong venom, because his head was too small to ingest anything of much size. I waited until the last moment and then pulled the trigger. The gun had more of a kick than I had expected, nearly dumping me onto the ground some twenty feet below. But the snake was hit. It writhed violently and then fell to the ground. I descended to find it lying there below, dead. Well, almost dead. The thin body continued to writhe for sometime. Now came the controversy. I knew that the natives ate some snakes, but which ones? Was this a delicacy that would salve my hunger, or was it deadly poison and its meat would surely kill me? There was no way to know but to try it. I pulled my knife from my boot, slit off the head and began to skin the animal. It was early in the morning and I had not planned to eat so early, but my stomach drove me to acts that I would normally not even consider. Next, I had to start a fire. That was going to be a real challenge. I decided to use a little gun powder placed in such a way that it would contact the driest material that I could find. That material turned out to be some flaky bark from beneath a fallen log that was suspended above the wet forest floor. I contemplated using the oil cloth from my report on the mutiny, but decided that I could not do that. I owed it to the Service to get those reports back dry and readable. With patience, fanning and blowing, I was gradually able to start a fire using the flint and steel on a flat place at the base of a tree which happened to have no water. It took half a day and I grew hungrier every minute. The waiting was killing me. But I was determined that this beast should be well-cooked and not just smoked. My reasoning was that if the animal was venomous, most venoms would be deactivated by heat. Mr. Ledyard, the surgeon aboard the *Faithful,* had told me that long ago. How I wished he were here now. When I had a good bed of coals, I wrapped the gutted snake in pieces in leaves and placed it on top of the coals. Yes, I had learned my lesson from the Broken Bridge, when as a child, I had tried to cook fish without gutting them. Piles of wet leaves atop the food would help to keep the heat in where it could do its work. I waited, trying to find things to occupy my mind in between.

Each day on my long trek, the vision of my Annie had appeared to me, leading me onward, coaxing with outstretched arms. I knew that I manufactured that image for my own comfort, but what did it matter. It helped me get through the worst of days. I could see her now, standing there, hands on hips, looking at me as if I were a helpless babe. I decided that cooked meals were going to be a luxury and that I dare not indulge in them often. They simply took too much time, but there was nothing to eat in this lowland jungle. I was sure that the natives would know what to eat, but I did not.

When the meal was finally cooked, I tore open the leaves and wolfed down the food as fast as I could. I could not have told you if it tasted good five minutes after I had eaten it, let alone now. I had no sensation of taste. All I knew was that my stomach was full and that, by the time it began to rain, I was ready to collect as much water as I could. I was thirsty. I had consumed most of the snake, but brought along what was left for tomorrow. There was no hope of saving anything cooked for more than a day in the heat. Sweat poured off me as I walked, struggling to stay upright. I wondered how the animals of the jungle could cope with the heat and the incessant insect bites.

The next day I was walking along, clawing at anything to stay upright and out of the black water when I started to step onto a log. But, it suddenly whipped sideways, a grotesque head flashing monstrous, deadly teeth. Its back was covered with huge scales and it looked like a fat snake with four legs. I had never seen or heard of such a beast before. I would examine my path more carefully in future. This one could kill a man in an instant with those sharp teeth, or that viciously strong tail. The jungle was fraught with dangers that were new to me.

Most of that day was lost and I was hardly able to walk five miles before the heat and exhaustion caused me to look for a place to sleep. I tried to climb a tree again, but it was not as comfortable as the last had been. Besides, I kept hearing things move in the tree tops, as if there was another snake headed for me. It was disquieting. The sounds of the jungle were all about me too. I heard crickets, strange howling sounds and other bizarre sounds that would turn a man's heart to lead. I was no longer comfortable in this jungle and longed to find a settlement of some kind.

Then I tried to catch some fish from the shallow waters. I had experience with this type of fishing at the Broken Bridge, but somehow, it seemed much harder now. I managed to catch several small fish, until one fish appeared from no where. It dove at me and bit my hand with razor-sharp teeth, drawing blood. I had heard of Piranha, and wondered if this fish belonged to that tribe. I went more cautiously now lest it should have me for dinner instead of the other way around. Four small fish fried over a smoky fire did some to lessen my hunger.

The next day I walked out into a grassland high above the sea. It was reasonably easy walking, but I felt strange. I had expected to turn sick any second from eating the snake, but nothing unusual happened. Now, my head began to ache and I felt sick to my stomach. It was too long after the snake for it to be that. I had passed most of the snake out of my system. It had to be something else, but what? I became dizzy, growing so hot that I could not continue to walk. I collapsed near a tree and lay there for two days, dying of thirst and boiling with fever. I was no longer aware of insect bites or of anything but the terrible fever.

When I awoke, I felt weak and faint. But I realized that my fever had subsided. It was gone in only two days. That suggested that I had suffered from swamp fever and that I might now be able to mend. I needed to continue my journey. The sense of urgency drove me to my feet long before I should have thought to get up.

I stood, hanging onto the tree when there appeared before me a vision that I will never forget. There loomed up from it seems nowhere the tallest woman that I had ever seen. She was easily seven feet tall, maybe taller. She was dark skinned with long, wavy black hair. All that she wore was a cloth around her waist. Her firm brown breasts were naked. She carried a long pointed stick in one hand and a sharp knife in the other. Behind her stood a tall man, but not nearly as tall as she was. He held a strange looking drum in his dark hands. His hair was short and crinkled, but more nearly brown. I shook my head. Surely this was a vision, something like my Annie. It was not real. There were no people out here in this wilderness, certainly none so large. I am a large man and was then nearly to my full height, but my head did not exceed her shoulders. She held her head high, proudly, walking with somewhat the grace that I had noticed in the big cat earlier. *They are much alike,* I thought. Surely this was the result of the fever, some hallucination. It could not be real, and if it were, I did not have a chance of surviving.

Just then, she spoke, a warm deep voice, "Tiene usted mucho calor? Esta usted enfirmo?"

I let go of the tree and fell in a heap at its base. I was still too weak to move and the strain of the approaching enemies was too much for me. I awoke hours later, my head cradled in the lap of the giant woman. I looked up into her dark eyes and realized that she was not an enemy, but she could be a formidable one if she took the notion. There were little smile lines around her mouth and she seemed somehow clean and sweet, not hot and sweaty.

"Quien es?"

"Soy una mujer de la Amazon," and she pointed, her hand rising high and then pointing far south. "El esta mi marido. Venimos para batir los tambores con la familia de mi esposo." Her Spanish was not perfect, but I got the impression that she had come from someplace far in the south to beat the drums with her husband's family. Many tribes had traditional times for drum beatings and this was what she had been doing. They were now headed home and it was easier to walk the llanos if one lacked a canoa.

"Y usted?"

I did not know what to say. Should I tell her that I was a British officer. I thought not. More than likely she would not know what British was, let alone His Majesty's Navy. "Soy un hombre pobre quien no tiene agua o comida."

She looked at her husband and gave a vigorous shake of her head. The man was gone for a short time and then returned with food. He had knowledge of the jungle and llanos and was able to find food that need not be cooked, palm nuts, other strange nuts and some strange fruits. He brought back a section of liana and showed me how to cut it to get water from its stem. We dined that night on a variety of delicacies from the jungle, most of which I had never seen or heard of before. But I would recognize them again and could collect them to eat. Among the food that he brought was conch, which he beat hard and then threw into a small fire that he lit from nothing but grass and twigs. I once again felt the wonderful taste of that sea food in my mouth and thought that I would now surely live. She also gave me the juice of a fruit that she had with her in a small sack. She called it 'lucuma' and it tasted quite good, sweet and strangely cool. It seemed to give me strength. I was soon able to get up and walk. The couple stayed with me for the night, but said, "Adios," as they walked on headed out in the early dawn. They spoke little Spanish, but regularly conversed in some strange language that I did not understand. She seemed to answer to Lilit, and he to Tombi. I never quite knew if these people were real or the product of my fevered mind, but somehow, they helped me immeasurably when I was about to give up all hope. At that Ben turned to me and said, 'If I had to swear on a stack of bibles, I could not be certain that I ever really saw them.'

I was recovered enough to travel on, but I had to stop early in the day. The fever took such a toll of my strength that I would not soon regain it. I expected to come to San Jose any day now, but it appears that somehow, I had missed it. For the past two weeks now, I had hobbled through grasslands, sometimes on the strand and sometimes on the llanos. Sometimes I was able to find conch and kill them. Those days I ate. The beach, when there was one, provided some fire wood and I learned how to start a fire so that I could get my meal in about two hours. Other days I could find nothing to eat. I learned to catch some of the small fish in the mangroves, but these soon disappeared, as had the afternoon rain storms. There were fewer and fewer storms, making it hard to find drinking water. It was the three rivers that saved me and kept me from drying up completely. I did finally stumble into Puerto La Cruz, having completely missed Barcelona. My map made it look as if Barcelona was directly on the coast, but apparently, it was not. I remembered that some ways beyond San Antonio, I would have to turn and walk north instead of east. If I missed that turn, I would have a long walk to Pedernales. There was also a good chance of staying too close to the ocean and finding myself on one of the long sand spits in this portion of the coast that might put me in danger if there were unusually high tides or a storm. I must make the right turn and I needed someone to direct me. Just before Barcelona, I was forced to move inland to cross two rivers. The chart had shown that. In moving inland, I had apparently gone too far. The first river was relatively easy to cross. There must have been a village nearby because someone had left a canoe tied to the west bank. I had only to crawl in and paddle across, hoping that the party who left the canoe had some easy way to get it back. When I reached the other side, I realized that there was a length of rope, quite long, intended to be used to pull the canoe back to the west bank. As I rowed east, the rope played out and the canoe could be pulled back to the west side with ease.

But the next river was wide and flowed fast. I pushed many miles inland on extremely sore feet to find a place where I might swim across. I had not been able to remove my boots for several weeks now and my feet were swollen and bruised. I knew by the squishy feel in the bottom of the boot that they were bleeding badly. A seaman's boot was never designed for long distance walking and I could expect nothing but trouble from these boots. After I crossed the third river, I found Puerto La Cruz. I hopped unseen aboard a small barge that was being towed across the river with supplies on it. Two donkeys pulled the barge and the barge man had all that he could do to keep the animals at their work. I climbed off on the east side, still unnoticed. Then I limped into the town.

I saw a small cantina and, fishing through my pack, I found some silver. Inside was dark and cool. It was the heat of the day. I asked for cerveza and comida. A tall, stately woman with her black hair pulled back into a bun brought me some beer and returned about half an hour later with a steaming plate of sea food. There were several kinds of fish, conch and other things that I could not identify. There was no time for worrying about what I was eating. I was famished and dug in eagerly to a fine meal. The bread was especially good. I really missed daily bread. I ordered two loaves of bread and four bottles of beer. That would last a few days, at least. Cumana should not be more than fifty or sixty miles away. I could buy food there. I paid the woman and then looked at my money. I seemed to have about twelve pounds left, but for some reason I could not remember how much I had carried with me when I left the ship. I must be careful with what little there was left. I stood on two feet that were so sore that I almost screamed. I might have to cut the boots off soon, if the pain did not ease up. I could not endure much more pain. My joints ached, all of them and it was an effort to walk. I must have at least another one hundred and fifty miles to go. I asked the woman as best I could how far it was to Macuro or Punta Piedras, but she shook her head. She had no idea. I had been gone some 21 days from La Guaira so far and was hardly half way to my destination. I could not see how I could continue without some decent shoes and time for my feet to heal, but I did not have enough money to eat and also to buy boots, if there were even any for sale. I walked through the market place and saw nothing but light sandals made from local grasses. They would not last long.

So, I headed off to Cumana. There was an endless panorama of grass plains on my right and ocean on my left. Had I not been in such pain, I might have found it most enjoyable. At Cumana, I bought another meal and some more bread. I was sure that the people were charging me too much, but the sight of my silver made them eager. Besides, they did not know what a British pound was really worth. My coins would probably end up as collector's items. But I found that I could not get a meal for less than a pound and I had no smaller change. A starving man has little choice.

I began to get diarrhea somewhere between Cumana

and Carupano. I was tempted to lay it to bad food at the cantina, but it was just as likely that in drinking from all sorts of leaves and puddles, I had picked up some vicious internal parasite that gnawed constantly at my guts. It was here that I had to make my first decision. There were trails now, well worn, some of them, but I could not be certain which one to take. One continued on to the east and one turned and led more northwesterly. I thought that there was an odd peninsula with one arm heading west and one east before I reached the final long stretch of land to Macuro, but I could not be certain. If I made the wrong turn in my condition, it could mean my life. These peninsulas stretched out into the ocean and were probably uninhabited. I could not find help or food on them, unless I stayed on the correct route. My memory of the ship's map was growing fuzzy. Besides, I did not know if the map was accurate or not. Land features were just sketched in, not boldly placed as were the reefs and harbours.

In the end, I decided to walk due east. That trail led through the grasslands and was frequented by horses. I stood a better chance of finding help and Macuro if I stayed with the eastern trail.

Travel now was agony. I walked about five miles a day and then had to rest. When the diarrhea hit me, I was so beset that I went to the beach and took off my trousers. They were no longer white but a motley of jungle colours, grime, mud and sand. I took off my undergarments and washed them. Then I slit the seat so there would be no more soiling and packed my trousers away in the canvas pack. I was contented to walk in my underwear, rather than try to get out of my trousers quickly enough to answer the frequent calls of nature. I needed only to squat. I became weaker by the day. Water was scarce now. The beer was all gone and I had no bread. But I was too weak to swim for conch. I tried chewing on grass, but it did not fill me up nor did it help the diarrhea.

When finally I reached Curupano, I knew that I was on

the last leg of the journey. I bought some bread and soup there and later some fried fish. It tasted good, but did not stay with me for long. I was thin as a marlin spike and hardly able to walk. I bought some wine hoping to pickle the varmints that were ruining my insides, but that did not work either. After a day's rest at Curupano, I set out due east through the grasslands for the fishing village of Macuro. It was perhaps a hundred and twenty miles but would be the longest walk of my life. Soon after I left Curupano, I began to feel feverish. The fever became worse by the hour until finally I was forced to stop and lie down beside the track. It was a lightly used track and I did not expect to see anyone along it for sometime. *I may well die here,* I thought. I was certain now that I would never see my Annie again. I lay quite still, using the grass for shade as much as I could and digging into the cool earth with my hands to find relief from the fever. I do not know how long that I lay there, but the day had passed and another come upon me when I awoke. The sun was a dull glow and it was going to rain. I welcomed the thought of rain. It would cool my fever-wracked body and give me relief. I tried again to remove my boots, but it was no use. I visualized the small insects trapped in the boots and eating away, maintaining a constant swelling. Sometime that day, I dragged myself to my feet and began to walk. The fever had subsided for the moment and I was just able to continue. I needed to get to Macuro, the only village for some 120 miles and I needed to get there rapidly. I felt my strength ebbing away and I frequently felt dizzy and fainted many times on the trail. But I was in a race for my life now. I walked for twenty miles that day, trailing fluid from behind. I could not imagine where any excrement could come from when I had not eaten for several days. But come it did.

That night I slept beside the trail, oblivious of the insects and rain. When I awoke, I had caught enough water in my hat for a good drink of water, which I badly needed. I drank every drop and headed off, telling myself that I could no longer feel the pain in my feet, which was partially true. My whole body became numb. But that afternoon the fever returned. I shook violently with fever, the heat consuming me and then I shivered as if I lay in a bed of snow instead of hot white sand. I was fairly certain now that I had contracted malaria on top of swamp fever. *That should kill even a good Englishman,* I thought. Nowhere along my route had I seen any of the herbs that were used in the Caribbean for fighting this fever, and so, I could do little but endure the misery.

The next few days were all the same. I pushed to within an inch of my life, trying to make twenty miles a day. I knew that I must reach medical help soon, or I would surely die. My feet now smelled like they were dying and I wretched every time I got wind of them. Finally, in desperation, I took my knife from the pocket in my boot and cut off the right boot. The foot was bathed in blood, red and swollen beyond belief. The lower leg was covered with an ugly green slime. Then I cut off the other boot. That foot was not quite as bad, but a green scum had begun to grow all over my swollen foot. I washed both feet in salt water, which bit and stung terribly, but the stench was almost more than I could endure. I pulled my officer's jacket out of the pack and cut it into pieces. I would use the arms to cushion my feet and cover them so I could continue to walk. *They won't last long, but then, neither will I.*Actually, cutting the boots off did help my feet some. They began to smell a bit better, but there were chunks of flesh that were starting to fall away. I had some form of hoof rot, I was sure.

As soon as my feet began to feel better then the diarrhea came back with a vengeance. At times I had to sit by the road and cry, I was so sore and so terribly hungry and thirsty. But, somehow, I willed myself to move on. Oh, yes, my Annie was there before me, always moving away, always beckoning. *I could not stop if I wanted to.* After six days with only the left overs from a few rain storms to drink and nothing to eat, I saw the village of Macuro up ahead. The image of shacks and boats by the water danced and shimmered in the heat of my fevered brain. Fishing boats were tied to posts and the houses were small, cozy one-room cottages. I started to go towards the first one, but felt suddenly as if a huge hammer had hit me in the chest. I fell in a dead faint on the strand.

Luckily for me, one woman was watching for her husband to come home with the day's catch. She saw me fall and came to my rescue. She summoned several other fishermen who were already in with their day's catch and they lent a hand. I was vaguely conscious of being moved, but nothing else registered in my mind. My body had finally collapsed under unrelenting punishment. Several days later I awoke and everything seemed to be good. I could see clearly, hear and even speak. I asked if I might have something to eat. The woman brought me a plate of cheese and some sauteed fish. I ate ravenously. She poured me a tall cup of water and I could not get enough. All this time she had asked not a question of who I was or where I was going. She was a kindly woman. I could see that in her eyes and who and what did not matter. What mattered was that I was there, in her house, very sick and in need of care. I learned that she was Senora Chiquita Romero. She and her husband, Miguel, had no children, which was most unusual for these people. She gave me ample care and attention and within a day, I was ready to ask to be taken to Port of Spain. I said that I had urgent business there that could not wait another day. She promised to speak with her husband who fished daily in the waters between Punta Piedras and Port of Spain. I offered to pay and held out silver in the palm of my hand.

When her husband returned, I learned that he owned his boat with a partner. "The partner, he is not willing to go into Port of Spain, for personal reasons," he said. Then I begged him to take me.

"I must get to Trinidad, I must."

The man promised, 'manana'.

But every day it was, ' manana'. After two days of delays, I could stand it no more. I had no shoes, just rags on my feet, but I was able to walk a bit. Sometimes great sweats would come upon me and nearly put me out of action, and sometimes I would get a bout of diarrhea that would send me running for the head, but I was healing.

As the two men went out to fish the next morning, I got out of bed and grabbed my canvas bag and followed them. I had kept my pistol out of sight for some time now. I did not want to appear like a pirate and these were simple fisher people. I had no fear of them. I pulled my pistol from my belt and in the dark, at the last moment, swung my leg over the bulwark of the fishing boat.

"We are going to Port of Spain," I announced in a quiet voice. I drew my pistol and they both looked at me in alarm. Then they looked at each other. "We go Port of Spain." But I sat there in the stern, shaking and unsteady. They could have taken the gun from me at any moment. I knew that. From their conversation I learned that they were not welcome in Port of Spain because of a fight that they caused over fishing rights some years ago. It seems that Miguel spent some time in jail because he was too cocky with the local magistrate.

I did not like to do this, but it was the only way. There was still the challenge of getting from Port of Spain to Barbados. I knew there was a hospital ship in Bridgetown and that the Admiral would most likely be aboard his flag ship there. I had to get news of the mutiny to them as soon as possible so they could send a ship to capture the *Hermione* and her crew.

When we landed at Port of Spain, I thanked the two fishermen and handed them each a silver coin. Their eyes lit up and they shouted, , "Gracias, senor, Gracias." I was short of money now. Something must have happened to my money while I was sick. I had no idea what, but I should have about ten pounds left. There were only three pounds here. What could have happened? Who could know. I may have lost some money when I was rolling around in the surf, or someone may have come by when I was in the fever and taken some of my money. I would have to beg passage to Bridgetown, but it was but a short ways.

I had no more than stepped on shore than the fever hit me, followed by severe chills. I lay on the beach, a hopeless wreck of a man, unable to do anything for myself. The fact that the fever subsided within about three to six hours and was then followed by chills convinced me that it was malaria. I would bide my time. I would be able to function in a few more hours.

When I came to, I found that the boat had just left for Bridgetown. There would not be another one for three days. I could have cried. I was so tired and exhausted. This was fate at its cruelest.

Somehow, I managed to get some food and drink down me and even kept most of it in place for the next three days. I found a small pub that had a nice older woman who took pity on me. She offered me free food when my money ran out and I 'ran' errands for her. To say that I 'ran' is inaccurate. I shuffled from on foot to the other. It took my mind off my problems. I slept on the beach at night, guarding my canvas bag with my life.

Three days later, a small lugger came into port, speedily unloaded and then took on cargo for Barbados. I walked to the pier and asked for the captain. Senor Wilson agreed to take me with him in the *Spitfire* if I would help load. We were carrying fruit mostly and speed was important. I was weak, but did my best to help with the loading.

We sailed the next morning and arrived at Barbados two days later. I would have stayed to help unload, but as soon as we docked, I was beset with the fever and had to lie down. I remember nothing of the passage. When we arrived at Barbados, the captain found a small boat to take me to the hospital ship. I doubt that he knew that I was a naval officer, but his sense of right and wrong led him to send me to where I could get help. That was where I needed to be. When I awoke hours later, I looked through a veil of sweat at Dr. Warcup whom I had met several years earlier on my last trip to Barbados.

I was desperate. "Please, sir, bring my canvas sack, please. Right now!"

"Now, lad, you suffer from a bad fever. Just lay back and everything will be fine." But it would not be fine. I had risked my life to bring the reports of the mutiny to the Admiral and I had to see to my duty.

"No sir," I said in a loud, commanding voice as I sat up. "I am a leftenant in His Majesty's Navy and I have important dispatches for the Admiral. I will have my pack, NOW!"

"All right, lad, if it means that much to you. I'll be right back."

The man moved aside as an aide brought my sack. I was ever so relieved

When I saw it, I expected that it might have been left behind or pilfered, but when I opened it, there was the crumpled white shirt. I pulled it out and motioned to the aide. "Take this to the Admiral on his flag ship at once. Tell him it is from Leftenant Rundel. GO!"

I was too weak to cut out the notes from the shirt, but anyone who handled that shirt would soon notice that there was something concealed there. The man ran off and I fell back to be greeted by the now too familiar chill, the feeling that I was lying in a bed of ice with no clothes on, my body trembling frantically to try to keep me warm. The surgeon put on more covers, but I lay shivering in a most miserable way.

About two hours later, I was just beginning to come out of the chill. I heard a great booming voice,"Get out of my way. Where is that young scalawag?" I recognized the voice of Admiral Horace Harrington at once. He stepped to my bedside and looked down at me.

"My God, it is Rundel! What on earth are you doing here? I thought that I sent you home and that you were in the Mediterranean with Lord Nelson. What happened?"

I was shaking still, but I managed to say that I had been sent aboard the *Hermione* and that we had sailed for

Barbados with dispatches. The crew mutinied in protest of the cruel punishments of Captain Pigot. I wrote an account of the mutiny, which you have in your hand, I believe." That took all of my strength and I lay back to endure another half hour of misery alone.

But the Admiral was not satisfied. "Look, lad, I can't believe half that you have written here. This just does not happen in the Navy. Surely you have made this all up. I'll have no fairy tales in my archives, I'll tell you that."

"Please sir, the man is very sick. He should be better in a day or so. I think he needs rest just now," said Warcup.

The Admiral looked somewhat embarrassed and stood looking at my piteous body for a few minutes. "I am sending you home day after tomorrow on the *Swift*." Then he looked at Warcup. "See that this man is comfortable and do all that you can for him. Have him aboard the *Swift* by six tomorrow evening." Then he turned back to me. "Lad, I see no account of how you got from La Guaira to Barbados."

"I walked, sir," I replied.

The Admiral looked even more astonished. Mr. Warcup stepped forward and lifted the covers so the Admiral could see my swollen feet, covered with cuts and sores. The Admiral stepped back in disgust. There was no doubt that he now believed my story, every word.

"Can you write an account of your trip from La Guaira to here so I can get it copied to send to the Admiralty? Have it ready by late this afternoon? I will have a packet of dispatches for you to carry to London when you sail day after tomorrow."

"I will try, sir. I was unable to take notes during my trip and I have lapses of memory when I was s-s-s-sick, but I will put down what I can remember."

"Sir, this lad is too sick to do any writing," protested Warcup.

"He'll do what he can, I am sure." At that, he took my cold hand and held it firmly, looking down at my trembling body. "You are one brave lad. I know of no other who could have done what you have done. Rest now. I'll see you later. I must dispatch a ship to hunt down the pirates and *Hermione.* If it were not for you, we might never have known what happened to her."

I slept for four hours. When I awoke, I was hungry and the aide served me a fine plate of eggs and ham, with bread and cider. I felt well enough after my repast that I called for pen and paper and began to reconstruct my arduous journey, complete with snakes, conches and wild boars, but I left out the part about the giant woman. I laboured for four hours, and for a sick man, this was labour. I hated to recall some of the pain that I had suffered and chose to make light of my sickness. After all, I was getting better and I would be ready to go back to sea in a week, at most. But Mr. Warcup did not agree. He said that I would have less frequent attacks with time, but I might expect a recurrence at the most inconvenient times. Severe stress might bring on an attack when I least expected it. But, he also said that I could expect the attacks to lessen in severity over time. I should avoid getting over tired, at all cost. I wondered how a British officer could manage that.

Finally, Ben had completed his report and called the aide to have it sent to the Admiral. An hour later they transported him to the *Swift.* He was delighted to be able to climb the battens on his own, although his feet were still extremely sore and he walked with a halting limp. *That will mend,* he told himself. It will require time.

He met Captain Willits, a dapper little man with a quick wit and ready smile. *There should be no mutiny here,* he thought. This has the appearance of a happy ship. Ben was given a bunk in one of the officer's quarters and assigned two seamen, Sam and Andy, to attend to his needs. Ben felt that all this was unnecessary since he was beginning to feel good, what with the fresh sea air and the prospects of a long sea voyage, his spirits were bound to be enlivened. But the men replied, "Admirals orders, sir." Ben had seen the Admiral talking with Dr. Warcup on his way out. Ben was led to believe that he was getting some special attention.

Ben was certain that he was considered 'special' when, at 5 a.m. the next morning, the old Admiral, who should have been in his warm bed, appeared at Ben's bedside, staring down at him. He shook Ben to awaken him.

"We haven't long, lad. You sail in a few minutes, but I have something to ask you. "Ben shook the sleep from his head and sat up, "Yes sir."

"Where were you when the crew mutinied?"

"It was my off-watch, sir. I was in my bunk, sound asleep. They burst in, grabbed me from a sound sleep and bound my hands and gagged my mouth. I was led to the deck with all the other officers. Some of the officers were already dead, as was Captain Pigot. Others were trussed up like pigs to be barbecued, as I was. They had already secured the ship's guns and were in possession of thc ship."

"Hmmm. Did you not tell Captain Pigot at any time that you suspected a mutiny?"

"Yes, sir. Many times, but he refused to listen. In my report I indicated that he was callous to any suggestions that there might be disobedience or mutiny on his ship."

"Yes, I remember. You need not fear a court martial. You cannot be blamed for the loss of the ship. There may be an inquiry, that is all. But we will capture the *Hermione* and her mutinous crew and the crew will be court martialled. You may be called on to testify, but your evidence in this report is complete enough that that may not be necessary. All England will be up in arms over this mutiny. It is so brutal and yet I can understand why it had to happen. We must guard against this sort of thing. It weakens us against our enemies and stirs up the citizens at home. Many of us knew of Pigot's evil ways. We are at fault for not acting earlier. I have already sent word to Captain Edward Hamilton to seek out and capture the *Hermione* and her crew at once. They must be brought to justice. I shudder to think what would have happened if you had not made so heroic a trip along the coast of Venezuela. I can't imagine that you thought that you could survive such a trip through wilderness."

"I had my doubts, sir, but there was no other alternative," said Ben.

"One other thing. How did you get sent to the *Hermione* in the first place?"

"I received orders at Gibraltar to transfer to her, Christmas Day. I was on my way to serve under Admiral Nelson, sir."

"But why *that* ship? I know that Admiral Nelson was beside himself when he heard that you were being sent off to the Caribbean."

"I may have made an enemy somewhere along the line, sir," Ben ventured cautiously. He had no proof against the Williamson family and he wished not to condemn anyone without proper proof.

"You don't think your transfer had anything to do with your testimony at the court martial that followed the Camperdown affair, do you?"

"I can't be certain, sir."

Then he screwed up his face and smiled down at Ben. "If I didn't know better, lad, I'd swear that every so often you get tired of the routine of the British Navy and strike out on your own for a little excitement and adventure. Why, there was the time with the slaver, a stint on a pirate ship in which you brought in three ships with only ten men and gave me a twenty-one gun salute to boot, and now this. You spend more time out of His Majesty's service than in it, I fear, but not by choice, I hope. Whatever it is, your reports sure do make interesting reading.

"Rest, now lad and have a safe voyage home. I hope we will meet again and soon, only next time, under more pleasant circumstances."

After a day at sea, Ben began to feel like a new man. He still had periodic bouts with fever and he suffered terribly from diarrhea, but just being at sea made it all more bearable. He felt a force within him that was wresting his health back from the clutches of death and he was relieved. He longed for home and more than ever now, he could close his eyes and see his Annie, beckoning to him. She was there now, real and he could almost feel her touch on his arms. But there were bad days too when Sam and Andy took turns nursing him through the fever and the chills. They would sit for hours, paragons of patience, waiting on his every need. Ben came to know them well and liked them both. Sam was a Cheshire lad, from a small farm and had run away because he loved the sea more than the plow. Andy was from a wealthy family and swore that he would find a place at his father's manor in Norwich for Ben, if ever he chose to quit the sea. But Ben knew that if ever he left the sea it would be just to settle in a small cottage overlooking the English Channel, like the place where he was born. He played whist with the boys. Ben never was good at playing cards, mainly he thought, because it was just play and not for real. They three, who were all single, set up a tontine of a few pounds, against which of them would be the last to marry. Sam bet that he would never marry because he liked the sea life too well. Andy expected to marry next year, but cheerfully put in his five pounds anyway. He had a sweetheart from his childhood that he was certain would have him. Ben wrote an I.O.Y., a note, to cover his bet. He had no money left. Whichever man held out the longest against marriage would win the tontine.

Otherwise, the trip home was uneventful. On good days, Ben brought out his balalaika which had suffered during his long walk. He retouched some of the gold ornamentation and brightened it up considerably. He found a bit of lacquer and refinished the case and put on the new strings that he was saving for it. The ship's carpenter lent him a bit of paint used for the figurehead and some fine brushes. For a few days, he actually felt well enough to play and Sam and Andy enjoyed his playing immensely, applauding his every effort.

The *Swift* lived up to her name and they were back in England at the Royal Dockyards sooner than Ben had thought possible. Ben felt quite well, but had relapses too frequently for comfort. He was to be transported to the Naval hospital at Greenwich for a period of rest and observation.

As luck would have it, he went into a deep sweat just as they were putting him into the carriage to take him to hospital. He emerged, drenched in sweat and had to be assisted to his bed. The wards were full of the badly wounded, those lacking limbs, eyes, or afflicted with fevers as he was. The call went out for the doctor and he came at once. Ben woke up some hours later, exhausted from the fever, to look up into the smiling eyes of Jim Ledyard.

"Jim," he said in a weak voice. "I can't believe it is you. Now I am sure to mend."

"Lay quietly for awhile. You'll be alright. I can do something for the demon that has seized your gut and is causing the diarrhea, but there is little I can do for malaria. It will lessen in time and you will be nearly normal again, but you must rest now."

"Did they get the dispatches that I was carrying to the Lord Admiral? Ben asked urgently.

"Yes. I found them on you when I examined you and had them delivered by medical courier immediately. There was a big whole page about the mutiny and your brave deeds in the *Chronicle* today. I'll bring it for you to read later on. I think the *Gazette* will have something about it too. From what I have heard, there is a great uproar in Parliament and the town folks are most angry with the mutineers. I expect the whole country will be in an uproar as the news spreads. They are calling for the immediate execution of the mutineers and the return of the ship, *Hermione*."

But Ben was more concerned about recovering and getting back to sea.

"Do you not have any herbs from the Caribbean to use on malaria?"

"No, lad. The medical board forbids their use. Anyway, I could not get the correct herbs here. No one knows what they are or how to ask for them."

"If only I could get back to Barbados, I might find the old witch doctor and get another supply. Herbs worked wonders on our lads when they had fever in the Caribbean," said Ben.

Then Ben told him of his experiences in the *Hawk* and explained how he had contacted an old shaman on Barbados who had sold him herbs that seemed to work wonders on the local fevers. He also explained how his successor had carelessly thrown the herbs away, even after Ben had explained their importance and the preparation of each to the new surgeon.

"That is not surprising," said Ledyard. "Most surgeons believe in only what they have been taught. If they were taught that herbals do not work, then they believe that. No one looks ahead to new cures or new medicines. I am proud of you for using herbs. It is a major step forward. Someone must have noticed that you saved all those lives. The more cases there are where the surgeons can see good results from herbs, the sooner they will act to accept them."

Ben spent the next two weeks resting and ridding himself of a host of unwanted intestinal parasites. At the end of the two weeks, he was more restless than rested. He was anxious to get back to sea. He would do anything to get aboard a ship. He made a few friends there and met a few men that he had known from former ships. They all wanted the same thing, to get back to the sea. They were like a pascle of flounder, ill-at-ease if they were not in the water. But most of the men that he saw there would never sail again. They were too stove up, a missing leg, or arm, blinded, or crippled beyond repair. He felt that he was lucky. His feet had healed on the trip home and he could walk nearly as well as ever now. He had his arms in tact and he had not suffered an attack of malaria for two whole weeks. The attacks of diarrhea had ceased, almost. He was gaining strength daily and asked permission to walk down to the Naval Academy which was just across the street. From there, he could look out on the Thames and all of the ships coming and going. He did not tell anyone that he climbed the hill to the Observatory which was the physical point of the Greenwich Meridian. All time and space for Englishmen started and ended there. The area afforded a fine view of most of London and he could see the tall masts of ships at the merchant docks and also the Royal Docks as well as the buildings. *The world below is a hum of activity, men going and doing, and here I am , an invalid,* he thought. It was balm for his tortured soul and he felt like a new man whenever he returned from his walks.

One day when he returned from a chilly walk on a cold day early in March, he was told that he had visitors. *Visitors? I don't know anyone here.* Ben sat on the edge of his bed and asked to have them shown in.

He could not believe his eyes when he beheld Betsy and Tom Fremantle. They had come to pay him a visit. Of course, they would have learned about his return from the *Chronicle.* "What a pleasant surprise," he said, grabbing her hand and kissing it. He remembered that it was she who had taught him how to greet a lady when aboard the *Seahorse* in the Mediterranean.

"Oh Ben, you did remember what I have taught you." She grabbed him and gave him a firm hug, as firm as she dared in her condition. She was due to deliver a baby boy in a month or so.

Then he turned to Tom. The taught muscles in his face told that he was still in pain with his arm after the battle of Tenerife. Ben thoughtfully reached for his left arm which was whole and took it warmly in both his hands.

"Well, lad you have had a most scary adventure," said Tom.

"That I have and glad I will be to get back to the Mediterranean Fleet and Lord Nelson. How does he fare?"

"Why, he is coming here to London at the end of the week. He has some business with the Admiralty and must see the Surgeon's Hall. I have had some dealings with them also. It has been a trying ordeal with this injured arm of mine. They must approve my injury before I may be awarded a pension. I think sometimes that the approving is more injurious than was the original wound.

Betsy broke in. "How are you feeling, Ben?"

"I am most well, thank you, my lady. I still have a bit of pain in my feet, but they are nearly healed and I have not suffered from the fever for over two weeks."

"This is such a dreary place, so depressing. Dear boy, why don't you come and live with us at Bolton Row and Curzon Street? It is not far away and you can always come back here if you are unhappy. We have an extra room and you would be welcome company. And with the holidays coming, you need to be with friends." Her smile was so charming that Ben knew immediately why Tom Fremantle had married her. She was an angel.

Ben looked at Tom and he smiled, indicating his firm approval.

Ben knew Betsy. She was looking forward to his playing the balalaika and telling stories of his adventures. She loved that, would sit there and eat up ever note, every word. He felt for her too. She was saddled with an invalid husband who required a good bit of care with his injured arm and must at times be cranky and out of sorts. She would refer to him as 'chrumpy'. She needed some cheering up too.

"I'll ask Mr. Ledyard, my surgeon if I may be released. I shall return shortly."

Ben found Ledyard tending a recent amputee, trying to comfort him and replacing his soiled bandages. When he had completed his task, Ben advanced. 'Sir, I have Betsy and Tom Fremantle here visiting. They would like to have me come to live with them on Bolton Row, if you will sign my release."

"I don't know, lad. You are only back a short time. I cannot be certain that the diarrhea will not return and the fever will come and go at its own pleasure. Are they equipped to care for you properly there?"

"But I am well, sir. I can walk some distance now and I have not been troubled by either the fever or diarrhea in the past two weeks. I am fit."

"I suppose that you are, as tough as you are. But you must promise me that you will return to hospital at the first sign of any trouble."

"That I will, sir."

"Come, I'll sign the papers."

So Ben headed off to Bolton Row with Tom and Betsy. He had resolved to visit the Admiralty himself tomorrow to see if he might be able to get a ship. On the way to their cottage, Tom explained that Admiral Nelson was in a storming rage when he heard that Ben had been sent off on the *Hermione.* He thought that it was some slighting of him since he had requested that Ben serve with him in the Mediterranean. He also thought that Ben may have made some enemies in the Williamson family as a result of his part in the court martial after the battle of Camperdown. "At any rate, Horatio is trying to talk the Admiralty into giving him the *Foudroyant* which will be commissioned early in January. If he gets it, I am sure he will want you well and back in his service."

"I would be honoured to serve with him again," said Ben.

So, Ben went the next day to See Lord Admiral Spencer. He did not have to wait long at all. Spencer was anxious to discuss the *Hermione* mutiny with him and asked to have other petitioners put off for an hour so that he might speak with young Mr. Rundel. They talked of the events that led up to the mutiny and of Ben's frequent warnings to Captain Pigot. Ben asked if Pigot had any family.

"None that I am aware of. There was a brother in there somewhere, but we have not been able to find him."

Ben asked about others of the crew. Most of the eighteen officers who were killed were single, but some had come from prominent families. "There is a big ruckus going on in Parliament over this mutiny. We'll not hear the end of it for awhile. But you have no worry, lad. You did all that you could. I commend you for your bravery. I understand that Admiral Harrington has sent Captain Hamilton to retake the ship and bring the mutineers to trial."

Ben asked some questions about ships and was assured that Admiral Nelson had already requested, that if he were seen to be fit, he should accompany him back to the Mediterranean. He had no worries there. Ben was anxious to see Lord Nelson now. He would arrive tomorrow.

Ben made a short stop at his bank and was delighted to see that the total had increased over what it was the last time he had checked. He needed more pocket money. He should pay Betsy and Tom for his lodgings and he needed a uniform since his old one had been demolished by the jungle. He was still wearing hospital clothes. The Fremantles clearly lived on a tight budget and he knew that the money would be welcome while he was there. Perhaps Tom's pension would come through soon.

Apparently the ceremonies making Nelson a Lord had taken place some months earlier in St. Paul's Cathedral. From what Ben heard, it was a most colourful affair and Betsy Fremantle told him all about it, smiling and glowing as she did throughout.

"Tomorrow Lord and Lady Nelson will stop by in the afternoon late and we are going to attend an opera by Mozart after supper. Would you like to join us?"

Ben almost flew out of his chair with excitement. "I would be most delighted to attend the opera with you both," he said. In his mind was the vivid image of a beautiful lady, his Annie, whom he had seen many months ago now but had not forgotten. He would almost certainly see her there at the opera and he could not wait. He was hardly able to contain himself with his great excitement.

But then reality hit him. He was wearing a plain suit of clothes given to him by Jim Ledyard at hospital. It was one of his older suits that he had outgrown, a nice dark green with black ribbing, but not suitable for polite society. He had no uniform or decent clothes to wear to a social function like the opera. He did not have time to get a new uniform made between now and tomorrow evening.

But Tom calmed him down. "I have a leftenant's uniform that is in quite good repair. It belonged to Tom Hardy. We were leftenants together on the *Culloden* some years back. Then Tom went and made commander and no longer needed his leftenant's uniform. He left the uniform with me. I have kept it, well, just because it belonged to Hardy, I guess. He is about your size. Come, let's try it on."

Ben went along willingly. Betsy helped to get out the uniform which had been packed away and found a good shirt and neck cloth of Tom's for him to wear. The uniform did fit him quite well. He thought that he was still quite peaked and thin as he looked in the mirror, but there was nothing there that he would willingly disown.

He decided to go for a long walk to cool off. *By this time tomorrow, I may have seen her,* he thought. He did find the offices of a good naval clothier where he would order his new uniform on Monday.

Besides, he had never been to this opera. It would be an adventure. He thought of all of those deadly hours walking across the Spanish Main, hoping to see Annie again, and now it might even happen. Betsy had told him that the opera was, '*Cosi Fan Tutte,*' and that it was supposed to be funny. His mind was in a whirl as he walked around London. *What will I say if she speaks to me, what will I do?* He was having all the pangs of anxiety of a teenager, well, he was still a teenager in years, but certainly a man in experience. *All but one kind of experience,* he thought. In matters of the heart, he was a newcomer and a total novice and he would be the first to admit it.

"That evening he pulled out *laika* and played for Betsy and Tom. He had considerable trouble getting the instrument in tune. It had suffered in all of his travels. They seemed to enjoy the evening and even sang some of the good old songs with him.

Betsy did not tell him until the next day that she had spent the afternoon running about the neighbourhood trying to find a lady for Ben to escort to the opera. She thought it totally improper for a handsome young gentleman like himself to attend the opera without a lady to grace his side. He learned that he was to take a Miss Pamela Grant to the opera and that she was a true beauty.

Late that afternoon, Lord Nelson and his wife, Frances, whom he called, Fanny, came to visit.

Lord Nelson embraced Ben with his good arm and seemed delighted to see him. He introduced his wife, whom Ben had never met. She seemed the quiet, efficient little woman, most devoted to her Horatio. She was not the least bit forward or flouncy. She was almost 'mousy' and delicate. They were staying just near by and Betsy convinced them to stay for supper. She thought that some good 'sea talk' would perk Tom up who had still much pain and often did not eat well. The men visited late into the afternoon and Ben sat, listening to every word while the women visited in the parlour. There was so much to learn about the politics of the Navy. He did not realize, that if he had been disabled from the Caribbean adventure and unable to work again, he could apply to the Admiralty for a disability pension. The pension would be granted, if Surgeon's Hall found him to be truly incapacitated by his injury. It seems that Nelson would draw 1000 pounds a year for life for the loss of an arm, but Fremantle would get only 200 pounds per year for his injured right arm.

Then they talked about the new ship, the *Foudroyant.* She was one of those being built quickly to beef up their naval power, but Tom thought that she would be a fine ship. He would not be ready for the sea any time soon, but Lord Nelson seemed as eager as a school boy anticipating holidays. Horatio spoke of another ship, the *Vanguard,* which might be ready to sail sooner. He hoped to get the command of either, but he felt that the latter would make a poor flag ship.

Betsy prepared a fabulous meal and Ben ate heartily. When it was over, the Nelson's called for a carriage for six. They sent a runner to the local stables. Once aboard, Betsy gave directions to the home of Pamela Grant.

The footman went to the door to announce that her carriage for the opera was waiting. A few minutes later, a most charming young lady of perhaps twenty emerged, beautifully dressed. She came from a fine London family and Ben was amazed to have her for his partner at the opera. He had expected some dowdy, fat young lady that no on else wanted. He climbed down from the carriage and introduced himself, bowing to her and kissed her hand. Betsy looked on with total approval.

At Covent Garden, long lines of finely dressed people waited to get in to hear the opera. This was its first performance in London, and there was great excitement. Some had heard Mozart's *Don Giovanni* earlier and were in great fever to hear a comic opera by the same composer. Ben bought Pamela a ticket and escorted her to a seat next to Betsy Fremantle. They would have a good view, and Ben knew he would watch constantly for Annie. *This is silly. Here I am with a most beautiful young woman and I feel nothing for her. All I can think of is the memory that I carried of an angel who sang like a bird and has captured my heart. For all I know, Annie may be married,* he thought.

He spoke to Pamela for a few minutes before the curtain rose. It seemed that she knew nothing about the sea or the war. All that interested her was fashion and the opinions of her betters and equals. Ben had to admit that he knew nothing of women's fashions and cared little about the opinions of his betters. Secretly, he did not even want to acknowledge that he had any *betters.* He was fast coming to feel that all men were created equal, but that they did not necessarily have equal talents. Anyone who was willing to explore his talents to the fullest might not need to feel that he had any *betters.*

But when the curtain went up, Ben sat amazed. The music flowed out of the orchestra box like a placid sea, engulfing him in a wonder of stimulating sounds. Ben had not had time to explore the libretto of the opera, but he thought that it meant something like, "Women Are Like That." The opera opened with a scene in a Neapolitan cafe where two young officers are arguing with a cynical old man about the fidelity of woman kind. Don Alfonso declared that the fiancees of the two officers will never prove faithful. Women simply do not have it in them to remain faithful to one man. The young, innocent officers disagree violently and in the end, Don Alfonso bets them 100 sequins that both women will betray them. The terms are that the two young men must do exactly as the Don tells them for twenty-four hours. The officers end the act by speculating on what they will do with all of that money when it is theirs.

But the catch is that the young officers are to woo each other's sweetheart, masquerading as Albanians. The girls have been told that their lovers have been ordered away on duty. Now the fun began, but for Ben, it was a lost cause. All the beauty of the music passed by his ears like a midnight wind when he saw who was singing the part of Dorabella. It was his Annie, with her vibrant, brilliant mezzo-soprano voice.. He heard nothing but her voice, saw nothing but her face. Nothing else interested him for the rest of the evening. He even forgot that he had a young lady that he was supposed to escort. Ben sat forward in his seat, soaking up every precious note, every movement in his vivid memory.

During the intermission, Ben excused himself and wandered back toward where the singers were gathered, cooling off, as it were. He did not see Annie there. The advertisement that he read outside said that she was , 'Annie Sutherlin'. He ventured forward and asked one of the singers where Annie Sutherlin was. She replied, "In her dressing room. She rarely waits out here." Then the warning bell sounded and the singers began to file back to their posts. Ben waited. Then a door to port opened and there she stood. He smiled. It had to be a stupid smile, he thought, because he did not know her. But their eyes met yet again. Her's said something urgent that he was not sure he could read. He was certain that she had recognized him from the sketch of him that had appeared in the *Chronicle* recently. It had been a fair likeness done by a talented artist while Ben lay in bed. There was recognition and remembrance there. She spoke just a word. "I must go, my call." Then she smiled warmly and turned and headed to the stage, waving shyly as she went. The last bell rang and she was on. Ben was especially handsome that night. He did Hardy's uniform justice and *I have just done a thing that Hardy would never do*, he thought.

Back at his seat, Betsy nudged him. "You are supposed to talk to the young lady, you clout." Ben tried, but his heart was lost for good. He loved Annie, no matter what it might cost him. She had brought him out of the jungles and llanos from the Spanish Main, and she would always be his. On his way out of the theatre, he ventured to ask an older gentleman who looked like an avid operagoer if Annie Sutherlin was married.

The old gentleman smiled and said, "No, but there's at least a hundred young bucks just like yourself who would carry her off to the altar in a second if she would only agree. Savin' herself, she is."

That made Ben feel better. So what if he would sail off to the Mediterranean in a few days. This accursed war could not last forever. It would soon be over and he would come back and claim Annie as his own. From there the fantasies grew more and more private, to where they had to waken him when he arrived back home. He went through the usual pleasantries with Pamela, thanking her for a lovely evening, but he knew that she would never go to the opera with him again and he couldn't say that he would blame her.

When he took his leave of Lord Nelson, the good man shook his hand and patted him on the shoulder.

"We'll sail again and soon Ben. I have asked for a

position for you as second leftenant on the *Foudroyant* as soon as she is ready to commission. Ed Berry will be joining us as Captain. He has just married, you know, a fine girl by the name of Forster from Norwich."

"I am ready, sir."

Ben went to sleep that night with visions of wondrous things before him. He would try to see Annie again before he shipped out. But the next three days were hectic with teas and parties set up by Betsy Fremantle. She was determined, in spite of their limited budget, to introduce Ben to a proper young lady. "A man at sea needs someone to think about him and worry over him," she said. He met a Miss Marquette, who was so proper that he had trouble speaking with her. Then there was a Miss Wimple, a bit of a snob and a Miss Hadley, who was pretty, but not Ben's type. He thought that he would float away if he had to drink any more tea.

He went to Covent Garden twice, hoping to get a glimpse of Annie again, but she was not there either time. Now he understood why Annie did not spend much time with the other singers. She was a diva, it was true, but she was more of a country girl, a loner, and felt out of place among them. He wanted to tell Betsy about Annie, but he knew she would only say that he had not a hope of capturing the affections of such a beauty as she. Half of the single men in London were after her and half of *them* could afford to buy the crown jewels.

Then, when a large manila envelope came for him in the hands of a naval courier, he felt relieved. Perhaps he could get back to sea and away from all this socializing and temptation. His fingers trembled as he opened the envelope. He skipped all of the officialdom nonsense and read,

'You are instructed to report to Portsmouth by the first of March, to Captain Ed Berry of the *Foudroyant*. You will serve us as second leftenant of that vessel.'

Ben made ready to leave. He had not taken the time to have his new uniform made and there were only three days left in which to do it. He set out as fast as he could to German Street to have his measurements taken. The man who waited on him was most businesslike and seemed to understand that he must leave for Portsmouth in three days. Ben thought that the tailor recognized him from the picture that had appeared in the *Gazette* . The man was extremely kind to him, asking him to take a seat while he completed his calculations.

"And would the young gentleman like a pair of boots, perhaps?"

Ben shook his head. He would always remember the pain he had suffered from swollen feet in boots that he could not remove. "No, sir, but I would like a pair of black shoes with gold buckles. *I am a man of substance now, I might as well wear fine clothes,* he thought. But the truth is that in spite of his expensive shoes, he would always be 'the Navy's poorest dressed officer'. He looked about as fine in Hardy's old uniform as he would ever look. He seemed to have a knack for sitting on a spot of grease or rubbing his shirt sleeve in a dab of spilled ink. It was just his nature. *Doers can't always keep clean. I wonder how the Admiralty expects a man to wear white trousers aboard ship where there is tar, rust, brick dust, grease and any number of other things to stain them. It is just not natural.* He resolved to change the uniform if he ever became Lord Admiral. He would require black trousers that would not show the dirt.

"Your uniform and accessories will be ready day after tomorrow at 2 p.m., Leftenant Rundel."

With that settled, he hired a carriage and went to see Jim Ledyard at Greenwich.

Jim turned dark, tired eyes to him when he came walking into hospital. Ben thought that his friend could not wait to get back to sea as well. He was being worked to death here.

"I have good news, Jim. I leave for Portsmouth in two

days to become the second leftenant of the *Foudroyant* . What do you think of that."

"I think that it is darned foolishness, lad. You are still recovering from a serious illness, three of them in fact. You should have a full month of rest. The rigorous work and demands of a full time commission are too much for you right now."

Ben looked alarmed. "You mean that you will not release me to my new ship?"

"I mean that I would prefer to see you rest here in London for a month more."

"But you will let me go, sir?"

"I should like to examine you first. Come this way," as he beckoned Ben to come to his examination surgery.

Jim Ledyard probed, looked, and listened to Ben, but could find nothing wrong that required beaching him any longer.

"You seem quite well, as far as I can see. How do you really feel? I want the truth now."

"Just fine, sir. Fine," insisted Ben.

"I will release you if you promise to take good care of yourself and not get overtired," said Ledyard.

"Oh, I will, sir. You can trust me." But Ben knew that the Service was not that way and that an officer must always do his duty, no matter how tired or sick he might be.

He hesitated for a moment. "Yes, I'll let you go, but I can take no responsibility if you have a relapse. Get all the rest you can, and the best of luck to you." At that he grabbed Ben's hand and shook it, smiling warmly. He liked this young fellow, even if he was a nut.

So Ben picked up his new uniform two days later, paid his respects to Tom and Betsy who had made his stay in London most pleasant. He slipped twenty pounds under his pillow with a note that said, "Betsy and Tom: This is for the new baby, a boy, I hope. Good Luck and thank you both. Ben." That way Betsy would accept it with glee. She was looking forward to the new baby and it should arrive any day now. He boarded a stage to Portsmouth the next morning early. He decided to buy some special supplies for his new appointment, but that could wait until Portsmouth.

The ride from London to Portsmouth was no smoother than it had been all those months earlier when he last made the trip. There was one incident that almost brought him to his knees. He sat in a small pub while they changed horses. He had ordered a scone and some milk. Suddenly a small furry creature climbed onto his lap and sat there on spindly legs looking up at him with sparkling green eyes. She (all cats had to be 'she' in his world) was a beautiful grey like his Tagon had been. She rubbed her soft head against his hand and began to purr. *She is hungry,* he thought. Ben ordered a scrap of beef and a platter of milk for her. She ate ravenously and as soon as she was through, she climbed back to his lap, leaving claw marks all the way up his leg as she hoisted herself aboard. Ben petted her and thought how lovely she is. He asked the serving girl if anyone owned her, but the girl shook her head, "no."

"She showed up 'ere a few days ago. Been feedin' off left overs ever since." Ben thought hard. He wanted the little gal, but he felt that he would not be able to care for her properly. His career was still too mobile. He never knew where he would be from one day to the next.

"I cannot take her with me. Will you promise me that you will feed her scraps every day <u>faithfully</u> and let her sleep in some warm place in winter?" said Ben. "I'll come by pretty often to check on her. Here, I will give you some shillings for your trouble. Will you keep her for me?" he pleaded.

The girl was young and not particularly pretty. She nodded her assent and said that she would treat it like she was her own. She reached her hand out for the shillings and smiled broadly at Ben. The stage was called and Ben was off. His last glimpse of the little animal was enough to nearly jerk out his heart. *She is so like Tagon.*

He arrived much more tired than he thought he should be and sore in every joint. He went aboard that day. Some ordnance had just arrived and was being stowed away. There were boxes and crates everywhere. He found the second leftenant's cabin and stowed his gear. The ship was so new that she smelled of tar and hemp and freshly shaved oak. He liked her at once. Captain Berry arrived two days later, leaving a bride with a tear-stained face waiting on the shore. She had come down to see him off, but was not made of the same stuff as Betsy Fremantle. She could not endure a long sea voyage in war time. The trip back to London would be enough for her.

Ben put his heart into his work, but took as much time to rest as he could. He learned that they were to sail the ship to London for final outfitting and provisioning. It would be her first sea trial. Captain Berry was anxious to get away and they sailed two days later.

After a week, word came from Lord Nelson that they were changing ships. "We will sail in the *Vanguard* from Portsmouth." The *Foudroyant* would be delayed too long in sailing and Nelson was an impatient man. We were to join him in Portsmouth as soon as possible That meant another bone jostling ride for Ben, but he was getting used to it. He could not help but remember with a slight smile on his face the time he had hired a horse named, 'His Majesty,' that turned out to be a wayward female that he preferred to call 'Vixen'. *What an ordeal that was.* The stage stopped at the inn where he had found the beautiful grey kitten. Ben went in and sure enough, there she was washing her face as she sat by the fireplace on a rug. *What a little gem.* He wanted to sweep her up and put her in his pocket and take her off to sea with him, but he knew that would be unwise. He spent all the time that he could with her and then left a handful of coins with the young girl who was caring for her. "Take good care of her for me," he said. She smiled and curtsied to him ever so gracefully.

Other good news came from Nelson also. It seems that Betsy Fremantle had been delivered of a healthy baby boy on the eleventh of March. 'She is recovering and doing quite well. Tom is still crumpy,' he added.

Chapter Nine

A Sultan's Beef or a French Prison

When the visiting women were all shooed off the *Vanguard* and the last pot of beef stowed on board, Nelson hoisted his pennant and declared this to be his flag ship. He was clearly less than satisfied with it as a flag ship. He would have preferred the *Foudroyant* but he could not have endured another month on shore. Ben had fared quite well. He did have one malaria attack in Portsmouth, but it was quite mild and almost no one noticed that he was suffering. It occurred during the night and he awoke lying in a pool of sweat. He hoped that the disease would wear itself out soon.

Ben enjoyed many fine meals with Lord Nelson and Captain Berry and the other officers, Mr. Harvey Pitts, first Leftenant and Mr. James Callan. Pitts was a tall, straight, serious lad from Cornwall and Ben took a liking to him at once. Callan was a womanizer from Norfolk who had a sharp tongue and a fast wit. He was a bit stocky of build and not particularly handsome. He and Nelson could tell stories that were beyond belief, and so, made fine supper company. There was an exceptional crop of young midshipmen aboard also and Ben came to know most of them and liked them. Ben improved his game of whist and learned how to play chess.

There was much to be done aboard the *Vanguard.* Besides his regular duties of managing his division, he went back to studying naval strategy and gunnery. He read eagerly to try to find out which strategies worked best in which situations. Nelson often teased him about burying his nose in a book. But Ben made up for his lack of social graces by playing 'laika' and singing for both officers and men. Ben was hounded for stories of his forty days on the Spanish Main, lost and isolated from all human contact. At first he thought to make a good story out of the tall woman, but later he thought better of it. He had no notion whether he ever really saw her or not. The crew thought it great sport of a Sunday to sit and ask Ben about his adventures. He was a most popular officer and much appreciated by Lord Nelson and his officers.

Leftenant Callan told him that he should write down the accounts of his adventures and become rich selling them to the public. "They are hungry for this sort of stuff you know, especially if you throw in a woman or two here and there." But Ben would not even think of writing about his life for another twenty five years. He had so much more that he wanted to do, that to write about his life now seemed pointless to him. His life had just begun.

During the passage out, Ben became more aware of the strange morbid nature of Nelson. He seemed to brood a lot and had a sense that the future of all England lay on his shoulders. He seemed to feel that fate had set a course for him and no matter how smartly he tacked or wore ship, he could not escape it. He was destined to do something great for King and Country and he felt drawn to the most dangerous scenarios in order to fulfill his destiny. He and Ben talked about serious matters from time to time, and Ben developed a deep respect for the man.

The trip to the Tagus was uneventful. Ben drilled his division at the guns until he was satisfied that they could hit a large barrel at a quarter mile. They were good lads, steady, seasoned and respectful. He treated them well and they respected his steady, unwavering discipline.

As they came smartly to anchor at the mouth of the Tagus, the smoke from the 21 -gun salute still lingering on the deck, Ben saw a flurry of flags from the signal halyards of the flag ship. Mr. Creer, ensign, came running to Captain Berry with his translations. "Sir, the Admiral is required aboard the flagship at once, and Mr. Rundel as well."

Ben wondered what he would be needed for, but he put on his best dress uniform and, for once clean shaven and neat, proceeded to join Lord Nelson in the ship's boat. When they arrived, Lord Nelson was announced first, after the boarding ceremonies, the piping, drumming and whistling that signaled that an Admiral was coming aboard. St. Vincent stood there himself to welcome Lord Nelson. "So good of you old fellow to heed a seaman's call and come back to us. You have been missed, you know." At that he took Nelson by the left hand and they headed for the Admiral's cabin. Ben liked John Jervis. True, he was an old war horse, hardened and tough as they come, in spite of a kindly face, but Ben had seen him in many situations. If a man was negligent of duty or seemed a slackard, he would bring down discipline as hard as he could. A traitor or a mutineer was dealt with speedily by hanging by the neck from the yard arm, but a man who had suffered bad luck and was sincere might get a kindly word and even some help. One sailor lost his life savings from his pocket during an action. St. Vincent refunded the man his money in full, from his own pocket before all of his assembled ship's company. He was most selective when it came to choosing captains and officers to carry out distant missions where there was much at stake. There were only a select few that he really trusted, but still his nature was such that most men liked him and he was, whether conscious of it or not, one of the 'brethren' who formed such a strong, winning team that the French and Spanish had not a chance against them. Furthermore, St. Vincent was constantly wearing down the points of his quills writing out orders that would make the life of his men more bearable and happy. He ordered the decks to be scrubbed before dawn so that the ship would be ready to come to action or chase if an enemy ship appeared on the horizon at dawn. He had a sense of humour too. One day when the seas were especially choppy, he ordered all of the chaplains to come aboard the flag ship for a conference. They arrived looking much the worse for wear and green in the face. Most were not true seafaring men. But he took stern measures when he sensed that his leftenants were running strongly to 'fat,' and was ready to arrest young officers who went ashore wearing round hats that made them look like landsmen.

After a few minutes, Lord Nelson emerged from the cabin, his face showing a bit of the one sided smile that he often displayed when not totally pleased. "The Admiral will see you now," he said to Ben.

Ben was announced and stepped into the bright cabin to face Admiral St. Vincent.

"I have read the dispatches that Lord Nelson brought out from England concerning your conduct in the Caribbean and I must say that I am blown away by it all. That was a dashed good bit of work, Rundel. Where do you come by all of this swish and nerve?"

"I guess a man does what he has to do in order to survive, sir."

"Well, from what I have read, you are a true survivor and have the makings of a fine officer. I have a duty for you. It's a simple duty, should take only about three weeks. We in the fleet are short of good beef. It seems that one of the food transports has gone missing and we have not had any meat brought in for over a month. I hear that the Sultan of Algiers has some fine beef animals in his flocks. I am sending you with a crew of twenty to Algiers to pick up 400 live beefs. We have enough men here to slaughter and salt the meat. You need only get it here in an efficient manner. I am loaning you a recently captured ship, the *Mignon* for the trip. She has been used in the Mediterranean for years as a transport for animals and grain. Should serve you well. You may have your pick of crew from the *Vanguard* . I expect you to be off with the next tide. Oh, and I will be sending Mr. Horace Peech with you as purser. He will do the dealing and will take charge of the money to pay the Sultan.

Ben's brow furrowed and he looked concerned. "Sir, the sky is turning an evil black and I fear that we are in for a bad storm."

"Oh, we get those storms every now and again. They

usually blow over in a few hours. If you can weigh anchor by, say, 6 p.m., you should be well on your way and out of harm's way by the time she gets here. Good luck to you now."

Ben would remember the Admiral's parting statement, 'Good luck to you now' for a long time to come. He had that strange seaman's feeling that this was not just another of those 'little storms'. Perhaps if St. Vincent had come on deck and looked at the sky himself, he would have reconsidered, but he was a busy man. There were other more important matters tugging at his mind.

On the way to the ship, Ben ran through his mind the names of the men he would want. *Dash! He had forgotten to ask if he could use Tom Murphy from the Culloden."* He had not seen Tom in many months, not since his injury and he wanted to see him before he sailed. Tom would be an asset on a trip like this too. He was raised on a farm and would know good beef when he saw it. *Let's see. There is Curran, Sharp, Gilmore, Moran, Frid, Roberts, Grist, Wallace, Mitchell, Wetmore, Tyrley, Marsden, Lapley, Hatton, Beetham and Cowley, with Tom and myself. That should be enough,* thought Ben.

Ben returned to the *Vanguard* and was not surprised that Nelson already knew about his orders. "Bad bit of luck having to sail on a night like this, lad, but if you hurry, you should be able to get through the Straits before the storm really breaks. It looks like it might be a corker," said Nelson.

"Sir, do you suppose that I might take midshipman Murphy from the *Culloden* with me? He is a man that I trust and he knows beef."

"I'll see what I can do. I'll get Ed Berry to send up some signals and see if we can get Mr. Murphy free of his present duty. What ship are you taking?"

"The *Mignon,"* sir.

"Hmmm. She is pretty old but otherwise suited to the job. But remember, lad, as soon as you complete this mission you are to return here to the *Vanguard* or whatever ship I am commanding. I agreed to lend you to St. Vincent only because I like beef and he agreed to let you return to me and serve at least six months of interrupted service. I need to prune off some rough edges on you if I am going to make a captain out of you."

"Yes, sir," said Ben most enthusiastically. He was delighted to think that Nelson even considered him as potential material for post captain.

Ben went off to get his gear. He would have to check for charts, chronometers, sextant and other essential gear on board the *Mignon* after he had boarded her. Meantime, he called Mr. Rose to see that his division was piped to assemble on deck. When Ben emerged from his cabin, his men stood there lined up smartly. They were a good bunch, all stalwart fellows. He could take any one of them. He began to call out names. "Step down as I call your name. Roberts, Wallace, Sharp, Moran, ..."

When he was finished he said, "If there is any man of you that would rather stay here on blockade duty than come to Algiers with me, you may step back in line now." Not a muscle moved. Their faces were glowing with smiles. Nobody liked blockade duty. A chance for an adventure was always welcome, but Ben preferred to take men who were willing and able, not men who came because they were ordered to follow him. Besides, they all knew of his adventures on the Spanish Main and they considered that his life was blessed with adventure. No red blooded seaman would pass up a chance like this.

"You men are to gather up your gear at once and report to the long boat. Mr. Rose, have the longboat lowered, if you please. Ben cast a sidelong glance at the *Culloden*, but there was no sign of a ship's boat that might be carrying Tom. Would he show? But there was much to do. He stopped by Ed Berry's cabin and explained his mission. He apologized for having to take men from his ship, but they were just out from port and had more than a full complement of men. He promised to return swiftly. Ed gave him a pat on the back and wished him God speed for the beef. "But, lad, I'd delay a few hours if I were you. See those mean clouds out there and the wind is freshening by the minute."

"I know, sir. I spoke with the Admiral about that, but he gave orders for an immediate departure, within the hour. I have little choice."

"Well, stay close in and perhaps you will miss the brunt of the storm. I think we are in for a tough night and a stiff blow."

"I certainly agree, sir."

Ben hurried off, the last to jump into the boat as it danced violently in the choppy water. A small cheer went up as he climbed aboard. His men were ready, storm or no. *It is good to get to know the men,* he thought. *Otherwise I would never be able to gather together so fine a crew in such a short time.*

"Pull for the *Mignon,* lads," said Ben.

Once aboard, Ben waited for a few minutes. He had so hoped that midshipman Murphy would be able to attend him, but there was no sign of him. Ben went about the preparations for sailing, securing his gear below and lashing it to the deck because of the threatening storm. He looked at the chronometer. It was only 55 minutes since St. Vincent had given the order. He should set sail in five minutes. Ben went on deck. He had to sail, in spite of the fact that all his instincts dictated that he would be safer in the mouth of the Tagus until the storm blew over. "Up anchor. Man your braces, clew up the heads'ls, main top fores'l there." he called. He dared not put much sail on her. It was blowing at near-hurricane force already. She was a merchantman, a brig which had ample, large hatches and lifts rigged for loading large animals or pallets of grain into the hold. She was old, that was plain. Ben hoped that she would be seaworthy in a storm like this. He ran below quickly to inspect her hull to be certain that she had no major leaks or damages. He saw none, but the groaning and working of the timbers seemed excessive to him. *Perhaps I am just imagining things,* he thought.

Suddenly he heard a hail from somewhere nearby over the roaring of the wind. He looked out to port and there was Tom in the jolly boat, waving for them to wait for him. Ben called down, "Pull, lads, pull! We can't come about on short."

"Send down a line," came the reply.

Ben turned to Mitchell who was watching. Send them a rope, Mr. Mitchell. It would be good to have Tom aboard. Even if he was still a midshipman, he had nine more years experience at sea than Ben. He would be a grand help. After several tries, the men in the boat caught the rope and Tom gave a mighty leap and made it to the battens. He climbed aboard, soaked to the skin from the driving rain that was now turning the sky into a black night. His mates tied on his gear and they hauled it up to the deck like some dead fish.

"Get below, lad. We'll bring your gear so you can put on some foul weather clothes. Ben decided to go below to finish putting on his own foul weather gear. It was turning a nasty cold, the rain pelting in from the west at hammer force. The men, as they came out of the tops, raced below for warmer, drier clothes. "Sorry, sir, but the cap'n didn't think you would sail in this foul weather. He was goin' ta send me over tomorrow."

"We would not sail if I had my way, but we have orders, Tom. Now get below. They'll be right along with your gear. Your cabin is just forew'rd of mine."

Tom was the only other officer aboard, so Ben would have to make some changes so that he could have someone at the helm at all hours and someone to carry orders. Ben crawled into his tiny cabin. He shook and shed his wet clothes and quickly put on dry ones. Tom's gear came down about then and he told the men to take it to the first leftenant's cabin.

As soon as Ben was dressed, he sat down at his desk, which seemed to be wandering all over his cabin. He'd have to see to having it fastened down properly tomorrow. He pulled out his quill and began to set up a duty roster.

“Let’s see. Who would make the best cook. He had not considered the cooks position when he had chosen his men. They would be better off with Mr. Rosco, who was a fine cook but preferred the tops. Well, he was not aboard, so they would have to do with, he ran his pen down the list of names, Mr. Lapley. Ben thought that he had served briefly as a cook’s mate. He should be able to cook for twenty men and be able to handle the helm for a few hours a day. Soon he had the topmen assigned to watches and that left his deck hands. *No need to plan for order of manning guns. We have none. Sure hope that we do not meet any French frigates in the Mediterranean.*

He was just about to complete his list and post it in the chart room for the men to see when Tom stood at the door. “Permission to enter, sir.”

“That was another annoyance. They had no marines so there would be no one to maintain order and stand guard duty. He had already checked and found that they had all of the navigational instruments that they needed, but he had not checked for small arms. He checked their course once again, due S, then SE and then E through the Straits, if they could even make it. But the storm was coming from the east and it looked highly unlikely that they could make a easting without a great deal of tacking, if even then. His mind was in a whirl.

“Come in Tom. It is sure good to see you.” As he stood up, the ship lurched and they both nearly went sprawling in a heap on the floor, as they had when they were young midshipmen together. Both men laughed at the joyous reunion. Both were eager for an adventure and both devoted to the other to the point of sacrificing his life for his friend.

“You’re looking good, lad, after your battle with the Spanish Main. I read all about it in the *Gazette*, but you’ll have to tell me all first hand, if this infernal storm ever abates.” The ship lurched again. She was anything but stable in a storm. Ben excused himself to go above deck to check on the sails and set their course. He was sure the luffs needed seeing to. "Mr. Roberts, see to your gaff," he called through the deafening wind.

He turned to Tom. "This little ship is bobbing about like a cork. She must have nothing in the hold. I hope that she is provisioned for at least a week or two. The Admiral said that she was ready to sail. I did not take the time when I was below to examine her food stores. Go below and check on her stores, will you."

"Aye, aye sir."

Ben went to check on the small arms, ammunition to be certain that it was stowed where it could not get wet. But that night, there was no place aboard the *Mignon* that would be dry. The wind blew water through men's thick woolen jackets, as if there was nothing there. Within an hour, one of the sails had torn away and was flying loose. The gaff sail went next. It suddenly split from top to bottom as if someone had taken a knife to it and slit it open. Sails were pulling out of their gussets and fraying at the edges. Ben put two men at the helm, but they were having trouble standing up. The deck was now awash and one man shouted over the storm that he had seen the deck house lift off the deck with the last wave. *So much for the duty roster,* thought Ben.

As they steered on a tack that would take them towards the Straits, the wind suddenly died, then picked up again, coming now sharply from the east. Each successive wave seemed to pound harder on the little ship, pushing her sideways, shoving her bowsprit deep under water. Great volumes of water rolled from the deck and until, with one gigantic wave, the ship's boat came free and carried overboard. At that point, Ben made his way forward and relieved the men at the helm. They worked together to lash down the wheel. Ben ordered his men below, just as he saw a great split forming in the foremast. It crashed to the deck and carried overboard with the next great wave. But the wind was now so violent that the ship heeled so far to port that she was lying on her side. Ben looked at Tom. No fires had been lit yet, so he could forget that threat, but the ship would certainly not be able to right herself. “Hold on, lads. If she rights herself, we are in for a mighty knocking about,” shouted Ben. Each one grabbed something solid and waited. It seemed like perhaps five long minutes before the ship finally picked up a tall wave that set it high enough so that the one remaining sail could catch some air. When that happened, she bobbed back to upright position with great force, throwing men about violently, in spite of their secure holds. Moran, a small fellow who was caught unprepared, lay on the deck, rolling with the motion of the ship. He seemed to be unconscious, but before anyone could get to him, the ship heeled sharply over to starboard, and she groaned as if she was going under for good. Water poured down the companionway and through every possible crack, no matter how small, and the men were knee deep in unwanted ocean.

Ben looked at Tom and shook his head, shouting. “We seemed to have sailed right into the eye of the storm, even before we knew it.”

“Aye, and that was the eye back there where she reversed her winds.” It was anyone’s guess where they were or what their compass bearing might be. Ben judged that they had made it through the Straits, or nearly so and that the winds had driven them that far in a record sixteen and a half hours.

But it was not over. The winds blew now from the west, or so they judged. They felt the main mast go, saw it splinter below deck clear to the chocks and then it flew to pieces above decks and was gone, trailing a mass of halyards, lifts and braces behind it. Ben noted that the mainmast, at least, was rotten through to the center and would not have been considered safe on any British ship, but this was a Frenchie.

There was nothing for them to do. The winds were so violent that when Ben tried to venture above deck after the mainmast had carried away, he was nearly blown over. The lads reached hands out to him, grabbing him by his clothes and saved him only by the greatest of luck. The ship continued to heel far over, threatening each time not to right herself.

They clung to bolts sunk deeply into futtocks and anything they could get hold of. It must have been sometime later before anything more happened. It was disquieting to feel the ship's timbers work, moving what seemed unreal distances as they clung to what was left of the little brig.

After many hours of being jostled about and beaten by the ship, Ben had fallen to near unconsciousness. He felt a sharp jolt and heard a loud scraping sound. *Oh, God, we are gone aground on some spit,* he thought. There were many, especially along the French coast. Ben disentangled his fingers from the hold that he had and ventured to stand up. He was waist deep in water. His legs were numb and he could not feel his fingers. He began to briskly massage his legs and to slap his hands together to restore the circulation. The men were coming back to life. The extreme motion of the ship had ceased, but she was still bouncing about, as if some devil had grabbed her bow and held on tightly while another toyed with her stern.

"Come, we must see what is left of this old tub," said Ben. "Did you find any food, Mr. Murphy?"

"Aye, sir. Enough for about ten days if we eat lightly. Enough water, too, but who knows what is left by now."

"Are there any spare masts?"

"Yes, sir, farther for'ard below deck. I don't know if there are enough yards to replace all those that have carried away, though."

"How about cordage?"

"There is very little of that, sir. We might get her masts and most of her yards in place, but we better hope that there is some cordage left that can be salvaged," said Tom.

Ben climbed out of the hold stiffly and could not believe his eyes. The deck had been swept completely clean. There was no chart house, no charts, or binnacle, no masts and no ship's boats.

"It looks like we have just about lost this ship," said Tom.

Ben turned on him angrily. He was tired and this was the third ship entrusted to him that had foundered for no fault of his own. "Don't you even think that, Mr. Murphy!" Ben said angrily.

The men began work. It was late the day after they had sailed. The wind had died down to a stiff breeze and the rain had ceased, but the pale sun would set soon. It was still early March. Ben sent Mr. Lapley below to kindle a fire and fix some food. He was happy for that duty. The work on deck was going to be strenuous and difficult. They quit at 6 p.m. and sat down like zombies to eat. They had not even eaten a meal together on this ship before. Tired men ate ravenously and even if the food was not good, it was filling and made them feel a little better. The work on the deck had cleared the two masts from the tangle of ropes and they had been able to save a goodly number of blocks and dead eyes. Most seriously needed was the stout rope and wrappings for the standing rigging. Ben figured that they could piece together enough for two masts and would come up short one yard. They saved all that they could and set the pieces in orderly piles on the deck. Refitting would take days and Ben doubted that the twenty of them could even step a mast on a ship that was severely tilted to port. Worst of all, they had no idea where they were. Ben could not guess. The Mediterranean vegetation is more or less the same for great distances of the coast. It could tell him nothing about their position.

Then suddenly, Curran said, "Where's Moran? I have not seen him since we started to get knocked about so during the storm."

"Best we all go and look for him," said Ben.

Half an hour later they found him stuffed between a large beam in the hull and a full hogshead. They gently removed the top beam and heard a groan.

"'E's alive, sir," said Gilmore.

They took the man to the upper deck and laid him out.

He did not seem to have any broken bones. After a few minutes he opened his eyes, but could not speak to them. He had chewed his tongue near off. There was little that Ben could do. He was thankful for his medical training. He found some rum and gave the man a stiff dose. Then he reached in with a knife that he had sent to the galley to be heated and slit off the rest of the tongue neatly and fast. Still the man made no sound. He seemed to have suffered a severe head injury. Ben was sure he was concussed and there was little he could do for that, except to wait. They put clean rags in his mouth and tied a rope from his chin to the top of his head to keep his mouth shut. He would have to endure hunger for a few days. Ben could slip liquids down his throat to keep him alive.

Ben volunteered to go overboard to check on the hull and to see if there was a chance that a high tide might lift them off. Tom came with him. The two men came back, dripping water and shaking their heads.

"The hull seems to be intact, but she has worked severely. Might always leak after this. It'll take a good high tide to lift us free. That is our greatest problem now. There is no need to refit if we cannot float her free. We have no cargo to jettison, so all we can do is wait," said Ben.

The men turned in early. It grew dark soon after they had eaten and each man tried to find a dry spot where he could curl up. There was nothing that was really dry on board this ship. Ben checked his cabin and found that the gear that he had lashed down before the storm was still there, well hidden under his bunk. That was a small miracle. But a fitful sleep came to Ben after several hours and he dozed off, his mind still struggling with all of the repairs and work that must be done to get them to their destination.

But Ben was never to see Algiers. About three in the morning, he felt something hard and cold on his cheek. As he struggled out of sleep, he could smell the unmistakable odor of garlic. His mind was not quite awake yet. *Good God! Frogs. Frenchmen!*

"Up, you stealer of French sheeps," said the man in broken English. Ben looked up into the dark eyes of a French sergeant. He struggled up. The man seized his hands and held them firmly behind his back, and then pushed him forward towards the deck. His men were all walking sleepily towards the side, faces contorted in pain and astonishment. He noted that some of the men had no clothes and it was March. Ben stopped dead in his tracks.

"I don't mind your taking us prisoner, but at least let us get some clothes. It is inhumane to walk a prisoner in March cold without clothes. You get no prisoner exchanges for dead men."

The man nodded to his troops and said something unintelligible in French. They turned the men around and took them back to their sleeping quarters. Ben grabbed his great coat, a second shirt, and when the officer was not looking, a handful of silver coins. Soon they were herded down the side of the ship into waiting boats and rowed to a French frigate that stood nearby.

"I thought we had driven you English out of the Mediterranean," said the officer to Ben.

"Just temporarily, friend," he replied. Suddenly Ben remembered Moran. Yes, he was there in the other boat. One of the crewmen had thought to see that he came along with them. He would perish on the wreck otherwise.

No sooner than they were put aboard the French ship, *Le Grand Croix* , and Ben began to feel a fever coming on. *Drat! Jim had said that the fever would return at the most inconvenient times. Usually when you are under severe stress, he had said. Will I always be plagued by this accursed weakness?* he thought. His face became hot first, but soon there was fire all over his body. He began to perspire violently, shaking, sweat running from his body to the deck. Ben slumped down and collapsed in a heap on the deck. They carried him below and he did not really come to his senses until they had reached port, which he judged was Toulon. Apparently Tom stayed by his side through the fever and subsequent chills and tended to his needs. Good that Tom was along.

By the time that Ben was able to drink and eat his first meal, they were already moving the prisoners off the ship and onto the quay. They tied their hands and shackled their legs. Ben was able to stand and walk, but was still weak. They were shuffled off towards the town, which seemed to be Le Seyne. Ben was certain that it was on the outskirts of Toulon. He had not found time to talk with his men or Tom, but they all seemed to be in good order, except for poor Moran. He stumbled along, a much broken and sick man. Ben learned later that he had not been able to eat since they had cut the tip of his tongue off. He no longer bled, but he had said not a word nor had he eaten anything. Gilmore tried repeatedly to get liquids down him while they were at sea.

They cleared the small town and moved along a road up hill, going generally northwest. Children came out with their mothers to stare at them and some jeered as they passed by, shuffling their feet along. Ben was himself again. He must make a mental picture of their every turn, of all aspects of the town and especially of time. It might help them to escape at some later date. There was no hope for escape now. They were flanked by twenty marines, all in their fancy uniforms. *There must be a garrison somewhere nearby,* he thought.

They walked up the road, climbing slightly, for about an hour. Then ahead, Ben saw a fort, complete with eight guns and a small turret outfitted for small arms fire. It snuggled back into a low hill and had a stream of water that seemed to pour from the leeward side. The stream was the same one that they had crossed earlier as they came out of the town. It was only about ten feet across. They were led up to two huge iron gates, and inside them, were two large wooden doors, strapped with massive, rusted steel bars. Once inside, they stood in a large courtyard with a parapet all around. Ben felt the nudge of the officers musket and he moved forward. They were taken to the blacksmith's shop and the leg shackles were removed. That was a blessing. Ben's legs were becoming badly chaffed. Then they were herded down into the dungeons, into a small cell that they would all share together. Ben was surprised that he, as an officer, was not separated from the men. That was usually done. But they probably thought that there was nothing that Ben could do with so few men. The French thought that officers were more likely to lead an escape than the men by themselves. *How many Frenchmen are there here,* though Ben. He guessed there might be about fifty soldiers and maybe twenty marines at the garrison.

Once they were locked in their cell, Ben went though his men, checking on the condition of each, trying to make each as comfortable as he could. He approached Moran first. The poor fellow had suffered so severe a blow on his head that he had lost his senses. He appeared to be incapable of speech. He would make only a few wheezing sounds and when Ben looked at this throat, he discovered that his voice box had been crushed. He might never speak again. His tongue had pretty much healed and it was no longer a problem. Poor chap. Ben looked around. Gilmore was a friend of Moran's and a good man. "Would you see to Moran and keep track of him for me? He is never going to talk again, I am afraid. Someone needs to see to him much of the time."

"I will, sir."

Everyone else seemed to be healthy and there were no other problems, not yet at least. Their small cell was made for perhaps ten men, but all twenty-one of them were crammed into it. They had brought along the purser, Mr. Peech, and he was most uncomfortable. He had not taken care to bring a great coat with him and now he sat shivering in the corner of the cell. This was not the kind of life that men of his cut were used to. He would suffer much from this confinement.

Their food came twice a day. It was always the same. In the morning there was a thin, cold pees porridge that was tasteless and bland. Ben could hardly get it down. It reminded him of his days at the orphanage when that was all they had to eat for breakfast. Dinner was a small bowl of rice, nothing more. Sometimes they got bread for supper and sometimes nothing. Even the bread was stale, dry and tasteless. This was not what Ben had heard about French bread. It was supposed to be some of the best in the world.

There were no sanitary facilities save for a leather bucket that stood in one corner. But one leather bucket for twenty men was far from adequate. When it started to overflow, Ben took it to the cell door and spilled it on the feet of the guard who stood outside. He let out some French oath and stood shaking his fist at them. But soon a poor scrub woman came and emptied the bucket. There was no way to wash or clean up. They would live in these clothes until they either died or were set free. Light from outside managed to creep in through a high window, allowing them just enough light to see to write and to distinguish day from night.

Ben was plagued by the inability or perhaps it was the refusal of Moran to eat. He did not know what to do about him. The man lay on straw in his cot and looked steadily at the ceiling. Something in his mind had snapped. He would never be normal again. Ben and Tom spoke regularly, speculating about what had happened and what might be their fate.

Just as irksome was the problem with the purser, Mr. Peech. He complained loudly about everything, the food, the sanitary facilities, the lack of air, dampness, filth, crowding, the smells, whatever there was that might make a prison cell uncomfortable was his favourite complaint. He came to Ben every two hours during the day with some complaint or other. It was getting on Ben's nerves and he did not know what to do about it. Sure, Peech was from a wealthy family and had never been made to endure such conditions, but he was a warrant officer in His Majesty's Navy now and he would have to learn to cope with unpleasant conditions. Ben told him as much, as politely as he could, but the man persisted. He was big, fat, a pinched up sort of fellow with round, pouting face. His complexion was a blank white. Chubby fists flew at Ben when he could not get him to change some condition that was unchangeable.

"I'll see you flogged for this, young sir. You are not fit to be a captain if you cannot get me some more suitable quarters."

"I doubt that this old prison has any more suitable quarters," replied Ben.

After the first day, Ben was taken to the office of the Commandant. He spoke fair English and asked Ben many questions.

"What were you doing in the Mediterranean?"

Ben could see no harm in saying that he was on his way to purchase beef for the Navy. That was no big secret. "I was sent to bring back beef for the British fleet," he said.

"And what were you doing on the Spanish coast?"

Surely the Commandant did not think that he was going to launch an invasion of Spain with a small brig and twenty-one men. "Our ship was dismasted in a severe storm and we were driven ashore, sir."

"Were there other sheeps with you?"

"No, sir. There was no convoy."

"How come one so young is captain of such a sheep?"

"I guess it is because my Admiral thought that I could handle the job, sir."

"And what is wrong with the one old sailor?"

"He was thrown about during the storm and was hit by a loose barrel. His tongue was severed and his voice box crushed. He seems to have been hit on the head so hard that he has lost his senses, sir."

"And what is your rank?"

"Leftenant Benjamin Rundel, sir."

"You have family, perhaps who would like to see you safely home?"

It had been too easy up until then. He did not know how to answer that question. If he said , ‘ yes’ the French would soon learn that he did not have any family. If he said, ‘no,’ they would not be eager to exchange him or to try to find someone who would pay for his freedom. But no matter. He would not leave without his men anyway.

“I have no family of prominence, sir,” Ben said most bravely.

For the first week, Ben was quiet and said little. He was brooding over the loss of his third ship. He ate little and said almost nothing, but did check on Moran several times a day. Finally, his silence became unbearable. Tom had to do something. The lad was his friend.

“It’s not your fault, sir. You did not want to sail into that storm. You were ordered to do so. No one can blame you for losing the ship,” said Tom.

“But Tom, this is the third ship that I have lost. I have no future in the British Navy at all. I might as well die here. It would be the kindest thing that could happen to me now.”

“No, lad.” He sometimes lapsed into the familiar in order to stress his point. He usually was most careful to use the, ‘sir,’ but now, he needed to get his friend’s full attention. He took Ben’s shoulders by both hands and stared directly into his eyes. “You were not at fault for the loss of any of those other ships either. The bean ship was holed below the water line and would have sunk anyway. You could not have held out against 240 mutineers all by yourself in the *Hermione.* An’ this ship was the victim of a storm. She was old, lad, old and worn out. You saw how her masts were rotted. She could not ride out even a small thunderstorm safely. Besides, most times when they have sent you off with one ship, you have come back with two or three. There’s no need to blame yourself. Tend to your luffs and lets find a way out of this Hell hole.”

“Where do you think we went aground, Tom?”

“Oh, possibly on some of them islands off the southern coast of Spain.”

"I think it was closer in, maybe Cabo de Gata. That is desolate country. But I am surprised that the French would come ashore for us on Spanish ground."

At least he had the fellow talking. Maybe he could draw him out of his misery slowly, if he could keep him talking. "No tellin' what these Frenchies will do. You got any ideas about gettin' out o' here?" said Tom.

"Not yet, but I do have one idea. I am still in His Majesty's pay. I should be doing something to earn that pay. I am going to learn French. It may help us get out of here." So Ben watched the four guards who came to guard their cell each day. They each served a six hour watch with a few minutes off during the third hour. The early morning man was a stilted, sober fellow and the two night-time guards seemed crude and uninteresting. But the fellow who came on at noon was a dapper little man, who looked like he might be from a good family. He smiled more than the others and he seemed more congenial. He had laughed when Ben spilled the night soil on the feet of Gaston, the nighttime guard.

Ben was fed up with just sitting there. The same thoughts bored into his brain day after day, *why did he let them take his ship?* He would go crazy if he did not have something else to think about. The vision of Annie that had so comforted him on the Spanish Main seemed to do little for him here, where he had no hope of ever seeing her alive again. He would give it a try. He hated even the sound of the French language, but he had no choice.

The next day he approached the small fellow when he came on at noon. He held out a shiny silver coin. He said slowly,

"I...will...pay...you...if...you...will...teach...me...French... Do...you...speak...any...English?"

The little man looked surprised and turned to Ben, "Oui, monsieur, I mean, yes, a leetle." His eyes bulged out at the sight of the coin in Ben's hand.

"Stand at attention and tell me from top to bottom, the

name of every part of your body."

But that had been too fast. Ben thought. Then he pointed to his head.

The man answered, *tete. Good, he has the idea.* Then Ben pointed to his eyes (*le oeil*), nose (*le nez*), mouth (*la bouche*), forehead (*le front*), chin (*le menton*), hair (*cheveux*), shoulders (*la epaule*), chest (*la poitrine*), arms (*le bras*), stomach (*le estomac*), legs (*la jambe*), foot (*le pied)* toes (*le droigt*), etc. Ben was disappointed that there were such distinct differences between the two languages. There was little there to even remind him of Spanish or English. This was going to be a hard task. The man gave him the proper word each time and Ben traded back its English equivalent. But Ben was perplexed. He could not remember things unless he wrote them down. He tried to remember those odd sounding words, spoken as if one had a mouth full of hot soup, but he could not. Ben soon realized that the little man could not talk without the use of his hands. He propped his rifle against his arm and then began to gesture with his hands. "Slowly...slowly, Ben cautioned with his hand to his mouth for silence. He had to be wary of the approach of another French officer, but the appearance of anything alive in that part of the prison, except the ample rat population, was unusual indeed.

The next day, Ben handed his friend a pound. "I ...need ...pen ...and ...paper, to ...write ...to... my... girl," he said. The man shook his head and took the coin eagerly. They did not work on French that day. But Ben was beginning to see some benefit in having a friend in the guards and in speaking French, especially if he wanted to make captain someday.

The next noon the guard came on time. He saluted the morning guard and took his place. Then Ben heard, "Pssst."

He drew near and the little man handed him a sheaf of papers, pen and ink which he had concealed somewhat awkwardly beneath his jacket. Ben took them and smiled, appreciatively. He pointed to himself and said, "Ben." Then he pointed to the little Frenchman and asked, "What's your name?"

The man smiled appreciatively and said, "Maurice Capulet." Now Ben began in earnest. He would ask the man for the French equivalent and draw the item if Maurice did not understand his question. Maurice soon began to learn the English equivalents, because Ben made a point of naming each thing that he asked. He would say, 'ship,' and then draw a tiny ship to conserve paper. Maurice would counter with , "Oh, sheep," and Ben would shake his head, 'yes'. It did not matter that a 'sheep' did not like water and had no sails. He was getting somewhere. But he took one sheet of paper and began to write down the proper French words. 'Yes' was. 'oui', but it sounded like,'we' to Ben so he wrote, 'yes=we'. He was fascinated that, like Spanish, words could be masculine or feminine. The English language did not give sex to its nouns, but then that was typical of the French.

Today Mr. Peech complained that he had a toothache. Ben had nothing that would help. He tried to explain to Maurice that one of his men had a toothache, but his command of the language had not progressed that far. The next day the toothache was forgotten and the man complained about the horrible smells. "This is like living in a London sewer," he said.

"And what do you expect me to do about it? Sprinkle the cell with flowers and cologne?" The man made no answer. He was hurting and lashing out in all directions. He sat there pouting like a small child that had been rebuked by his parent.

Each day the two men went at their exchange of words. Ben had some trouble getting verbs and adverbs, but with persistence, he was making progress. Maurice seemed to enjoy the exercise. It made a boring six hour stint on guard duty much more interesting. The crew watched all this with interest, but could see no way that this would ever get them out of there.

Peech came howling at Ben again today. He had a stomach ache from the food.

"Too bad, sir. Perhaps it will go the same way of the toothache," said Ben, now totally out of patience with the man. Their confinement was hard on them all, but Peech was making it that much more miserable for everyone. They all suffered the same tortures. Ben was just thankful that during his four months there, he did not suffer another malaria attack. He did have two bouts with diarrhea, but he blamed that on the food. Others suffered the same affliction.

Moran remained unchanged, although at times they were able to force a bit of rice down his throat. He could swallow, but he seemed to have lost all interest in life. Then it struck Ben. This fellow had a fine singing voice. He was the main attraction whenever Ben brought out his 'laika' to play when they were on the *Vanguard.* His pain was that he would never be able to sing again. No wonder the poor devil wanted to die. Ben tried to soothe him, but could not make any progress. Moran became so weak that he could not get out of his bed. The men had to tend to his every need and that, at least, gave them something to do. Most of the time they sat in small groups and talked. There was nothing else for them to do. Some found pebbles and invented games, trying to lob a pebble into a small hole in the ground or playing other games with straw and pebbles. One thing that Ben neglected to consider when he choose his crew was that both Mitchell and Wallace were Scotsmen. They got along just fine as long as there was plenty for them to do, but now in the confines of a tiny cell, there was nothing to occupy their time. One was a highlander and the other a lowlander and these two sorts rarely see eye to eye on anything. They began to fight, first verbally but that soon turned into ugly brawls, with both men coming out much the worse for wear. This bothered Ben. He had to keep harmony in this small crew. They would never get out of there if they fought all of the time. Ben was beginning to get a glimmer of a plan for their escape, but it required that each man be willing to die for his fellow seaman. He tried to interest the men in learning French, but he soon learned that he was greatly reduced in their eyes by simply talking to the French. They hated the Frenchmen and everything French. Even Tom refused to learn the strange language. He had turned sullen of late and said little, keeping off to himself. Ben thought that he longed for action, anything that would get them out of there and back aboard a ship. When they did speak, it was matter of fact and lacked the warmth of olden days.

After several bad fights, Ben took action. "Look, lads, I cannot get us out of here just any day I wish. We have to abide our time, and Moran has to be fit to travel. As he is now, he cannot even walk. I suggest that you gentlemen leave off fighting for awhile and try to find a way to coax him to eat. We don't leave until he has two good legs under him."

But the next day, the two were at it again. "That's it," said Ben. I am going to give you men some work. You are all getting weak. Weak men cannot hope to escape this place. If my plan works, you will need all the strength you can get. I will set up a schedule of wrestling matches. You are to wrestle each other, each man for half an hour a day. That way, we may be able to keep our strength. The man with the most matches won will be the first to walk out of this Hell hole."

The lads cheered him. They would never think of such a plan on their own, but the thought of something to occupy their minds and keep them reasonably fit was welcome.

"I don't want to see any injuries, now. We'll put some of that fresh straw in the center of the room and you will get your chance to wrestle any man in this room that takes your fancy. Mr. Murphy and I will do some wrestling too," as he stepped over to Tom and touched him on the shoulder. Tom simply turned his sad face towards Ben, but he could see a gleam of the old friendly competition in his eyes. *This might just work,* Ben thought. He was still a good surgeon whenever he could find the right medicine.

Just about then, Mr. Peech came forward and complained bitterly that he would not be subjected to such rough scallion fighting. He would not allow it."

"And who are you to say what my crew will and will not do?" said Ben.

Joe Curran stood up and walked over to Peech. He was a big fellow, one of the strongest men that Ben had ever known. He calmly hit Peech on the chin, a mighty blow, knocking the man off his feet and unconscious. "We're tired of your chrumping around and griping all the time. That should shut you up for awhile." Then, turning to Ben, "Beggin' your pardon, sir, but there ain't nothin' you can do to make things better fer 'im. He's just a daft old man."

Ben smiled and thanked Curran. "I was just about to do the same thing myself, there Joe."

After that, they heard no more from Mr. Peech. He sat silently on his straw, his mouth set in a pout, and spoke to almost no one. Ben did interest him in speaking a little French now and again. Apparently he did speak some French and it pleased him to be able to speak in a language that the rest of the crew did not understand.

There was eager talk now about who could whip whom and who would fight whom. Ben made out a schedule and the lads went at it. There were bets too, so many pieces of straw for a man's bed if he won. It was good therapy and the men took to it eagerly.

The men regularly caught rats and killed them, but, as hungry as they were for meat, they had no way to cook them, so they were thrown out through the cell door where they lay until they stank or until the bent old cleaning woman came to take them away. Ben would not have been surprised if the fresh ones did not end up in her pot at night. Peech made his disapproval of the whole process known, but never uttered a word. He was now quite afraid of Curran. All Joe had to do was to stand up when Peech was about to speak, and the man would clam up immediately. The men joked about his yellow streak. "That Peechy bird, 'e has a yeller stripe clear down his back," said Joe Beetham.

But Ben would not give up the progress that he was making with the French language. As much as he hated it, he could see it being of value sometime in a fog when his ship might end up in the midst of a French fleet instead of a Spanish one as it had done months ago in the Mediterranean. Even Tom could see that benefit, but he remained silent much of the time.

What does a man in prison think about? For Ben it was either the loss of his ship, his Annie or some new French word that he had learned. Some of the words seemed so unlike the English equivalent that he could not easily remember them. He had to run them through his mind over and over again, visualizing the thing that the word denoted. He was starting to put together sentences, and he had no idea of how the verbs might be conjugated. He would try a sentence on Maurice and the good fellow would correct him, always with a pleasant smile, and sometimes almost rolling on the cobbles with laughter.

Ben paid Maurice by the week and his money would soon be gone. When he told Maurice that he would not have any money next week, Maurice simply waved his hands and said that it would make no *difference*. He would continue to teach Ben. Clearly, the teaching was improving Maurice's lonely life and he was learning some English as well. Ben learned that Maurice had a lady friend in Toulon named Bridgette. Ben spelled it, 'Bridget'. But the two young men spoke often of their loves and their respective beauties. Maurice was not quite as reserved as Ben and had become Bridgette's lover long ago, but her father hated Maurice. He called him a 'little mouse in a soldier's uniform,' and forbade him from seeing his daughter. But that did not stop Maurice. He was determined to see her anyway and managed to find her in strange places out of sight of prying eyes, waiting for his fond embraces.

Months wore on and they had been there now almost four months without any place to walk in the sun. It was warm, most days steaming hot, clear into June. The prison cell stank terribly in the hot weather and there was little fresh air to breathe. Ben decided to ask Maurice if he might be able to get them privileges to walk and take their exercise in the sun. "My men are pale as ghosts, old friend," he said in his not perfect French, but not so bad French either. He had applied himself to his studies of the language and he was doing quite well. He knew that he would never be able to read the language, but he could get off quite a few common sentences that might serve him well at some time in the future.

Maurice came back the next day, all smiles. He drew out his key. "You may walk in sun for four hours today," he said in his improved English. Commandant says it permitted." He still had trouble with verbs and tenses. He bowed ever so politely and opened the door to the cell. Mitchell had the highest score in the wrestling derby, but Wallace was one match behind him and the two were in contention, so Ben invited them both to walk through the door together.

Once in the courtyard, they had to run for the cover of shade. The sun burned their eyes and they could not see a thing. They sat huddled together like a flock of pigeons for over an hour until their eyes grew used to the strong light. The sun was hot and it felt good on their skin. They had endured months of damp, mouldy prison and the warm sun was a blessing. But Ben was concerned about their getting sunburned and being in serious trouble from loss of skin. Open sores would never heal in that filthy hole where they slept. He ordered the men back to their cells after only an hour in the sun. There was much grumbling and complaining, but he told them they could have more time in the sun each day until their skin was hardened up again.

Tyrley came to Ben's rescue. "Our lads from the *Placid,* spent too much time in the sun once after being in a cold climate and we were burned so badly that we could not sit or sleep. Best do like the cap'n says. Too much sun can make a man sick to his stomach too."

On the way back from the courtyard, Ben thought he noticed a place where the stream ran right under the fort. That was a most interesting arrangement. In the old days they could withstand siege for a long time if they had a supply of fresh water, and the stream seemed to flow summer as well as winter. It looked as if the stream was used as a place to dispose of sewage today, but it had once been a pure source of water, Ben was sure. Back in the cell, he spoke with Tom. The sunshine had brightened everyone's spirits and even Peech seemed a bit happier. Moran had a weak smile on his face. He was able to walk to the courtyard and back.

"Tom, do you remember how far that waterfall dropped when it left the fort? You know, we saw it on the way up the road the day we arrived."

"Let's see. That seems like such a long time ago. Maybe forthy feet, sir," he ventured.

"Ben said, "It looked more like twenty feet to me. Let's ask the men. He went around the cell, quietly asking each man what he remembered. Some had paid no attention to it. Others said it was anywhere from ten to fifty feet to the pool below. The one man whose judgment seemed to be almost infallible was Carl Frid. He would call a snake a snake and tell you how long it was, to within an inch. Carl answered, "It seems like it was a bit over twenty feet, sir. Course, I wasn't close enough to be really certain."

Ben went back to Tom's side. I am getting an idea, Tom. I'll need your help tomorrow. See how far you think it is from where we cross the bridge over the stream to where it breaks and falls off to the pool below. We'll compare notes tomorrow, but say nothing to the men just yet." Tom knew that Ben was hatching a plan and he was delighted to see some progress, even if ever so small.

The next day they went to the courtyard and Ben pretended to be interested in his French lesson, but his mind was caught up in a welter of details. How big was the courtyard? How many guards were on the wall above? Did any of the men ever swim in the pond by the fort? He dared not ask Maurice these questions, but he put his eyes to work seeking all that must be known before he could put his plan to work. Judging from the lack of cleanliness of the guards and their clothes, he was certain that they did not swim in the pond and that it was a disposal for sewage. He longed to stand on the bridge and look down into the cool water on their return to the cell, but he dared not. His eyes took in all that he could of the grating that covered the opening on both sides of the bridge.

That night he and Tom compared notes on the length of river before the drop-off down to the pool. Ben thought that it was at least twenty feet. Tom said closer to twenty-five. That night Ben laid awake for a long time. He though about his plan, examined it from all perspectives and tried to think of everything that could go wrong and cause them trouble.

For the next few days, Ben examined the fort as carefully as he could from his limited access to the courtyard. The soldiers were housed in rooms above their cell. There were three empty cells before they came to the turn that led to the bridge. The stream looked to be about four or five feet deep, about eight feet wide. Hmmm. I wonder how far it is to Le Seyne if one follows the stream?

One interesting thing happened that day. Maurice told him that he was being sent away. He could no longer help him. He was going to a place on the Nile called Dumyat. He seemed quite excited about it and would be glad to be free of the fort for awhile. Then he said something about the blasted heat and that he would enjoy a good swim in the 'pool' that afternoon when his duty was done. That was interesting to Ben too. Apparently the pool at the bottom of the small waterfall was deep enough to swim in. That is, if he were talking about *that* pool. Did the French mind swimming in a pool that had small amounts of sewage in it? Possibly not. The depth of the pool was a critical element to the success of his plan. If it were too shallow, a man dropping into it might break his legs and drown.

Earlier, Ben had heard the Commandant, who happened to come into the courtyard, talking to a naval Captain about 'the force in the the Nile' and 'plans for India..." What could that possibly mean?

After five days, he had a plan in hand and was reasonably confident that it could succeed. He drew the men close together that night and spoke in a whisper, lest their evening guard might know some English.

"Lads, I have a plan to get us out of here. You know the grating that covers the starboard side of the bridge where it crosses the stream? Well, I have looked at the hinges. They are old and rusty, but I believe that ten or so strong lads could lift the grill off its hinges, even though the other side is locked with stout locks. If we could move it enough to allow a man to slip under the grating, then we could follow the stream down the rock surface to where it drops off into the pool. The problem is that we do not know how far it is from the edge of the rock where the stream drops off to the pool below. If it is too far, we might be killed in the fall, or drown. But our best estimate is that there is a drop of twenty to thirty feet. I think that all of us can manage that," as he looked at Mr. Peech. There was no response from the man. Apparently he was ready for 'out,' no matter what it took.

"But won't they see us, sir?" volunteered Sharp.

"Not if we leave when the moon is in its quarter or on a cloudy night. I have been watching the stars through the window above and I think that it will be quarter moon in two days. That would give us enough light to see where we are going and enough cover so that they will not notice us."

"What about the noise, sir. Won't we make loud splashes as we hit the water?" said Tom.

"Aye, but we will have to take that chance. I have

learned from Maurice that they often swim in some pool by the fort at night to cool off. It has been unbearably hot. We will have to be certain that no one is swimming there when we decide to make our escape. That is where you men come in. We do not need our blankets at night in order to sleep. I suggest that the day we decide to leave, you will cut up your blankets and knot them together to make a rope at least twenty-five feet long, longer of possible. I will use that to slip out to the edge of the rock when we have opened the grating so I can get through. If all is clear, I will yank the rope two times and you will each start down the rope, one at a time, but as close together as you can. I will jump down into the pool and I believe there is a clump of dense shrubs to the far side. I'll wait there for each of you to catch up. If it is not clear, I will tug once on the rope and then crawl back upstream using the rope to move myself against the current and we will have to abort the plan for that night."

"But can we get the grating back on its pins, sir?" said Bill Marsden.

"I think that we can, but if we cannot, then we will have to admit to our plan and be discovered."

"But how are we goin' to get out of the cell and past the guards at night," asked Charlie Wetmore.

"That's where you come in. You are a strong lad. We will tie two of your belts together and I will coax the guard close to the bars. The after- midnight guard often stands dangerously close to the bars anyway. We'll attack him just as soon as the guards change duty so that will give us about six hours start before they find that we have gone missing. You just loop your belt around his neck, hold on tight and we will take his keys. Kill him if you have to," said Ben. "You, Kenneth Lapley, will grab the keys and open the door."

"But I think it's too dangerous to flee at night. We don't know where we are and we will not be able to see anything," said Horace Peech, offering his first objection in several months now.

“I have learned that there may be some troops leaving the fort tomorrow during the morning. If that is so, then it will be an excellent time for us to escape. Besides, it will be some time before there will be a quarter moon again. It will be even better if we get clouds and it is totally dark. I am sure we sailors can find the ocean, Archie,” he joked. The man’s name was really ‘Horace,’ but the men had taken to calling him, ‘Achy Archie’ and ‘Horrible Horace’.

“Oh, and Dick Gilmore and Jim Grist. I will ask you to take charge of Moran. He will not be able to understand what we are doing. He may call out or make some sound that would betray us, unintentionally. You’ll need to gag him and see that he gets down the waterfall safely. Mr. Peech, you will stay close to Mr. Roberts who will see you off in style,” said Ben.

No one had said much of anything funny for a long time and it suddenly felt good.

“Any question, lads?” said Ben. There were none, but he spoke with several of them about special jobs that they would need to do to be ready when the time came.

The next day when they were in the courtyard, they heard a large number of horses riding off. *Perhaps that is Maurice and his men off to the Nile, and I could not be more delighted,* thought Ben.

Ben worried that night that they might be planning to escape too close to the troops leaving and that they might only walk into the whole French army holed up in port. He spoke to Tom about it. “There’s no way of telling, Ben. We just have to take our chances, but I think that if you delay much longer, the men are going to get mighty ornery.”

So, the next day a new guard appeared at noon. He was a big fellow who had been wounded and walked with a severe limp. Ben wondered if the midnight guard would be the same stodgy fellow or someone different. After it was dark, Ben ordered the men to begin making rope. They did it all quietly with their backs to the door and the guard never once looked inside the cell.

At midnight, Ben could see a slit of a moon outside. The guard changed and their usual guard took over. As soon as the footsteps faded from the stone walkway, Ben motioned to Charlie Wetmore to move forward. The guard was standing about six inches too far away for Charlie to get his belt over his head. He looked to Ben in desperation. Ben went to the fellow and called, quietly, *'Quelle heure est-il?'* The man turned to him, quite astonished that he could speak French. He moved closer and said that it must be just past midnight. *Minuit.* He had just come on duty. As he turned, Charlie reached high over his head and brought the belt down over his head, cinching it up tightly. The man gagged and gasped, squirming like a startled fish. Ben quickly put his hand over the man's mouth and motioned for Lapley to grab the keys. Eager hands reached out to grab the guard by the throat and within a few seconds, he lay dead at their feet. Lapley turned the key in the lock and the rusty hinges squeaked as the door flew open. Ben froze. He had forgotten about those rusty hinges. They might set up an alarm all by themselves. He motioned for everyone to be silent while they strained to listen, but there was not a sound, save a rat scurrying into one of the beds on the far side of the cell. Ben motioned for the men to drag the dead man into the cell and close the door. The corridors were silent. It was stifling hot and Ben began to fear that he would have a malaria attack just when he was needed most. *No! I will fight it. I have to get these men free of this place.*

He stepped forward and picked up the lighted lantern that hung by the cell. The men crept quietly past the last three empty cells. Ben shone his light into the cells, to be certain they were empty. It would be a shame to leave a good British seaman behind because he did not know about him. But all he saw were rats and one skeleton. *Too late for that poor fellow,* he thought.

At the bridge, the men lined up next to the grating. It was made of iron, about six feet long by perhaps two and a half wide. The metal was an inch thick. Ben had estimated its weight at over six hundred pounds, what with rust and all. The men fitted their fingers into the holes and six of them lifted the grating off its' hinges quite easily. They slid the bottom of the grating outwards so that a man could crawl through the opening at the end. The air came up fresh and warm to them, but the water was inviting, in spite of a faint whiff of sewage. Ben tied the rope to the grating and motioned for Wallace to put the light out. They would operate in darkness now. He motioned for Tom to stand by the rope to feel for his signals. Tom was to be the last one out so that he might help anyone who had trouble. Ben strained to listen, but it was quiet, all but his heart which beat a full, 'clear for action' tattoo in his chest.

Ben slipped down to the floor of the bridge, crawled through the narrow opening between the grate and the wall and grabbed the rope firmly. As he let himself down into the water, he felt its cool, refreshing embrace. He had not had a bath for over four months. If nothing else, this would give him a good cleaning. His clothes smelled terrible and he stank. He slid down the rope, and then let the current carry him to the edge of the rock which formed the lip of the waterfall. As he approached the edge, he stopped and looked down. There was a good twenty foot drop below him. The water cascaded down, making a pleasant sound as it hit the pool below. Was there anyone about? He could not see the wall of the fort which was directly above him, and he knew there must be guards there. But how many? There was no one near the pond. An old cow ate grass in a field a bit below the pond, but there was no other life visible.

How much rope did he have left? There might be three feet left. He would have to fall about seventeen feet into the pool. That should not be too bad. He gave the rope two firm tugs and then let himself over the lip of the waterfall. Then he let go. He fell for what seemed a long ways. Then he was being drowned by the water as it rushed up over his head. The pool was deep enough. If it had not been, he would have broken both legs and would be left there to die. He had not taken a large breath before he fell and now he was gasping, desperate to breathe, but as his head popped out of the water, he caught a big breath and held it. He could already see a dim figure in the moonlight on the rim of the waterfall. He moved slowly, quietly over to the clump of brush and watched.

There, two, three, now four. He could not recognize the men, but they were following him. He hoped that they all could swim. He saw several being helped by swimmers as they came across the pool. It was only a forty foot swim, but he would hate to get his men out safely and then have them all die from drowning. He glanced up at the wall of the fort. No problem there. He could see a sentry, but he seemed to be looking far out to sea, perhaps wishing that he had been lucky enough to go with Maurice to the Nile.

The first men had reached Ben now and then settled down in the moss, dripping from their refreshing swim. *Ten, eleven, twelve,... fourteen...* Ben counted. No one spoke. They were too much overwhelmed that this scheme had succeeded. There were nineteen of them there now, huddled silently in the small patch of brush. Ben waited anxiously for Tom and, who else was missing? Peech! He strained to see if they were near the lip of the falls, but he could see no one. Moran lay back against a small tree, a moronic smile on his face. Even he was beginning to like the taste of freedom.

Where is Tom? thought Ben. Could he have run into trouble? There was no way to get back to him if he did have a problem. He would be trapped there and charged with the murder of the guard. Minutes dragged on. The men looked at him anxiously, but what could he do? He could not go back. This was one adventure from which there was no going back. Tom had to come soon.

A cloud obscured the moon and Ben still could see no sign of his friend. Minutes dragged by. The men were restless.

Then at the lip of the falls, appeared Tom with his arm

around Mr. Peech. Peech was obviously fighting the descent into the pool, but Tom would have none of it. He clouted Peech beside the head and sent him unconscious. Then he jettisoned his body down into the pool, following as soon as he could see that the man had surfaced.

Tom swam quietly to the brush, hauling Peech behind him by the nap of the neck. Peech was just coming to and Ben had to reach out and silence him.

"Sorry, sir, but I had a bit of trouble getting that grating back in place, but I had a lot more trouble with this old geeser," whispered Tom.

Ben motioned for the men to advance. They walked down the stream, feeling their way as they went. The cloud slipped off the moon for just a few minutes before another came to hide it. Ben could see that they had about a mile to make it to the town. There were no lights in the town, except those by the quay. The way was rough, strewn with large rocks and briars. They walked on silently, ever wary. *There will be a few sprained ankles and skinned shins after this hike,* thought Ben.

As they approached the town, Ben signaled for a halt. He looked out at the quay.

They were totally dependent on finding a boat large enough to take them back to the Tagus, and on being able to capture it. Ben saw many small fishing boats tied up at the pier. There was a guard at each end of the pier. But there, at the end of the pier was a small brig.

He whispered to Tom. There is a brig tied just there, See her?" The moon was playing tricks on them again and she was hidden by darkness.

"And I do believe that she might be the *Mignon* with newly stepped masts, new yards and sails bent on. What do you think?" said Tom.

"By jove, I think you are right. Wouldn't that be too much if we could take her back."

Ben watched the guards for awhile. There seemed to be no one else about. The waterfront was silent. He turned to his men, pointing to Wallace.

"You and I will walk naturally towards the first guard as if we are a couple of fishermen returning to our boats. Everyone expects a few Frenchmen to be out and about after midnight trysts with their lady loves. When we get to him, you strangle him and I will quickly take his rifle and take his place. From the far end of the pier, the other guard will not be able to see that I am not in uniform. With luck, we may be able to make the exchange when the far guard is looking out to sea. Then," he whispered," lead the men down the walkway at the side of the pier to the far guard and take him out. I will come running when I see that you have him and then we can board her. Be wary that there could be as many as thirty or forty men aboard if they are ready to sail, or perhaps only three or four guards if the crew is ashore."

He looked at the guard's position. They would advance on him while he was looking towards the far guard. "Go," whispered Ben.

He and Wallace, walking tall, strode directly toward the back of the guard as he stared towards the ship. With a speed and agility the Ben could only marvel at, Wallace put his hand over the man's mouth and skewered him with a short knife that he had taken from the prison guard, all while pushing him over the edge of the quay into the water. It happened all in one smooth motion, no fuss, no hesitation. The poor fellow never knew what happened to him. Ben barely had time to collect the man's musket. *This Wallace is a born killer,* thought Ben. *I am glad he is on our side.*

Ben assumed the position that the guard had held and then heard something plink down at his feet. Wallace had stripped the man of his powder flask and shot and had sent them up to Ben. So excited was he that he had completely forgotten that their lives might depend on having a musket and shot. Tyrley had the musket from their prison guard, but the rest of the lads were unarmed. Ben saw out of the corner of his eye the shadows of the men as they crept across the street to sneak down the walkway to the end of the quay. *Thank God there is some cover for them,* he thought. They could crouch down a bit and stay out of sight since the walkway was part way down the side of the quay.

Ben waited, hardly breathing. It seemed to take a long time for the men to make it to the other end of the quay. The far guard did not appear to be alarmed. He would have great difficulty seeing that Ben was not his colleague in this dim light. Then he saw Wallace seem to bob out of the quay and pounce on the guard just as he started to turn, but Wallace had dispatched him with the same brutal efficiency that he had used on the first man. Ben's feet seemed glued to the quay, but he forced them to run towards the ship. His men were already climbing aboard, Tyrley first with his rifle, but there was not a sound. Ben heard a faint gurgling sound as he approached the ship and grabbed the rope to climb aboard. Then it struck him. He had not checked to see if his rifle was loaded. What if he needed it and it was not? He would have a bad time seeing to load it in this gloom. The moon had taken a short vacation and clouds ruled the sky. As his foot hit the deck, Wetmore came up to him.

"Sir, we 'ave taken the two guards. They're checkin' below, but I don't think there is anyone else aboard."

The lads found two men sleeping below and speedily dispatched them, but there was no one else there. They were in luck. Ben sized up the situation quickly.

"To the tops, lads. We must get under way as soon as possible. Man your halyards, man the braces, cast off your bow line," he whispered.

The deck exploded with activity as the men went gladly to their duties. Just then the moon chose to sneak out from behind a cloud and they had some light, which was good for setting sail, but bad if someone happened to be looking from the fort.

Mr. Peech stood there in the midst of it all, quite bewildered and very much in the way. But poor Moran stood to one side. He knew what to do, but his mind had deteriorated so that he could not quite get himself to do what was needed. Ben felt the ship drift free from the quay. They were in luck too, because the tide was going out. There was no way that he could have obtained that information from the fort. They had to gamble that they could get under weigh. Ben was prepared to tow her out into the open water using the ship's boat and oars, if needed. He looked up as the tops began to blossom out in sails, their corners quickly sheeted home and secured. He moved to the helm and took over. They had about a mile to sail before they were out of range of the fort. The winds were light but steady from the west. As soon as he took the helm, he was certain that she was the *Mignon*, refitted and ready for service. *That was nice of the French to repair our ship for us while we rotted in prison,* he thought.

Just then, as if from nowhere, a round shot flew through the main tops'l, leaving a hole about the size of a man's head. Instantly he heard the report. He could see shot falling all around them. The fort was awake and found them gone missing. As soon as they saw the ship move, they knew what was afoot. It would be a tedious fifteen minutes until they could get free of the fort and away from the town, but try as they might, the French could not hit them again. Shot fell like rain at times, but not another one touched them. Ben shouted encouragement to his men. They were vexed because they had no cannon to return fire. "We are on our way to some good English beef, lads. Hold her as she goes."

Tom was serving as first leftenant and began to shout orders now. There was no more need for whispering. Ben brought the ship as far out to sea as he could and soon the shots ceased.

"What do you think, sir? Will they follow us?" said Tom.

"I doubt that they can right away. All that is left in port are fishing boats. They might be able to get a ship out of Toulon, but it would take at least an hour to get there and more to get her ready to sail. This ship is a fair sailer and we should be well out of harms way by then," said Ben.

After about an hour, when they were safely at sea, Ben turned the helm over to Grist and sent for Lapley.

"Fire up the galley stove lad and I will get you some food for the men. Don't spare anything. We are in need of some good English beef.

This was the first chance that Ben had to check out his old cabin. He found that things had been knocked about by the storm and had been put back, generally as they were originally. He was amazed when he looked beneath his cot and found his sea chest there, intact, with all of his belongings, even his money. Apparently the French had towed the ship to port for repairs at Toulon, but had never taken her out. The cabin had not been occupied. *It's a good thing that I lashed my gear down before that storm,* he thought.

Then, as he approached a pile of crates in the middle of the cabin that were covered by canvas, he stopped in amazement. *These French can be magnanimous when they have a mind to,* he thought. As he lifted the canvas, there before him were crates of eggs, pots of jams, bags of fresh bread, racks of fancy wines, and all manner of delicacies. Apparently they were getting ready to sail soon, perhaps as early as tomorrow. The captain must be a gourmet, judging by the quality of food that he had put aboard for his own use.

But Ben was not cut out to be a cruel captain. He took away most of the wine, leaving only what the men could use for that meal. Then he went to Lapley and directed him to use from the captain's private stores anything that he needed.

"Mr. Peech, if you please," yelled Tom as Ben requested the attendance of the fat purser.

"He has lost a few pounds in prison, don't you think sir," said Tom.

"Aye, and he is about to lose a few more. I am going to put him to work," said Ben.

"You should have seen his fat rump bumping over the rocks as we came out of the prison, sir. It was a sight to behold. I could hardly keep from laughing and waking the whole garrison," said Tom.

Ben turned to Peech. "Sir, I want you to go below and take a quick look at the stores. This ship is riding low in the water. What is her cargo? Then report directly back to me."

There came a reluctant, "Aye, sir."

An hour later Peech came waddling onto the deck, his hands gesturing wildly. "Sir, the hold is full of, well, you would never guess what."

"No, Mr. Peech. I could not guess what. That is why I sent you to have a look," said Ben.

"Sir, it's English beef. They must have intercepted one of our prize ships, off-loaded her and they are taking it to the French troops."

"Good, Mr. Peech. Now take Mr. Marsden with you, and Roberts too and go below and broach a barrel of good beef for the men. Take it directly to the galley. We will all eat properly tonight," said Ben.

"There were three eager, "Aye, aye sirs," and the three men were off. Ben was pleased to see the return of enthusiasm in the men, especially in Peech who had lived a miserable life in prison for one gently born.

After turning the conn over to Tom, Ben went to his cabin to study their course and gave instructions for a change of course that would carry them away from the Spanish coast and closer to Algiers. He wanted to sail a jagged pattern so that the French would not know where to find him. They would assume that he would take the direct, shortest course straight along the coast of Spain to the Straits. But Ben thought better of that.

Then he went through the Captain's belongings to see if there were any valuable papers. He was one Gascon Villiers of Toulon. *Poor fellow, now he has no stores and no ship,* thought Ben. He found signal books, charts of local waters, documents for someone named Admiral

Bilbou in Egypt, charts of the waters around the coast of Egypt, and a host of other documents that he thought St. Vincent would like to examine. Ben felt angry with himself. He could speak enough French to carry on a limited conversation, but he could not read a word of that horrible language. He checked his things again and was delighted to see that all was there. Now he busied himself with plans for their entire trip. They would be extremely hard to track in these waters if he followed his set course.

By the time he emerged from his cabin, it was light, the sun resting like a giant red orb on the eastern rim of the sea. He could not see a sail anywhere on the horizon. He called to the lookouts, but they said there were no sails in sight. At eight, Mr. Lapley sent Grist to Ben to tell him that their food was ready.

The men sat all together on the deck in the warm morning sun, talking cheerfully, joking, and eating to their hearts content. By Ben's order, four men had been allowed to eat early so they could take over the helm and lookout duties. No one seemed to mind. As they spoke and ate, Ben learned that they had found most of their gear intact as well. That was strange. The new crew had brought their duffels aboard, but then had gone back on shore, presumably hastily for one last night of revelry with the women. Ben thought about that. There would be no harm in letting the lads have the belongings of the French sailors. They had abandoned them.

They ate great greasy, lovely chunks of beef, boiled potatoes, boiled carrots, fresh French bread, that was nothing like what they had eaten at the fort, fine cheese, and drank wine. Mr. Lapley was not a real cook, but he saw the need clearly, and as a good British sailor, he had gone out of his way to prepare an excellent meal for them. At the end he brought out a figgy dowdy with a sauce on it that was just heavenly. "Made with real butter, sir, an' lots of it," said Lapley. Fortunately, he had made extra, for each man wanted seconds. Even Moran's eyes brightened and he made gestures to show his happiness as he took his second helping. Old Peech shook his head in definite approval as the sauce ran down his ample jowls onto his coat.

With the meal completed, the men began to clean up. They had not bathed for four months and the grime could almost be scraped off. The pumps were at work for four hours. It was a Sunday and clear sailing weather. As long as there was no sail in sight, Ben felt comfortable letting the men play and clean up. They shaved, cut one another's hair and seemed to be having a most jovial good time. Clean clothes were brought out and put on, bringing smiles of pride back to the men's faces. There was a good bit of clothes washing and mending to do too. Frid sat to one side making himself a new pair of boots. His had been lost on the way out of the prison. Ben made sure that the lookouts were alert and changed them frequently so they would be wary.

Dinner was served on time, steaming platters of fried eggs, ham and bread with cheese. The men fell to with a will that can only explain how they had survived starvation all those months. These were tough, determined lads, made of the best stuff that England had. Ben was proud of them and thanked them for their patience in prison. He knew that in these men he had a crew that would never fail him. He had kept faith with them and they had served him well. He also made an effort to thank Lapley for the grand meals that he served since their return to the ship. Lapley smiled a shy smile and said, "Sir it was your personal stores what gave us that gran' cheese, plums, and wine. Couldn't ha' done it without ye, sir." A great cheer went up from the men. They liked this fine young captain, who was only acting like a captain, but apparently his 'acting' met with their full approval.

Lastly, he put his arm around Moran and pulled him back into the group. He seemed to want to shrink away from his fellow men, sensing his deficiencies. But Ben spoke of his bravery all that time in prison and how he was beginning to handle the ropes again. The man gave him his first full smile in a hundred days and seemed to melt back into the crew. Everyone took care of him from then on, sharing special things with him and being friendly. They honoured him for his efforts and the more honour, the more effort. He would soon return to being a good deck hand, with considerable strength, only lacking the power of speech.

Then Ben surprised them all. "You have all taken berthing space below and found the belongings of French sailors who, had things gone badly for us, would be in your places today. They have abandoned their duffelss and according to sea law, it is legal salvage. Each man may have the gear that he found in his place and may he prosper from it. The only exception would be personal letters or anything that represents the French Navy. I forbid you to look like Frenchies, but use your imaginations and do with their clothes what you will."

A great whop of joy went up as the men raced below to explore the duffels. Ben knew that they had already been into them, but no matter. Within minutes, the bags were hauled on deck and a great trading session began. "Hey, anyone want this pink shirt?" "Oh, mate, I fancy them checkered trousers. Would you take this coat for 'em?" The rest of the day was spent in enjoying their new finds and not a man went to his hammock that night but did not feel quite happy and relieved. They were still free of the French.

The rest of the voyage was routine, except the meals. Lapley kept up his fine cooking and the men ate well, each recovering more of his lost strength every day. Ben's plan to sail to the Algiers coast and then east had fooled the French completely. They never saw a single sail all the way to the Tagus. The best news of all was that Ben did not suffer from a malaria attack, not since they had been taken aboard the French ship off Spain. They had made a fast passage, of necessity, only eight days.

As they entered the bay, Ben regretted not having any cannon with which to fire a 21-gun salute to honour the

Admiral, but he would do a good job of making port in all other respects. The men had worked some on the little brig so she was in top condition when they let go her anchors and came to a most professional anchorage.

As Ben had expected, the Admiral's flag ship began to sprout flags on the signal halyards. "Captain repair aboard flag ship." "Who the devil are you?" "Get over here at once."

Once on board the Mignon again, Ben managed to piece together most of the time they were in prison, often not day by day, but at least week by week. There was really little to report after the storm and their capture. He had all of his reports ready, except certain ones that the Admiralty would require: the needs reports for the carpenter (we had none), the munitions report (they did find several tons of good dry gun powder in the hold), the surgeon's report (there was none), and several other obscure reports that Ben was hoping he could get by without.

He set out in the jolly boat in his best uniform, determined not to look like the Navy's worst dressed officer, at least not this time. He had lost a lot of weight and his uniform hung on him as if he were a hanger, but he could do little to remedy that. That was the job of time.

As Ben climbed aboard the flag ship, he was greeted with the full captain's welcome, pipes a twitter, drums beating, first leftenant Ames standing at attention with his glass under his arm, marines lined up in spit and polish order. Ben realized that they did not know who he was, so they had to welcome him as a captain. Nevertheless, such a warm welcome sent shivers of happiness through his body. He was beaming. As he stepped onto the deck, Admiral Lord St. Vincent bellowed out loud, for all to hear, "Good God, it's Rundel!" Where on earth have you been , lad? I just sent you for a load of beef. Where's the beef?"

"Ben saluted smartly and said, "Sir, Leftenant Benjamin Rundel reporting. I have brought your beef, all slaughtered, salted and barreled."

"Welcome home, lad, from wherever you have been hiding. What happened to you?"

"We were beset by a fierce storm, sir and dismasted, driven onto the Spanish coast about Cabo de Gata. The French captured us, rescued the *Mignon* from her shoal, and repaired her. Meanwhile, we spent four months in a French prison. We were able to escape the prison and recaptured the ship, which brought us home, sir."

"Come to my cabin, lad. I have to hear all about this adventure. Oh, Mr. Ames, call Admiral Nelson aboard too, if you will."

The short explanation of anything was never good enough for John Jervis, so Ben handed him his file of reports and told the whole story beginning to end. They waited until Nelson had arrived, exchanging pleasantries while they waited. When Ben was through, St. Vincent said, "I never should have sent you out on that fateful day. That was a terrible storm. It scattered our fleet, doing considerable damage to many of the ships. Even sunk two smaller ones. I am surprised that you survived in that egg crate that I gave you. Well done, lad. Nelson was delighted to hear about the barrels of beef and especially the powder. He swiftly sent off orders to transfer some barrels of beef to his ship. He complimented Ben on spending his time learning French. "Not every young officer would be so conscientious," he said.

"You have not been able to follow things here, lad, but we think that the French fleet is out and headed for the Caribbean. Lord Nelson here is about to leave within the hour to pursue them. He has played tag with them all over the blasted Mediterranean. You and your crew are being transferred back to the *Vanguard* under Captain Berry to assist Lord Nelson. You are to report at once.

Ben hesitated. "What is troubling you, lad?" said St. Vincent.

"It's just that I heard something about a large deployment of French troops to India and Egypt, sir. They must have pulled out of Toulon just ahead of us. Lucky we waited as long as we did to escape. There are papers there that verify the whereabouts of the French Fleet, sir," as Ben pointed to the file of papers in the Admiral's hand,

Ben returned to his ship and ordered his men to gather together their things and head for the *Vanguard.* Tom strode forward. "Sir, does that include me?"

Admiral St. Vincent said, "Your whole crew, and you are one of my crew, so let's not question it, lad. Pack up your things and come along. We should see some real action soon."

The squeal of the capstan could be heard as they climbed aboard and there was that ever-present smell of warm hemp as the huge cable smoked on its way through the keepers, so eager were the crewmen to set sail for the French. They were off again.

Chapter Ten

Aboukir Bay

The trip across the Mediterranean to the Caribbean was full of work and excitement. First, they had to get their crews in shape. Ben had long been absent so he had to get to know his division again. The other divisions were well-trained and in good order. Shot and powder was checked. Supplies shifted to speed their sailing and everything done to guarantee readiness.

After a whirlwind cruise to the Caribbean where they learned that the French fleet had just departed for the Mediterranean, they headed back to the east under full sail, skys'ls included. They were now quite certain that they would find the French fleet at Alexandria, Egypt. Admiral Nelson sent out a frigate to scout for the fleet. Each day, the Admiral called his captains and some of his leftenant's aboard and held lengthy discussions on battle strategy. Ben was lucky that he was able to attend many of these meetings and he took in every word. Some good suggestions were made.

Lord Nelson suggested," We want to smash their gun decks, disable their guns and damage their rigging. Leave the hulls intact if you can. This way, we bring confusion and destruction to her war machine, her guns. The more confusion and rubble on the gun decks, the better. Anything that delays their fire or disables their guns gives us an advantage."

There was a general nodding of heads. No one would dispute that tactic.

"Now gentleman, I know that you have all studied the teachings of Cloudisley Shovell of about 1702. You would never have made leftenants without Shovell. I want to disagree with that strategy, even though Lord Jervis made good use of it in 1778. I would agree that if two fleets of roughly equal size are matched one on one in line of battle, there may be no distinct outcome. But think you on this. We are 15 ships to their 17. That's a close match. If each one of our ships picks an opponent in line and hammers away at him, we will both end up severely damaged. Neither may feel a winner nor be willing to surrender. The mess to clean up when it is all over will be horrendous. But, if we cut out a portion of their fleet, say the rear half, and hammer away at it, two of our ships to their one, we are bound to bring them to their knees rapidly. A victory where we capture 8 or 9 ships is a true victory, especially if we suffer little damage to our own ships. So, when we have finished off half the fleet, we can proceed to destroy the other half, if we are able. If not, we still have a great victory to report to Whitehall. Thus, two fleets of comparable size can engage in battle and one succeed, *if one fleet is sharp enough to cut out a portion of the other, isolating it from all help and then totally destroying it.* I call it divide and destroy. It will work, gentlemen. Be assured."

Again, heads nodded and several of the captains commented. "Looks like we will have to be on our own a bit to decide which ships to attack, sir," said Foley.

"I will be delighted to give you that freedom, and I trust that you will execute the battle handsomely, Captain Foley," replied Nelson. Ben stood there with the others and watched Admiral Nelson forge together the most effective team of captains in naval history. When they were through preparing, they would know his mind to perfection. Each would be able to act just as he would want them to. *A shrewd man is Nelson.*

Ben spent his few spare hours helping Tom with his navigation. He had not been able to do much for Tom in many months. They had tried to remember some of the navigational problems in prison, but they were at a loss without adequate writing materials and books. So they had given it all up. Now they began to make real progress and Ben was relieved to see Tom back to his old self again.

The next meeting with Admiral Nelson proved to be

most interesting. With the captains gathered around, he began to discuss strategies. “If they are aligned like so,” as he laid out a series of books on the table, “and we come at them from here, with the wind to our advantage, they will be unable to move. If they are at anchor, that requires one tactic. We must rig to anchor with sheet cable in abaft and springs. That will allow us to handle any winds blowing along the shore and to move our ships in a wide arch so that we can bring our guns to bear on the enemy. I wish each of you to prepare sheeted anchors ready for use at a moments notice. Also, have an array of shot available to our gunners. We may need to act quickly if they are in a position where the enemy might escape. I will signal if we need certain shot or to use the sheeted cables. If I fail you, use your own judgment.”

The ‘brothers’ as they were becoming known in the fleet, nodded their heads in strong approval.

“Now gentlemen, the people at home are in poor spirits. The French control most of Europe and they are afraid that we have lost our dominance of the seas to Napoleon as well as dominance on land, specially since we had to withdraw from the Mediterranean. King George needs a victory that will raise spirits at home. We cannot win a war alone, you know, but if we take control of the Mediterranean, Napoleon and his 40,000 troops in Egypt will suffer severely. It will put an end to any hopes of conquering India too. This man Napoleon Bonaparte appears to be growing in power daily and we fear that he will become the ruler of France and most of Europe. He is as good as there already.”

Ben realized more each day how much political pressures and events in far-distant places affected what they were doing, and that the outcome of their battle was much more than a personal victory. Every man there knew that all England would benefit from a victory.

The Admiral continued. “Now, if they are anchored just so, as he ran his finger across the chart along the coast off Alexandria, we should be able to flank them on both sides. Much depends on which way they are headed. If they are headed this way, they will expect us to come in from the west. But, we may surprise them and come in through these islands, if the water is deep enough and if the wind is in our favour. If they are headed in the reverse direction, having come to anchor under a different wind, then we can surprise them by slipping in here. We would engage their van and leave the rear isolated and ready for us to attack later, if necessary."

Now James Saumarez spoke."You do not propose to place our ships on both sides of the French ships, do you?"

"Why not? We can control our fire so that the enemy is the prime target," offered Nelson.

"I would be concerned about cross fire and damaging our own ships, sir, especially when we are aiming for rigging. It poses a grave danger," said Saumarez. The two would discuss this strategy for hours, and would never come to agreement on it. Saumarez was to be second in command under Lord Nelson for the battle.

The discussions went on day after day. That day they considered what they would do if they found the fleet sailing, first to the west and then to the east, using their knowledge of the prevailing winds. It was like a big chess game with too much at stake. They considered all possible contingencies, which was Nelson's way, and a way that Ben had used all of his life. He was learning a great deal about men and about naval strategies. He ventured a question. "Sir, will we attack at night?"

"By all means. That is the one thing that they will not expect us to do."

In the end, Lord Nelson rose from his seat and said, "I believe that we have considered every possible position in which we may find the enemy, and no matter where he hides or sails, we have him. He is ours."

He thanked the captains for their ideas and suggestions and they left to return to their own ships, each a man trained in the Nelson tradition. Yet, each with a chance to distinguish himself by free interpretation of their plans. Ben felt a certain pride in his participation in the discussions. He was ready to go and do whatever Lord Nelson might bid, to shed his blood and die if needed. Every captain and leftenant felt the same way, he was sure from their conversations. This was a most unusual group of men.

Early on 1 August, 1798, our scout returned and said that the ships were drawn up close to shore at Aboukir Bay, some thirteen miles east of Alexandria. Vice Admiral Francis Paul, Count de Brueys was in command. He had placed his flagship in the midst of the fleet which was strung out over about two miles in a gentle ark. His van was formed by the weaker ships, with the strongest in the rear. They were headed east, with four frigates inshore in the shallower waters. They might have a shore battery as well, but Captain Gould could not be certain of that. By the time they approached the bay, it was late in the afternoon. It was fast growing dark. They reduced sails on all ships to slow their approach. It was clear that the British would have to come to anchor.

Ben's division was on the starb'd side of the upper gun deck. He could just see the *Culloden* off far to starboard. She had a prize ship in tow and was moving more slowly than the rest of the fleet. His men were ready. They had eaten and the guns were loaded, ready to run out and train. Captain Foley was leading the van in the *Goliath.* He had the only copy of the latest charts showing the depth of water and presence of shoals on this part of the coast.

From the lack of activity aboard the Frenchmen, Ben deduced that they did not expect the British to do more than come to anchor. It was nearly dark and De Brueys would assume that the British would hesitate to sail into these shoal waters in the dark. He would assume that they would come to anchor for the night and then bring them to battle in the morning. What he did not know then was that de Brueys had sent a large number of his men ashore to water, so that he had only small crews left aboard some of his ships. He sent out frantic signals for his boats to return at once, but many of them did not comply or did not make it back in time.

The *Vanguard* was sixth in line as they approached the French ships. As Ben turned to look back at the stern, he noticed that the *Culloden* came up suddenly with a sharp blow. She looked like she had gone aground just off a point of land to the north. The prize that was in tow had stopped moving also, so something was definitely wrong with the *Culloden*. The *Mutine* and *Leander*, which had been detached to reconnoitre the port, looked as if they might be going to her aid. Ben closed his glass with a snap and went to tell the Admiral about *Culloden*. *Tough luck, that,* he thought.

Then Ben watched the *Goliath* slip handily between the *Guerrier* and her buoy. Apparently the French Admiral had signaled his ships to pass cables between their ships, but only a few did so. Cables would have prevented them from penetrating the French line and engaging the French ships on both sides. Most were open so that the British ships could pass between if they wished. After the battle, Captain Foley explained his reasoning. It occurred to him as he approached that the French had anchored by the bows only. That meant that the water must be deep enough for the ships to swing in a full circle. If they could swing, then there was enough room for him to slip the *Goliath* in between the Frenchmen and the shore. He also suspected correctly that the French had not loaded their guns on the starboard side, since they expected no attack at all, but if one did come it would have to be on their port side. They were wrong. The wind was in Nelson's favour for an attack from the north, not from the south. Ben saw *Goliath* drop anchor just inside the *Guerriere* and commenced firing about 6:20 p.m. Lord Nelson was delighted at this clever maneuver, so professionally executed. Foley was anchored in only five fathoms of water, but he was free and clear to fight.

Then Ben saw the frigate *Serieuse* open fire on Foley's *Goliath*, but Foley soon silenced the frigate with a couple of broadsides. But the broadsides had caused him to overshoot his position abreast of *Guerriere,* so he anchored between *Conquerant* and *Spartiate.* Now Captain Hood, in the *Zealous,* saw what had happened to Foley's ship, so he cut away his sheet anchor and took up the position opposite *Guerriere.* Then, Saumarez who was Captian of the *Orion* came on and passed both Hood and Foley. He fired a few more rounds into the *Serieuse* and finished her off. Then he anchored between the *Aquilon* and *Peuple Souverain* and engaged them both in ravaging fire. The *Vanguard* was moving quickly into position, but Ben could see the *Audacious* under Captain Gould cut across the stern of the *Guerrier* and came to anchor opposite the *Conquerant's* larboard bow. Finally, Captain Miller took his *Theseus* between the *Goliath* and *Zealous.* As he passed down the line of his ships, the British crews cheered, but their cheers were met with feeble shouts from the mystified French. The British only laughed at their feeble reply. The French were apparently distraught at having to fight a night battle at anchor, with no way to escape. Miller sent off a broadside at each enemy ship that he passed by, making some dents in their gunnery. He finally anchored *Theseus* astern of the *Goliath* and abreast of *Spartiate.*

It was now the moment when Admiral Nelson would have to decide whether he wanted to take the rest of his ships inside the French line or leave them on the seaward side. Ben said to Tom, who stood nearby. "Bet he doesn't go inside. It's getting too dark. There are enough ships there already. If we anchor outside, we can rake them from both sides."

Tom smiled and said, "You probably are right. There goes the order to the helmsman. We'll know in a few seconds what he intends to do."

Apparently the French had not prepared for using their port guns as Foley had suspected. Some of the sailors saw boxes, lumber and bags piled up next to the lower deck gun ports of the *Guerriere.* It would take them some time to get ready to fight. Now was their chance and Captain Hood was wasting no time. Hood managed to completely dismast the Guerriere with only a quarter of an hour of intense firing. This was a great victory because the *Zealous* was largely undamaged.

Then they watched as the *Conquerant* crumpled under intense fire from the *Goliath, Audacious* and *Theseus.* They had drawn up two on one side and one on the other and had pounded her into submission in only twenty minutes. Nelson's divide and destroy philosophy was working quite well. They could see occasional flashes from the shore guns, only about six of them, but they were just wasting powder and shot. They were too far away to be effective.

They were now dropping anchor abreast of the *Spartiate.* The other British ships had followed in line to seaward to attack the remaining ships in the van with a brutal crossfire, aided by those ships on the land ward side. Now Ben was so taken up with the excitement of the moment that he told me the rest of his story in his own words.

"We received the order to open fire as we came to bear. My lads were eager and ready and poured broadside after broadside into the *Spartiate.* We were able to get off about two broadsides to her one. The French were never known for fast or accurate gun drill. The smoke became so dense that I could not see and it was hard to breathe. I gasped out my orders, "Fire!" and the lads did their best. We suffered some damage in the first fifteen minutes, but after that the *Spartiate* was weakened enough that even at such close quarters she could not do us much harm. Some of the taller ships like *L'Orient* failed to do our ships much damage because she fired too high, firing over our heads and missing her shots altogether. I was impressed with the bravery of the French, but their gunnery was abysmal.

I was asked to find where the *Alexander* and *Swiftsure* were so that they might be signaled to come to our aid, but they were still some miles away. *Culloden* under a steaming Captain Troubridge was definitely out of action. She was firmly stuck with apparently a large hole in her hull and a damaged rudder. I felt sorry for those lads, saddled with a sinking ship and being able to do no better than to watch our fire and follow our progress from afar.

After awhile the darkness seemed not a problem. The frequent and intense fire from the British ships kept the sky lit up and we could see one another most of the time. Admiral Nelson had made a wise decision before the battle. He required that all British ships display four banded horizontal blue lights at the mizzen and that they should fly white pennants so they might recognize one another in the dark. Nelson was determined to fight in the dark if he must, and he was ready. Ben learned that advanced planning and anticipation of your enemies possible moves can save lives and win battles. It was working, but the miracle was that there was no real order to the fighting. Each man reacted as he knew Lord Nelson would want him to and it worked extremely well. Nelson sent up only six orders during the entire battle, mostly directed at bringing the ships to bear on the enemy.

Then a brig came out to attract our fire, She was a decoy, but she quickly skipped back into the shallow water. It was clearly a ruse by the French, trying to lure us out to attack the easy prize and run our ships aground on the shallows. Admiral Nelson did not take the bait and we stayed at our post, pounding the nearest ships with withering fire.

For the next two hours the battle raged, with such force and vigour that I thought my men would drop. They were becoming fatigued, but still stuck to their guns, firing as regularly as humanly possible. I was getting tired and my ears ached. We actually saw people drop dead without a mark on them. I figured it was from the force of concussion after a series of close firings. I saw men shot in two, heads rolling about the deck free of any body and atrocities that only a huge gun could deliver. But the musket fire did its damage too. I saw men disemboweled with a single lucky rifle shot from the enemy tops, a horrible thing to contemplate. Men fell regularly from the decks of the French ships, either dead and thrown over board or wounded and having lost their balance, plunged into the sea. The water was full of floating debris, dead bodies and cordage. I was near sick at the sights, the deafening sounds, the smells and the fear that comes when a musket ball whizzes past ones' ear. I had forgotten how steamy and hot a man's insides are when they are first opened and what a peculiar smell comes with pools of blood freshly drained from warm bodies. But I was proud of my lads. They fought most valiantly and showed no sign of cowardice. The marines stationed at the entrances to the hold said afterwards that not a man tried to bolt from his duty to run below decks to safety.

But there were some odd things that happened. Some of the powder boys were killed and some of the women on other ships who carried ammunition for the gunners were wounded. One lady decided that it would be a good time to divest herself of her baby. She delivered a boy during the hottest portion of the battle. She must have taken care of things herself for no surgeon or surgeon's helper would have time just then to attend to her. Lord Nelson did not permit women aboard ship when at sea, because he thought them to be too disruptive. I agreed with him, but some of the captains had officers with wives who came along, war or no, and some of the men brought their wives to serve them while at sea. One woman aboard the *Orion* worked with the surgeon throughout the bloody mess, assisting with amputations and all manner of disgusting work. I knew what she must be suffering for I had been there once myself when I was surgeon's helper aboard the *Faithful.* I heard tales afterwards of women bringing their men water or wine to drink to lessen their thirst, which, by midnight was terrible for us all. The acrid smoke from the guns cut our throats raw and drove men to drink from the swab buckets to assuage their thirst.

I heard a call though the smoke and Tom's smiling face emerged, offering me a ladle of water. I grabbed it and blessed his skinny Irish self at the same time. It gave me the will to go on through the rest of the night. I had sent a ship's boy off for water for my division about half an hour ago.

All of the enemy van was either defeated or engaged by nine o'clock. We waged on, never letting up the pressure of our gun fire, never ready to lay back until the enemy struck their colours.

Captain Louis in the *Minotaur* went to work on the *Aquilon* just ahead of us. I could see intense fire and loud action from those ships. Captain Peyton set his *Defence* against the *Peuple Sauverain* and a heated battle ensued. All around us I could see flashes of flames from the guns, hear shrieks of pain, smell the smoke and feel the vibrations that ran through my body with each salvo. I was becoming a zombie like my men. All we could do was repeat the same actions over and over again until our enemy hauled down his flag and we were free to seek another. Strange as it may seem, we had no time to put aboard prize crews. By the time that the French ships surrendered, they were reduced to such a state of chaos that there was no hope of fleeing. They just sat calmly amid their rubble and awaited the time when our men could break free to come aboard and accept official surrender. Then we would take the prisoners and arrange for their transfer to shore. We set up prisoner cartels because some of the French wounded could better be served by their own surgeons ashore. Our surgeons were all busy. I would see many more battles during my lifetime, but never one like this.

It was sultry and hot. The air stirred too little for my liking. I was sweating and my throat burned and I could not stop coughing. The ship's boy came by with water again which I gratefully accepted. I must say that the French were poorly trained, but lacked nothing in courage. I saw one of the Captains, a Du Petit Thouars of the *Tonnant* lose both his arms and one leg, but demanded to be patched up, placed in a tub on his quarter deck where he could continue the fight. We happened to be close enough by her that I was able to determine what was happening. Aboard the *Vanguard* we learned later that a shot had come right into the magazine, but a ship's boy ran for the carpenter. He was able to come at once and plugged the hole so that the powder remained mostly dry. It was our grand organization, and our lack of express orders that made it all happen so well. Each man knew his duty and none held back.

About a quarter to eight, we took in on our spring so as to engage the *Aquilon,* while still firing on the *Spartiate.* The firing was non-stop by now. I needn't even give the order. The men had been at it so long that they were timed to perfection. But I could see that they were tired, weary to the bone. Such work exceeds all other in its demands on a man's strength. Lads were falling from exhaustion and thirst. I ordered one ship's boy to get yet another bucket of fresh water and a ladle and serve the men at the guns first. I marveled at how little damage the *Vanguard* had sustained. Yes, we were holed in a place or two and we had lost some of our rigging, but we were nearly intact otherwise.

Just in a short lull, I heard a scream from the quarter-deck. I looked up and there was Admiral Nelson, reeling and then he fell. He had been studying a map taken from a ship captured by Captain Hollowell. He had sent it over to Lord Nelson at once, thinking it would aid the fleet and keep us from going aground.

I ran to him, glancing at Tom. "Take over, Tom," I called through the din. When I had reached the quarterdeck, the Admiral's face was covered with blood and I feared for the worst. He said to Captain Berry who had come running, "I am killed. Remember me to my wife." Then he fell unconscious on the deck. I rolled him over and wiped away the blood. It was oozing from a triangular-shaped wound on his forehead made by a piece of langrage.

"Let's get him to his cabin," I said as I helped to lift him up. But the Admiral did not stay unconscious for more than a minute or two. He soon came to and was calling for someone to hail Captain Louis to come aboard. He was supposed to be related to Louis XIV and was fighting on our side. Meanwhile, I secured clean cloths from the steward and wiped the blood from his good eye. I managed to fold the flap of skin back where it belonged and bandaged his head tightly to stop the bleeding. "Head wounds always bleed excessively, sir," I tried to comfort him. "You will be fine if you just lie still for awhile. We'll get you to the orlop deck in a few minutes."

He looked up at me. "I had forgotten that one of your many talents Rundel was that of surgeon. I feel better already. You need not rush me to the orlop now. I am fine and can wait my turn for the surgeon. Thank you for your help, my good man."

So I returned to my post and we battled on. About 8:30 p.m., *Swiftsure* and *Alexander* had caught up with us and came to join the fight. While sailing into position, a dismasted 74 floated by *Swiftsure* in the dark, not a light aboard her. Hollowell almost opened fire on her, but something was just not right. He called to his men to hold their fire. Just in the nick of time he recognized her hull style in the dim moonlight and realized that she was the battered remains of *Bellerophon.* The Admiral had taken all precautions against this happening, but no one could have predicted that one of our ships would have all three masts blown off her. A disaster was avoided and the *Bellerophon* was able to limp into port and was repaired later on. She had come up unexpectedly too close to *L'Orient,* the 120 gun French flag ship and had taken a severe beating. She fought the huge ship for over an hour, but, refusing to lower her colours, she cut her cable and drifted away. Captain Darby and a third of her crew were casualties. They could not fight on against such a large ship.

Captain Hollowell of the *Swiftsure* was a dare-devil.

He made directly for the position that *Bellerophon* had vacated and came to anchor abreast of *L'Orient.* Now he began to pour a steady fire into her, aided by the *Alexander* which came to anchor close on her larboard quarter. The men of these two ships were reasonably fresh and were able to seriously injure the huge French flag ship. Just about the time they took up action, a stray shot severed the cable of the *Peuple Sauverain,* which was in very poor shape indeed. Captain Thompson in the *Leander* saw an opening and guided his ship in where the *Sauverain* had been anchored. That gave her access to fire on the French line and particularly on *L'Orient.* With three ships now pounding away at her, the French fortress began to crumble. She lost her masts and soon her guns were unable to fire regularly.

By nine o'clock, the intense fire from the *Zealous, Audacious, Goliath, Theseus,* and *Orion* on one side and their partners, the *Vanguard, Minotaur* and *Defence* on the seaward side, the enemy van was completely subdued. There was only sporadic fire to be heard anywhere in the van. I could look out and see hulks floating by or still anchored, with nothing of the substance of a fighting ship left in them. The *Guerriere* had stubbornly held out against Hood's demand that she surrender, but now I could see that it was over for her too. Three-quarters of her crew were either dead or wounded and the ship was completely dismasted. The other French ships of the van stood silent, their guns not able to murmur a sound and the ships too devastated to sail away. Shortly after, the *Peuple Sauverain* ran aground on the shoals to leeward.

The only action now was between the battered *L'Orient* and her three bulldogs, *Swiftsure, Alexander* and *Leander.* They hung on with all their firepower. Suddenly, some one on the *Alexander* threw an incendiary device onto the deck of *L'Orient.* No one would own up to the nature of the device afterwards, but it was most effective. *L'Orient* caught fire at once and within a few minutes there were flames raging far out of reach of the sailors who tried to extinguish them. Apparently she had barrels of paint on board that immediately caught fire and spread the flames at an unusually fast rate. The three British ships soon ceased to fire and brought in their anchors and moved off from the huge ship. The ship was useless and would be a total loss. She was certainly going to explode if there was any powder left in her magazine. It was just a matter of time... Everyone left off his duties to watch, mesmerized by the brilliantly lighted spectacle. The moon shone brightly now, although there was still a haze of smoke. But the flames illuminated the entire sea, throwing sparks to sizzle and go out as soon as they hit the cool water. I had seen a ship burn once in the English Channel as a boy, and again as a young man off the coast of France, but this far surpassed anything that I had ever seen or imagined. Even Lord Nelson, when he was told of it, demanded to be taken from his cot and brought on deck to watch it. There was much going on aboard that embattled ship. Apparently De Brueys had been hit in the legs by a cannon ball and had lost both legs. After bandaging his wounds, he made his men bring him back to his quarter deck and he stayed there to direct the fighting until another shot nearly cut him in two. He had said after the first injury, "A good Admiral should die on his quarter-deck, nes pas?" Great numbers of his men were wounded and unable to escape. Some who were still whole began to jump into the water and swim for the nearest ship. We plucked a number of men from the sea. Admiral Nelson dispatched a ship's boat with Mr. Galway to pick up as many as he could find.

What a grand and yet horrible spectre lay before us. Cold moon light and the heat from the giant ship which carried even to our decks, illuminating tired, grimy faces. Tom stood by my side and I looked at him. "Any time now, lad." We could see men sluicing down their decks, especially Ball and Miller in the *Theseus.* Captain Saumarez closed the gun ports of the *Orion* because she was anchored quite close. He secured the magazine and furled the sails, wetting them down as best he could with the pumps. Even the French ships to the stern of *L'Orient* veered their cables to warp their ships out of danger. A few of them had managed to rig springs.

Then about three minutes after ten, the air hot as a blast furnace, the ship blew up. The fire finally reached her magazine. She blew with a sound that was deafening, the impact of the explosion made men reel on their feet. The explosion was heard ten miles away. Sparks, huge chunks of wood, burning rigging, all flew in every direction. It was a spectacle that a man would see only once in a thousand lifetimes and it was splendid enough and sufficiently horrible to last that long too. Tom and I watched as the pieces dropped into the cold sea, hissing and smoking. The remaining hulk began to sink almost at once and within a few minutes, the last of her was gone, with the mangled body of Admiral de Brueys, and 600,000 pounds in gold and silver as well as art treasures stolen from the Egyptians, all lost. Commodore Cassabianca died with the ship too. He had refused to leave because his son was wounded in the leg and was unable to leave. Some where in the vicinity of a thousand men died with that ship and that was enough to turn the heart of any sailor. Only seventy of her 1010 men were picked up and taken aboard other ships to safety. "What a horrible death, even for Frenchmen," said Tom.

One incident was talked about later. One body, naked except for his officer's hat appeared at the tumblehome of the *Swiftsure*. Hollowell greeted him with, "Who the deuce are you?" The man answered that he was Leftenant Berthelot of *L'Orient* and had swum part way to this ship when he decided that he had best go back and claim his hat so he would be accepted as an officer and not a common seaman.

After the explosion, there was an unreal silence. Men stood and simply looked at one another. They were too stunned to act and too tired to even think of doing anything more that night. But the night was not over with the battle still at ragged ends. After about ten minutes, the firing broke out again. Nearly two hours later, at midnight, the *Franklin* struck her colours.

By that time, three of the French ships had veered out of the line of fire, the *Tonnant, Heureux* and *Mercure.* Firing had ceased from the fort on land long ago. It was useless because it was about 1.7 miles away and none of its shells could reach the British ships.

By midnight, Lord Nelson had to be confined to his bunk. He was faint from the loss of blood and could not give orders to press the fight further. The men were exhausted beyond imagination and could not execute orders. Some men had fallen asleep at the capstan when they tried to up anchor. They were simply worn out. Most leftenants and captains gave orders for their crews to sleep beside their guns and everyone on both sides observed a well-deserved 'nap time,' as Tom called it. He and Tom sat down on the deck, back to back and slept like babes.

Just before dawn, Hood came aboard and roused men to get back with the battle. Lord Nelson, somewhat recovered, ordered his flag-leftenant to signal all ships that were not disabled to move forward to join the *Alexander* and *Majestic* which were engaged with the rear of the French fleet. The *Zealous, Goliath* and *Theseus* complied almost immediately and the rest of the battle was about to go forward. *Leander* joined them straight away and the four went to finish the job. The *Hereux* fell first to Captain Miller in the *Theseus.* Within a few minutes, the *Theseus* engaged the *Artemise,* which appeared as if she might make a good fight of it, but morale was low and she soon struck her colours too. Most of her crew fired one broadside at *Theseus* and then abandoned their guns. They knew what lay in store for them if they decided to fight any more. Miller commented on their dishonourable action and would always consider them cowards. It was not long before they had secured the surrender of the *Mercure.* That left the *Tonnant* now dismasted, drifting to leeward and having lost her cable. She went aground soon after.

Only three French ships were left that were more or less whole. The *Genereux, Guillaume Tell,* and *Timoleon* now saw the handwriting on the sea and weighed anchor, setting sail for the open sea. Rear Admiral Villenueve was with them and had to go back to France to answer to the worst defeat in French naval history. Ben thought that he would rather die than try to fill his shoes. One of his tiny fleet, the *Timoleon* had been crippled by heavy fire from the *Theseus* and was soon wrecked on a nearby beach. Captain Hood made off to chase the two remaining French ships, but Nelson needed him close by. There was much work to be done before they could head for a friendly port and make repairs. Prisoners had to be organized into cartels and transported to shore, emergency repairs were needed and he did not want to disperse his fleet. He signaled for Hood to return.

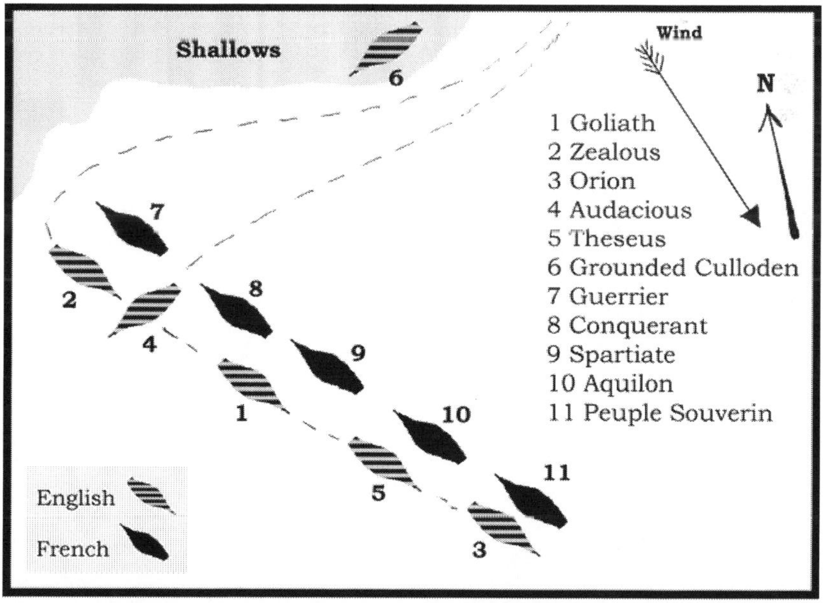

DIAGRAM OF A PORTOIN OF THE DEPLOYMENT OF THE SHIPS DURING THE BATTLE OF ABOUKIR BAY
Adopted from Blake and Lawrence, 1999, Chatham Press
The Actual battle positions were much more complicated.

Chapter Eleven

The Aftermath of Battle

When the sun rose the next morning, it shone down on an incredibly tragic scene. The water was full of debris, floating rigging, boxes, wood, barrels, dead bodies, spars, spare severed limbs, and there was here and there a red cast to the sea. It brought home most painfully what it was that they had just experienced. Men who have been through such an ordeal become bonded in a special way that their women can never understand.

After the fighting had ceased and when the sun rose, the British sailors assembled on deck, requesting a brief memorial service for the dead and thanksgiving for their deliverance. It happened throughout the British ships. Men gathered in solemn thanksgiving, certain that they had narrowly escaped death and mourning for their lost shipmates. The French sailors looked on, amazed at the devotion of these men to their country, their King and their God. Many praised Admiral Nelson for having carried forth such a successful battle. Only James Saumarez was critical. He began to lament the lack of a firm plan, when Nelson reminded him that their success had come from the decisions of well-trained officers, brilliant leaders all, not from any rigid master plan that could not be adjusted for unforeseen contingencies.

"No one could have 'planned' this battle."

As soon as he was up and about, Admiral Nelson dictated a short account of the battle to send to the Admiralty in London. He dispatched two copies, one with Ed Berry and Captain Thompson in the *Leander* 50 which was the only British ship to lose her captain. On her way out to the Straits, she ran into the *Genereux,* of 74 guns. The French ship had on board 900 additional crewmen from the Nile and so could man her guns most effectively.

Unfortunately, there was no escaping a fight, so Berry and Thompson settled in for a hard fight. It was a bloody battle and in the end, the Leander was dismasted and lay helpless in the water. Captain Thompson was wounded four times and Captain Berry was wounded also. When asked by the French if they would surrender, they looked at each other and with heads hung in sorrow, agreed that there was little other choice. They asked to be taken to Naples where they knew they would meet up with Nelson in time.

The second message concerning the glorious victory was sent to Naples in the *Mutine* under Leftenant Capel and it arrived safely. Capel had replaced Thomas Hardy who was now promoted to Captain of the *Vanguard,* which remained the flagship. He would serve as Nelson's captain much of the time until the latter's death in 1805. The message was sent on to the Commander-In-Chief in London overland with Leftenant Capel. The command of the *Mutine* he turned over to Leftenant Hoste. Ben had so wished that he might be given the command of the *Mutine*, but that was not to be. There were often too many capable young leftenants in the fleet so that the one chosen for a particular duty might be the one nearest by, not always the one best suited for the job. Captain Bailey had warned him of this problem and of the problems associated with his humble birth many years ago. He would have to be patient. Soon all of England was celebrating. But there were some hard feelings about the victory message.

"...Nothing could withstand the squadron your Lordship did me the honour to place under my command. Their high state of discipline is well known to you, and with the judgment of the captains, together with their valour, and that of the officers and men of every description, it was absolutely irresistible. Could any thing from my pen add to the character of the captains, I would write it with pleasure, but that is impossible."

(Nelson's Battles, Tracy, 1996)

Some officers, particularly James Saumarez felt that individual captains had distinguished themselves and should have been duly recognized in the victory letter. Perhaps Nelson felt that he did not want to exhault any one of the 'brothers' above the others which might make them less brothers in the future. That is what Ben thought, at least, and Tom agreed. But few had any complaint to make. All felt as if they had slaved together for a good common cause and now they could bask in the glow of victory. After all, now Bonaparte and his men were bottled up in Egypt with no way to return to France. The Mediterranean was no longer their private sea, but was now in the control of the British once again. The British left the French only two ship-of-the-line in the Mediterranean. They were hopelessly weakened and could not threaten the shores of England for some long time.

As soon as the service was over, the men began to make repairs. There was so much to do that Ben and Tom did not find time to talk to one another until late that night. It would be several days before they would be able to sail together back to Naples.

During the repairs, Ben and Tom tried to collect data on the number of ships lost and the casualties for the Admiral. Ben figured that the French lost all but four of their seventeen ships. But the great news was that the British had lost none of their ships. This news brought smiles to Lord Nelson's face and was a cause for rejoicing throughout the fleet. The *Bellerophon* needed major repairs, but was salvageable and the *Culloden,* although badly holed from her encounter with the shoal, was repairable. Some five thousand Frenchmen, by actual count nearly 5,235 men, appear to have died, some were missing, but no one could ever get an accurate count. The British losses were 218 killed and 677 wounded, an unbelievable record considering the closeness of the fighting and the intensity with which it was carried out. Captain Wescott of the *Leander* was killed and Captains Hood, Miller, Saumarez and Ball all had minor injuries. They were joined by Lord Nelson, but he would soon recover.

One strange thing happened while they were busy at repairs. This was before Leftenant Capel was sent off with dispatches. It seems that now Captain Hardy had gone aboard the *Serieuse* to check on the progress of repairs. As he stood by a hatch, it suddenly flew open and a disgustingly bloated corpse of a dead marine popped onto the surface of the deck at his feet. Hardy jumped backwards wriggling his nose in disgust. Within seconds, a second naked body emerged, but this one was quite alive and held out his hand in greeting. It was Leftenant Capel who had been diving in the ship to check on her condition. The incident made good telling during, no *after* supper around the wardroom table and captain's tables.

The first day, Ben and Tom were sent over to assist the *Culloden* which was still aground. Ben took three ship's carpenters and their mates and they were able to stop the leak which had been letting 120 tons of water into her hold per hour. Her pumps had worked steadily day and night and were overwhelmed. The men heaved a great sigh of relief when they learned that the carpenters had the leak stopped. They were able to ease her off the shoal during high tide and refitted a rudder on her so that she might be able to get back to sea. Once the emergency repairs were made, Ben and Tom returned to the *Vanguard.*

But their stay there was short. Ben was ordered to go aboard one of the French ships that had sunk in shallow water. The Admiral was distressed because all of the French captains had managed to destroy their code books before they died or were taken prisoner. Ben thought that the bottom of the bay must be littered with code books, but no one could find them. The captain of the *Mercure* had been killed before his ship went aground. There might be a chance that his code book still remained in his cabin. The ship had touched on a shoal, then swung around so that her stern was just out of water. It was possible that enough of her stern was above water for them to seek out the code book. Ben had orders to burn her when he was through with his search. He took Tom with him and called up his division from their labours at splicing and knotting.

"Any man here a good diver and swimmer?" said Ben.

Several men stepped forward. Ben selected William Feeney because he was thin and might be able to get into tight places. "Dismissed, men. Back to your duties."

He took a small crew to handle the jolly boat and set Tom at the tiller. Feeney went below to collect a pry bar and tools and then they were off. They lashed onto the stern of the ship which sat only about five feet above the water. Ben gave Feeney his instructions. "You are to enter the Captain's cabin and search for the code book, you know, like the one I showed you on board the *Vanguard.* Also look for any other things of value to a ship of war." Feeney shook his head, smiling to reveal a mouth almost devoid of teeth.

Feeney, a spidery little man, with a long, leathery, wrinkled face, climbed up the transom and disappeared through a window into the captain's cabin. *It is an easy job,* Ben thought. But that did not prove to be the case. A gun had upended in the cabin and blocked the passage into the cabin itself.

Ben and his crew sat in the sweltering sun, waiting for Feeney to return. They had brought along the powder and gear to burn the ship, but Ben hated to begin work on that until he was certain what was in the cabin. But Feeney did not come back. "He has been gone for over an hour," said Ben to Tom. "I wonder what has happened to him?"

'I don't know, sir, but I wish he'd hurry. It's God-awful hot out here," replied Tom.

So they waited, scorched by the Egyptian sun. It was almost two stifflingly hot hours before his skinny head appeared above the transom, sticking through the broken window. There was a broad smile on his face, *but his eyes seem glazed and strange,* thought Ben. He crawled through the window quite awkwardly and tumbled into the sea. Then he appeared to be unable to swim. He was drowning before their eyes, flailing his arms about like one who had never been in the water before. "He could swim like a fish when he went in, sir," said Tom.

Ben stripped off his clothes and dove in. He reached for the poor struggling wretch and dragged him aboard the jolly boat. "What's wrong with you, anyway?" asked Ben as he propped him up against the gunnels. But the man's eyes closed, a placid smile on his scrawny face. He slumped down and settled into the bottom of the boat, a wet mass of flesh.

"'E must be sick, sir," said Roamer, one of his crew.

Ben leaned over and looked at the man. "There's no way he could get sick under water in a sunken ship," said Ben. He smelled the man's breath and then stood up. "Gentlemen, he is stoned drunk," Ben announced. He stood there shaking his head for a few minutes, not wanting to believe what his eyes and nose told him. But it was true. The man was drunk. How he had done it was more than Ben could guess. It would soon be dinner time and he had to make some attempt to find the code book. So Ben jumped back in and swam to the ship. He climbed aboard and dove into the cool water. It was pleasant on his skin after the heat of the sun. When he found an air pocket and came up for breath, he quickly realized what had happened. The air pocket, only a few feet square was in the far corner of the cabin. Right below it was the captain's store of fine French wines. Some bottles had survived the wreck and were still in the rack. Feeney had clung there just under the ceiling and had dove down to retrieve wine bottles. There were several empty wine bottles floating in the cabin. So that was it. That was how Feeney got drunk aboard a sunken ship.

Ben dove to the desk, but the drawer was stuck or locked. Feeney had not brought the pry bar back with him and now Ben needed it. He dove looking for the bar. Logically he might have dropped it just beneath the air space. Ben looked, but in the gloom, it was hard to see anything. He dove again and again. Finally he found it, lodged against some blue cloth. As Ben reached for the bar, he suddenly froze. There, wedged under a huge wooden chest, lay the dead captain. His face was a horrible blue and his eyes bulged. Ben panicked. He raced to the window and hung out, breathing frantically. But it was really his nerves that were in disorder. He had seen just such a face on a corpse floating in a wrecked French fishing boat when he was a small boy and this sudden appearance of the dead man brought back the pain of that day in his life. *I should not be afraid of a dead man.* He had seen hundreds dead and dying in the past twenty-four hours. Why was this different? It was because the dead man stared up at him, helpless yet accusing. Ben imagined he could hear the man saying, 'It is because of you Ben Rundel, that I lie here now and if things had been different, you might be here instead of me.' That was what Ben saw in those horrible eyes, bulging from the man's head and what his overtired mind told him.

Ben took several deep breaths. *I have to get a hold of myself. This is not the way a British officer reacts. I must be in command at all times.* He stiffened his resolve and dove back down into the cabin. He had retrieved the bar and now he averted his eyes so that he could not see the corpse. There was a good chance that this captian had not jettisoned his code book and it was his duty to retrieve it if at all possible. He worked the pry bar into the space between the drawer and its frame and gave a mighty heave. The drawer slid open. *Yes, there was the packet that he wanted. It looked like a code book wrapped in oiled canvas and tied with heavy string to which there was a weight attached.* Ben surfaced for air and set the packet aside. He was into it now and he would finish the job. He went through the other drawers and came out with a beautiful gold cup engraved with 'R.C.' Then his eye caught sight of a large box like structure in the corner of the cabin, now tipped as if it might fall over any minute. He surfaced, breathed and then went back to the box. It was as he had suspected, a large safe. He worked the pry bar between the hasp and the lock and to his surprise, the lock flew open. *Not very secure,* he thought. As the door fell open, several bags of gold coins fell out. Ben reached for one of them and decided to take it with him. He looked inside the safe. There were perhaps enough coins there to make some 100,000 pounds plus some other treasures of gold and silver. *I'd best get back to the Admiral with this,* he thought. So he swam to the window, collected his code book and the bag of coins with the gold cup and made his way with difficulty to the waiting boat. The men looked like lobsters, fully cooked, but he gave orders to pull for the flagship with all haste. As they pulled away, Ben looked at the way the ship lay. The best way to get the money out would be to bring the safe through the deck. That would require drilling holes through the upper deck and sawing out a place about four feet by four feet. There was just a stub of a mizzen mast left, but it would serve to attach a lift to bring the safe out. Ben closed the door of the safe before he left. He dressed hastily as the men rowed towards the ship. Everywhere he looked there were ships with men crawling all over them, mallets, saws, adzes in hand, busily getting the ships ready to sail. The noise of work met his ears from all quarters. These were good sounds.

Once on board, he asked to see the Admiral. He had not had a chance to see Lord Nelson since the night his head was injured and he wanted to see how well he was recovering. *He is a frail sort of man,* Ben thought.

"Oh my saviour, my leftenant surgeon, please do come in. I have not had a chance to properly thank you for your ministrations when I was injured during the battle. Please, you look tired. Sit, lad."

Ben came and sat next to the Admiral. "You look fine, sir. You should be healed in no time at all." But Ben thought that he really looked very tired and haggard. He noted that the Admiral had already handed over some of the responsibilities for repairing their ships and the prizes to James Saumarez and some of the other captains.

"I have brought you a signal book, sir, but I am not certain if it will be readable. It has been in the water for sometime. I think you can make out most of the entries, though. There are ghost letters left on the pages." Ben handed the book to Lord Nelson, who extended a thin hand for it.

"Good work, lad. This is the only one out of fourteen that we have been able to recover."

"There is more, sir. The *Mercure* appears to have on board a sizable safe with I would guess somewhere in the vicinity of 100,000 pounds in gold, plus a number of silver and gold pieces. It is risky business trying to get the treasure out through the cabin window. I propose that we saw a hole in the deck and lift the entire safe out through the deck, using the stump of her mizzenmast for a place to secure the lift."

"Wonderful! My luck will never end," said Nelson. Ben knew that the Admiral seemed to have continuing money problems and that he, a mere leftenant, was probably more wealthy than this great man, but he would say naught of that.

"Take what ever help you need Mr. Rundel and see if you can retrieve the treasure. It will look good on the final reports to the Admiralty that not all of the treasure went to the bottom of the sea with *L'Orient*." Ben could tell that the Admiral was pleased. He was smiling that strange smile of his and he seemed much relieved.

Ben sent his crew to dinner and then picked them up again, all but Feeney. He had been sent into irons for drunkenness on duty. Captain Hardy would deal with him later, when the work of repairs was less pressing. Feeney's antics would appear in Ben's report and would be worth a good laugh at dinner for some time to come. The men would say, "I'm going to do a 'Feeney'," or "Don't do a 'Feeney' on me." Back at the wreck, the men brought out large augers and drilled several holes through the deck just over where the safe lay. Unfortunately, that portion of the deck was under water, so the men would dive down and drill for a minute or two, surface and another man would take his place. Once they had six holes close together across each end of the planks, then they took turns diving with the saw. A man could stand the work of sawing beneath water for about a minute and a half and then would have to surface. But the work was progressing well. Ben was relieved not to have to go back into the cabin to look at the dead captain. It was bad enough that he was stealing the dead man's safe, but he could not look the poor fellow in the eye ever again. While the sawyers worked, Ben and several sailors rigged a dummy tackle on the stump of the mizzenmast and prepared a sling to haul out the safe. Someone would have to go into the cabin to put the sling in place, but Ben had swimmers to do that. He found two more men who were good in the water. They worked with a will. A good night's sleep had revived them and the cook put extra effort into preparing good meals for them.

Two hours later, the safe emerged from the cabin, dripping, the ropes straining to hold its great weight. They were able to swing a short gaff over to the waiting long boat and let the safe down onto her deck. The longboat sunk dangerously in the water, but soon righted itself. Now the men were able to prepare for firing the hulk. The opening in the deck made an excellent draft so that they could burn the above-water portion of the ship easily. The men laid out the incendiary materials and within an hour, the ship was ablaze. The men made it back just in time for supper. There was great excitement as the safe was hoisted aboard the *Vanguard.* Ben was hailed by his fellow officers for recovering it. The safe yielded many interesting papers, but most had been severely water damaged. One told of the 32,000 or more French troops who had been left in Egypt and who now had no way to get home. Others told of plans to invade India, to make all of that huge country part of Bonaparte's vast domain. None of that would come to pass now. They had seen to that with a brutal efficiency that amazed everyone, including themselves. Tom often commented that he could not believe that they had succeeded so well. He was certain that he was back in the French prison dreaming of what might have been.

The next day, Ben and his crew were sent to the *Timoleon* which was about to be burned. They watched as work progressed on the ships around them. The British ships and their prizes had drawn close together for safety and for the convenience of sharing parts. A spare spar here might be just what was needed on a ship close by. Captain Hollowell salvaged all that he could of the wood from *L'Orient.* Some would reappear in strange places aboard British ships as a vital piece here or there, to splice together a rail or whatever was needed. British sailors were among the most resourceful in the world and they showed both their resourcefulness and good spirit during the arduous duty of repairing two badly battered fleets. In all, they had to repair nearly twenty-eight ships. The worst hit of the British ships was the *Bellerophon.* But a thorough inspection showed that she could be made seaworthy and so, she was under intense repair efforts.

Ben was to examine the *Timoleon* and then burn the wreck if there was nothing useful aboard. His crew soon became the 'search and burn' crew. Ben checked all of the officer's quarters and found nothing of interest. He went below and although there were considerable amounts of supplies there, too many of them had been water damaged to be worth a salvage effort. He had his crew busy removing several bits of rail and other wooden parts that were still sound and they were ferrying them back to the *Bellerophon* where almost any ship's part would be welcomed.

Ben stepped back into the officer's quarters for a second to examine something. He found an abandoned night glass and a sextant, always useful on any ship. It was then that he noticed a small shadow scurry past his feet.

He thought it was only a rat hoping to find a way off the ship before she sank, but the animal was black. Some rats were black, but not *that* black, and this one had some white on it. He had never seen a two-coloured rat before. Besides, rats usually came larger than what he had seen. He stepped quietly towards the door where the animal was headed and looked down into the darkness. It was pitch dark there and at first he could see nothing. Then, with no effort of his own, it raced out from its' hiding place and ran to his leg, rubbing its head on Ben's trousers. He looked down in amazement. "Where in the devil did you come from?" he said and then laughed at himself. *Of course, you cannot speak English, You are French!* By that time the tiny kitten was standing on his hind legs and rubbing his head on Ben's trousers for all he was worth. *Poor little devil. He knows what is about to happen and he has spotted me as a soft touch. Well, little one, you are right. I am a sucker for any lost small animal, but kittens are beyond all possible resistance.* He reached down and lifted the feather-light body, just some black fur and skin stretched over a few bones. He held the small cat up to look at its face. It had the usual white face, but there was a most amusing black patch around the mouth, reaching up to his nose. She had a comical face. Her ears were velvety black and she promised to be a real beauty someday, but she surely must have suffered severely from malnutrition. Then he did the inevitable. He lifted the kitten's tail and looked. He was sure up until now that it was a female, but all that vanished in an instant as he realized that it was a fine male kitten. "Well, little fellow, I guess I own you now." He stuffed the kitten in the front of his shirt and went about the day's business. The small animal snuggled in close to Ben's heart, contented that he would be safe there.

He cuddled the small ball into his hands and took it back to the *Vanguard.* It was amazing what could be found when men put their minds to it. Leftenant Galway had found some chickens that had survived the battle, although he thought that they had been nearly scared to death. They had lost most of their feathers. A pig was found, too, and he was most distressed because the water was coming up fast on his pen. He squealed and snorted frantically. But he had not long to suffer. The crew of the *Vanguard* made a meal of him. Most of the livestock that were found alive were shared around the fleet with the officers and crew, so Ben knew there would be chicken that night and pig tomorrow.. One of the Midshipmen found some freshly baked bread and that was appropriated for supper, along with some vegetables that must have come from Egypt because they were fresh. That was possible. The officers could have gone ashore at Alexandria and picked up some fresh provisions. There were other delicacies too. Most of the officers were delighted to get the wine from the cabin of the *Mercure* which was rescued by some of the men working on the safe. There was a fair good bit there and that was shared around the fleet too. Certainly if the French had been victorious, they would have plundered the British ships to the limit. They were notorious for that. They needed fresh supplies and this was the best they could do.

Ben took the kitten gleefully because he had been wanting just such a pal. He found ample scraps for him that night and as he sat at mess with the leftenants he decided that the kitten was definitely a 'keeper'. He sat on the bench next to Ben or in his lap, ready to snag any scrap that came his way. When the meal was completed, the little black fur ball had a stomach as round as a cannon ball. He promptly crawled into Ben's lap, began to purr and soon fell asleep.

He picked up the small bundle, marveling that life could reside in one so small and that the animal had survived the hell that must have roamed the decks of that ship during the great battle. "What shall I call you?' he said. "Some French name? No, I would only grow to hate you if I had to call you by a French name. Hmmm. What about Tom for *Timoleon?* That might work. Tom is a good English name too. He looked at the cat again. Yes, you are a Tom, maybe even better, a Tomid. And so it stuck. Tomid would be his name and he would come to love only Ben. Not even Tom could get his affection for more than a minute or two. He was Ben's cat and always would be, his closest companion and mate.

On 6 August, Saumarez gathered together all of the prize ships that were seaworthy and headed out of the bay for England. He took the *Bellerophon, Majestic, Minotaur Defiance, Audacious* and the *Theseus* with him to escort the *Peuple Sauverain, Spartiate, Aquilon, Franklin, Conquerant,* and *Tonnant.* It had taken nearly a week to get ready for sea, and there were still many things left to do. None of the ships could withstand a severe storm. They would be holed up in port for weeks for more complete repairs once they reached England. But everything considered, the *Vanguard* was not seriously damaged. There was a hole below the water line, but the carpenter had plugged that. Some other repairs were still in progress. Although they had to leave behind the *Guerriere, Heureux,* and *Girond,* and these were ultimately all destroyed, Admiral Nelson wrote the Admiralty asking that these ships be paid off so that the men could receive the prize money for which they had worked so hard. They talked much about the prize money and the rewards for other achievements. It was all there was to cheer the men up. Nelson was tired and sick. He could scarcely carry on, so he turned over the affairs of the fleet to Captain Troubridge. He, with the help of Ball, Hood and Hollowell completed the refitting of the remainder of the fleet.

Chapter Twelve

Naples

It was 19 August before they were finally able to up anchor and leave Aboukir Bay, but there was still much to be done. The *Vanguard,* a heavily patched *Culloden* and the *Alexander* set sail for Naples where there would be time to complete their repairs. The men needed rest too and they might find some in a friendly port. They left behind the *Zealous, Swiftsure* and *Goliath* with orders to blockade the bay and Alexandria. Napoleon was not going to get supplies to his men by sea. Ben wondered how he would handle that problem. Finding food and ammunition in Egypt where they fought with scimitars and primitive weapons might be a true challenge for even Napoleon.

It was well into September when they made Naples. As soon as they dropped anchor at Naples, the celebrating began. They had already heard of the battle from Capel and Hoste and so, there began a series of elaborate celebrations. Lord Nelson was invited to move ashore into the home of Lord William Hamilton, a man whom he had met five years ago. Hamilton was the chief diplomat from England in the Neapolitan court. As an officer of the *Vanguard,* Ben was often invited to teas, evening dinners, musicals and plays.

On 29 September, the Hamiltons put on a grand display of fireworks and a play for all to enjoy. Great sparkling bits of flame and exploding packets flew over the bay, shedding light over all Naples. It was a balmy night and everyone was out to watch the excitement. During the day their ships were being repaired and put into top condition. The men were even given some shore leave. Between the showers of fireworks, men from the ships would cheer Lord Nelson. Everyone was in a festive mood and they ate and talked well into the evening. The work progressed at a slower pace now and Ben was needed only to supervise repairs during the day.

But there were disturbing reports of French troops marching from the north towards Rome, not far from Naples. Napoleon had ruled most of Italy for sometime now and even in his absence, his troops were making their presence known. It appeared that Naples might come under attack at almost any time. They watched, danced, dined and waited, which was the Neapolitan way. Ben was introduced to Lord Hamilton and his wife Emma for the first time. He became aware that there was a strong friendship between Lord Nelson and Lord Hamilton. They met about five years ago when Nelson, then a captain, had come to negotiate with the King of Naples for troops to help in the war effort. It seems that Lord Hamilton had been the ambassador to Naples for nearly thirty years now. He married Emma late in his life, she being some thirty years the younger. She was at one time Lord Hamilton's nephew's woman, but when the nephew tired of her, William Hamilton collected her and made her his wife. He had a wonderful love of fine and beautiful things and was an avid collector of art objects. Ben visited the beautiful house of the Hamiltons several times. Lord Hamilton was a collector of all things beautiful and was beginning to worry about the possibility that his belongings might fall into the hands of Napoleon and the French army. He showed Ben and Lord Nelson his extensive collection of fine paintings and sculpture and they discussed what might be done to protect it. One thought was to seek out a cave in the hills where the art works might be stored safely, although not necessarily dry. But the Lord rejected that, "Most caves are damp and there is always a chance that they would be found anyway and destroyed or stolen," complained Lord Hamilton.

In the end, they decided to pack them aboard a smaller ship that was headed for England and send them off to Lord Hamilton's residence at Merton. Ben was put in charge of the packing of Lord Hamilton's rare art objects and later he complained that he would rather fight another Aboukir Bay than to serve in that capacity again. But it did bring him in close contact with the Hamiltons and their household for a period of several weeks. During that time, he met the King of Naples and his family. He told Tom that he was not at all impressed. "They seem to worry more about what The French army's coming will do to their next party than what it might do to their country and people," he said. "The Queen seems a sensible sort, but her husband is not at all competent as a king. All he thinks of is himself."

While Ben was at the home of the Hamiltons, he met Commodore Carracciolo, senior flag officer of the Neapolitan Navy. He seemed a pleasant fellow, although to Ben's thinking, he was an idler. He sat around sipping wine while the French were advancing on his homeland. He should be out getting his fleet, such as it was, ready to withstand the French assault. He seemed to be most unhappy with King Fernando too. Ben heard bits of conversation that would be considered treasonous in his country. "The king thinks of no one but himself. Did you see how he ignores the needs of his people? We are ill-served by such an incompetent king." said a servant.

Ben wondered how the man could get away with such talk and he often heard Lord Hamilton trying to silence the man. "Kings are who they are. We cannot change them to be what we would like them to be. You must remain loyal to your king and country," said Hamilton. Ben did not particularly like the fellow, but he could well appreciate how he felt about the Neapolitan king. He was a useless fop. Worse still, his children were growing up to be just like him.

Ben also became aware of a strange relationship between Lady Hamilton and Lord Nelson. They seemed to be forever in each others company and never out of sight of each other. Nelson was most obliging to her and from the looks that he gave her, Ben knew that he had more than a casual interest in the woman.

The packing began on a Monday and Ben brought some of his oldest, most trusted crew men to do the packing.

They were supposed to be helped by the servants of the household, who, for some reason, seemed contented to stand back and admire the work of the seamen, jabbering all the while in Italian. Once in awhile Lady Hamilton would appear and set the servants back to work, but it appeared that she had to say,"Move that box and put it here," or nothing would get done. Ben's lads went to work as soon as he had explained what they were to do. Ben was constantly treading on eggs trying to keep this from being scratched or that from being handled too roughly. "Remember, Lord Hamilton, these lads are used to handling barrels of beef and water, not art objects such as these." Tom was a great help in this work because he had the patience to see things through. He was everywhere, guiding this, ordering that, playfully tucking a bit more padding in next to a marble bust. Ben was blessed to have Tom with him and he knew it.

In the midst of the moving, word came that King Ferdinando had ordered his small army to advance against the French with hopes of defeating them. Daily messengers arrived with ever more grim news. "The men are trapped at Cisterna di Latina." Then it was, "We have no more ammunition, your excellency." Followed by, "We have been completely routed. The troops have scattered to the hills and there is no army left, your excellency."

The sad part of all this is that even Ben could see that this poorly trained army would not stand a chance against a well-disciplined French force. The French were too many and too well equipped.

Each night Ben crawled in beside Tomid and and they curled up to keep one another comfortable. He found little time to work on Tom's problems of navigation, but he did take the time to assign him a new problem each day. "I'll check them over in a week or so when I am not so pressed as I am with this damnable moving," he said. He had felt badly during the repairs at Aboukir Bay because neither of them had time to help Tom with his studies. Tom was a poor student at best and tended to fall away quickly if his studies were not brought to his attention almost daily. Ben's greatest comfort in life was the presence of Tomid, who was beginning to grow. He was a sprightly little fellow, full of fun and one who loved to play. He had some strange habits about him that took some getting used to though, like sitting on Ben's shoulder while he read. But in the end, they came to know one another and a strong friendship grew and flourished.

Ben was forced to learn Italian. His limited vocabulary from his former exploits in Corsica were not adequate for the situation. He was delighted when on the second day of moving, Lord Hamilton appeared with an Italian lexicon and handed it to Ben. "Here. You need this more than I do. I think you will go far as an officer. You have a way with your men that is most effective."

Ben smiled. "Thank you, sir."

Ben spoke with Lord Hamilton often and learned that the ambassador held Lord Nelson in high esteem. "He is one officer who will make a difference in this world that we live in. In fact, he has already. He has put an end to the plans of a mad man to rule the entire world. There is no way now that Napoleon can rule Egypt or India. Lord Nelson's decisive battle at Aboukir Bay ended that dream forever." The Lord's admiration for Nelson only strengthened Ben's belief that he was the most successful and perfect of leaders that any navy could have. Ben worshiped Nelson, as did so many other men.

When the paintings were all packed and the other art objects wrapped in cloth, then they began to haul them to the ship. That was a task in itself. Ben had to hire a local drover who had nothing but dung carts to offer. He went in search of others but learned that this fellow had a corner on the market and that he would not find anyone else unless he went far out into the country. Ben hired a horse and small carriage and went out in search of a clean wagon. The Lord would not hear of having his precious things hauled in a dung cart. Eventually he found a farmer who had a hay cart that he would send with his son. His hay was in the barn and he did not mind letting Ben use the cart, for a lot less than the first fellow had wanted to charge. Eventually they had all of the pieces aboard, each numbered, recorded on many sheets of paper so that they could be inventoried once they arrived in England. With the ship provisioned and a good crew aboard, Ben finally sat back and said, "Bon Voyage." He was glad to be rid of all those paintings and all that artwork. Tom teased him afterwards saying that he lacked a taste for finer things, especially art. "Why, he said, look at this nude lady. Doesn't she look inviting enough that you would want to crawl right in bed with her?" Then he went on to explain the delicacies of painting as if he were an artist himself. "You see the torture in the mind of the artist when he made these strokes. Can't you imagine how he anguished over whether her gown should be pale blue or passionate pink? And look here, he didn't even finish this portion of her shoe, so distraught was he with the beauty that he had created," teased Tom. At that he gave a great Irish laugh and slapped Ben on the back. Lord Hamilton stood in the doorway watching the two boys and he smiled a sad smile at the folly of youth. "Wasted on the young," he said to himself.

But Ben was weary and could hardly see the joke in it all. He saw many women while on shore, some Neapolitan beauties associated with the King's court, but he had not been attracted to any of them. He could think of only one woman, his Annie. She never left his side, day or night. He had to get back to London to meet her. *This time I am not going to act like any bashful youngster. I will come right out and ask her to dine with me.* he thought.

The day after the *Albatross* sailed, Ben was called to Captain Hardy's cabin. "I know that you have been busy with moving Lord Hamilton's belongings, but I need you for another duty." Ben liked Hardy. He was a bachelor and a straight, traditional fellow whose advice and guidance Ben coveted. He was all 'no nonsense,' all sailor. Ben liked that.

“I want you now to move the King’s Court and the Hamilton’s to Palermo. We will take them and their personal gear aboard the *Vanguard*, to leave the day after tomorrow. We have reports that The French army is not far off, perhaps only twenty miles or so. Naples is already lost with the defeat of the King’s feeble troops. I will need you to escort them and find berths for them. Oh, and I hear that the *Foudroyant* may be on her way out to serve as our new flag ship. What do you think of that.”

“That is good news, sir and I am sure it will please Lord Nelson. And where should I put Lord and Lady Hamilton?”asked Ben.

A strange look came into Hardy’s cool eyes. “You know your duty, Mr. Rundel, now do it. No moping around,” he replied with a most amusing smile on his face. He knew about Lord Nelson and Lady Hamilton and the look on his face told Ben that the two of them were in agreement on the impropriety of the matter. Although Hardy would never say anything against his good friend Nelson, Ben knew that it grieved him to see the Lord so recently covered with honours and laurels, behave so in public with another man’s wife. They would speak of it sometime in the future, Ben was certain. It struck too deeply at both of them to remain buried forever. Both loved and revered the seaman Nelson, and both men felt that it was not right that he should be so ‘imperfect’.

But the first ship out from England brought news of the great joy occasioned by the victory over the Toulon Fleet. King George had exclaimed, “Almighty God has blessed His Majesty’s Arms,” when he heard the news at Weymouth. The news spread like fire in a fire ship. As each town heard the news, church bells began to ring, people gathered and planned bonfires, marches, parades, plays, musicals, readings, teas, all to celebrate Nelson’s great victory. That victory was just the medicine that an ailing country needed, prescribed professionally and delivered in just the right dosage. A wave of rejoicing spread all through the country, beginning at London and moving all across the country. When Lord Spencer of the Admiralty learned that not a single British ship had been lost, he fell to his knees, overcome by joy and emotion. There were banquets, torch light processions and some landlords offered free beer to their tenants. It was a time for great rejoicing. Everywhere "God Save The King" and "Rule Britannia" were sung, in taverns, at musicals, plays, anywhere people gathered. The Fremantles heard the good news in London and were beside themselves with joy. Even Emma Hamilton when she first heard the news, made great preparations for receiving Lord Nelson, even though she had met him for only a short time five years earlier. Lord Howe, now retired from Port Admiral at Portsmouth, received Nelson's message, written with his left hand, with great enthusiasm. He returned a note congratulating Nelson with high praise for his accomplishments. He said, "It stood unparalleled and singular in this instance that every captain distinguished himself." (Kennedy, Nelson's Captains, 1951). Nelson himself said, "I had the happiness to command a band of brothers."

When the first wave of excitement was over, the country settled down to a more lasting show of gratitude. News came almost daily. Parliament offered Nelson a peerage carrying the title of 'Baron Nelson of the Nile'. With it went a trip later on to both houses and an annual pension of 2,000 pounds per year. The East India Company gave Nelson 10,000 pounds in appreciation of the protection of its interests in India. King George III ordered gold medals struck for all the captains who were present at Aboukir Bay. The City of London had swords forged and engraved to be presented to the captains. Mr. Alexander Davison had gold medals struck for the captains, silver for the officers and copper for the crewmen, commemorating the greatest battle fought and won in British history. Davison was the agent who handled the disposal of all of the prize ships and moneys. Most of the first leftenants were promoted to post captains. But for Ben, who was second leftenant, that did not mean an automatic promotion to first leftenant when Galway left as he had supposed it would. He remained a second leftenant and a Mr. Hayward took the position of first leftenant. Ben did not mind too much. He felt as if there was still a great deal to learn, especially about people and the workings of politics and governments. He still felt like a babe lost in a huge forest when it came to dealing with political matters. But he was learning.

The captains of the fleet wrote a grand letter commending Nelson as their brave leader and presenting him with a sword. They also requested that he have his portrait painted and ordered that it be hung in the room belonging to the Egyptian Club. This was a most suitable testimony to the high regard in which his fellow officers held him. *No man could ask for more,* thought Ben.

So Ben hauled his weary body back on shore the next morning and roused the household of the Hamiltons. They had been alerted to the dangers and it was like a double alarm fire, servants running every which way and no one accomplishing much of anything. All was a twitter until Ben, in disgust, stepped in and began to give orders. "You get my lady's clothes packed. You see to His Lordships immediate wardrobe. You find household items that they must have with them to be comfortable." In the midst of all this Lord Nelson and Lady Hamilton walked in the gardens as contented as two doves. Both of them were needed to give the servants direction, but that now fell on Ben's broad shoulders. He packed the Admiral's personal belongings himself. They were ready by late afternoon and luckily Ben had kept the farmers cart. The farmer's son had taken a liking to one of the serving girls of the Hamilton household and was more than willing to spend the night in Naples. The cart was used to ferry the household goods to the ship. Sailors laboured to haul their belongings aboard. Ben shepherded the women and their household attendants and children down the hill and into waiting carriages so they could get to the ship on time. There were screams of female joy, giggles and women running back for some forgotten unneeded item, but he managed somehow to get them all aboard and all into berths. It was necessary to put most of the women in one room and the men in another, for they did not have private passenger space for so many persons. At the last minute, Commodore Caricciolo insisted that the Royal Family should be transported in a Neapolitan ship under his command, but Nelson would hear none of that. "The Royal Family will be much safer in one of our large ships," he said. Caricciolo was clearly offended and came along at the last minute, somewhat put out by the whole move.

Ben and Tomid slept on the deck that night, but it was warm and they did not care as long as they had each other. Ben thought how much he preferred this warm ball of fur to any of those giggling females from the Hamilton's household. *There must be something wrong with me,* he thought.

But midway through the night, the wind came up. They had to reduce sail twice and finally, when the rain came, they knew that they were in for a rough passage. Ben called, "Furl all sails save the foretopmast sail." It was a short sail to Sicily in miles, but even a short passage can be arduous in a storm.

With so many seasick passengers crammed into such a small space, life aboard ship became unbearable. Ben hated to order his men to their duty, but it became necessary to empty the night soil from the pots in the cabins every hour. There were so many sick persons and the people suffered so much misery that the sailors hated to go into their quarters. The stench of vomit permeated the ship and the fickle wind seemed not in any hurry to carry it away. Ben spread the duty around so that no one had to do the same task all day long.

Ben slept under the bunk of Mr. Hayward in order to get out of the storm. It was not only cramped for one so tall, but most uncomfortable. Captain Hardy managed to find out about it and offered Ben a place to sleep on the cushions in his cabin, which was really a storage space, his cabin having been given over to the women and children. It was much better than under the first leftenant's bunk. Ben secretly thought that Hardy enjoyed playing with Tomid and that was why he offered Ben cabin space, but whatever the reason, neither of them got much sleep. When he actually caught the captain playing with the kitten, there was a childish smile on his face, a sort of, 'Well, so you caught me' look. So what?

Lord Hamilton remained in his tiny cabin through the worst of the trip, clutching two loaded pistols. He said, "If the ship goes down, I am not going to gasp my last in the water. I will die like a landsman." The King's Confessor was thrown out of his bunk during the storm and broke his arm. There was great bowing and fussing over his arm, much more Ben thought than there had been when a man was cut in two by a cannon ball during battle. One of the ladies, a duchess of something or other, lurched forward while trying to use the pot and cut her head on the Admiral's sideboard. Nelson was sick most of the time and the only soul who seemed to weather the storm was Emma Hamilton. She was about, nursing to the sick and injured, smiling the whole while.

During the passage, the Queen's youngest child, Prince Alberto died from convulsions. He had several seizures early in the voyage and then on Christmas Day, after a good breakfast, he suddenly went into a violent convulsion and died in Emma Hamilton's arms. She was a godsend because the royal servants were all laid low with seasickness and fear. Only Emma, always Emma, was there to care for the distraught royal couple and their children. The death of the child made for a most difficult time. The Queen would not hear of a burial at sea and no one wanted to stand out in that storm, hats off, to witness a burial, so the dead child was closeted below. The King paid no attention to the whole affair, claiming cavalierly he had a dozen sons by town's women to make up for the loss.

The ship was in constant need to attention. She was handling the heavy seas most awkwardly. The ship lurched, rolled and carried off tons of water as she fought her way through extremely heavy seas. It was well into winter and severe winter storms were to be expected. They would be lucky to make Sicily in ten days, the way the storm was forcing them to the east. Strong west winds heeled the ship far over and made things slide and fall from their proper places. Some of the men were sick too and there was much moaning and groaning that was not the fault of the ship's timbers.

When finally they arrived at Palermo, the sun came out and it was a glorious day. But the Queen was crying over the loss of her child and Emma was grieving because of the tortures of the trip. Lord Hamilton had a bad bout of bilious and they were generally still an unhappy lot that moved into Government house at Palermo. Lord Nelson moved in with the Hamiltons. He was not feeling at all well and needed considerable rest. The house was a grand palace, painted walls, murals, tall columns. Ben saw it when he was supervising the moving of the belongings of the Royal Family. He helped Lord Nelson to his quarters and made him as comfortable as he could. "If you need me sir, just send a boy to the ship. I can be here in fifteen minutes."

"I may ask you to serve as my scribe on shore. Tom needs the scribe that he has aboard ship."

Not long after their arrival, they learned that the French Republican Army had taken Naples. Reports came to them of murder, rape, plunder, burning and needless destruction of life and property. It was sickening to think that these French people who were allegedly fleeing from tyranny could so easily visit the same atrocities on another people, without even thinking about what they were doing. *Revolution defeats its purpose if it results in just a new set of tyrants practicing the art of tyranny on yet the same people. Where was the reform? Where was the change?* wondered Ben. He and Tom spoke of the matter often. Tom was coming to a strong awareness of the weaknesses of man, as was Ben.

Life settled down on Palermo. The King indulged in his favourite sport, hunting wild boar. Ben happened to go along on one of these so-called hunts. He had been at the palace to call on Lord Nelson who had sent word for him to serve as scribe. Ben came to his door and knocked softly. It was while the hunting party was forming in the courtyard. Apparently his knock was mistaken for that of a faithful servant because when he was bade to open the door to enter, he saw Lord Nelson in his dressing gown lying on the bed, with Lady Nelson scantily clad and lying beside him.

She jumped up, explaining that the Lord had a fever and she was needed to tend him. “Mr. Rundel can run along and join the hunting party that is drawing up in the court yard. It will be a good experience for him,” called Nelson with a guilty smile.

Ben bowed and with a sagging heart, withdrew from the room. He never came to the royal palace again unless he was called for. He had found his hero in a most compromising position, and he hurt more than he could tell anyone. He resolved then and there not to discuss what he had seen with anyone, not even Tom. If his suspicions were true, there was no need for the whole Navy to know about the Admiral’s weakness. He would be a man of honour, no matter what it cost him. He headed down the stairs towards the courtyard, dragging his feet. He had no desire to join a hunting party at just that moment. His derriere did not need to spend hours on the back of a horse. He needed time to hide somewhere by himself and to think. What he had just seen could have only one explanation. His head pounded with the same question, over and over again, *Why must my hero be a fornicator, why why!* Ben reached the bottom of the stairs and someone grabbed him and before he knew it, he was being ushered to a horse. Apparently everyone able to stand at court was expected to share the King’s joy in the hunt. Ben managed to stumble into the courtyard at the wrong moment. He tried to explain, but the two pretty girls who had shanghaied him had their own plans for him after the hunt, but he would have none of them. He was too hurt inside. He felt as if he had taken a broadside in the stomach, and after two hours on the horse's back, he felt as if his rear had ridden a 32-pounder all through the Battle of Aboukir Bay.

Ben learned that the object of the hunt was to run the wild boar into a small pen and then stand back and admire the King as he shot the poor beast, with however many shots it took. Ben was sick. He had not only learned how corrupt his Admiral was that day, but he had seen a degenerate King who knew nothing of honour or valour. He was a coward who would let others do the dirty work for him. He gloated in his ability to kill a helpless wild animal in a cage. Ben watched the King wallow in the blood of the dead animal as if killing it had been a great feat, an insurmountable victory. Ben suddenly hated Palermo, in spite of its pleasant trees and beautiful houses. He longed to be back at sea, where he felt free. No matter what his duty, his mind kept going back to Nelson. *He is a Lord, honoured above all others by me and my country and he is a married man. And she is married too. There can be no excuse, none at all.*

As soon as they reached Palermo, Admiral Nelson began to experience many troubles. He was more beset with problems than any man that Ben had ever known. Foremost among his troubles was his health. The injury to his head was more than a simple head wound. Ben was sure of that now. He suffered terrible fits of depression and was extremely irritable, at times waving his one arm frantically to shoo everyone away for no apparent reason. He also suffered impaired vision in his good eye, apparently from nerve damage from the recent injury. It was during one of these days when he had trouble seeing that he called for Ben. Ben went on to tell in his own words all of the problems that were eating at the famous man, many unseen even by those close to him. Because Ben was given the task of writing his letters and reading his correspondence, he came to know a great deal of the madness in the Mediterranean.

"I have difficulty focusing my good eye, Mr. Rundel, you will serve as my temporary scribe, won't you? I know, I have a scribe aboard ship, but Hardy needs him. Hardy is a poor writer and needs someone. Besides, the man is a skinny fop and a tattle. I don't need someone around me that I cannot trust. You understand, lad?"

"Aye, sir."

And so Ben became the personal scribe for the Admiral and came to know all of the strife in his life. Besides his immediate health problems which irked him sorely, there had come a strange event into his life. The former warm friendship with Lady Hamilton had turned into a hot intimacy. Although the Admiral must have enjoyed her company without reservation, once he was by himself his conscience ate at him as will any honourable man's conscience when he has cuckolded his best friend. For, although Lord Hamilton undoubtedly knew about the love affair, he was not ready to give up his beautiful young wife, nor was he ready to censure a man whom he admired as a great leader and warrior. Nelson must have thought now and then about what his affair with Emma would do to Fannie, his wife. She was a fine, simple woman, not gay and full of life, but suited to a stodgy forty-year old man. He must have salved his soul by reassuring himself that she was not there and did not want to be there. Nor did he want her there, particularly after he learned that Emma might be pregnant by him. Surely no one would blame Lord Hamilton for that deed. He was an elder of at least sixty five.

It was during one of their dictating sessions when Emma came to the door of Nelson's drawing room. She beckoned for him to come to her, making cute signals with her hands. She frequently came into the room when the Admiral and Ben were working and thought nothing of planting a kiss on his head or teasing him in any number of ways. Ben would sometimes get up and walk away. But this time he could not shoo her off. "Go away, Emma. Can't you see that we are busy?"

"I know my lord. That is why I need to see you at once," she called.

So Nelson went to the door to speak with her. They whispered, but Ben distinctly heard the word 'pregnant'. Nelson put his hand to his forehead and threw his head back. Ben would never know if he was delighted or distressed, but sensed that some of both emotions must have been tugging at his already embattled mind. In the end, he would be happy with his only child, but it was apparently quite a shock.

Another nagging problem was that of Captain Troubridge and the *Culloden.* When Nelson wrote his report of the battle of the Nile, he purposely left out the part about Troubridge running his ship onto a shoal for fear that Troubridge might lose out on the honours and awards. But he should have known that one cannot keep a secret of that magnitude in the Navy, even fourteen hundred miles from the Admiralty. When Lord Spencer wrote his letter to Nelson telling of the medals to be struck for the captains of the Nile, it read, 'those captains *engaged* in battle' shall be rewarded. Nelson took exception to that and Ben, under the direction of Lord Nelson, prepared several letters extolling the virtues and fine seamanship of Captain Troubridge. There were not superlatives adequate to describe Nelson's regard for Troubridge. It would take almost a year, but eventually the King ordered that Captain Troubridge should receive a medal with the rest of the captains. His first leftenant had already been promoted, which was a sign of weakening on the part of the Admiralty. When Troubridge came to visit Lord Nelson, both men were in a state of black depression and both were most unhappy. Whenever Nelson felt in a glum mood, he would reflect on the slight that he had received after the battle at Calvi and Bastia. He never felt as if he received his true rewards for that battle. Troubridge was sad because he felt that he had sinned and let his King down in a time of need. He had an inferior opinion of himself that would drive any lesser man mad. Troubridge wrote to his colleagues asking to have his name removed from the Egyptian Room because it would only cause him pain in future to see it there next to those who so truly deserved the honour. Instead of the breath of fresh air and strong arm of advice that Nelson wanted and needed from him, all he received were complaints, moanings and regrets. It was not at all a happy meeting.

But the spring of 1799 brought many other troubles to Lord Nelson. He began to confide freely in Ben and often called for Captain Hardy. Hardy was just the opposite of Nelson, solid, disciplined, of the old school although Ben doubted that he was more than 26, a man of great honour and strong sense of duty. It was surprising that the two men rarely quarreled. They exactly complimented each other, one trading weakness for the others strength. Ben often thought that if one could take the best qualities of each man and create a new man, he would have the finest, bravest sailor ever to sail the seas.

It was during this period that Ben came to know and respect Captain Hardy. He was a tall, bony fellow like Ben himself, every inch a sailor and a fine seaman in every respect. When he saw that some of his crew did not know how to go aloft and take a reef in a sail, he tore off his coat and climbed the ratlines, taking the sail in hand and showing them what to do. He made a strong impression on his crew. From that day forward, they respected him and would do their best for him. But he was of the old school, never negligent where discipline was concerned. He had his boat crew flogged when they got into trouble over some Italian woman and asked Emma Hamilton to speak on their behalf. Hardy was not going to be told what to do by any woman aboard his ship and he made that plain. They received their twenty-four lashes just the same. But he treated Lady Hamilton with all courtesy. The incident did not seem to interfere with the firm friendship that was growing between Nelson and Hardy.

When some of the officers were bored in port and walked the deck with their hands in their pockets, Hardy became upset with them. Their minds were not on their business and he gave orders that the pockets of all of the officers should be sewn up until such time that they discontinued the unmanly practice. Ben sewed up his pockets so as to be 'one of the brothers,' but he was not guilty of the offense it was intended to cure. In fact, Captain Hardy treated Ben well. He and Ben were much alike in many ways. They shared the same goals and could speak easily with one another. Hardy laughed when Ben told him about borrowing his old leftenant's uniform when in London. Ben explained that he was visiting the Fremantles and had no uniform to wear after his release from hospital. Tom Fremantle loaned Ben Hardy's old uniform. Hardy said that he had outgrown it and left it with Fremantle, hoping that he would grow into it someday. The two men often shared supper together, with the other officers. Ben came to look up to him as the best officer under whom he had served.

Ben knew that Hardy strongly disapproved of the Lord's affair with Emma, but he would not let that interfere with his professionalism or his duty to Nelson. Troubridge was less lucky. He fell out with Nelson after awhile, unable to resolve in his mind the conduct of the Admiral toward Lady Hamilton. Even the Admiralty was in irons over Nelson. Their staunch British morals were compromised when their greatest naval hero turned out to be a wife-stealer.

But storm clouds blew in from the north in the form of a Captain Sir Sidney Smith of the *Tigre.* One of his sailors told Ben his story. "This fellow had already shown his metal in accomplishing many astonishing minor victories. Among other things, he was knighted for his bravery in the Swedish Navy in the war against Russia in 1788. When the French War broke out, he was serving as a volunteer in the Turkish Navy. He wanted to be in the centre of things, so he bought his own ship and outfitted it with as many good English sailors as he could find. He arrived to help with the evacuation of Toulon and then he and Captain Miller blew up the arsenal and shipping in the harbour as the British fleet withdrew. He was appointed to sail the *Diamond* and spent his time effectively ravaging Atlantic ports to harass the French. But he managed to get captured in the mouth of the Seine and was held in a French prison for several years until his final escape."

His position in the British Navy was unusual in that he carried credentials naming him as Plenipotentiary to Turkey. What riled Nelson was that Lord Spencer assigned Smith to the blockade of Alexandria, which should have been done with Nelson's consultation. The young pup had the impudence to write to Lord Hamilton telling him that he was on his way to Alexandria and would take charge there, Captain Hood being his natural junior. Of course, the letter found its way to Nelson quickly, and Ben was forced to read it to him. Nelson railed about the impudence of young Smith for days and the blistering letters that he dictated to Ben for St. Vincent and Lord Spencer were something to read. Ben would often stop him and ask, politely, "Do you want to say it <u>that</u> way, sir?"

"Yes, you damned fool. Write down what I tell you," was his angry reply. He wrote to St. Vincent that he longed to be relieved of his post and returned home, if such was to be the policy of the Admiralty. The whole thing was resolved when Nelson's captains returned from an unsuccessful blockade of Alexandria and Smith was left with only Dixon, not one of Nelson's men, under him.

The telling shot came when Smith, totally lacking in finesse and manners, wrote to Lord Nelson on some paltry matter. He introduced himself as: *"Chevalier Grand Croix de L'Ordre Royal et Militaire de L'Espee de Suede, Ministre Plenipotentiare de sa Majestie Brittanique pres la Porte Ottomane, et Chef de son Escadre dans les Mers du Levant."* (Kennedy, Nelson's Captains) The use of French irritated Lord Nelson, as well it might, since the French were the enemy, but the impudence of the young man to write using so many titles was just too much. Ben had to leave the room while the Admiral stormed about and even Lady Hamilton could not quiet him. Finally, Nelson called Ben back into the room and he dictated a short reply, which said, in effect, that the young fool should find some way of introducing himself in English so that his commander would know who he was, if he wished to get his concerns properly attended to. Because Smith held his ministerial duties jointly with his brother, Nelson had a good point that he could not tell which of the two men were seeking his services. Ben should have liked to have seen the man's face when he read that letter.

Then there was a battle between Nelson and Spencer for the services of Troubridge. Nelson wanted him to stay in the eastern Mediterranean under his command. Nelson was still Admiral of the detached fleet. But he sent letters flying back and forth to Spencer concerning the proper duty for Troubridge. St. Vincent was getting on in years and was much distressed that his two finest officers, Nelson and Troubridge were both depressed, one wanting to go home and the other unhappy over his performance at the battle of the Nile. St. Vincent wrote to Spencer pleading for help.

In the end, Nelson won, but it was a trying battle. Each struggle these days seemed to take more and more of Lord Nelson's energy, leaving him weaker and even more depressed. Troubridge stayed on and helped to chase the French from the off- shore islands near Naples.

There were some sixteen British ship-of-the-line in the Mediterranean and each one had some problem or other. Those ships serving the Island of Malta were beset by a disease known as the Maltese fever. Mr. Wood, the surgeon of the *Goliath,* died of the fever and some of the officers were badly infected with venereal disease and there was need of mercury to treat them.

Nelson would often complain that he had more writing

to do than any man with three good arms could accomplish. He sent off broadsides in ink to Lord Spencer at the Admiralty on all manner of subjects. Letters came from Hollowell when he was at Alexandria telling of the poor condition of the *Swiftsure*. The seams were leaking badly and the galley boilers were rent, making it hard to prepare food for the men. He needed to refit badly. Foley's ship was taking on thirteen inches of water per hour from stressed seams. Here a ship's parson needed to be returned to England for health reasons or to settle his personal estate. Hood had lost his brother during the battle and was needed in England to settle his brother's affairs. Everyone needed something and Nelson was too sick to give much to anyone.

There was a Portuguese squadron anchored off the Tagus. This was led by a French Royalist and the ships manned by ex-British merchant captains. One could not expect much of such a conglomerate. When ordered to set sail by Troubridge, they had sat there and thought about it for sometime. deNiza was in charge and he offered Captain Hood anything that he needed, but when Hood replied that his men needed water, none was forthcoming, not even as a gesture. Nelson wrote St. Vincent that the Portuguese squadron was of no account and of no help to His Majesty in the Mediterranean.

Then there were many letters from Malta. It seems that Captain Ball had been sent there to wipe out the French garrison. On the surface, it seemed a simple task. Many of the French were sick, venereal disease was rampant as was the Maltese fever, they were short on rations and their munitions were low, but they managed to put up a stiff fight, driving the British marines and local Maltese back each time. It seems that that small island did not really belong to anyone, nor did it have any stable government. Naples, Britain and Russia all expressed interest in Malta and agreed to support it jointly. The agreement was not working. As a result, the few loyal natives who banded together to fight the French were poorly equipped, half starved and nearly naked. There were many of the daily functions of government needed there. In the end, when Ball could not summon Nelson to help him, he asked permission to go ashore and serve as temporary administrator for the island. He arbitrated, judged, helped the people find food and shelter and did his best to drive the hated French out of Malta. When the French appeared to be ready to capitulate, the Maltese asked Ball to stay on as their governor. He was well-suited for the job and the Navy allowed him to serve for a short time. Ball was most grateful for the service, but was insistent that his term as governor should not interfere with his career in the Navy. His letters to Nelson were full of gratitude.

In December of 1798, the Russians allied with Britain, joined by Naples, Portugal, the Ottoman Empire and the Vatican, and later Austria. As squadron commander in the eastern Mediterranean, Nelson had business with all of these leaders. There were letters to St. Petersburg, Constantinople, the Consul at Smyrna, Egypt, the Turkish and Russian Admirals, Trieste, Vienna, Tuscany, Minorca, Earl St. Vincent and Lord Spencer of the Admiralty. As a result, Ben was becoming well-acquainted with the names of world leaders, their titles and the politics of handling them. Nelson, although brash at times from his head wound, was still an excellent teacher. Ben was learning and as always, eager to learn more.

But by August of 1799, Russia had left the Coalition after forty-five thousand Russian and British troops failed to take the Netherlands. The good news was that the Batavian Fleet was captured.

Ben found Tomid in his bunk that night, his nose running as if he had a terrible cold. The little animal wheezed and had extreme trouble breathing. Ben did not know what to do. He could not get the little fellow to eat any food, nor drink much water. He went back to the galley repeatedly to see if there were any aromatic fish fragments that he could snag and he made all sorts of things that would tempt any cat to eat, but the tiny body lay there, the chest rising slowly with each tortured breath but he remained unwilling to eat. He even caught a mouse and presented it to him, still kicking, but there was no response. Ben held him close all that night hoping that his body warmth would help the tiny cat, but he was still poor in the morning. How he loved this little bit of animal. Ben figured that if he could smell, he might be tempted to eat. He did drink a bit that day, but that was all.

The next day news came from the mainland that Napoleon's troops were about to destroy all of the unoccupied private property around Naples. Commodore Caricciolo and some others from the court who had extensive lands and properties there begged permission to leave the court to see to the safety of their lands. The King granted them permission and wished them well. Lord Hamilton and Caricciolo were good friends and Ben watched them as they said 'Goodbye.' Something did not seem right between them, but Ben could not discern what it might be. They seemed estranged and distant, not close as they had been for the time he had known them both.

Ben was one of the most handsome young officers in the Navy. He was nineteen and stood tall, a strapping lad with broad shoulders, narrow hips, huge hands from his days as a common seaman and a most pleasing continence.

He felt awkward around women, especially the girls at the court. He could sense their eyes following him whenever business took him there and he knew what they wanted. It was perhaps just because they wanted it that he felt obliged to deny it. He longed to be back at sea with nothing but the wind and sea to trouble him. Most of all, he wanted to go home to see his Annie.

Captain Hardy invited Ben and the other young officers to share supper with him aboard the *Vanguard* one

August night. The young men gathered in the Captain's cabin, eager for a chance to relax and visit. Hardy was not a sparkling conversationalist, but he could encourage others to speak. The young men talked of the miserable state of the war, of the problems at Malta and about the weather. They ate a wonderful ragout of beef and good, fresh vegetables with it. The meal was fine. Ben sat quietly, eating slowly and enjoying his meal, but his mind was taken up with other matters. He rarely spoke or seemed to enter into any aspect of the social occasion. Hardy could not have helped but notice his young officer's withdrawal.

Eventually the conversation came around to women as it always does with young men at sea. And although they were in port and all had enjoyed shore leave, women were still their favourite topic of conversation. Midshipman Rawlins started the blasphemy by commenting on the Admiral's absence and speculating that he had other things to occupy his time. From there, the conversation deteriorated.

"He's got himself a regular mistress, I hear," said one midshipman.

Another offered, "He rarely comes aboard anymore."

"I've seen him at the gambling parlours with Lady Hamilton until way late, after I was due back aboard ship. Oh, pardon, sir. I did make it back by midnight, most nights, that is," said Wilson with an apologetic smile to Captain Hardy, fearing that his candor had let him in for a good stiff bout of discipline.

Ben sat there, distressed. He looked at Captain Hardy and the pain in Ben's face must have read like a book. Ben was saddened by the unprofessional behaviour of the Admiral, but he had made an effort not to discuss it with anyone, let alone discuss it so openly and shamelessly at the supper table. Ben could half understand the Admiral. He was sickly, far from home and his wife, who chose not to be here with him, and he was obviously lonely. He was a man who needed a woman's tenderness and awe to feed his ego. He could understand, but that did not make it right. Sure, Lady Hamilton was voluptuous, in her prime, gay, a born caregiver, and married to a man twice her age, but that did not change the fact that they were both married. Worse still, Ben could not understand how Lord Hamilton could stand by and watch all this affair and not do something about it. Yes, Lord Nelson was a good friend and he did pay him honour, but one does not usually pay honour with his wife's favours. Ben was lost in his own sad thoughts when he was vaguely aware that Captain Hardy was talking to him.

"Oh, sorry, sir. My thoughts were elsewhere," said Ben.

"I asked if there was anything wrong. You are so quiet tonight," replied Captain Hardy.

"Oh... no, sir. I am just tired, I guess. We had a long session of letter writing today."

Then one of the midshipmen, Sparks, I think it was, offered, "I hear that the Admiral has gotten Lady Hamilton with child." with a sense of glee in his voice which hardly suited the thought, especially when applied to an Admiral who was wooing someone else's wife.

Ben looked to Captain Hardy with a wounded, sad look in his eyes. The look that Hardy returned was every bit as sad and miserable, his long face drawn and solemn.

Hardy made quick work of changing the subject. "It would serve you young gentlemen right if the Admiral walked through that door right this minute and caught you in the midst of your calumny. What about your romantic exploits on shore? I bet each one of you has a story to tell, if he is man enough to tell it."

Ben feared that Hardy would regret his choice of topic, but at least it would leave poor Lord Nelson's butchered carcass alone for awhile. Neither he nor Hardy really wanted to hear about all of the beddings that had gone on while the young officers were on shore. Indeed, such stories only brought grief to captains because the more the men had pursued the ladies on shore, the more sickness a captain would have to deal with on board ship. The common sailors had to make do with whatever wenches were brave enough to come aboard and bed with them there. But Hardy had done the right thing. He had changed the topic of discussion quite artfully, Ben thought. Ben rummaged through his mind to try to find some other topic to attract their attention, but they were together daily and had discussed every aspect of the war, what was happening at home, the ship, and the weather until they were bored with it all.

The officers began to describe their romantic exploits on shore. Most were the usual drivel, but one poor fellow, Midshipman Collins, had escorted a young lady from a fine Neapolitan family to a fancy ball. They were having a grand time until suddenly her petticoat came undone and fell about her feet. He told his story with some humour. "She stopped, dead still, and just looked at me. For a second I could not fathom what had happened, but I followed her gaze to her ankles and there, splayed out on the floor, was her petticoat, almost as big as a forcsa'l. Well, you know old Collins, always a good man in a crisis. I simply reached down and pulled the thing up. She turned many shades of red and grabbed the d... thing and ran as fast as she could. I never saw her again and dare not go to her house. I hear that her father has put a price on my head."

One other fellow had a good story to tell. He sat next to Tom, who had been quite reserved during all of this racy discussion. Midshipman Percy had met a nice young lady in church. They were so taken with one another that she invited him to supper to meet her family. But she was a Roman Catholic and poor Percy was an Anglican. Once the girl's father learned of his religious beliefs, he refused to let him see his daughter, but they had been meeting in secret for weeks now. He was so love sick that it made them all laugh, even Tom and Hardy got a jolt out of his misery.

When they came to Ben, he sat looking for a few seconds at Tom Murphy, who had passed when his turn came.

Ben was in the habit of making up wild love stories and attributing them to his own efforts, just to amuse Tom. Ben was an avid reader while Tom had to be dragged to the books. They both knew that these extraordinary stories had not a shred of truth to them, but they were a good way to wile away a dull evening. Tom always loved a good story. He sat there now, glowing with his eager Irish smile, mouth hung partly open in anticipation of a great guffaw, but Ben was not in the mood. He could not bring himself to invent any wonderful romantic exploits this night. He was hurting too much inside. He simply shrugged his shoulders, spread his hands before him and smiled an empty smile.

"Come, Ben, you have spent every day at the Royal Palace. You must have run into some juicy bits about the Admiral, if you did not find some tempting wench for yourself. I can't believe that you have been celibate here in port," not a handsome devil like you." said Collins.

"Believe it, Mr. Collins. Not all leftenants are as promiscuous as you midshipmen," said Hardy somewhat sternly. He knew that Ben was not a womanizer, and that made him a better officer who thought most of the time of only his duty. The steward brought in the cheese platter and port. *Thank God the evening is nearly over,* thought Ben.

As the other young officers filed out of the captain's cabin, each thanking the captain for a fine evening, Captain Hardy touched Ben on the shoulder. "Stay a second, Ben."

Ben stood back while the others filed out. Then Captain Hardy turned to him. "Lad you are young and the world is still all black and white. There is no grey. I know because I was there not long ago myself." Hardy had been a captain only a few months and he was about six years Ben's senior. Then he continued. "As you grow older, you will find that the world gets grayer every year. Things are not just all right or all wrong any more. It's disturbing, at least to me and I suspect that it is to you also. A man is great because he does one thing extremely well, better than anyone else, but that does not mean that the man is perfect. None of us are perfect and the older we get, the less perfect we become. But it is human nature to expect perfection in our heroes. Well, lad, it is just not to be found. Think back on history. Every great man had some significant flaw. Some were womanizers, some were homosexuals, some downright scoundrels in their private lives, but that does not destroy the good that they accomplished as fighting men and leaders. It's no one's fault lad, but it is something that you will have to learn to deal with. Would you believe that much of my job is in finding ways to live with the imperfections of humans?"

Ben looked into his eyes. "I have never said a word about Lord Nelson's personal life to anyone, sir. You must believe me," said Ben.

"I do, Ben. You know that the Admiral's, ...er indiscretions are the topic of conversation throughout the fleet and even to the parlours of London, and it is no fault of your own. Learn to love the man for the good that is in him, and try to overlook the imperfections. It is what I have to do every day, and it is most difficult, most difficult," said Hardy. There was pain in his face as he spoke gently to Ben, and Ben knew that they would have to speak of this yet again. It was too big and important for either of them to overlook it for long. Ben felt as if Hardy had been trying as hard to convince himself of the truth in his words as he was to help Ben through a difficult time. They were much alike.

It was many years later that Ben came to realize that the wild, daring nature that allowed a man like Nelson to plan an attack on another man's bed was the same quality needed to plan and execute a major naval battle successfully. That knowledge put some grey into his life, but no joy in his heart.

Word came the next day from a man who fled the terror in Naples that Commodore Caricciolo had joined the French Republicans and was working disguised as a common peasant. That was one more blow to Ben's concept of a perfect world. Here was a man who had been an officer in the navy of his country and who had not only defected, but joined the opposition. He was accused of firing on his own flag ship, the *Minerva,* off Procida. From what Ben heard of the atrocities being committed in Naples on the local people in the name of liberty, brotherhood and equality, he was certain that Caricciolo would soon regret his decision to join the French and Neapolitan insurgents. *They do not have any idea what it is they are fighting for. None at all.*

The King raged for days against Caricciolo and vowed to have his head at the first possible instant, but he stayed in his palace at Palermo, contented that someone would soon bring Caricciolo's head to him.

Tomid was getting weaker each day and now Ben knew that he would lose him. He talked with the surgeon, Mr. Ross, and they decided to try some strong-smelling ointment that might open up his nasal passages, but he still refused to eat. Ben went off to his duty with a heavy heart. When he returned that night, little Tomid had expired. Ben was distraught. This was the one time in his life when he needed an animal, a friend, and he could not bear to lose Tomid, not just now, not with all that was happening. Tom Murphy understood and tried to comfort Ben as much as he could. Tom was the only one that Ben really confided in and trusted. Together they shared their grief for the loss of a tiny ball of fur that had amused them for many hours. Tom Hardy showed compassion and understanding when he learned of the little cat's demise. He had enjoyed playing with the little fellow too.

Well into the summer, Ben was still at Palermo. The *Vanguard* had not budged. She sat bobbing in the water, waiting the arrival of her Admiral with some plan to put her to work. Then word came that a man by the name of Cardinal Ruffo had led a band of local men against the French and had retaken Naples.

At this point in his narrative, Admiral Rundel hesitated,

cleared his throat, and then sat for sometime looking off into space. I sat and watched him, asking if he was well. He replied that he was well, but that he needed some time to think about the events that so blighted his life during the last of 1798 and into 1799. So much happened during those few short months that ate away at the image that Ben had built of *his* Navy. He had, until this time, loved everything to do with the Navy and was devoted to his service above all things in his life. I went forward to complete the story in a sketchy way. I knew that someday before he died, he would call for me and my pen and we would take up these events that had caused him so much pain. I knew that when that happened, the Admiral would be close to death. The events below are but an outline of the agonies that Ben endured during those last months in the Mediterranean, while all that he loved was eroding and falling into the sea, to be dissolved in the frothy foam and never formed again.

Now, the 'Band of Brothers' that Lord Nelson had brought together and had made into such a superb fighting force, was beginning to break up. There was fighting and continual bickering and it seemed that everything that the Navy tried to do failed. There were some exceptions. Captain Troubridge had taken the castle of St. Elmo in ten days, a feat that everyone said was impossible, and had brought Capua to capitulation. Ben was there and would tell me about St. Elmo and Capua at a later date.

Then St. Vincent struck his pennant and headed for England, a tired and sickly man. Everyone would miss him and everyone knew that no one could ever replace him. Only he, with his great vision had been able to bring together the men who won such a splendid victory at Aboukir Bay. Nelson wrote to St. Vincent, begging him to stay, but the old man had already packed up and left by the time that Nelson's letter arrived. Ben remembered helping with that letter and it gave him great pain to see the fine old war horse leave the field, broken and worn.

Keith, who eventually brought *Foudroyant* to Lord

Nelson, was named to replace St. Vincent as Admiral of the Mediterranean Fleet. Nelson was unhappy and he explained his feelings to Ben. He considered himself as better qualified to manage a fleet in the Mediterranean because of the many years that he had spent there. He neither respected nor liked Admiral Keith. Keith was to bring Britain no glory. He chased Admiral Briux and his fleet all around the Mediterranean without ever bringing the enemy to action. Keith returned to his home port with no major victory to report and Briux failed to achieve his goal of evacuating the French troops in Egypt and on Malta. Both men had done no great service to their countries, save to cruise the Mediterranean for five months.

Then when Nelson did not honour Keith's order when he was told to go to the defense of Minorca, Keith was livid. Nelson flatly refused and later on, he failed to execute Keith's orders because he claimed to be in too poor health to proceed. By this time, Lord Nelson had become so enarmoured with Lady Hamilton that he would refuse any order that took him from her side for any length of time. His judgment was impaired by his extreme concern for her safety. He was interested in protecting only Naples and Sicily, the rest of his domain could get by as best it could. Ben saw the truth through all of the fluff that he heard about the Admiral.

Malta was a good example, although it is unlikely that Lord Nelson could have done more for the Maltese than he did. King Ferdinando of Naples sent some corn to aid the starving Maltese, but no supplies were forthcoming from England. The Russians suddenly had other priorities for their food and none came from there either. Nelson sent Captain Troubridge to help Captain Ball in defeating the French on Malta. Soon Troubridge saw the miserable conditions under which the Maltese were living and dying, and he sent word to Lord Nelson to send food. But none came. Nelson refused to ask for more food from the Neapolitan King until the British and Russians sent their fair shares. Troubridge paid out of his own pocket for food for the suffering Maltese and captured a supply ship to keep the people alive, but it was not enough. Ben was there and saw it all. Captain Ball was ever their hero, doing for them all that he could, but it was the vitriolic pen of Troubridge that sent the message to the world that Malta needed help. Nelson tried to help, but failed. Malta was a terrible blot on the fine reputation of the British Navy that Ben loved so much.

Then when Ruffo took back Naples, he and Captain Foote of the *Seahorse,* Fremantle's former ship, negotiated a capitulation with the Neapolitan insurgents, allowing them to go free. When Nelson arrived from Palermo with the Hamiltons, his sails were taken aback. He said that the capitulation was an outrage. That these men were traitors to their King and should be hanged, not turned loose to do more mischief. He ended by calling Cardinal Ruffo a 'fool,' and signaled a reversal of the treaty. He put the insurgents in transports in the harbour and left them there for weeks with little food and water. In the end, he put most of them to death.

During the retaking of Naples, Commodore Caricciolo was captured, dressed in the dirty clothes of a peasant, half starved, with a beard and most dirty and unkempt. When he was sent aboard the *Vanguard* , Hardy recognized him as an officer and demanded that his shackles be taken from him and his arms untied. He put the man in an empty cabin and offered him food and drink. That morning Lord Nelson ordered a court martial for Caricciolo, which was his duty as Commander-in-Chief of the allied Navy. Count Thurn, Captain of the *Minerva* presided over the court martial, and the man was speedily found guilty of all crimes of which he was accused and sentenced to be hanged from his own flag ship at 5 p.m. Ben and Tom were both there to witness the hanging.

During his brief period after the trial, Caricciolo was visited by Captain Foote and Lord Hamilton. He begged them to intercede for him and to get him a priest and allow him twenty-four hours to prepare himself for death.

When Lord Hamilton brought Caricciolo's request to Lord Nelson, he stoutly refused, saying that the hundreds of men whom Caricciolo had killed while acting with the insurgents had died without benefit of clergy or twenty-four hours to prepare for death. Many were shocked when promptly at 5 p.m., Captain Hardy did his duty and ordered that Caricciolo be hung from the yard arm of his flagship by his own crewmen. After he was dead, he was cut down and allowed to slip into the sea with no Christian burial. Some sailors said that three days later his body surged to the surface, his eyes staring at heaven in a most ghastly manner. There was much discussion of this ungallant treatment of an officer and Lord Nelson was severely criticized in many quarters. Ben thought and brooded.

Some time later, Troubridge became ill, diagnosed with fever and jaundice. He was at times too sick to even write. When he recovered, he had withdrawn into a shell of hatred and misery, lashing out at any one who displeased him. Things would never be the same between him and Lord Nelson.

The further loss of the 'brothers' came when Captain Miller was accidentally blown up by some errant bombs aboard the *Theseus.* They were lying off Acre with Captain Sydney Smith in the *Tigre* when the accident occurred. The *Theseus* was badly damaged and thirty-five men killed, forty-five wounded. Captain Miller had been liked by all and was sorely missed.

Then Captain Edward Berry returned to take over the *Foudroyant* which meant that there was no employment for the most capable Thomas Hardy. Nelson pleaded with the Admiralty to let Captain Hardy have the *Princess Charlotte* which had no captain. But communications were slow in those days and the new Captain, Stephenson, had already left England and came prepared to take over the *Princess Charlotte.* Poor Hardy had to be sent back to England where he would fret on the beach until he could get another ship. He and Nelson made a fine team, each understanding the other completely, even though they may not have accepted each others philosophies. Hardy was a fine captain and left the *Foudroyant* in top condition. The crews were well-disciplined and the men respected him and liked his steady discipline. "He is stern, but also human," one man said. But Berry was a different type of leader. He was not good at organizing and running a ship and unfortunately, Lord Nelson also suffered from the same affliction. It took good men like Hardy to keep the Navy in shape, to allow dreamers like Nelson to do their thing and produce great victories. Berry was a dreamer and planner, Nelson a strategist and Hardy an organizer. No wonder they had made such a fine team in the past.

By this time, Captain Hood had returned home to settle family affairs and Captain Blackwood had come on the station to replace him. It was during the long siege by Smith in the Levant that he finally won the praise of Lord Nelson, who might not forget insults, but would always rise to praise a man when good work had been done. Lord Nelson thrived on praise and much of his problem in life was that he sometimes failed to receive the praise that he thought was due him.

When the *Culloden* ran aground a second time in her career, Nelson was beside himself. The grounding was hardly predictable since it occurred in the middle of the channel. Troubridge was angered beyond words. He had grown farther and farther away from Lord Nelson, largely because of Lady Hamilton. In spite of that, Troubridge always depended on Nelson to call the major moves. He needed Nelson and so, became more depressed when they were not on friendly terms. Eventually, Troubridge was ordered home with the leaking *Culloden* and Troubridge became flag Captain for St. Vincent who had been coaxed into serving as Admiral of the Channel Fleet. But Captain Ball kept close contact with the good Lady Hamilton. He was fond of her and had known her for sometime. Captain Ball was assigned as temporary governor ashore at Malta and was no longer under Nelson's direct command.

Louis left the *Queen Charlotte* when she was devastated by fire. Most of the original 'band of brothers' were now gone, leaving Nelson mostly alone and sick. Ben doubted that any Admiral could ever again assemble so able a group of captains and he felt as if England had seen her greatest hour at sea and would never be so strong again. Maybe he was right?

During one tour of duty, Captain Berry almost lost the *Guilliame Tell*, which was under Captain Dacres, one of the remaining French ships that got away form the Battle of the Nile. But Captain Ball came in the nick of time and helped to convince Berry that he must attack and take the *Tell.* They succeeded and managed to brighten the sadness in Ben's heart, for a short time at least.

About now, Captain Hollowell had his ship's carpenter prepare an elaborate coffin from the wood of the main mast of *L'Orient* which blew up during the Battle of the Nile. He presented it to Lord Nelson, who was so flattered that he carried it with him wherever he went until his dying day. When officers stood admiring it, he cautioned them that they might look but should have no plans of inhabiting the box. It was *his.*

After the failure to bring the French Fleet to battle, Lord Keith went home, leaving Lord Nelson as Commander-in-Chief for some six months. Nelson was convinced that he could hold that post indefinitely and that Keith would not return. But return he did and Nelson was now most despondent because he had been superseded once again, made redundant as it were. There was general discontent among the officers now on the station. None had much confidence in Keith and they deplored the way that Nelson had been treated. But Nelson's prejudice towards securing the safety of Naples and his affair with Lady Hamilton set the Admiralty on its ear. They were not ready to entrust Lord Nelson with any more major campaigns. He had lost their trust.

During that time Napoleon managed to sneak out of Egypt with two French frigates, leaving behind most of his remaining 30,000 troops to fend for themselves. Ben was disturbed when he learned that the British ships had not caught the frigates and that the French had returned safely to Toulon. What had happened to the old fighting British Navy? Were they lost forever? Would there never be another battle like Aboukir Bay and had all courage died?

Finally, a month after the Battle of Morengo where Napoleon routed the Austrian army, Rear Admiral Nelson struck his pennant and packed up to leave for England. Everyone was amazed beyond words when it was learned that he would not travel by sea, but was going back by land to the Channel where he would enter England through Dover. The Admiral's barge crew wrote a fine letter expressing their grief at his leaving and the officers did much the same thing. Ben could not believe that he would opt for so arduous a journey in his poor health. And there was Lady Hamilton's condition to consider too. She and Lord Hamilton would travel with Lord Nelson. Days of jogging along in a carriage over bad roads would do a pregnant woman no good. But apparently Lord Nelson had requested a ship to take him home sometime ago, but Lord Keith did not send one when Nelson wanted it. Nelson, ever an impatient man, and impetuous, sought to find his own way home. He dragged a good bit of baggage with him, the Hamiltons, the Queen of Naples, a Miss Knight and all their servants and retinue. Included in the mountain of baggage was Hallowell's gift to Lord Nelson, his coffin from the remains of *L'Orient*.

Chapter Thirteen

Egypt

Ben sat alone in the wardroom of the *Vanguard.* He had just seen Tom off in the *Ardent* bound for the Tagus. Nelson had left with his long entourage overland. Ben had stood for an hour watching them make their way along the Italian coast. The trail of dust finally settled and Ben sadly returned to his ship. With Hardy off to England, and the Band of Brothers pretty much disbanded, Ben had never felt more lonely. He was to stay on with the Neapolitan Court for yet a few more days. Then, who knows?

Rosco, a ship's boy, stepped into the wardroom and handed Ben an envelope. It was the usual sort that comes from the Admiralty. *Perhaps I will not languish here for long.* With nervous hands he opened the letter and read, "Leftenant Benjamin Rundel is to report to Admiral Keith at once aboard his flagship."

Ben had seen the flagship drop anchor but an hour earlier. He arose and headed for the flagship. He was met on deck by her first leftenant and taken to the Admiral's cabin. Ben had never met Admiral Lord Keith before and all he knew of the man was what he had heard Lords Nelson say. None of that was good.

The sentry announced Benjamin Rundel and a voice from within called for him to enter. Ben stepped into the dim cabin and faced a smallish man, not of unusual contenence, in fact he might have been someones solicitor. He seemed to be a quiet type, lacking in the barely restrained yet dynamic energy that Ben had known in Lord Nelson and St. Vincent. He saluted smartly and stood wondering what was next.

"Welcome, Mr. Rundel. Please be seated."

"Thank you, sir."

"I suppose that you have heard that Napoleon has escaped with some of his generals in two frigates and made it safely back to Toulon."

"Yes, sir. I have."

"What do you suppose will become of his some 30,000 soldiers that are left in Egypt?"

"I don't know, sir, but I imagine many will desert, some may make it back to France, eventually."

"Well, the Admiralty needs to know if there is a viable and sizeable fighting force there in Egypt. If there is, Napoleon may find some way to get them back to France and there they would pose an invasion threat to England. France still has some six rates and can still move a few soldiers about. You come highly recommended by Admiral Lord St. Vincent. I am entrusting you with a most dangerous but important mission. Step over here, please."

Ben stepped to the window of the flagship.

"See that ship over there?" as he pointed.

"She is a Zebec, I believe, sir."

"You will board her this evening at 4 bells and Captain Hugo Rossi will sail you to Egypt, to a point about five miles west of Alexandria. There they will set you ashore and you will proceed to town. We have two operatives there. Here are their names and addresses."

Ben read, "John Enfield and Richard Smythe."

Keith continued. "Enfield was due to come out of Egypt two months ago with reports on the French army, but we have heard nothing from him. Smythe should have come out over three weeks ago with a more recent report, but he has not shown. I want you to find these men, get their reports on the numbers, strength and morale of the French army and return here within the month. Is that clear?"

"Aye sir."

Lord Keith added, "You shall masquerade as a Frenchman down on his luck. You'll have to borrow tramps clothing."

"Sir, I do speak some French but I have trouble understandinmg spoken French and cannot read it. I would prefer to go in the disguise of a Spanish sailor who is temporarily beached. I do speak Spanish quite well, sir."

"Very well, if you wish, but you know that if the French get wind of your presence they will take great pleasure in slitting your throat. You'll need some Egyptian money. This is mighty hard to come by here on the Tagus, so you will have to make do with what I could scrape together." At that he tossed Ben a small bag of coins.

"You should be ready to return by, say, the 20th of January. Rossi will cruise by your drop off point once every four days on his daily trips out to the east. If you build a fire at night, he will be able to spot you and send a ship's boat. Now get along with you. You have only two hours to get aboard the merchant ship."

"Aye, sir." There were many questions that Ben wanted to ask, but clearly the Admiral was finished with him and he had to up anchor. *There'll be no tea and scones here,* he thought. He headed back to the *Vanguard* and went to the sailor's quarters. He met up with Crowe and Gentry.

"Lads, I need to get some seaman's clothes suitable for a Spanish fisherman. Do you have anything handy?" Both men were tall and either might be able to supply him with worn but clean clothes. Crowe produced a pair of mended duck breeches and a pair of worn leather shoes that fitted quite well. Gentry came up with a short blue jacket and semi-white shirt, but no one seemed to have a hat that would fit. Ben paid the men for their kindness and went to the wardroom to change into his clothes. He gave Crowe some extra money and showed him where he had stowed his duffel and laika. He asked him to take care of his things while he was away.

"He's off for a rendezvous with some fancy lady, I reckon," said Gentry. But Ben had no time to explain. He was off swiftly to the Zebec. He appproached the ship and called to the man at the rail. "I wish to see your captain."

The man turned and called out in Italian. A swarthy, dartk haired man ambled to the rail.

"What you want?"

"May I come aboard. I need to speak with you." The captain motioned for him to board.

I am Benjamin Rundel and will be sailing to Egypt with you. You are to let me off at a predetermined location."

"I know naught of thees. I sail in minutes for the Straits. I go west. You wrong."

Then Ben caught a glimpse of a smaller ship, a Polacca, which was anchored behind the Zebec and would have been out of sight from the flagship. His mind was in a whirl.

"You are not Captain Hugo Rossi?"

"No. He sails there," as he pointed to the Polacca.

"Sorry to have bothered you, sir," said Ben as he raced over the side and began to run along the wharf to the small merchant ship. He wondered as he ran why Admiral Keith had not told him that he was to board a Polacca and not a Zebec. *Does he think that I don't know the difference?* Ben could see men scurrying about unfurling the fore lateen sail. Others were working to set the main and mizzen square rigged sails. They had just let loose the mizzen lateen sail. Ben made a mad dash racing at top speed, managing to grab the rail just as they cast off her bowlines. He clambered aboard awkwardly. When he had regained his footing, he looked to the nearest sailor. ""Your captain?" he said.

This time Ben was not going to make any mistakes. "You are Captain Hugo Rossi?"

"And you must be the late Leftenant Benjamin Bundel," he answered.

"Leftenant Rundel, sir." Things had happened so fast that Ben had not taken time to think of a good name to go with his disguise. He thought for a second. "For this voyage, I am a Spanish fisherman who goes by... Antonio Valera. You are to drop me off west of Alexandria and then pick me up in about three weeks."

"I talk with your Amiral an' he say nothing about pick you up. He say only drop you off west of Abu Qu."

"We must have an understanding, sir, that you will

pick me up as planned. I cannot be left stranded in a foreign land."

"You will not be alone. There are many Frenchmen there who also want to go home." Ben let it ride for the moment. He had no power over the Italian captain.

The voyage to Egypt was surprisingly swift. Ben tried several times to pin Rossi down concerning his plans to rescue Ben, but he seemed to get nowhere with the man. Apparently his English was poor enough that he had not understood the Admiral when he asked to have Ben brought back to Italy, if he really did ask for his return. Ben found himself an unwanted guest on an Italian merchantman and he had little to do but sleep and eat and try to learn some Italian. Then it struck him hard. *I don't know a word of Egyptian. How will I get by? This is another one of those fool's missions where a nobody is sent to do the impossible so that no great family will suffer the displeasure of the King if I fail. I am getting tired of these assignments. Why can't I just serve as leftenant and sail the seas like everyone else?* Ben amused himself reading old copies of the London Gazette which were in the officer's quarters. They used them for toilet paper. He had to adjust to Italian food once again, but that was to be a minor challenge.

Twelve days after sailing they were off Alexandria early in the morning. Rossi said, "I leave you here at Abu Qu. I send you ashore with small boat."

Ben: "You will return in three weeks and watch for my signal?" The man made no attempt to answer. He had the Admiral's silver in his pocket and could care less what happened to Ben. *There is no going back. I am committed now and must hasten to my duty.*

It was ten in the morning when Ben finally set foot on the Egyptian shore. He instantly wished that he could be back in England doing almost anything but what he was about to do.

He passed a number of small huts and headed east along a path that led to Alexandria. It was supposed to be only five miles, but it was the longest five miles that he had ever walked. Late in the afternoon he arrived on the outskirts of Alexandria. He pulled out the paper and began to make motions towards the address. One man stopped to speak with him. "He live there," as he pointed down a long alley. But Ben could find no such address anywhere along the alley. Then he stumbled onto another street. If he understood the letters correctly, it might be the one that he saught. He found the address about dusk, but no one answered his persistent knock at the door.

Discouraged, Ben decided to try to find an inn for the night. His first attempt failed. The house was an inn of sorts, but one where only elderly dying people lived. The inn keeper pointed to another building. It said "Molly Brown's Boarding House" over the door. Ben was heartened. *Surely Molly Brown can speak the King's English.*

He entered and a stubby, brown-haired woman about forty with an amazingly white complexion came to answer his call bell. She had hands on her hips and left no one wondering that she meant business.

"What ya want, sailor man?"

"I would like a room for the night, madam."

"Ya understands that there's to be no drinking, fightin', or womanizing within these here walls," she said in a voice so loud that all within hearing distance looked her way.

"Ya look like a sailorman to me. Never seen one of them what didn't indulge in every vice in the book. There's no room here for the likes o' you."

"But madam, I have come a long way and am most tired. I want only a place to lay my head for the night."

"The rooms are cheaper by the week."

"I'll buy a room for the week then," said Ben as he laid some Egyptian coins on the counter.

"That'll buy you a room with meals fer a week. Go in there an' eat," as she pointed to a small dining area where several men sat and smoked pipes.

Ben was very hungry and he ate a fine Irish stew. Then

the woman led him to a second floor room, just a bed and a chamber pot, nothing more. *It'll do,* thought Ben.

The next day he headed out for the house where John Enfield lived, but again there was no one there. Then he spent most of the day trying to find Smythe's house. All this was proving much more difficult than Ben had ever dreamed it would be. Many of the streets did not have names posted and when they did, he could not read them. Finally he met a Egyptian soldier, finely dressed. He asked the way to the Smythe's address and the man showed him with sign language. Ben was off and the numbers on the house matched the address. But again, no one was home. It looked as if no one had lived there for months. Dust piled up against the door and there were no footprints. He spent the next week trying to find the two operatives, but finally came to the conclusion that something had happened to both of them. It was extremely hot and Ben wished that he had been able to bring a hat with him. *It's hot here even in winter,* he thought. He stayed and ate at Molly's, even though he loathed the old woman. But his meagre money was running out fast. He decided to spend a few nights sleeping in a grassy area near the water. That way he could save some money to buy food. He was baffled at the disappearance of the British agents. *If only I could go to the authorities. They might be able to help me find the men, but I dare not risk arrest and compromise the entire venture.* The last time that he went to Enfield's house, a fat dark lady with six small children answered his knock. She spoke little English, but she hinted that the former occupant was no longer there. *Does 'there' mean living here or alive?* She obviously had just moved in and was not yet settled. *Something has happened to Enfield for sure.*

Ben often went to a nearby pub to sit and listen. He thought that he might be able to pick up some information on the French army from straggling French soldiers who stopped by. He sat many evenings watching and sipping a glass of beer. Most of the Frenchmen who came by were looking for women and almost nothing was said about the French army as such. He was getting no where most slowly. He did learn that there was an encampment to the west a few miles, but nothing about how many men were housed there or their morale. He judged from the number of men who stopped by the pub minus their uniforms that many were deserting, but that was all that he could learn.

Then one evening just as he had sat down, a group of well-dressed Frenchmen entered the pub and began to talk loudly. At first Ben thought that they might be officers, but that soon proved incorrect. One man began to speak about a Sphinx, which Ben judged was some collosal statue to the south. Then he spoke of Giza and huge pyramids, his hands flying as he described the wonders of ancient architecture in the land. Then another man stood up. He had many plants with him, pressed between old newsprint. He showed many of the specimens to his fellows and often exclaimed that, "this is a new species!" Now Ben began to understand. *These are a group of French scientists. Napoleon must have been so certain of his ability to conquer Egypt that he had brought along sientists to study the history and natural history of the country. Ben decided that this was not too far out of character.* Napoleon had not been defeated so resoundingly until Aboukir Bay. He was known to have plans for improving the roads, schools, parks and hospitals in France and also for improving the economic system. Others spoke also, covering history, the people, geology and even their libraries and books. One man seemed to be in charge. He lamented the fact that there was no way for them to take their valuable finds back to France. The men ordered wine and sat around talking for sometime. Ben was tired and could learn no more from them. He left.

He was returning to Molly's when suddenly he felt a sharp blow on the back of his head. Ben felt his body slump to the ground and he lay there for sometime. When he awoke, he checked his shirt and found that someone had robbed him of all of the coins that Admiral Keith had given to him. All that he had left were the three silver coins that he had stuffed into his shoe. *They won't last more than a few days,* he thought.

Ben was losing weight and he was not feeling at all well. One night ten days after his arrival, he laid down on the grass and within seconds he knew that he was going to have a malaria attack. He began to feel hot, boiling, weak and helpless as a babe. Sweat poured from his body and he writhed uncomfortably. The grass felt as if it were on fire. Ben decided to crawl to a small boat that was tied close to shore. He crawled in and lay with his hot back against the cool wood of the boats hull. It did give him some relief. After about six hours, he began to feel cold. He had no great coat and nothing to put over him. He shivered until the dull sun arose in the morning, shining with its life-giving warmth on a scorched earth. Ben sat huddled up in the boat, mostly past the chill and wondering what would happen to him now that he was a penniless beggar. *Keith was right. I will end up as a penniless beggar in this forbidding land, but by God, I'll not pose as a Frenchman!*

Just then a group of sailors came walking along the bank. One of them stared down at Ben. He looked back. They were all dressed in odd clothing, brightly bedecked with much jewelry and mostly expensive too.

"What have we here, mates," said the closest sailor. He smelled of garlic, and wore a red turban, no shirt, but a yellow vest, multi-coloured waist band, faded tan trousers, more like bloomers and no shoes. Gold necklaces hung from his neck and his fingers sported half a dozen gold rings.

"Marsillo, he sleep in our boat. Drown heem!" said another of the sailors.

"No, ...No. Look at his broad shoulders. He very strong man," said Marsillo. "We use him. Up, there poacher. We take you with us." At that he pulled a pistol from his waistband and pointed it at Ben's head, cocking the hammer.

Ben, still not fully recovered, could do little to resist these men. There were at least twenty of them and they seemed quite bold and determined. He stood up causing the small boat to rock violently.

"Come. We row to the sheep," said Marsillo who appeared to be their leader. The men grabbed the oars of a larger boat nearby, tied on the small boat and rowed towards a small cargo ship that Ben recognized as a Mediterranean Pink. He looked at her three short masts with lateen sails and possibly one square sail on the main mast. Her stern was long and narrow but she had a round bottom perfectly suited to carrying cargo.

As they rowed, Ben, now somewhat recovered, looked at the sailors, his captors. Marsillo was probably Italian or Greek and so was his second in command, Rudolfo. Two men he knew spoke Spanish. Several others were probably Dutch or German, but all seemed to understand Egyptian. The remainder of the men were dark like the Egyptians. His first impression was that they might be pirates. Ben ventured to speak to one of the Spaniards, Juan.

"Donde vamos?"

"Somos pescaderos y buscamos a los pesces," he said with a mirthless laugh. Manuello, his friend, began to laugh also. "Muy rico estos pesces, eh hermano."

Ben sat wondering what would happen next. He was not used to waiting for things to happen but preferred to make them happen, but something told him that he would do well to not anger these men just yet. He said, "Cuando comemos?"

Juan answered, "We eat aboard sheep. Josepha she cook good." They boarded the Pink and Ben sat with the others on the deck. Soon two women, one Josepha, who was dark and pretty and one Sophia who was short, chubby and not attractive, came with platters of food. The men sat in a tight circle and pulled slabs of meat and bread from the platters. There was a pot of rice and some beans as well. They waited out the day, mostly talking and playing games. Ben became friendly with Juan and Escobal. He could speak in Spanish with them, but he sensed at once that they knew that he was not Spanish.

During the day, Marsillo came to sit next to Ben. He was a muscular man from the tips of his mighty fingers to his toes. He had the thickest head of jet black hair that Ben had ever seen. And he spoke in a soft voice to Ben.

"Who you are?" He apparently could speak some English.

"I am Antonio Valera, a fisherman from Malaga. My family is all dead, killed by Napoleon and his men." Ben gambled on the fact that these men might not like the French and the fact that he had called at Malaga once when he was aboard the *Faithful.* At least he knew what the port was like and a little about the town. Marsillo began to ask questions about his home and his childhood. At first, Ben was able to make up a good story that anyone could believe, but as the questions became more personal, he began to have trouble. Finally, he excused himself to go to the head. Marsillo said nothing, but Ben was certain that he did not believe him.

They lived aboard the ship for three days, eating, playing games, wrestling and sleeping. But always either Marsillo or his second in command, Rudolpho, sat in the stern watching out to sea with a glass handy. Ben wondered what they were looking for. *Surely they cannot see the fish swimming in the sea,* he thought. He noticed something a bit unusual. He had been aboard many ships over the years, but he had never seen one so totally stripped down as this one. It had two swivel guns which could be mounted either fore or aft and one boat. She carried only a few barrels of ammunition, not enough to last for an hour's firing. The galley was nothing but a small ship's stove with two or three pots and pans. There was no gear aboard, no duffelbags for personal belongings. The men slept and ate on deck. She had the usual number of sails and yards, but there were no extra sails or yards below should one blow out in a gale. And there was no fishing gear at all, no nets or lines. There were no paint pots, okum, no cordage or spare sail. In fact, there was nothing below except empty space. The hull had been completely gutted with access through two large hatches. Even the captains cabin was stripped of all comforts, just a small table and a chair, nothing else save a large safe in the corner. It looked as if there had been cargo stored there recently from the scratches on the deck. Ben wanted to ask but thought better of it. Juan told him that her name was *Sheba.* "She very new, fine sheep."

On the afternoon of the second day, Marsillo brought out a small stringed instrument with a rounded body. Ben thought it might be a Greek Bouzouki, but he had never seen one before. Marsillo had aparently not played the instrument before, although from the crew's reaction, Ben judged that he had played with it and drove them all most crazy. Men got up from their rest and went to the other end of the ship. Rudolpho was on duty looking for whatever. Ben soon realized why the crew hated the instrument. Marsillo, whatever he was, was not a musician. After about twenty minutes, Ben asked playfully if he might give it a try. He thought that it was enough like 'laika that he might be able to play it and spare his crewmates further pain. Marsillo seemed quite happy to turn the little instrument over to Ben. He began slowly at first, tuning the strings and trying them for sound. But soon he was playing a fine Russian tune and singing in Russian too. He had learned to play the balalaika from a Russian sailor who had also taught him the words in Russian. He dared not play the English aires of which he was so fond since it would mark him at once as a Englishman. He had no idea where the English might stand in the minds of these strange people.

Now the crewmen began to come back to the stern, a few at a time, all curious. He had succeeded in establishing himself as a mystery man, someone who was a bit unpredictable and it would serve his purpose well.

Late on the afternoon of the third day, Marsillo, who

was on watch, jumped up, his glass in his hand. He opened the glass and squinted at some far off object for sometime. Ben strained to see what he was watching, but didn't want to seem too curious. Soon a large merchantman appeared, heavily laden from the looks of her hull. Now everyone crowded to the rail, watching the new ship. She dropped anchor about four cables away. Ben could just see her name. She was the *Athena* and most probably Greek.

They watched as the crew lowered a boat into the water and the captain and probably the purser climbed down to be rowed ashore. *Probably off to arrange for sale and offloading,* thought Ben. Soon two other boats were lowered and quickly filled with sailors. They rowed off towards shore also. Ben wondered how any captain could expect men to work after a night in town in the stews where loose women were abundant and liquor flowed freely. He would not dare to let a crew ashore if he had a ship to offload. As soon as the two boats were out of sight, Marsillo called, "Man the capstan, hoist the foresail. We go."

Ben was now more suspicious than ever that these men were pirates, but he was still recovering from the malaria attack and needed their help. At least he was eating well and that would help him to recover.

Within minutes the *Sheba* was along side the *Athena.* Men threw grapples to her deck and tied them securely, while others rushed onto the deck of the merchantman. What happened next was a miracle that Ben would never understand. No one gave any orders, not for hours, but the men went to work as if they had been training all of their lives for this one moment. Someone shoved a cutlass in Ben's hand and before he knew it he was on the deck of the merchantmen, facing about a dozen crewmen who had been left behind to guard the ship. The twenty pirates quickly disposed of the merchant crewmen. Ben used the method that he learned when first he was forced to serve as a pirate. He hit the opponent's head so hard that he became unconscious. That way he did not need to kill him. The crew was confined to the captain's cabin, after Marsillo had rifled it for valuables.

Now the real miracle began. With not as much as a word, the men began to knock out the chocks from the cargo hatches on both ships. Soon the hatch covers were thrown aside and the sailors brought out two large wooden chutes. The hull of the *Athena* was just a bit higher than that of the *Sheba.* The chutes were set so that cargo could be delivered from the deck of the merchantman directly into the hold of the Pink. While the chutes were being set in place, others of their crew set up jeers or lifts to haul the cargo out of the hold. Ben stepped in and helped wherever a hand was needed. Now four men loaded the cargo in the hold onto the lifts and three more hauled on the line to bring it on deck. There were two such teams offloading at one time. Ben was set with a haul line in his hand. Six men worked in the hold of *Sheba* and stowed the cargo. It was about six in the evening when they began and they were finished about midnight. There was never a halt in the work and after two hours, Ben's back began to ache. Soon his arms grew tired from the heavy hauling on the line to work the blocks. But the men worked on, frantic efforts to secure the cargo.

Early in the night Ben noticed that Marsillo went to the stern and mounted the two swivel guns on *Sheba.* Out of the corner of his eye he saw him load the two guns. He set a bucket of water close by with a slow match burning over the water. *He is ready for trouble,* thought Ben. Marsillo never left the stern for the rest of the evening, standing watching out towards the shore, ever watchful. About 11 pm, he saw a ship's boat being rowed rapidly towards the *Athena.* A man stood in the stern and was shaking his fist at *Sheba.*

Ben continued to haul on the ropes, but kept an eye on Marsillo. When the boat was less than half a cable away, he heard the swivel gun fire and he could see the small boat fly into pieces of kindling from a direct hit.

That was probably the captain and purser come to claim their ship from the pirates, thought Ben. He now knew that he dare not cross these men. As he had suspected all along, they were dangerous and ruthless killers. He took a deep breath and gave another heave on the rope. By now his hands were blistered from the rough rope. When about a quarter past midnight, the hold of the merchantman was empty, Marsillo called the crew together. They had already stowed the two chutes aboard the *Sheba,* but no one had battened down the hatches. Ben looked at the little Pink. She was sitting extremely low in the water with only inches of freeboard. *One good wave and she will founder and sink,* he thought. To his surprise, the grapples were taken from the deck of the merchantman and, with open hatches, *Sheba* set sail for the shore.

As the ship glided towards the quay on shore, Josepha and Sophia brought out wooden platters heaped with rice, spicy meat and jugs of wine. Ben was forced to drink the wine to asuage a terrible thirst, but he would have preferred water. Within minutes the men were throwing the bow line and stern line over the pilings and they were along side a long dock. There was a large warehouse closeby. Ben figured that they would sleep for the night and unload in the morning, but he was wrong. As soon as the lines were secure, the men brought out the chutes and set them so that cargo from the hold of *Sheba* could be slid out onto the dock. *This is stollen cargo and I suppose they cannot risk being caught unloading by daylight,* thought Ben. Men rose like zombies to the burdonsome task of offloading the Pink. Ben managed to get the job of shuffling the barrels and bags of grain to the warehouse, which would give his sore hands a rest. The cargo had been mostly bags of grain, barrels of wine and olive oil.

Ben saw Marsillo walk slowly towards the warehouse manager. They shook hands and now Ben knew that the warehouseman probably knew which ships were due and approximately when and what they would be carrying. He managed to get word to Marsillo who would wait for the arrival of the ship and then capture it and bring the cargo to this warehouse for sale. *But why take the time to load all of the cargo onto Sheba? Why not just sail the merchantman to the wharf after overcoming her crew and save all the back breaking work of handling the cargo twice?* Ben would never get the answer to that question. When he asked Juan, he said that it had something to do with if they were interrupted during offloading, they could still sail away with the Pink and not be caught.

"On shore the crew could find us and claim their cargo if it were in their hull, but they could not claim any cargo that was in *Sheba.* She is not theirs. And there is something sentimental about Marsillo and this Pink. She is his lady and he would never trade her for any other sheep."

When the cargo was finally offloaded, it was about half past six in the morning. The men stood like zombies, almost unable to move. Josepha came by with pitchers of wine and a plate with bread and cheese, but no one was interested in eating just then. Men were asleep on their feet. Ben saw Marsillo come aboard with a broad smile on his face and a large bag of coins in each hand. He heard him stow them in the safe in his cabin. The chutes were stowed and the order came for loosing the bow and stern lines. They set one sail and let the tide carry them back to their anchorage of a night ago. As soon as the anchor hit the sea floor, men dropped onto the deck and fell instantly asleep, Ben included.

They slept until three in the afternoon. Then Josepha came by, kicking them playfully and taunting them with the smells of hot food. Ben was famished and he was soon awake and diving into a plate of rice and spicy chicken with fruit. When they had finished eating, Marsillo began to give orders. "Man the capstan, loose the sails there, we go."

Ben wondered where they might be sailing, but soon he realized that they were hugging the coast and then they rounded a point, giving it wide berth. They dropped anchor just beyond the point. The women served another meal and they ate heartily. Juan encouraged Ben. “Eat good because it may be sometime before we see food again.”

After the meal and towards dusk, Marsillo said nothing, but he divided his crew in half. Ben was to stay with the ship at anchor. Ten men went with Marsillo in their only ship’s boat and began to row towards the point. It was then that Ben realized that there was a tall pole on top of the point with a lantern set upon it. Someone had just lit the lantern.

Have I stumbled into a nest of pirates who are also ship wreckers? he wondered. He could see no other reason for the men to go to the top of the hill where the beacon stood. He could see them now slowly ascending the hill, creeping up on what appeared to be an Egyptian guard of about six men. And as he suspected, there was gun fire, distant shouts and soon the lantern was extinguished. Ben had noticed a shallow reef with jagged rocks as they had sailed around the point, but that was at high tide. The tide was going out fast now and soon those rocks would be within inches of the surface. With no light to warn them off, a ship could easily pull in too close to shore and founder on those rocks, ripping out her bottom. Ben wondered if these men had ever turned an honest day’s work in their entire lives.

Now they sat and watched. Rudolfo held a glass to his eye, looking out towards the reef. They waited about three hours. Then, a tall ship hove into view. At first Ben thought that she might be a frigate, but as the moon came from behind a cloud, he could see that she was a merchantman of French cut. Juan said, “She fine sheep. Too bad we going to wreck her.”

Half an hour later there came a loud crash, the masts fell forward as the ship, under full momentum, came to a sudden halt on the jagged rocks. Rudolfo now flew into action.

“Up anchor, loose all sails, qweekly!” Ben saw the boat and Marsillo’s crew begin to row towards them rapidly. They met about half way and Marsillo and his men clambered aboard as fast as they could.

Marsillo urged the crew to speed. “We mus’ get to her

first. There is another sheep just the other side of the point. If they saw her go aground, they may seize her first and we will have to fight her for the prize. Full and By."

They reached the ship, the *Oriole*, out of Toulon first. The other ship decided not to contest the prize and veered off to the north. The drill was much the same as it had been two days before. The chutes were set in place and soon they were offloading cargo at an amazing pace, This time the cargo was mostly grains and some barrels of wine. And this time they were racing the sea which was trying desperately to claim her cargo. Fortunately, the bow of the ship had ridden up on the reef and most of the grain was stowed far forw'rd. They had to leave some of the wine barrels that were under sea water in the stern, but they could never have put all of the cargo on the Pink anyway. *Sheba* had cargo stuffed all over her decks, crammed below decks and even in the captain's cabin. The *Oriole* was a much larger ship than they had tackled earlier. After five hours of frantic labour, the ship began to slide from the rocks and would soon slip beneath the sea with her crew confined to the captain's cabin.

Marsillo let out a low whislte and the men slipped quickly into the overladen Pink. Within two minutes they were cut loose of the sinking ship and were free of her. Before they were half a cable away, they saw her sink beneath the cool waters of the Mediterranean, never to see the light of day again. Bubbles drifted to the surface to temporarily mark her grave. There was a sudden whoosh of air and bits of debris began to rise to the surface. Just before she sank, the ship let out a low moan, like a dying person. Ben wondered how many other ships had met a similar fate on those very rocks from the treachery of these ship wreckers.

They set sail for a point slightly west of Alexandria. Ben saw no town there, but there was a long, low warehouse and a wharf. They hauled *Sheba* in close to the dock and tied her to the piers. No sooner had they tied on than two Frencmen, probably officers, appeared. Ben strained to hear what they had to say.

The older officer said, “What have you brought for us this day, friend?”

“We have much grain and wine, monsieur. Have you money?” said Marsillo.

“We can pay you in silver for part of the load, but we need food desperately. Gentry, here will go back to the camp and get rifles to pay for the rest.”

“We do not want rifles without shot and powder,” said Marsillo.

‘We bring you shot and powder, as much as we have. It is no good to us here. We are starving.”

The older man spoke up, apparently impatient with the bickering. “I have seven thousand soldiers still under my command and many have not eaten in three days. We need to offload at once.”

“We will begin at once, monsieur, if you will show me the colour of your money. The smaller man brought out a bag of coins and showed it to Marsillo.

Marsillo turned to the crew who stood by the rail of his ship. “We begin to unload at once, Go!”

So another six hours of strenuous work followed. Ben was beginning to toughen to the work, but he was always hungry and thirsty. When the cargo was all ashore, the Frenchmen brought the bag of coins and set a pile of half rusted rifles on the quay. Marsillo looked at the rifles in disgust. “How I going to sell theese mess,” he said mostly to himself.

Ben wondered at the gall of ship wreckers who would take a French ship, wreck it, capture her supplies and sell them to the very same French soldiers for whom they were intended in the first place.

They set sail and ate another fine meal. Ben continued to look for an opportunity to escape, but with no money he could hardly hope to survive for more than a week or two. This time they returned to Dumyat. Marsillo said that they were going home. Ben learned from Juan that they had a small warehouse which they used as a place to eat and sleep ashore. “The women can cook there and it is safe from harbour police.”

At the Warehouse as they called it, Marsillo set up a table and began to count out money. He figured that he was counting their take for the week but soon realized that they had captured much more money than could set on that small table. Then Marsillo began to distribute pay to his men, the old timers first, but he did give Ben a fair amount of money, saying, "You good strong man. You work hard. I pay."

That night the women decided that they did not want to prepare a meal. So Marsillo called his men together. "We go eat at the Sphinx." Ben learned that this was a restaurant where they often ate when ashore. The food was good and they had musicians to entertain the customers as well.

They stayed at the Warehouse (Entrepot)for five days and often ate at the Sphinx. Ben was beginning to wonder if he might not just wander off some night after the others had gone to sleep. Just about that time, Marsillo announced that they were sailing back to the point. *That means another ship wrecking,* thought Ben. *I will not have a chance to escape just yet.*

This time they wrecked a smaller merchantman from Portugal. She carried a varied cargo of mostly foodstuffs. When they landed at the French quay, the two French officers were waiting there anxiously. *How do they know that we have just taken a ship?* When Marsillo told them of the cargo and the many delicacies aboard, they were eager to get hands on the cargo. But Marsillo was wary. "I see your money first. No more rusted rifles."

The two officers stood looking downcast. "Monsieur, we are starving. Hundreds of men desert each day. They take up with Egyptian women and some try to get back to France. We soon will perish here on this shore. Napoleon has forgotten about us. We are no longer loyal to him. All we want now is something to eat."

Marsillo looked hard at the two men. The crew had just begun to unload cargo onto the quay. Marsillo put his hand up. "No more! These dogs not pay, I no give." At that he turned away, climbed aboard and we threw off the stern and bow lines, leaving three bags of grain on the dock as a gift. They sailed to Dumyat and sold the entire cargo there at a huge price.

Then they retired to Entrepot for several days. One night they had dined at the Sphinx. Ben was just finishing up a fine fruit dessert when a singer completed her tour. Then a strange figure walked upon the small stage. He wore trousers of a French soldier, but a plain tan shirt. He began to juggle, taking things from the tables, forks, knives, even plates and including them in his act. Ben had the uneasy feeling that he knew the fellow. *He looks most familiar, that mousy mustache...it's Emil...Emil Capulet! He taught me French when I was in Prison near Toulon. It can't be! He came over here as a soldier with Napoleon. He wouldn't desert, but there he is, oops, he just dropped a knife.* The fellow looked towards Ben and halted for an instant, a glimmer of recognition in his eyes.

Now Ben's brain was racing. *I must get to speak with him. But the risk is great, especially if he is still a loyal French soldier. He could have me killed. Since he is out of uniform, he may no longer be loyal to Napoleon. I may at least be able to get some hard figures from him on the strength of the soldiers here.* He planned to wait until the act was finished and then pretend to go to the head. He could intercept the man behind the stage and out of sight of the pirates.

Ben waited. "Emil, my friend. You recognize me? I am the prisoner that you taught to speak French when I was in prison. Surely you remember?"

Emil grabbed Ben in a bear hug and said, "An' you taught me English. So what you do here in Dumyat?" Ben noted that he smelled of wine.

"I have little time. I need to know what you are doing in Dumyat?"

"I sail last year with Napoleon for the glorious conquest of Egypt, and then you Eengles come and blow up the French fleet. Now we have no support, no sheep to sail back to France. Napoleon he desert us, leaving us stranded here on this hot shore with no food, no ammunition, nothing! I no longer can be loyal to one like that. But I mus' eat, so I juggle, an' not so good either," he said with a muffled, sheepish laugh.

Ben decided to come right out and ask the critical question. He knew that he would be missed from the pirate band soon. "How many French soldiers remain here in Egypt who could still fight?"

"I doubt there are more than five thousand who have rifles and ammunition for them. They are sick, many have deserted, some try to find sheeps to take them to Italy, some take up with local women. We are no longer strong. Morale is very low and many starve."

"How many do you think will make it back to France?"

"Oh, perhaps a few hundred. They have no pay and cannot hire sheeps."

Ben thought, *This poor fellow is so naive that he does not realize why I am asking these questions.*

"So how come you in the Sphinx?"

Ben had to think for a second. "I was captured when I brought a cartel of your wounded men ashore. I managed to escape and am now trying to get back to England."

"You want to go home too, to your Annie. I want to see my Bridgette too."

Ben thought, I should be able to trust this fellow. He is of a simple mind. "I may have a ship that will call for us in...two nights, but we will have to walk a ways."

"Oh! Would you take me with you?"

"I will if you agree not to tell anyone that you have seen me, an English naval officer, here in Egypt."

"Oh, dear friend. I will tell no one, if you will tell no one that you have seen Emil, a deserter here in Dumyat."

"Agreed," said Ben. "Meet me by pier # 8 at eleven in the evening."

"I jus' finish my act at 10:30. I will be there."

"Take care that no one follows you."

The next day they sat in wait for another ship, but the

cargo was light. She had already offloaded at another port and they turned her back to sea. Ben was lucky to be free by the next evening at 10:30. He slipped out of the Sphinx as the pirates sat talking, laughing and mostly drunk. *That was too easy.*

He met Emil and they walked all night. The next night was when, according to Ben's records, Rossi was supposed to cruise by and pick him up. He seriously doubted that Rossi would appear, but now he had to give it a try. They sat and ate cheese and Egyptian bread for four days, but there was no sign of Rossi, not by day or by night when they built a fire for him to see. Finally Ben said, "My contact has abandoned me. We must give it up, my friend. I am sorry."

"I mentioned earlier that there are a group of French soldiers who are trying to get a boat to France," said Emil. We can go now and see if they have succeeded. It may not be too late to join them. I have a few pieces of silver from my juggling."

"I have a few coins from work on the docks," said Ben. So they walked back to Dumyat and found Emil's friends. Emil had warned Ben, "These are all Frenchmen. They will slit your throat in a second if they think that you are English and the reason that they are stranded here like thees. You mus' not speak in their presence. You do speak fair Fench, but a true Frenchman will know the difference. Do you think that you can keep your mouth shut for six or seven days?"

Ben thought. *If I can get back to English territory, I could give up speech for the rest of my life.* They hid for the day and then went aboard the small fishingboat that evening. Just as Ben's foot hit the deck, he realized that he was in for another malaria attack. He had told Emil about his attacks and it was good that he had. Emil immediately took him aside, telling his friends that he was sick. He brought Ben water and gave him cooling towels for his head during the fever and blankets for the chills. Ben had to be careful not to call out or to groan as he went through the terrifying phases of his illness. *Why now?*

Sixteen men were crowded on the deck of the small fishing boat. Emil explained in French that one of his soldiers had fallen in with a young Egyptian girl who had inherited a fishing boat when her father had suddenly died. "Some of my men they talk to Enta and they convince her to let them sail this sheep to France. They promise to sail her back as soon as they can. Then others join us. It is the best we can do. Rest now, my friend."

Ben thought that the French soldiers would never sail the fishingboat across the Mediterranean to Egypt, not ever. The young woman had been diddled. On the third day Ben was much recovered and he felt fine, but he realized that the malaria attack had been a blessing in disguise. He surely would have said something about the weather, the tides or their handling of the little boat if he had not been feeling so poorly. That same day, a squall blew up and when it was over, the fishingboat was headed in the wrong direction. Ben realized that these man were soldiers, not sailors. Thcy had not a cluc about sailing a boat anywhere. *They'll be lucky if they even find Europe the way they are handling this boat,* thought Ben. By evening, he could stand it no longer. He got up when most everyone was asleep and took the tiller from the steersman. He had to rely on his judgement of winds and tides since the tiny compass appeared to be stuck. When he had the boat back on course, he turned the tiller back to the steersman, pointing for him to stay on that course.

Now Ben began to wonder what their intended destination was? Surely they did not plan to sail clear to France. But some Frenchmen were still in parts of Italy. They would be best off to sail there. He knew that he might meet up with an English ship if they ended up anywhere near Naples. He watched the steersmen from that point on. Emil had said nothing about their destination and Ben dared not ask.

When they finally arrived at a landfall, Ben learned that it was Reggio di Calabria on the southern tip of Italy. Naples was a long ways off, but he was so glad to make a landfall that he could not care less where he was. He turned to Emil as they brought the small boat to the quay and shook him by the shoulders, smiling. He offered his hand, which he realized later was a very English gesture. *I should have rubbed cheeks with him,* he thought. In an instant Ben was on the wharf and headed off to find yet another fishing boat. He made his way north over a week's time hopping from one Italian fishing boat to the next. Once at Naples, he was discouraged but not surprised to see that the flagship was not there. *I'll have to make my way to the Tagus.*

Ben found a British brig in port and managed to get a position as fourth leftenant aboard her. He hated to take a demotion, but he was glad to be out of Egypt too. On his dog watch he tried to write a daily report for the Admiral, but found that his memory of the past three months was a scrambled mess of pirates, fighting, hard work and frustration. He settled for a weekly report and hoped that the Admiral would be contented. He had brought home all of the information that the Admiral had requested and he was happy at that.

He boarded the flagship and was announced at the Admiral's door. When bid to enter, he stood there, a disheveled wreck of a man. He lived up to his reputation as the Navy's worst dressed officer in grand style. There had been no time in Naples to procure a uniform, so he had borrowed bits and pieces for the trip across the Mediterranean. Nothing fitted him, not a single piece.

While Ben was concerned about his dress, the Admiral boomed, "Good God! It's Rundel. I thought that you were supposed to be back here several months ago. Where have you been?"

"Things did not go as planned, sir. Captain Rossi did not appear to pick me up as he was supposed to. I had to make my way here by whatever boat I could find. But I do have all the information that you requested. It's all here sir, as he handed him his reports.

"Mind you, I don't approve of young leftenants going

off on long vacations when I give them an assignment. If I expect you back here in three weeks, then you had better appear in that time or have a good reason why."

The old admiral settled in to read Ben's reports without as much as a single compliment and Ben went off to find the *Vanguard,* his ship. As he climbed the battens he came nose to nose with Midshipman Thomas Murphy, his old friend. They grabbed one another in a bear hug and went off to find Ben's belongings. Members of the crew who remembered Ben let out a cheer. It had been bruited about the Tagus Station that he was dead. Both men had grand stories to share and they sat well into the warm evening telling of all that had happened to them over the past three months.

We must leave Benjamin Rundel there, sitting in his chair in the sun of a warm September afternoon by the English Channel. He would tell me more, someday, I was sure, but for now, he needed rest and time to recover. He seemed to relive every moment of his life as it had actually happened, often leaving him drained and emotionally exhausted. The events that were yet to come were the most painful of his career.

Benjamin Rundel stayed on in the Mediterranean, but that is another story.

THE END